I0772355

THE LENOIR LEGACY

BOOK ONE

CRISTEN JENNETTE

DRAGONNOOK

PUBLISHING LLC

THE LENOIR LEGACY – BOOK ONE

Written by Cristen Jennette.

Published by DragonNook Publishing LLC.

ISBN: PB: 979-8-9851800-2-2; eBook: 979-8-9851800-1-5; Ingram Spark HB: 979-8-9851800-3-9; KDP Hardback: 9798480209358

Cover by Stefanie Saw; Edited by Karen Robinson; Map by Jared Faulkenberry; Chapter Icons by Josh Kaul.

*To all my family and friends, without whom
this dream never would have happened.*

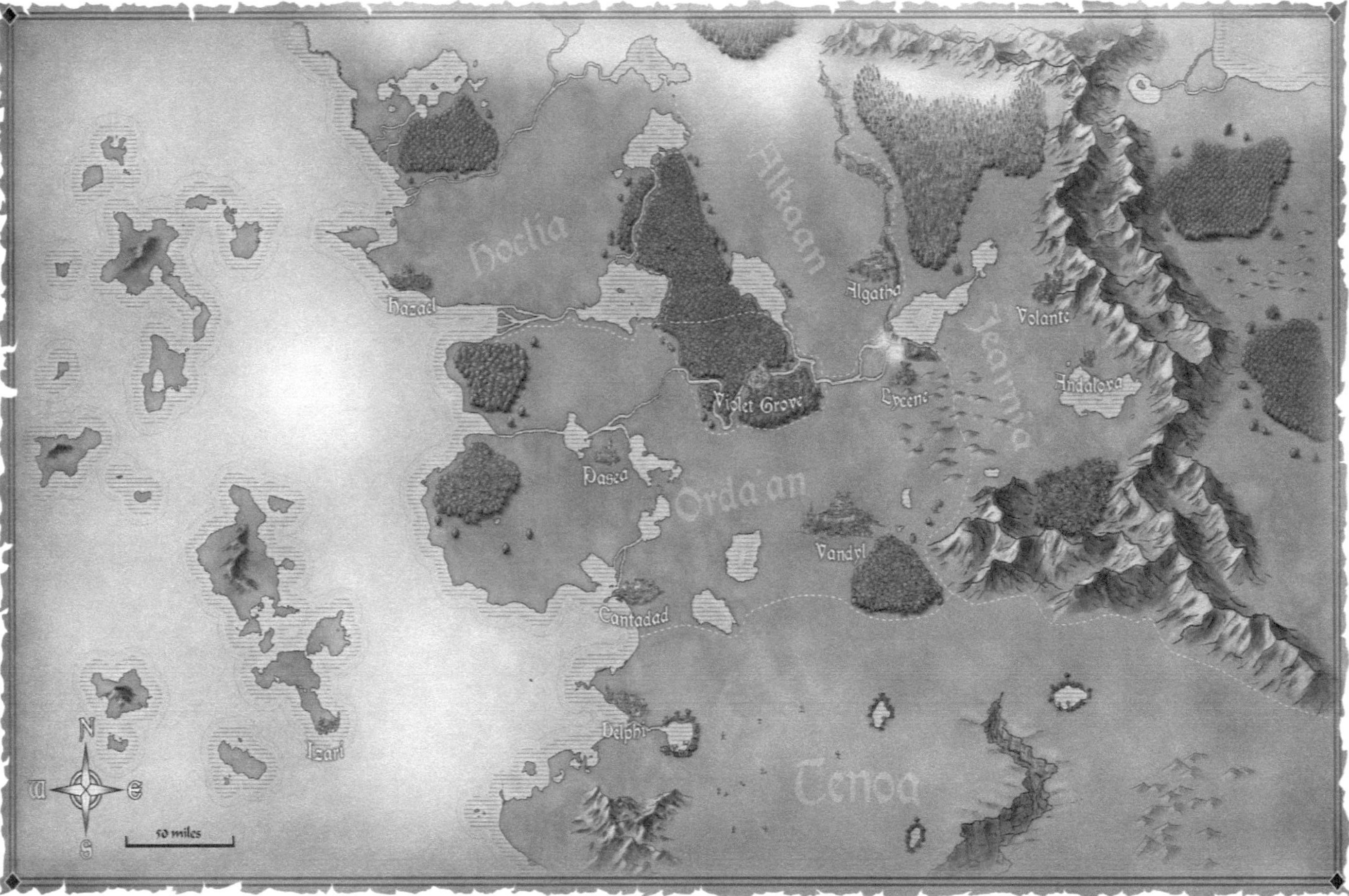

Hoclia
Alkaan
Jearnia
Algatha
Volante
Andalora
Lycene
Violet Grove
Hazael
Pasca
Orda'an
Vandyl
Cantadad
Delphi
Isari
Tenoa
N
E
S
W
50 miles

Part One:
A Country's Status

1

An agreement. The words seared into Charles's mind again. He leaned forward in his chair to lay the book he had been trying to read down on his bed. There was no use continuing, not when *those* words were drifting across his mind instead. The mention of the agreement was subtle, but the words were no less poignant than when King Phillippe first created it.

"As if I need a refresher," he muttered to his empty room in the barracks, wondering why else the king had requested his presence that evening.

He ran one hand through his dark brown hair and made a mental note to cut it before the curls appeared again. Princess Rosealyn had not only asked questions about them, she still mocked him for how they looked. Few here had curls. Before he could stop it, a smirk tugged at the corner of his lips—sometimes the way he toed the edge of "proper" was a source of amusement for her, and for him. But the king's words would stomp through his head again, reminding Charles of his role.

His bed sat snug along one wall, sheets disheveled from use with the small book lying face down in its center. The book was fraying at the edges, and a ragged white crack was widening along its spine, reminiscent of the small scar marring his own chin. Given it was his only book from home and written in his mother's flowery hand, he had read it time and time again. Even when pages fell out and had to be stuffed back in, he read it.

He kept glazing over the words that morning though, glancing instead at a thin slip of paper with General Azeiah's crooked hasty handwriting. It stared at him from the small desk a hand's breadth from the door. Between the desk and closed door, hooks held a long-sleeved black coat with white-rimmed cuffs and large white buttons. And his sword.

He moved the chair back and knocked into the small water basin on the opposite wall. He shifted the chair again, angled so he could stretch his legs, though his feet reached beneath his bed. A deep breath in and out, he reread the words the general had sent.

King Phillippe requests your presence tomorrow evening. ~A

He pushed away the swirling anxiety about his meeting with the king. It was almost time to relieve Moss from night-guard duty—and for the princess's next training session. He stood and donned the coat, closing every button despite how the topmost one in the collar's midst threatened to choke him. After a quick tug at each sleeve, he cinched the sword belt around his waist.

Eyes falling on the singular line of the note again, Charles debated what the king wanted to discuss this time. Their agreement was well established after ten years, and Charles had upheld every term so far. As had Phillippe. But still he wondered. *A secret? No, though Orda'anians can be petty. Or maybe she…*

Charles shook the thoughts from his head. Neither Princess Rosealyn nor King Phillippe had reason to distrust him, and her training was going well. After receiving his assignment to train the princess, Charles had insisted she read the books and study the images of the techniques, only to discover she had already read all there was to know. And he was positive she had spied on his training long before her father had given her permission to hold a weapon herself. He smiled. He was proud of her continuous improvement and wondered if she would attempt a new move on him today.

Charles opened his door and walked through the officers' wing of the barracks, noting the glow of sun lighting the castle's walls. Those tall, formidable walls prevented him from appreciating the display of color when the sun crested the horizon. Most mornings he could be found outside the castle walls for a brief run or meandering walk, but sleep had been hard to find after reading General Azeiah's note.

The halls of the castle were quiet in the early morning, and the soft thud of his boots echoed. Dragonstone, as some called it, lined the base of the walls before transitioning into the common gentle gray of regular stone. Wind carrying the smell of morning dew gusted through well-placed windows, making their deep purple curtains billow into the walkway. A winter-like scent lingered on the breeze that shifted his brown hair just into view before he pushed it back.

Charles turned into the main hallway, walking down the center to remain out of the way of servants dashing about with loads of linens or clothing. It was odd to see so many still, given Vandyl's castle housed only the royal family, necessary soldiers, a handful of priests, and enough servants to keep the palace running smoothly. Any excess staff stayed with Duchess Adela at the old castle in Cantadad.

Visits to Vandyl, the capital where Charles currently resided, weren't prohibited, of course, but they had become a rarity as crops dwindled and Orda'an's neighboring countries issued more threats with each passing day. Charles believed the king and his family should have already moved to Cantadad, which was much further south and therefore further from the dangers which continuously approached from the north. Though the eastern country of Jearnia remained silent, he feared what they would try in the future. Instead, the king accompanied the battalions, fighting alongside the soldiers, much to the queen's chagrin.

Servants ignored Charles as he walked, and he grinned inwardly. He spent so much of his time walking beside the princess he had grown accustomed to the honorifics they offered her. A silent chuckle accompanied the invisible grin as he recalled Princess Rosealyn's scowl for each servant who insisted on bowing or curtsying to her.

Lieutenant Flynn Moss stood outside the princess's door, leaning against the wall with one foot propped against the gray stone. His head jolted back up when it touched the wall, and Charles shook his head at the youth. Moss's light hair was short, barely visible above the scalp, and his deep brown eyes were wide, as though only mental effort kept him awake.

"Long night, Moss?" Charles asked.

The younger soldier snapped to attention. "Quiet night, Captain," Moss responded while fighting a yawn.

"I told you, Moss." Charles shifted his weight to one leg and rested his hand on the leather-bound hilt of his sword, fighting a yawn of his own. "Sleep during the day, at least the morning hours. You can't function as the night guard if you don't sleep sometime."

"Yes, sir," Moss mumbled, fist still held to his chest at attention.

"You're relieved, Lieutenant. Of this post, that is. Your orders are to sleep. If I catch you this exhausted at the morning change again, you *will* be reassigned. Understood?"

The younger soldier bristled but nodded. Charles watched Moss's careful, albeit wobbly, steps down the hallway. The gray stone to each side was even lighter in some places, a tinge of white providing evidence of the tapestries which once adorned the walls. Charles turned back to the princess's chamber door and gently rapped his knuckles against it.

"You can come in," came the princess's melodic voice.

Charles opened the door and leaned against the frame. Chairs in their haphazard organization and the colored rugs scattered across the floor greeted him. From her chosen seat in the middle of the room, she looked up from the book she was reading. Rosealyn's brown eyes twinkled as she snapped the book shut and stood.

"Come to relieve Moss, I see?"

Charles nodded, fighting to cool the rising warmth in his cheeks. "Same as every morning this week, Princess."

She wore the beige dress designed for training with the soldiers. And with him. Pale against her skin, the beige looked almost white rather than a lighter shade of brown. After their first few sessions, she had slit the skirts along the sides for ease of movement. The billowing arm-sleeves received similar treatment. It hugged her torso, framing her rather than cinching her like her court dresses. In this dress, she moved with ease—shoulders relaxed, breathing without strain, and no fidgeting.

"Dressed for training already, Princess?"

"Same as every morning, Captain." She flicked a stray strand of auburn hair back over her shoulder and set the book down in the chair behind her.

Charles looked away and studied one of the obnoxiously bright rugs she insisted cover her front rooms. The chaotic mess could make one dizzy, but he'd studied every inch often enough. If danger arose for her here, the designs and strange colors would not distract from his position as her bodyguard. His gaze snagged on her breakfast plate still dotted with food, and he frowned.

"You should finish your morning meal, Princess." He nodded at the plates of wilting fruit and bread. A hint of cooked meat lingered, meaning she had at least eaten *something*.

"No need." She waved a dismissive hand toward the plates. "I told Lori to share the rest with those who need it. That lady-in-waiting of mine would stuff my face every hour if I let her."

Charles studied the princess for a moment, noting the subtle clench of her jaw. King Phillippe had tried to keep her from learning too much, fearful she would act without thinking, but the princess was crafty. She befriended the servants, conversing with them and learning what they overheard. Meaning she knew how the crops continued to grow scarce across the country and had overheard the reports of one burning field after the other.

"You need to eat too, Princess." He approached one of the random chairs.

"I ate several fine pieces of broiled ham," she responded, walking toward her door instead. Charles took two long strides, blocking her path before she could exit first. She gave him a disapproving stare. "I hear the rumors, same as you, Captain. Lori says there is just enough for the castle occupants, much less for the servants. And, for probably the hundredth time now, I'm positive I can enter the hallway without you scanning every inch first."

He nodded but did not move until she waved her arm with a dangerously playful grin. "After you, Captain. Since you'll insist anyway."

Charles glanced to each side of the hallway and waved her through. Two paces behind her, he walked in time with the click of her boots. After a few moments, she slowed to walk beside him rather than in front of him.

"You know it's unlikely an attack will occur here, yes?" She shifted the free-flowing portion of her wavy hair to no avail. Each time she moved one strand, the wind would pick up another and replace it. Two taut braids leading from each side of her forehead held the remainder. Even without the small circlet she wore only in the throne room, those simple braids gave away her station.

"Then why give you personal bodyguards, Princess?"

She sighed. Loudly. At the title, doubtful. He always referred to her that way; it helped remind him of the differences between them. This meant the overexaggerated sigh was in response to his question. "Because Father worries too much."

They continued walking, listening to the increasing bustle of footsteps as the rest of the castle awoke. "The reason probably lies in that Gift of his he never intentionally uses."

The pained yearning in her voice as she spoke sent a small chill down Charles's arms. He could add nothing. Charles was well aware of how the king used the LeNoir Gift and understood the strain with which she spoke of it. The Gift could only be held by one; she would receive the Gift only after King Phillippe's death.

"Father returned last night," she added after a moment.

He glanced at her, a quick break in the monotony of studying the surrounding hallways. With no adornments on the stone walls, it seemed Charles and the princess had been standing still rather than walking several minutes toward the practice yards.

"I'm aware, Princess," Charles acknowledged in barely more than a whisper, grateful the door leading outside the castle proper had come into view.

"He wants to speak with you again, doesn't he?" she asked. The strain of worry had disappeared, replaced with curiosity. He nodded and held the door, watching as she wrinkled her nose at the onslaught of musky sweat. Had he not been distracted, he would have laughed. The princess practiced outdoors with one of the soldiers every day, and the smell of sweat still bothered her.

"Curious." She walked past him, removing a string from her wrist and wrapping it around her hair to hold it at the nape of her neck. "Swords today, right, Captain?"

"You practiced swords yesterday, Princess. Time to pick a different weapon."

She shook her head emphatically, steps measured but quick in their approach to the rack of practice weapons. Without hesitation, she grasped two practice swords. They were created of the lightest hue of wood, and could have been mistaken for parchment rather than a blunt force weapon. He chuckled at her mischievous grin which made her brown eyes sparkle while the rising sun brought a glow to her brown-tinged skin. In many ways, she was still the girl he had first met a decade ago, not a woman of marriageable age. At twenty-two, Princess Rosealyn was a few years younger than he and a rarity among nobility. Sole heir to her father's throne as an only child and not yet wed, nor even promised to another.

"Swords today, and then you're stuck with the quarterstaff for all of next week," Charles countered. "But not against me, Princess. Against a well-rested Moss."

She squinted at the suggestion but did not relinquish the swords. "Does that mean you'll be my nighttime guard next week?"

She voiced the question over her shoulder and approached one of several empty practice rings. Others contained sparring soldiers of various ranks. Sword against spear, quarterstaff against sword, spear against quarterstaff. The thwack of wood meeting wood sounded often, while the periodic slap against skin made his arms tingle with memories of the occasional hits the princess managed. Charles paused at the opening between the gates of the ring she had chosen, unbuckling his sword and setting it against the fence, all while watching the princess to see what she would do with the second practice weapon.

He tugged at his sleeves and undid the topmost button. At Princess Rosealyn's smirk, he considered re-buttoning it but decided against it. Given the beads of sweat trickling along his skin beneath the long-sleeved black coat, the entire thing would find its way draped across the fence soon. The wind that continued to swirl the princess's hair around her face brought a dry heat rather than the refreshing coolness of the mountain winds. More than likely, it would be one of the last warm days before the winter winds took hold.

She twisted the second blade, holding the hilt out to him, but he waited. Her shoulders moved first, forecasting where the rest of her body would follow, so he pivoted in the opposite direction. With one hand, he snatched the second practice sword from her and tapped her in the side with the thin slab of wood. She glared at him and shifted into a proper fighting stance.

"I wasn't ready," she grumbled, gripping the weapon in front of her.

"You should always be ready, Princess," he responded, unbuttoning the rest of his coat and laying it atop the fence. Beneath was a simple, loose shirt, one that wouldn't constrict his movement like the tight sleeves that were not long enough for his arms. "An opponent in battle will not wait for you to be ready. They'll use that hesitation against you."

She scowled at him but nodded her acknowledgment of his instruction, though she didn't take advantage of his own lack of readiness.

Charles's grip tightened on the practice weapon, the natural hue of the wood barely lighter than his own skin, and he tapped her poised weapon, taunting her. She waited, and their gazes met, making that new tension rise up inside again. He looked away first, and she lunged. A slight flick of his wrist knocked her downward strike aside.

Princess Rosealyn grounded her heel and shoved against his block with unexpected strength, but he pivoted away, tapping her back as she almost face-planted into the dirt. He silenced the rising chuckle, leaning left to avoid her wild swing and backpedaling a few quick steps until his back met the fence.

She followed his movement, sword point reaching for his midriff, but he knocked it aside again. Her forward foot dug into the ground, chest rising and falling as beads of sweat made loose hairs cling to her neck.

"Think, breathe, watch my feet and shoulders. Look for the movement before it happens, Princess."

Her gaze darted between his shoulders and feet as he had instructed. She shoved the blade straight at his middle again, her balance growing unsteady when the two weapons met with a loud thud. He grabbed the hilt of her sword and wrenched it away. With both blades firm in his grasp, he shifted his balance to prepare a kick and noticed the king observing from the garden balcony overlooking the training grounds. The simmering adrenaline disappeared, replaced with the common tension that accompanied the king's presence.

Charles put down his barely risen leg and turned so his back faced the princess, lowering both weapons. From this distance, Charles could make out the king's smooth yet hardened features, like the aging man was burdened by an invisible weight. Sunlight made the king's blond hair turn gold, especially since he wore the solid black coat. With a shake of his head, Charles shifted the wooden blades so he held one in each hand and faced the princess again.

"What was that about?" Rosealyn held out her hand for the wooden blade.

"Nothing, Princess," Charles muttered, glancing back up to the balcony again.

The rising sun illuminated the playfulness in her gaze as she followed his eyes to where her father stood watching. A teasing smile softened the sharp features of her face. "Worried what Father will think still? You should be over that by now. Your command is to train me, not coddle me. Again."

"You did well today, Princess." Charles set the two practice blades against the fence and donned the high-buttoned coat. The princess frowned with arms crossed, and he added, "Still need to watch my feet."

Her frown turned into a scowl. His instructions hadn't changed in months, but he was sure he would have to remind her again despite the singular nod she gave. *Especially since she'll be going up against Moss and his quarterstaff again.*

"And *you* need to stop holding back, Captain."

Charles grimaced but tilted his head forward as he clasped each button of the coat. The king's presence above did nothing to assuage the growing apprehension inside. She was right; he was still holding back, but nowhere near as often as before. "As you wish, Princess."

"We *can* continue training. Just because Father is watching doesn't mean we have to stop for the day. We've barely begun!"

"Library, Princess?" He knew they could continue, but the king's steady gaze and his later meeting with the man made Charles hesitate.

"Not until we're done here." She stepped around him and grabbed both practice swords.

Smirking, he allowed her the small victory. It wouldn't take him long to seize both from her hands. Again.

The jitters of his later meeting with the king gave way to adrenaline as he ducked and pivoted away from her twin slashes. Soon he forgot the king watched from above, losing himself in the push and pull of dancing with swords. Rosealyn's youthful demeanor shifted to frustration with each stumble and fall. Smudges covered her skirts, and the streaks of dirt were barely visible along her arms. Each time she fell, she jumped back up, insisting they continue until the sun was well past its midday height.

2

The throne room doors stood open when Charles arrived. King Phillippe sat alone on his white throne. Not even the young kitchen boy who filled the plates was present. Charles wasn't surprised to find the king alone for this meeting; no one else knew of their agreement. Charles tugged at each sleeve, squared his shoulders, steeled his nerves, and entered.

It was plain, as throne rooms went. Alternating black and white swaths of cloth swung from post to post on either side of the path down the center to the raised dais at the other end on which resided two thrones of solid stone. One white, the other black. A larger cloth adorned the wall behind the dais, the LeNoir family crest prominent in its center. The middle of the crest featured a gray cloud. To one side, a black dragon held an equally as dark sword; to the other a white dragon held a white sword. The legends Rosealyn repeatedly read called those two swords the Twin Blades.

"Ah, at last," King Phillippe said when Charles stopped and knelt several feet before the raised dais. "Oh, stand up, Charles. No need for the show when we're alone."

Charles stood, shifting to rest one fist atop the hilt of his blade, the other over his chest. King Phillippe shifted and sipped from his metal cup.

"Azeiah must have left my message in your quarters. Making me wait on you, I'm certain," the king said with a soft chuckle. Charles chose not to correct him, though his back stiffened. "No worries, the peace of this sizable room is enjoyable." He took another sip. "I wish its walls could speak to me."

Charles remained at attention and adjusted his grip on the sword's hilt as his gaze studied the familiar striations of the marbled floor. From above, he heard the rustle of clothes.

"How does my darling Rose fare in her training?" It was the tone of simple curiosity. No different than their last conversation.

"Well, my King. She has taken to the sword most often, though I have pressed other disciplines."

The thumping of his heart in his chest quickened; he was certain there would be more to this meeting. He looked up, fist still held against his chest, trying to read the king's expression. King Phillippe wore his simple castle garb rather than the stiff court attire. A pristine white shirt was tucked into straight black pants, and the man's blond hair rendered the solid gold crown almost invisible. Recent travels had tanned the king's skin, though no amount of sun would make his complexion match his wife's or daughter's. Those same recent travels continued to steal the kindness Charles had so often found in King Phillippe's presence.

"Good, good." Phillippe held the cup to his lips without taking a sip. A smirk lit his aging green eyes. "I've been spying on your training sessions with her."

Charles shifted a foot, following the line of a striation until it disappeared at the crack between the stones. *How many times did he see me knock her down?*

"You can't hold back, no matter how much you care for her," Phillippe said. The smirk lingered, but a shift in the king's tone made Charles's fingers clench around the hilt, the nails of the hand held fast to his chest digging into his palm. "And no matter how she looks at you."

"Sire?" Charles dared to meet the king's gaze again, resituating his hand to rest on the sword's pommel.

The king's amusement faded, betrayed by a tightness to his features. "Oh, my boy, I still see everything. I am truly sorry about your past, you know this. But my daughter cares for you. And I see how you look at her." Phillippe paused, the last hint of the smirk disappearing. "I know the awkwardness this post has placed you in, but please do not resist growing closer to her. Her—" He grimaced and stared into his cup. "Orda'an's future is tumultuous."

Charles tensed, unsure of how to respond. These meetings were often short, especially after the first few, once he had gained the king's trust and earned back his sword. Before his assignment to train the princess, Charles had accompanied King Phillippe on multiple journeys. Minor arguments with Hoclia and Alkaan, their northern neighbors, grew into small skirmishes as crops withered and each country blamed the other. But the soldiers still talked of the battles against Jearnia, amazed Phillippe had not sought significant retribution for his own father's death at Jearnia's hands.

"The LeNoir Gift," Phillippe reminded Charles when the silence lingered.

Ah… His steady nod continued, gaze darting between meeting the king's eyes and studying the stones. That same gift had led to Phillippe's offered protection, and Charles would be a fool to disobey the king's requests.

"Make sure she's ready," Phillippe said, and Charles recognized the edge of exhaustion in the king's voice. The king took another sip from the cup and set it on the table next to him. After shifting in the chair several times, he leaned to one side.

"Expand her training further. Be more persistent that she spar against other soldiers. And not just Moss." His lips ticked down. "Someday soon she will be the ruling monarch, and knowing my darling Rose, she will not sit quiet in here while others do the hard work."

"As you command, Your Majesty." Charles leaned into a deep bow. *Someday soon? What has he seen?*

"General Azeiah will accompany me on my next journey. My brothers and sister in Cantadad have requested a meeting. It will be brief, as our northern borders remain threatened. Banner-Captain Rake will assume command here in Azeiah's absence. Keep Rose safe, and as always, remember our agreement."

King Phillippe's intent stare awaited Charles as he stood straight once more. His younger self had often flushed at that stare, at those words. Phillippe need not say more; the phrase still made Charles's heart flop around his chest.

The king leaned forward with an unwavering scrutiny.

"As always, Your Majesty," Charles whispered.

Before he could turn to leave, the king stood and approached. Charles tensed. The king walked like the warrior he was, each movement intentional, no different than the first time they had met. Pausing at Charles's side, the king placed a firm hand on his shoulder and spoke softly, as though worried someone might be listening despite their being alone.

"The time is nearing for you to honor your portion, Charles. I know you will want to fight it, that you may prefer to live out your days here no differently than you have for the past ten years, but remember what you have learned."

Charles swallowed and faced the king. As Charles turned, his hand strayed, touching the small scar along his jaw. The simple change from the previous meeting, especially knowing what he would have to do, made his heart race. Were the attacks on Orda'an's border solely from Hoclia? Had Alkaan finally joined the fight? It'd be logical for Alkaan's youthful king to be rash. Or had Jearnia finally broken their silence?

But the greatest question of all was if honoring his portion of their agreement would truly help.

"When, Sire?"

The flickering torches around them cast the king's face with an orange hue that made his expression more somber. "If I can finally understand this revered yet cursed Gift of my family, the when will occur before winter takes hold."

Winter was close. Too close for Charles's liking after this conversation. His mouth turned dry and scratchy. All he could do was nod. He had known this would happen someday, so why did it scare him so much?

"That is all," Phillippe said, giving Charles's shoulder another squeeze and walking back to the table next to the dais. He grabbed his cup and added, "You look like you could use some rest."

After a nod of his head rather than a full bow, Charles left and turned opposite the direction he had come, unsure if the flips of his heart were because of the approaching change or because he had to inform the princess her father was leaving. Again. *Mountains be cursed, why am I always the bearer of such news for her?*

He tugged at his sleeves, scrutinizing the hallways out of habit. The so-called dragonstone of the walls always made the coming darkness of night bleak, stealing what little color the moonlight might reflect.

Rosealyn occupied the lone table to one side of the library, surrounded by shelves of books. Before her sat her ancestor King Gailin's journal, behind her stood Lieutenant Moss, who—she noticed when she glanced over her shoulder at the sound—held a fist to his mouth to stifle yet another yawn. After a tsk and a shake of her head, she turned back to the journal lying open on the table before her. She had it memorized, yet something was intoxicating about its pages, about learning of her ancestor's actions through his words. Of all the LeNoir kings who had ruled Orda'an, Gailin was the only one who had written about himself. The other rulers, her father included, relied on the court priests and historians to record their lives.

She tugged at the bodice of her dress, annoyed with the shallowness of her breaths. Her mother had not been happy with her sweat-ridden hair or clothing after the lengthy training session with Charles. At her light chuckle from remembering her mother's appalled expression, she heard the click of Moss's sword against his belt as he moved. A quick glance back and another shake of her head made the young soldier settle back into a stiff standing position near the wall. Moss was a recent recruit, but he had risen through the ranks quickly. Thinking of his rise brought her back to how quickly her ancestors' lives had changed not long after the founding of her country, and her attention returned to the journal.

It alternated between succinct lines and rambling diatribes. It was also the only written record of Xannan, whom the leading historians believed to be a figment of Gailin's imagination. Xannan was supposedly Gailin's twin brother. A few of the historians labeled Xannan "the Lost Prince," using the name to create obviously fictionalized stories. But Rosealyn had found Xannan's portrait, hidden among a stack of simple landscape tapestries. His piercing green eyes haunted her. It made what Gailin wrote more real, even if the historians she questioned insisted the man was a myth. *Strange how they trust what Gailin says of our family Gift, about the civil war, and even about the Twin Blades. But not what he says about Xannan.*

Rosealyn surveyed the shelves of books surrounding her, eager to discover more of their secrets. History books grew dull after a time, a repetition of one king angering another leading to war and death. Stories of love sometimes captured her attention, whisking her away on a whirlwind of emotions. Gailin's journal, however, held secrets she longed to unlock.

She flipped through the pages, hunting for the entry describing Xannan's disappearance. With each page she turned, Rosealyn wondered how long her father would stay home. Each time he left, more days passed before he returned. In her youth, he'd travel mere weeks at a time. Now it was often months. His absence meant endless days of being subjected to her mother's disapproving stares.

Moss's sword clicked against his belt behind her again, and she rubbed her arms. Bruises were forming where Charles had whacked her several times with those practice blades, but she smiled at the thought of how many hits she had given in return. Her smile faltered, recalling her father's demeanor while watching them from above. He had appeared analytical and calculating. Almost judgmental. *Is Father unhappy with my progress? Is that what he's talking to Charles about?*

Not for the first time, Rosealyn wished she had discovered an inconspicuous place near the throne room to eavesdrop on their conversation. The one time she had come close, Azeiah had found her. That was the day the general had replaced her other guard with Moss. And if Charles caught Moss sleeping again, Rosealyn was sure she'd soon have yet another guard to figure out. Since she liked Moss, Rosealyn had decided escaping him would cause more harm than good. Instead, she read the words she had read a thousand times and still did not quite understand.

The right passage found, Rosealyn set the journal flat on the table in front of her to shift the bulky skirts that never lay right. An hour had passed since she'd changed into "proper" attire, and she was desperate to know if her lady-in-waiting, Lori, had washed the beige training dress Rosealyn preferred to wear.

She ran a finger along the page, pausing, as she always did, at the mention of the black cloud engulfing Xannan. One moment there, the next gone. Like magic. No one else wrote about Xannan's disappearance, and Gailin acknowledged he was alone with his twin brother when it happened.

The entry transitioned to Gailin's despair within a few lines; Gailin lost his entire family within a week's time. She tugged at her bottom lip with her teeth, knowing her own fears mirrored Gailin's. All it would take was one arrow, one strike, and her father would be gone, too.

She often urged her father to use the LeNoir Gift. Gailin made it seem simple enough. Images, feelings, or even sounds of events before they happened. Her father accepted the Gift.

Acknowledged what it showed without forcing its use. He hadn't wanted it, but he had been the one to receive it.

A soft click at the far end of the room, opposite the table, made her look up. Charles's insistence on being perfectly proper, especially when her father was home, amused her. The black coat was completely buttoned, even the topmost one he always tugged away from his throat. His pale blue eyes met her gaze and darted away before she could read the emotions hidden within. Brown hair, curly when long, mixed with the unique color of his eyes, made her question his heritage. Once he stood next to the table, Charles and Moss exchanged a glance, and the younger soldier left, hopefully to get some rest, but likely to spar against his peers instead.

"Why did Father want to speak with you?" Rosealyn continued to flip through the pages of the journal. Sometimes she could read the hint of an emotion, but the captain was reserved. *Something is bothering him today.* "A new command?"

"No, Princess." Charles shifted his blade to sit in an empty chair on the opposite side of the table. "I am still one of your guards and your trainer."

She faked a grimace and flashed a smile, heart swelling when the hint of a smile tugged at his lips too. "Stuck with me?"

"Yes, Princess," he said.

Rosealyn fought the urge to laugh at his stiff posture. "What else did Father want? Surely he didn't hold a private meeting with you to confirm you are to maintain your post."

Charles leaned back and straightened again, avoiding eye contact with her. Though she knew of the agreement, she didn't know what it entailed. All she knew was that each time her father spoke privately with the captain, he crawled back into his shell as though he had been admonished.

"Father…" Rosealyn paused when Charles grimaced. She stared back at the journal as the edges of her vision blurred. "He's leaving. Again."

"To Cantadad, yes," the captain said in a gentle, albeit cautious, tone. She pursed her lips. The elation she'd felt at her father's return descended into dismay as she continued flipping through the journal's pages absentmindedly. The words blended together, but she refused to let the tears come. When she looked up, Charles's demeanor had softened enough for her to recognize warmth and worry.

"When?"

"Soon, Princess," he replied, speaking barely louder than she had. "His Majesty's siblings requested a meeting, and then General Azeiah will—"

"He's taking Azeiah with him?" she interrupted. The last time the general and her father had traveled together was before their neighbors had signed the original treaties. "Usually he takes Rake."

Charles nodded, and though he tried to hide it, she saw the quick flash of concern darken his features. "You know what I know, Princess."

Her muscles tensed, reminding her of the soreness from the day's training. Something was different this time, something her father hadn't shared with the captain. She frowned at the pages before her, ignoring the feel of Charles's gaze studying her, blocking out the slowly growing anger. *Trained yet sheltered.*

Rosealyn soon tired of pretending to read the journal, of sitting silent and still. So she walked the castle hallways, smiling at passersby with tight lips, contemplating how she could change her father's mind. Or, at the very least, convince him to allow her to join him for the journey. Cantadad was not in danger, and it would be good to venture outside the castle's walls again. With minimal effort, she managed to avoid her parents.

She couldn't avoid Charles, though. He followed her step for step, listened without comment when she said *anything* about going with her father, and stood at her door when she decided to eat the evening meal alone. By the time her lady-in-waiting helped her change from the court attire into something much more comfortable, Moss had arrived and Charles had left.

Dusk arrived, then the darkness of night, and Rosealyn could not sleep. She opened her door and tiptoed into the hallway, making sure her boots met the stone without a sound. The door closed, she glanced to her right to find Moss awake and muttered an inaudible curse. She had no desire for company on this midnight walk, but her father's orders were clear for the soldiers. *Keep me safe. Inside a castle. Full of armed men. An army who has yet to lose a battle since Azeiah took command. What has he seen to make him worry so much?*

She settled onto her heels. "I can't sleep," she said, her voice booming in the still of night. "I'm just going to sit in the gardens. You can stay here."

Moss's lips worked to form words, but before he managed to speak, Rosealyn released an exasperated exhale. "Fine, follow. I know you'd rather not get in trouble," she grumbled, wrapping her arms around herself and no longer trying to hide the shuffle of her boots against the stone floor. Moss followed a few seconds later, his sword hilt clanging against his belt with every step. Rosealyn gritted her teeth and shot him a glare.

"Sorry, Your Highness," he mumbled, gripping the hilt to stop the sound. And then silence, the perfect silence of the moon-filled night, greeted her. Familiar shadows danced along the hallways, and the distant howls of wolves floated through windows bordered by moving streams. No one else to bow or curtsy to her amid their task, no one else to stop and murmur a quick "your highness" or "princess." Peaceful, glorious silence. And Moss, with the occasional chink of metal against metal when he released his hold on his sword.

The garden balcony overlooked the training yards, so she took the same path she had with Charles earlier that morning. She despised not knowing what her father had told him. Throughout the years, Rosealyn had thought of multiple reasons why her father spoke with Charles in private. But none had come to fruition.

She arrived at the stairs leading to the second level of the castle and went up them carefully. It was late enough the torches along the stairwell had burned down to a flicker, providing just enough light to distinguish the outline of each step.

Though it had turned dreary in recent years, the garden balcony was more like home to her than anywhere else in the castle. Faded purple, blue, red, and yellow blossoms sprouted amidst dulling green leaves. Vines grew like snakes along the castle's walls while others spread like puddles, covering the dirt below them. She bypassed most of the displays until she reached the edge of the balcony where two rectangular bins were placed on either side of a bench. When she sat on it, she faced her father's favorite flower: the black rose bushes. The bottom petals of the black roses had fallen, revealing a strange green hue covering their base.

Rosealyn became lost in the abyss that her namesake flower provided, not realizing her father had joined her until his arm wrapped around her shoulders, pulling her closer to his side. She laid her head on his shoulder and sniffled, desperate not to repeat the angry tears from the last time he left.

"When?" she whispered, breaking the comfortable silence.

His grip on her tightened. "Within the week," he replied. The rumble of his voice did not calm her as it often could.

"With Tate?"

Rosealyn lifted her head from his shoulder when his light chuckle shook it.

"You know he's always preferred to go by Azeiah."

"True," she acknowledged, crossing her arms and resting her head on his shoulder again. "You're avoiding my question."

"Aye, Azeiah's coming with me this time," her father said with resignation. He shifted her off his shoulder and angled himself so he could look at her. "My brothers and sister need to speak with me, probably about the faltering trade routes. And then I must see for myself what is happening at Pasea."

"But—" Rosealyn stopped at her father's raised hand and distracted herself by picking at the folds of her skirts.

"There is *something* developing at Pasea." He faced the row of black roses whose green leaves shimmered in the moonlight dancing through the occasional cover of clouds. "The scouts aren't hiding anything, but they can't describe it."

She swallowed, eyes darting from one flower's shadow to the next, voicing the same question she always did. "Can I com—"

"No," came the sharp interruption, and her heart sank. "Especially not now."

"There's more you're not telling me, isn't there?" She gripped her skirts tighter. "You can't keep me in the dark forever, not when you constantly put yourself in danger. I'm not ready for the day you don't return. I *need* to come with you."

She stared at him with all the defiance she could muster, but it disappeared when she recognized the fear across his features. Rosealyn knew that look, knew its implications.

"Be cautious, my darling Rose," he whispered, pulling her close and kissing the top of her head. "And stop trying to evade your protectors. I told them to stay near for a reason."

Despite the dread and concern, Rosealyn grinned. "I know." She adjusted her position next to him, shivering as his words replayed. "You really should tell me more about how the Gift works, Father."

"No different than that journal you've memorized," he murmured, hugging her into his side and standing. "Get some rest, Rose. I'll see you at the morning meal."

"I will, soon," she told him, rubbing her arms. Before he left, her father whispered something to Moss and the young soldier nodded curtly. Rosealyn knew it would be more comfortable to return to her rooms, to lie down in her bed and sink into the mattress. Her thoughts returned to finding a way, any way, to convince her father she could help. After a time, she curled up on the bench, and before she knew it, Moss was gently prodding her awake. A faint pink sky greeted her, and she stretched and stood. Her footsteps back to her rooms were heavier than those from her midnight walk, not eager to dress for the day that would be, once again, colored by her father's leave-taking.

3

Phillippe cinched the already tightened strap of the saddle, knowing that once he turned around he would face the disapproving stare of his wife. A hundred armored men surrounded him, a combination of jangling and stomping and neighing.

"Is Azeiah incapable of doing this patrol on his own?" his wife asked.

He turned, already envisioning the solid frown plastered on her dark-skinned face. Roseanne's light brown eyes looked down at him, despite the fact he stood at least a head taller than her. The tightly wound crown braid of Roseanne's dark hair provided a stark contrast to the dual braids which relaxed into flowing locks on his darling Rose.

His daughter stood stiff, tugging at the edges of her taut white dress, and kept her distance from Roseanne. Or perhaps it was Roseanne who kept her distance from Rose—it was hard to tell who avoided whom these days. The ever-watchful Charles stood behind, tight-lipped and tense. *Sheltering him was worth the risk.*

Phillippe returned to checking over the brown mare.

"My brothers and sister don't like to be kept waiting," he said, a cross between an apologetic husband and ruling king.

Phillippe turned back to her, reins held tight in one hand, and brushed the woman's cheek with a soft kiss she almost turned away from. He winced, reminding her, "And I must learn more. Ruling a country cannot come without sacrifice. You know that well, Roseanne."

Lips pursed, arms crossed, Roseanne's voice turned the monotone which indicated a veiled anger. "It would be safer for you to stay here, in the castle. You said you can't tell—"

"That uncertainty is why I am going, Roseanne," he said, always a tad more forceful than he intended when speaking to her. She tried to hide it, but Phillippe noticed her clenched fists almost imperceptibly shake at her sides. Phillippe let a small smile tug at his lips, appreciating how Roseanne had risen to the challenge of monarchy. The smile widened as his gaze fell on Rose again, watching the wind tumble strands of her hair behind her.

"I love you, my darling Rose," he said. At his wife's glare, he added, "I love you both."

When Phillippe mounted, both Roseanne and Rosealyn took a step back. His gaze found Charles, not wishing to see his own feelings mirrored on his wife's or daughter's face again. "Keep them safe."

Phillippe motioned for Azeiah to lead the way, but the king waited a moment more, surveying the bare training grounds, eventually resting his gaze on the alcove which overlooked them. Within the garden balcony, he could just make out the falling petals of his favorite black roses. They flitted along a gentle breeze and rested atop shimmering white stone. It took more effort than he cared to admit to pull his gaze away. He did not look back again and trotted to join Azeiah at the front of the battalion. They settled into a steady walk southwest, toward Cantadad, though Phillippe continuously fought the urge to look north instead.

The pattern of hooves meeting packed dirt allowed his thoughts to wander. Four soldiers, whom Azeiah had deemed necessary as his personal guard, surrounded him and followed everywhere he went. Not much different from his order for Rose to have her own personal guards. And Roseanne.

But these soldiers could not protect him from the LeNoir Gift. No one could help him escape the screams which woke him at the most inopportune hours. Less than a week within the castle's walls had been no different. Each night they sounded. Soft at first, and he could do naught but listen in agony until the Gift relinquished its strange hold. He inhaled, tucking away the concerns he held as a worried husband and father, and released his breath as the resolute king his people needed. Behind him, Vandyl's walls shrank, giving way to open plains which would not be broken until the land met the sea. *But those screams which wake me. Roseanne? Rose? The people?*

Though he tried to quench the stories before they became rampant, rumors of destroyed fields, burned beyond recognition, spread like weeds. Meeting with the other countries in Violet Grove had been his idea and a fruitless endeavor. Ramon, his wife's cousin and the praetor of Tenoa, agreed to remain an ally. But Hoclia and Alkaan, their northern neighbors, blamed him for the destruction of their fields. He surveyed the widening plains, unable to stop himself from glancing north.

Azeiah motioned for another to take the lead, slowing until he rode alongside Phillippe.

"I know that look, Sire," Azeiah said, blunt and gruff as usual. "What says the Gift?"

Phillippe gave a dismal shake of his head. "Says? Nothing. Shows? Nothing. It *screams*. Faint echoes of a haunting scream like none I've heard before."

He paused, shifting in the saddle and focusing on the true sounds surrounding them. His insides turned cold when the faint screams returned. A shift, a thought, a wonder, another dismal shake of his head. The feelings from trying to see what accompanied such pain were worse than the screams themselves. But it was becoming difficult to push them away.

Soon, the screams would be real.

"Even in my sleep, I hear the screams of the Gift. Whether it be the voice of my people, my wife—" He grimaced. "Or, the Blaze take me, my daughter, I know not."

Another pause, another futile attempt at shoving the sound away. Phillippe studied the reins he held loosely in his gloved hand.

"Never-ending screams. Sometimes accompanied with flashes of battle, sometimes a…" He left the last unspoken. That one was too real to say aloud, too real to change. A calm dread met him as he closed his eyes, greeting him with an image of a black blade.

No need to fight the inevitable, but he could not stop his own turmoil from bubbling within.

"When the time is right, you'll tell me, Sire?"

"When the time is right," Phillippe agreed, examining the aging bearded general's expression and adding with a mischievous grin, "We grew old, Azeiah."

"Aye, no thanks to those treaties you crafted."

Phillippe's grin faded, remembering the exchange of threats. Through a miracle, none had attacked before his return to Vandyl, and through an even greater miracle, no reports had come of an advancing army at his northern borders. He resisted the urge to look north again, wishing the ache in his gut was from the jolting movement of the horse while knowing it wasn't.

"Hoclia and Alkaan broke the treaties they signed. All of them, not just the few we've fought the last few years." Phillippe's gaze roamed over the surrounding plains as he spoke. "And if not for my marriage … Tenoa may have done the same. The rumors of fire-breathing beasts, the destruction of fields throughout the known continent." He pressed his lips together and exhaled through his nose. "They both think I am responsible, that I have control over whether or not the myths of my ancestors are real. And, for all I know, Tenoa agrees."

"I'm more concerned about Jearnia's silence, Sire," Azeiah said, his own mischievous glint darkening with the somber reality. "Their crest—"

"The fire itself, ours the beast which creates such flame," Phillippe finished. "A history inexplicably twisted together. But I agree, such silence is strange."

"I wonder where those scouts you sent—"

"I didn't send them, Azeiah. No need to poke the sleeping beast." Phillippe grimaced. *Not yet, at least.*

"And the rumors," Azeiah said, his voice hushed, though just loud enough to be heard above the steady beating of hooves against the well-traveled dirt path. "Fire-breathing beasts—"

Several shouts sounded down the line, leading to a halt of Azeiah's voice and of the battalion. Phillippe and Azeiah guided their mares to the front.

"One of ours," Phillippe muttered, watching a mounted soldier approach them. They'd barely made it an hour's march outside Vandyl's gates. He had no need to hear the scout's tone; Phillippe already knew their path would change to the north. He'd known as soon as they left the gates by how his stomach twisted and turned, as though trying to pull him from within toward the path the Gift intended.

"Sire!" the soldier exclaimed as he came to a halt, nearly throwing himself from the horse. The boy gasped, hands resting on his knees in a half-bow before standing to attention.

"Well?" Azeiah asked. His horse pranced a step to the side. "An attack?"

"No, sir, but Hoclia's army, at least two hundred, maybe more, approaches the border, north of Pasea."

Phillippe glanced southwest, though the city of Cantadad would not be visible for several days. "As I suspected." He squeezed his legs against the mare's thighs to quiet her fidgeting and spoke firmly to the scout. "We do not attack, but we will always defend and protect our own. How many days before they arrive, Corporal?"

"A week at most, Sire." The scout's words sent shivers down Phillippe's spine. A week was not enough time to visit his siblings and return to Pasea before Hoclia attacked. Phillippe muttered a curse; his brothers and sister would have to wait. Another chill spread over him as he wondered if he would ever speak to his siblings again.

"Then we go to Pasea now."

At his decision, the general shouted loud enough for all to hear their change of direction. And what awaited them.

"Return to Vandyl, Corporal." Phillippe searched for blank paper in his bag, scribbling hastily as he explained, "Inform them my battalion goes to protect Pasea and send Banner-Captain Preston's battalion to join us. Then, make sure this message makes it to Cantadad, to Duchess Adela."

The message to his sister was simple: "Keep our brothers on the proper path, as you always do; Rosealyn will need your assistance. Do not forget what I have shared with you that the Gift has imparted to me—it has never been wrong about whom to trust."

The young soldier took the folded paper, saluted, and mounted his horse. Phillippe watched him gallop away, forlorn and distraught. The succession of screams sounded too clear, as though the one who made them stood at his side. *Blaze help me if Rose follows the soldiers.*

4

Roseanne frowned at the lone soldier who followed her through the castle. An order of Phillippe's, she was positive. The man was becoming more cautious with each passing day, but he still ran toward danger rather than away from it. Though she had joined Phillippe during his short stay in the castle, she preferred her own rooms when her husband was away. Roseanne hated the emptiness that spread around his usual abodes in the castle. She pushed thoughts of Phillippe aside as she hastened her walk; dinner was not far off.

In her distraction, Roseanne returned to their shared quarters, still prepared per Phillippe's request. But all of her belongings remained in her rooms since it was useless to move them, knowing Phillippe would leave soon. And she had been right. Roseanne opened the door, half expecting to find Phillippe sitting inside. Everything was in its place, as though he had not left. But he had left. Again. She did not release the handle, closing the door and backing away, and quickened her pace to her private rooms.

The soldier tried to follow her inside and visibly blanched when she pinned him with an icy stare. Instead, he took up position outside the door and Roseanne furrowed her brows. *What good will one soldier do if the castle is attacked?*

She could take no more than a shallow breath while hindered by the tightened laces roped along the back of her bodice, but this space comforted her. Roseanne's sitting room held several chairs around a low table, though no other noblewomen were close enough to join her for an afternoon tea. Her sister-in-law, Adela, and brothers-in-law, Theo and Alan, had all ventured southwest months ago, taking up residence with their cousins in Cantadad.

Nevertheless, she loved the ambiance of the plush chairs in bright colors next to the deep brown wood. The setup created the perfect complement to her writing desk in the farthest corner of the room. This was her space, where she could reminisce, where she could wear dresses that did not utilize tightened strings roping up the back, cinching her into the cloth. It was a pity the much more comfortable loose-flowing Tenoan style had not taken hold after her arrival to this country.

Roseanne sat in one of the chairs, knees bumping the low table as she did. Atop it were her mementos from home—a box of smooth sand housed the small plants that coated the air with a sweet perfume, a scent which reminded her of plump fruits. Those tiny tan granules could be gritty, annoying, and dull, but they were home, too. The plants had spiked leaves that glistened in the sunlight poking through the small windows set at intervals along the walls. She kept several plants in each room of her chambers, allowing her to breathe in a reminder of where she had grown up, of what she had been instructed to leave behind.

But most of all, the plants were a reminder of her missing sister. Catarina loved all plants and had marveled at the beauty of Vandyl's palace gardens during their first visit. Foolish to think of her long-lost sister on the same day Phillippe left. Logical, but foolish.

She drug her hand through the sand to circle each plant as she let the tension in her shoulders ease. After dwelling on the past a moment too long, she stood. Her swift steps clicked against marble stone, occasionally muffled by rugs. One a solid black, the next a solid white, the rugs formed a running pattern of the LeNoir family colors. Walking through to the next room, she was surrounded by a rainbow of fabric in an otherwise dull castle. From the same deep blue she used to see in the ocean to the pale pink of dawn and every color in between, her dresses hung on either side of the narrow room.

To her right hung the typical Orda'anian garb which held snug from her bosom to her hips, a slight flare leading from the bodice's lower edge and down to the floor. Tenoan dresses crowded the other side, her favorite dresses from her faraway home. Phillippe didn't mind that she preferred to wear the Tenoan dresses, though he insisted she wear the proper attire in the courts, and she constantly had to remind the princess to do the same.

Tenoan dresses did not cling to her body like the dress she was struggling to remove. She could just reach the laces tied at the top between her shoulder blades, tugging until they loosened. Released from their hold, Roseanne took a proper deep breath. It felt good to fill her lungs.

Shoving the tight garment to the ground, she stepped out of it and grabbed a Tenoan dress in her favorite red hue. The same shade as the one she had worn for their wedding, it reminded her of the deep crimson of the morning sun as it first kissed the horizon, flaring against the diminishing darkness of night which it overcame. Roseanne pulled the dress over her head and relaxed. It was a perfect translucent and billowed in the breeze floating through the open window in her bedchambers, making her feel like she was floating.

A soft knock sounded at the outer door. Roseanne opened it to see Leila, one of her younger servants, waiting in the hallway, bowing. "There you are." Roseanne snatched the paper from Leila's hand and squinted at the unbroken Tenoan seal. *This better be from Ramon.*

"Send word to Rosealyn I will join her soon," Roseanne said as she lowered herself onto one of the plush chairs. "And make sure one of you is here when I return from the evening meal."

Leila's cheeks flushed. She curtsied and squeaked an almost inaudible, "Yes, Your Majesty."

Roseanne did not wait for the door to shut before her steady fingers ripped the seal open. She scanned the few words quickly. Then again.

Young Lord Desmond has been voted onto the council. Do not fear for my position as Praetor. As always, I have a plan. He will find you and help you.

~Ramon

His failure to prevent the addition of a councilman did make her worry about his role as the council's praetor. The man was smart and had led them well, but not all appreciated the abrasiveness Ramon had brought to their country.

"And if he is removed, will any of our borders be safe?"

The empty room offered no answer.

Roseanne glanced at the final line again while repositioning the crown which had shifted during her quick perusal. The paper crinkled as her hands trembled. *He will find you and help you.* Standing with a steadying breath, she approached the hearth with a crackling flame and tossed in the crumpled paper. Its edges curled and reddened as the fire consumed it. *What does that mean?*

Roseanne decided to decipher the phrase later; it was time to join her daughter for dinner. The hours following Phillippe's inevitable departures led to her walking through the hallways as though blind, ignorant of those who offered quick bows and curtsies. Every piece of decor reminded her of him and of the danger he insisted on placing himself in. Compounded by the fact she had a guard as well. Though she did not recognize the soldier, she found his presence irritating. It was another sign the peace Phillippe had worked so hard to find was unraveling.

A simple dining room awaited her. Sparse walls, simple furniture, same as the rest of the castle. Dark brown table, dark brown chairs, glow of the sunset through the one open window mimicking the flickering torches lining the walls. An already seated Rosealyn smirked when the soldier entered behind Roseanne. She pressed her lips together as her gaze raked over those present. Two servants, one behind Rosealyn, the other behind her empty chair. She took her position at the far end of the table, sidelong to Rosealyn and opposite Phillippe's empty seat.

They sat in silence as plates filled with chunks of meat and bread were set before them. A miracle, really, to have this much. Scouts brought daily reports of more blighted fields across the country. If rumors were to be believed, the destruction came from dragons. Stories created to fend off reality. Man could create fire, too. The destruction of resources, such as the burned fields across the entirety of the continent of Ebios, was no more than a fight for survival. A competition of control.

"Did the captain not wish to join us?" Roseanne asked. Though the plates were full, the colors were dreary, as though everything were cast in gray.

Rosealyn gestured toward the youthful soldier standing by the door. "Don't fear, my armored shadow is near, just like yours. Captain Charles is only my guard for part of the day, Mother, as you are well aware."

"Yes, right." Roseanne shifted her plate so the meat rested closest to her, though she had little desire to eat. "How goes your training?"

"Well enough," her daughter said, consuming a large bite.

Roseanne smoothed her expression, wishing Rosealyn would stop being so nonchalant in her responses. The rift between them seemed irreparable. The years Roseanne had spent wallowing in despair after her sister's disappearance had been a waste of time and damaged what chance she'd had at a decent relationship with Rosealyn.

Roseanne flicked at the pieces of meat with her fork. "Phillippe asked me to give you more responsibilities," she announced, controlling her features when the princess sat taller. "You are to join the morning briefs with Reeve. It seems you will have to pull yourself away from those ancient texts you enjoy so much."

"History, Mother," Rosealyn said. The expression of excitement on her face at the announcement flashed to frustration. "They are not mere ancient texts." She took another bite and washed it down with a small sip of wine. "Any news from Cousin Ramon?"

"Yes. There are now five to the council, and I worry about his position, especially since it's uncertain if we can maintain the trade routes with how many fields have been destroyed."

"Father will find the culprits soon."

The two women fell into silence. Try as she might, Roseanne could not form a connection with Rosealyn as her husband did. A knot formed in her stomach, and she set the fork across the plate, signaling she was finished. *So foolish to attempt this dinner on the eve of Phillippe leaving.*

Roseanne settled back into her seat and gently repositioned her crown. Raised the eldest daughter of a councilman, she knew the importance of leadership, but in Tenoa one could present their hair however they wished. Shaved, braided, flowing to any length regardless of station—Roseanne missed the feel of her locks tickling the back of her neck and shoulders. By now, her hair would likely brush against the majority of her back, coming to rest just above her waist. But it was pulled taut, tugging against her scalp and the edges of her forehead, every strand in its proper place.

In Tenoa, the braid had been her least favorite. A braid could not emulate the ebb and flow of the sea, nor could it mimic the swirl of sand caught in a rotating wind. Here, the braid *was* a second crown atop her head, protecting the solid gold circlet that always seemed to stray. The memory of her free-flowing locks brought a pang of nostalgia, colored with her sister's laughter from when they both had failed to create the Orda'anian royal braid as youths.

She massaged the edges of her scalp, trying to ease the pressure to no avail. Rosealyn's hair was in the dual half-braids, allowing it to flow down her back while keeping it away from her maturing face—only the Orda'anian queen could have a braid resembling a crown. The pang of nostalgia turned to worry as she thought of her daughter's hair wrapped like her own.

Rosealyn flicked her fork at a chunk of meat. "I wish Father would let me go with him."

"As his only heir?" Roseanne gave a slight shake of her head, just enough to indicate her disapproval. "That would not be smart. Your father, and I, would worry too much."

Rosealyn harrumphed, and her fork clanged against her plate. "Mother, I've barely been outside the castle grounds in the last year. The city of Vandyl flows outwards from these walls and seems to grow every day and I—" She clenched her hands into fists. "I'm told to stay here, to stay safe, to avoid the dangers along the borders."

Roseanne grimaced, letting the silent pause linger; the forming knot turned her stomach against her. *The dangers Phillippe always runs toward.*

Her daughter leaned forward. "Why not join Father? I've studied battles, I've studied mediations, I've studied every king who has ever sat on Orda'an's throne and know their stories better than anyone. But instead—"

After flattening both palms, Rosealyn leaned back in her chair and continued in a half-mocking tone, displaying her naïveté. "Keep training, keep improving." She paused again, adding more forcefully, "Captain Charles believes I can protect myself well enough, and it's not as though Father would let me go anywhere without that man. He's the most prominent shadow of all my guards."

As if summoned by her words, the captain appeared in the doorway with his ever-present unreadable expression. Rosealyn straightened and rested her hands in her lap, cheeks flushing as she stared down at her half-empty plate.

"Care to join us, Captain?" Roseanne asked.

"Thank you, Your Majesty, but I am here on business." The captain offered a slight bow to each. "Banner-Captain Rake sent me to deliver this information tonight rather than at the morning briefing."

Roseanne waited, one eyebrow lifting expectantly.

"The king's battalion heads to Pasea, Your Majesty." The usually stiff captain's shoulders slumped a smidgen. "The scouts returned with the news moments ago."

"Hoclia?" Rosealyn whispered.

Roseanne's stomach tightened further, remembering Ramon's last line to her.

"According to the scout, yes, Princess," Charles said with a curt nod.

"I must return Ramon's message." Roseanne rose from her seat and left Rosealyn alone with the captain.

Roseanne hastened back to her quarters and sat at the small corner desk, snapping at the servant girl to leave despite having insisted the young lady be present at her return. The same anxiety which arose when Roseanne tried to write to Catarina reared as she attempted to respond to Ramon. A blank page stared back at her. She rubbed her eyes and set the pen down to turn and stretch.

When she craned her neck, her crown shifted, and she nestled it back atop her head while surveying the room. Every piece in its proper place. She squinted. Almost every piece. What appeared as a pebble-sized speck of dirt lifted from the floor, and her fingers gripped the back of her chair more tightly. The small black cloud hovered in midair above the low table. As though it knew she was looking, it moved closer. Roseanne froze, grateful she had consumed so little at dinner. Moments stretched, her breaths shortened, but nothing more materialized. *Can this "he" of which Ramon speaks bring Phillippe home? And keep him home? Does this "he" have a way to stop a war before it's too late?*

"Roseanne?"

Her heart jumped as her insides fell. She surveyed her room quickly. The soldier stood outside, and the voice had not been loud enough to be heard through the walls.

"He will find you and help you," she whispered.

"Good, Ramon told you," the disembodied voice replied. Roseanne shook her head, positive she had fallen asleep atop the blank page on her desk. *No harm in listening to a dream.*

"Apologies I cannot come myself. Soon, you will meet me. But first—"

The cloud shrank and Roseanne strained to listen. Snippets of suggested trade routes. She tugged at her lower lip, reviewing the list she had created. Some were logical enough she had already considered them. Others were useless as they would supply abandoned towns. What could one extra wagon of food provide to towns which struggled to survive after the destruction of their fields? Yet, as this unusual disembodied voice explained, providing for those who had lost—no matter how small their group—would resow the seeds of trust Phillippe may have lost.

The pen fell from her grasp to roll along the paper. *What have you roped me into, Ramon?*

5

As the days turned into weeks, Rosealyn fell into the routine she had created during her father's prolonged absences, choosing to linger in the areas of the castle which made her feel closest to him. When she wasn't training, she meditated in the gardens or sat at his desk—as she did now.

King Gailin's telling of how Orda'an descended into a civil war was the first story she had reread. She spoke the words aloud, one hand tracing the stitched outline of a black rose just above the waistline of her emerald green dress as she did. *"Lord Edmund moved to the small town of Vandyl, paying men to join his army and build a castle of his own. It's ironic he used dragonstone, considering dragons no longer exist. Nothing more than a name for creatures designed to scare young children from their dangerous adventures, though the stone is beautiful. Strange how he believes in a beast he has never seen."*

She looked up to inspect the wall of her father's study. A solid stone wall, blacker than the darkest night. Dragonstone. A smidge to her right, the heavy wooden door stood open. She glanced up every few minutes, despite knowing her father would not appear there today. Instead, she was greeted by Daniel's too-fake grin.

Behind her, a small window allowed the noonday sun to shine on the desk, lighting the aging pages of the journal. Grunts and clashes sounded below, pulling her from her reading. She strained to look, to see who was sparring, but the palace garden balcony blocked a view of the training rings. The sounds echoed from one stone wall to the next until their muted thuds met her ears. Each concussion was a reminder of the many bruises she had received in those same circles, her opponent besting her more times than she cared to admit. Recent months had led to her beating her opponents more and more often. Her primary trainer and bodyguard, the methodical and resilient Captain Charles, still managed to knock her down every time they sparred. *One day, I'll knock him down.*

Rosealyn was sure the captain would soon insist on her practicing with more weapons. New locations, new arenas, new opponents. Turning back to the journal, she could no longer focus on the words. The increased vigor of training since her father last left surprised her. But despite her questioning, the captain was ever cautious in his responses.

Scout reports arrived regularly, as her father had promised. Skirmishes, he called them, but the returning wounded told a different story. Doctor Alvin was skilled in his craft, but even he did not have the magical liquids of the elves' stories. Rosealyn believed none had ever held such magic which could knit a wound back together, soothe a stinging burn, or draw out a poison. Stories. Myths told to her as a child.

Rosealyn moved the journal's thin ribbon back between the pages, closing the book with a gentle reverence, and stood, taking one more survey of her father's study before leaving. Her slippered feet whispered against the gray stone floors. *And thank the Blazes Daniel knows how to keep his sword belt silent.*

Her dress seemed to shift from green to black as the open windows let in wide rays of the midmorning sun. She passed her mother's private chambers, the ones the queen kept when her father was away, on her path to return the journal to its place in the library. A moment's hesitation, Rosealyn reached for the handle and paused. No matter how the conversation began, even if it started with an apology, it would end in an argument. All of their interactions did. Neither could ever provide the other any ounce of solace or comfort while her father was away.

Rosealyn lowered her hand and fidgeted with her skirts for a second while staring at her mother's closed door. She wanted to understand her mother, to connect with her like she did her father. But since Rosealyn was not in the mood to argue, she chose to continue her steady walk down the hallway.

Her mother seemed to live in a different world. Often, with her father away, Rosealyn wondered if her mother was harboring secrets, crafting lies about the messages received from Ramon, but she dismissed the thought. Just because their personalities clashed did not mean her mother was doing anything wrong. The journal returned, Rosealyn continued to her own quarters.

Chairs of varying sizes and hues created a haphazard circle in the vast front room of her quarters. Though she often read in the library or her father's study, choosing a different chair each evening had become a nighttime ritual. She strolled toward the hallway connecting the front room to her bedchamber, passing the closet and washroom connected to either side.

Lori approached from the inner room, carrying a new gown, to find Rosealyn struggling to remove her dress.

"No need to strain yourself, my lady." Lori pulled the strings loose, and Rosealyn took a deep breath then shoved the bodice of the dress down. The dresses were gorgeous, and she loved how she looked in them, but she much preferred being able to move and breathe.

"Thank you, Lori." She ran a hand along the dress Lori held. "I like this dress, too. Simple, elegant."

"Perfect for your visit to the city streets of Vandyl, my lady." Lori held the dress out for Rosealyn.

She stepped into the gown and stiffened when Lori tugged on each string and tied them in a bow between her shoulder blades. The bodice fit snugly against her chest, making her breaths shallow again. The material itself was plain. No decorative flowers, no ornate designs, not even her signature rose bloom outlined on the waist. Both the bodice and skirts were a gentle white, no different from the papers she used to write letters to her father while he was away. Letters he had been returning with less frequency the longer he remained at Pasea.

She glanced at herself in the lone mirror, admiring how well the solid color of the dress showed off her darker skin. The only person in the castle with skin darker than hers was her mother.

"Is it a recent design, Lori?" Rosealyn shifted her hair onto her back, running her fingers along the half-braid on either side of her head to where they met, smoothing the unbraided locks which flowed just past her shoulders. An unadorned circle of solid gold rested on a table just below the mirror. She glanced at the circlet and moved to reposition a few strands of hair off her shoulders instead. Wearing the circlet in the city streets, Rosealyn decided, would present the wrong impression to the citizens.

"Yes, my lady, arrived just this morning," Lori said, gathering the dirty bed-linens she had set down.

"It's perfect," Rosealyn said as a knock sounded.

Lori opened the door to find Captain Charles in his usual garb. Black coat with white buttons, black pants, and a sword with a leather-bound hilt wrapped around his waist. Rosealyn smirked at the unclasped topmost button. Of her three guards, the captain toed the line of "proper" most often. Neither Daniel nor Moss seemed to even consider unbuttoning their coats, not even when the bold red sun beat down upon them in the sparring rings.

"Perfect timing, Captain, as always." Rosealyn walked over to Charles, wondering if her cheeks flushed as often as his did. He gave his curt nod and led her through the hallways toward the castle gates in silence.

The captain's gaze darted about, hunting for the smallest signs of danger, while Rosealyn watched the bustle of the surrounding castle. Servants scurried from the pantries to the kitchens in their drab brown with darker spots, bright white aprons soiled with the remnants of food, carrying pots, pans, and even bags of produce. Mildewing and rotten food, with bags nowhere near as full as the previous year.

Maids in pristine white with a black apron wrapped around their waists walked with purpose, some carrying fresh linens, others walking with wrinkled noses at the stench of the soiled bedclothes. Different livery, different services. The stable hands were nowhere to be seen as she walked. When she wasn't reading, Rosealyn watched the servants, learning their mannerisms and habits and their names. *Mariah with the clean linens, not so young anymore. Jack with the large full pot. Little Charles who no longer responds to Charlie with the dismal basket of barely rotten fruit. All with jobs, tasks to keep them busy, occupy their minds.*

The castle gates stood open, as her father commanded they should, but she could see the metal rods hiding within the grand walls of solid dragonstone. Beside them rested a cart of food.

She rummaged through it, frowning. "Half of this food isn't worth giving to others." She picked up an apple, wincing as her nail pierced its skin. "Or eating for that matter."

"It's all the kitchens could spare, Princess," Charles said, scrunching his nose as he lifted the handles of the cart.

Rosealyn nodded with tight lips as she walked beside Charles and into the city. The occasional clash of weapons behind her dissolved into silence for several paces. As their ambling walk continued, the sounds of squeaking wheels, rumbling voices, and shouts resonated around her.

The castle gates gave way to haphazard buildings. One main street stretched through the city with alleys branching off at awkward angles. Rather than be designed before its construction, Vandyl developed as it needed the space. When a building no longer fit one's needs, they added onto it. Sometimes that meant making their buildings taller. Other times it meant adding accommodations where no one else had. None of Vandyl's homes or shops matched. Not in color or in size. Taller buildings resided closest to the castle, diminishing in height the further they walked.

The city came more alive with each step she took, but her frown deepened. A stench which made her appetite flail into nausea permeated the dry air. The occasional waft of freshly baked bread did little to assist, though she was positive that scent would have made her mouth water without the other turning her tongue bitter.

"Has food gone so scarce?" Rosealyn eyed the commoners sitting along the sides of the streets who appeared to wither into the wood behind them.

"There are many blighted fields, Princess." Charles concentrated on avoiding the pits and falls of the dirt road with the cart he pushed. "And Her Majesty rerouted some of the trade lines, sending food to the smaller towns along the northern border. Even to the half-deserted towns of Lobelia and Lycene."

"Curious," Rosealyn whispered, distracted by finding her footing. "How far are we going?"

"Not far, Princess." Charles shifted the cart down a side street. Rosealyn followed, glancing behind her to see a few people follow them. She moved close enough to Charles that the sheath of his sword bumped against her leg.

"They're following the supplies, Princess."

Rosealyn nodded, tripped on a tiny mound of dirt within the road, and muttered a curse. Sprinkles of brown dust showered the bottom of her dress, and her toe throbbed. The cart Charles held stopped squeaking.

"There's no one—"

Small children, pale skin smudged with grime, lingered in the crevices between decaying buildings. Those who appeared a few years older than the rest grasped the hands of the younger children and inched their way forward with careful, cautious steps. Her heart fell, watching them each amble forward with wide eyes. Young girls clung to the thinning cloth hanging loose against their bodies as they curtsied. The boys held fists in the air, as though holding invisible skirts, imitating the girls. Despite her dismay, Rosealyn smiled, but it disappeared when she noted the large holes dotting the children's clothing. She rummaged through the cart, trying to find the best pieces of fruit for the children.

"There are several more groups like theirs, Princess," Charles whispered beside her, and she gave him a sidelong glance. The muscles of his jaw clenched, making the small white scar along its edge more apparent. Beyond the stoicism, beyond the pensive smoothness, Rosealyn found compassion and sorrow. Her gaze flicked back to the scar she had asked about once. In response, he had remained silent for almost a week, speaking only when absolutely necessary.

"It's best to offer only one piece at a time, Princess."

"Where are their parents?" Rosealyn whispered back, halting her study of the newfound emotions awakening the sharp lines and smooth edges of Charles's face and handing another piece of fruit down to a small boy. The little boy bowed at the waist, squeaked out a quick "thank you, Princess," and ran back into the recesses between the buildings.

Charles shrugged, holding a piece of bread out without looking down. "His Majesty and General Azeiah discussed strange disappearances all over the country before they left. They planned to ask your aunt and uncles about it, especially since it is not just soldiers anymore. I wish I could tell you more, Princess."

Rosealyn tensed, staring down at another dirt-ridden face. The child's enormous brown eyes were full of awe. He plucked the food from her hand and scurried away, biting into the half-rotten apple as he went. "Any news from Father?"

"His Majesty remains at Pasea," Charles said, with a tone indicating he had nothing else to say on the matter. A gentle, calloused hand pulled hers back. "Princess, they all have a piece to eat now. I know it's not much, but it's time to move on."

Rosealyn bit her lower lip while rubbing the fabric of her dress between the fingers of her right hand and studied the gaunt faces of what her father once described as a thriving market street. Tears would not become the future queen and certainly would not become a princess. But the edges of her vision fogged, making it difficult to visualize the withering frames of the people. *Her* people. Orphans, homeless and hungry. Families, broken and battered. While her greatest worry was nursing the bruises from her training sessions, those living just outside the castle gates starved.

Burned fields meant dwindling crops, she knew that. She had acknowledged it. Even her own stomach grumbled in protest when she left half the food untouched, insisting others eat it. The food on her plates had grown scarce. Before, the vibrant colors of fruits and vegetables covered every inch. Over the past several months, the painted clay became more visible. Visiting the streets of Vandyl should have been exciting, but every new sunken face was like a stab to her chest.

A few paces later, Charles led her down a different side street to witness an identical scene. His voice became softer, gentler, and more caring as they continued. His hands provided quiet guidance through the streets, showing her a side of him she had not yet seen. Her resolute bodyguard did feel, though she was unsure if it was his care for her or for the people. Rosealyn's mind was too preoccupied to decide. They continued down several more side streets until the cart of food stood empty. She wrung her skirts with each hand, wishing she had more to offer. *How can I convince Father to let me help?*

Their walk back to the castle grounds encountered more groups of eager children braving the market in hopes of goods. Each step back to the castle made it harder for Rosealyn to hold her head high. Part of her role, and her parents' role, was to protect and provide for the people. Questions rested on the tip of her tongue: what more could they bring, what shelter could they offer, how would they keep the people from dying, from starving? Her lack of answers made it impossible to look at anyone, and her chin sank lower.

Silence lingered until they were back inside the castle's walls. Her throat clenched, suffocating the sobs which threatened to escape. This was not the city of Vandyl she remembered. It was not the city where children ran together, laughter echoing off the sturdy, well-maintained buildings. It was not the city where families ran businesses together, passing bakeries or shops from father to son for generations. It was not the city she and her father had visited together less than a year ago. *Is this why Father insisted I stay in the castle? Did he not want me to see their suffering as he has? A cart of spoiled food… We are better.*

The smack of wood against wood was like a warm embrace, but the hollowness of the children's faces tugged at her heart.

"Another training session, Princess?"

Rosealyn shook her head, shivering at the cool breeze, wiping the sting of escaped tears from her cheeks. "I need to speak with Mother. We must ensure we feed the people."

Charles bowed and resumed his grip on the cart, pushing it back to the kitchens where scraps would refill it to be delivered the following day. Rosealyn wiped at her cheeks again. She could do more than provide rotten food. Mind racing, she stood like a statue in the castle's bustling entrance until her armored shadow returned to her side, asking another question she chose not to hear.

A commotion near the stables pulled her from her thoughts. Soldiers gave their mounts a quick scan and rode out the same gates through which she had just returned. Unlike Rosealyn in her white dress with a dirtied hem, the soldiers wore armor and weapons. They went to battle. They went to replace the wounded who survived the journey home. They went to join her father. *I can fight, too.*

6

With the second battalion came proper supplies for setting up camp near Pasea. Seated at a desk barely large enough to hold a single piece of paper, Phillippe stared at the envelope he had just sealed, wishing he could deliver the message in person, and tucked it into his inner pocket. He rubbed at his nose when a waft of his own stench reached it, making him reminisce about the perfumed baths servants would insist on providing for him when he returned to the castle. No amount of soap could clean what he had seen or done nor how he felt. The grime hid the LeNoir colors running along his sleeves, helping his coat blend into his plain mud-caked pants. No matter how many times he scraped at it, the dirt and sweat continued to accumulate as his battalion defended Pasea.

A set of dull armor rested by the tent's thin wall, propped near the roll of material some called a bed. Phillippe's sword lay next to his small desk, always within arm's reach. Two steps separated the so-called bed and desk, reminding Phillippe this was not his quarters in the castle.

He patted the letter tucked into his pocket, idly wondering what Roseanne would say if she found it or read it. Faint screams crescendoed—again—and his thoughts shifted to the nearby town he had come to protect as he rubbed his eyes with his palms.

Close to the circles of tents which formed the camp, Pasea had transitioned from bustling thoroughfare to solemn tension. The largest border town between Orda'an and Hoclia, Pasea was a target in need of protection. Phillippe rested his elbows on the small writing desk, vision glossing over the map and its markings as he rubbed his temples to ease his aching head. More than Pasea was in danger.

"Morning reports, Sire."

Phillippe lifted his gaze, dry eyes flinching at the glow of the morning sun. The Gift often startled him awake at night, oscillating between visions not even exhaustion could prevent. Visions involving screams and a plummeting dark blade.

He leaned back, smudging his face with ink as he massaged his temples and rubbed against his cheekbones. "Any changes, General?"

"More missing. Privates. Here for the evening, gone by morning," the general said. He sounded distant, strained. The man often reminded Phillippe of an immovable cliff, but the continuous skirmishes grated on them both, as did the strange disappearances. "A few Under-Lieutenants missed their morning reports."

Each day, more soldiers went missing. By choice or by force, Phillippe was unsure. He grimaced and leaned forward, resting forearms on the desk and stifling a yawn. "Suggestions?"

The general shrugged, and Phillippe rubbed the growing stubble of his chin.

"Only the lower ranks so far, Azeiah?"

"Yes, Sire." Azeiah paused, shifting the helmet he held against his side. The general's hint of mischief dissipated with each day, returning to the formality Phillippe disliked. "We must adjust the rations again; the last shipments have yet to arrive, and Pasea needs the funds of selling their produce."

Phillippe's stomach grumbled at the mention of food. Between lack of sleep and food rationing, he grew weaker by the day over the past month.

"Any change in Hoclia's position?"

"Not since the last report, Sire."

"A minor relief," Phillippe muttered, one-handedly rubbing his temples. His eyelids drifted closed for a second, but he forced them back open lest he see the blade again. The screams were impossible to escape.

Phillippe, who always relied on the power of words, had failed. Both Hoclia and Alkaan accused him of lying during the brief summit in Violet Grove. He attempted reasoning, showed kindness, and even drafted new treaties. It all meant nothing. Words meant little when every resource his northern neighbors had was gone while his country still managed. It was ironic, really, that a budding war over resources caused the destruction of what few resources remained. Despite the fruitful fields of their southern ally in Tenoa, Orda'an's resources continued to dwindle.

Phillippe frowned at the jangling sounds of soldiers running, followed by loud shouts. He looked at Azeiah, but the general was already outside barking orders. Phillippe donned his breastplate, strapped his sword belt around his waist, and grabbed his helmet before exiting the tent.

Remnants of the soldiers' morning porridge scattered across the ground formed interlocking rivulets as their poor excuse for sustenance stained the dirt like blood. The Gift's screams were no longer distant. They threatened to overtake his senses, crescendoing when he recognized the lone horse riding into camp. Breaths came shallower as Rosealyn rode closer, slowing from a trot to a walk, until she stopped and dismounted next to him. Both Rosealyn and her horse were matted with sweat, and the flowing beige dress he had seen her wear so often when sparring with Charles clung to her body. A cooling wind whistled around them, blowing stray locks of her hair across her face. The skirts of her dress billowed, one side held fast by the lackluster blade hanging at her hip.

He wanted to bury his head in his hands to quiet the screams. His daughter was here.

A triumphant grin plastered on her face, she embraced him. "I couldn't sit and wait any longer."

She stepped back when he made no move to return the embrace. Around them, the soldiers continued their tasks, rallying together in hopes to push back Hoclia's advance. Again. Each day Hoclia tried. Soldiers died. On both sides. Nothing changed. But Pasea's fields, their produce, remained protected. That was why he stayed, to protect his people. A muscle twitched in his jaw. That was why she had come, too.

Phillippe grimaced in return. "I told you not to evade your guards."

Rosealyn waved a dismissive hand. "Mother is as aloof as always, and my armored shadows taught me well."

The screams of the Gift surged, and Phillippe tensed. "You shouldn't be here, Rosealyn."

His daughter tilted her head to one side, squinting; he never called her by her full name.

"What did you see?" Rosealyn's hand moved toward the hilt of her sword, pausing before grasping it.

He looked away, unable to hide the tremor in his voice. "Heard, felt, not seen," he muttered. "You shouldn't be here."

Rosealyn threw her arms up in the air. Then, more steadily than he believed she could, she pulled the blade from its sheath, testing its weight in her hand as others do before sparring. "Then why teach me to fight?"

"Sire, they're attacking." Azeiah looked between Rosealyn and Phillippe, and back again, before speaking directly to Phillippe. "The forward troops are in position and await your command."

"Send the Hoclians back to their lands." He clenched his jaw until his teeth ground together. "For good this time."

Phillippe removed the weapon from his daughter's hands and returned it to the sheath resting on her hip. Every muscle in his shoulders tensed. "Do *not* follow us, Rosealyn."

He held his breath until she gave a simple nod. Wrapping her hands in his, he gently kissed her forehead. *Blaze protect her while I cannot.*

Rosealyn watched her father stride away and followed. Walking with the sword around her waist was awkward, un-natural. With every step, it shifted or bumped against her, and a bruise was forming where it had dug into her side during the ride to Pasea.

Her pace slowed when the throaty shouts, roars at the tops of the soldiers' lungs, reached her ears. No matter how many times she read Gailin's entries or any other accounts of battles waged, she was not ready for the sight before her. It was like a thunderstorm appeared in the midst of a calm blue day, threatening to rip apart the ground with each shudder of the darkening sky. Clashes of steel reminded her of blinding bolts of lightning, appearing and disappearing more quickly than she could blink.

Her father blended into a sea of men wearing identical armor, identifiable by his blond hair shimmering in the sun. But soon he donned his helmet, and she lost track of him amid the others. A sea of black armor waited for the Hoclians' approach.

The men racing toward her father's soldiers seemed to multiply, covering the green grass of Pasea's fields with their brown and tan coats. Many tripped over the uneven ground in their haste. Not tripped, Rosealyn realized, seeing the minuscule sticks protruding from chests, shoulders, and heads. She had missed the release of a volley of arrows, had not seen them rain down on the approaching enemy. A shout shifted her gaze to her father standing with his sword. Another volley of arrows released. Her breath froze when the lightly armored Hoclians did not hesitate to plummet into the line of Orda'anian soldiers.

Nausea welled inside at the mixture of sweat and blood. Her knees met the ground beneath her, sending a tremor through every inch of her body. Palms pressed tightly over her ears, she looked in desperation for her father. But all she saw were Hoclians breaching the camp. Her eyes widened, horrified, while the cacophony of metal against metal, blade against blade, shout versus shout continued. Each new concussion quickened her already racing heart.

Rosealyn gasped for air, clutching a hand to her chest, standing to search the battlefield for any sign of her father. Her line of sight broke, invaded by a burly unarmored man prowling toward her, his mouth curled in a strange smile. She swallowed forcefully, attempting to focus on the new threat. All the soldiers were fighting. None remained in the camp. None remained to protect her.

The gasps continued. Had she forgotten how to breathe? Had Charles followed her? She worked to calm the rapid movement of her chest. *I came here to help. I can protect myself.*

Rosealyn gripped the hilt of her sword. She stepped backward with each stride the man took forward. Lips tightened, jaw set. His smirk twisted the scars along his face like the tiny cracks of a broken mirror. Her insides churned. She lost control of her lungs again. Air escaped without replacement. She could see the discoloration of the man's scars, could see the shape of them. The sword felt foreign against sweating palms.

"W-we…" She tried to speak but was too winded. Her lungs burned.

This scarred, aging man could *kill* her.

Several days ago she had been proud of escaping her guards, sneaking out of the castle with them unawares, eager to be of use for her people. For the first time since her father had insisted she train, she truly wished for his protection. She held one hand behind her, jaw clenching when the hand met the thin outer shell of a tent.

"Why?" Rosealyn managed in a hushed whisper, other hand tight around her sheathed sword. The burly man's laughter added an odd harmony to her heavy breathing. *Count. Breathe. Watch the feet.*

"Resources," came the guttural—and expected—response. The ribbed edges of his sword dripped dark liquid, but he did not raise it. His steps were quick, much quicker than a man his size should move, and he was upon her. His free hand grasped her arm while the strange smile turned sickly. Rosealyn dropped her shoulder, ducking beneath his hand and bracing to knee him in the gut. Or lower.

His outstretched hand glistened in the sunlight. His second blade, an imperceptible knife, flew with rapid speed. She twisted to avoid the slashing knife but hissed with each small gash. Tiny streams ran down her arms, blood smearing along her dress sleeves when she wiped at them.

With a gulp, she met his grim gaze. Certain her heart would burst from her chest at such speeds and fearing her lungs would fail her again, she backpedaled, trying to gain distance. Her back pressed against the tent's outer shell. Legs wobbly from the ride threatened to tumble her to the ground, but she pulled the sword free. The burly figure tilted his head and laughed. Grinding her teeth together, she swung the unbalanced sword. His blade met hers, and though she grasped the hilt with both hands, the strength of the blow threatened to knock her weapon from them. She took a step forward, inwardly counting her breaths, eyes darting between the man's shoulders and his feet.

No taunting, no waiting, no chance meeting of the other's gaze, no pause between the clashes. Rosealyn moved her feet when he did, parrying each thrust with diminishing strength. The journey to Pasea had been quick only because she had not stopped.

A millisecond of succumbing to the tiredness gave way to desperate slashes, then pain—a pain so sharp she could not withhold the scream.

His blade dripped with fresh blood.

Her blood.

A slight movement, another scream. She looked up to see his sickly smile return. Fury ignited. His foot shuffled forward, and she fell to one knee, thrusting her blade up toward his abdomen, her gaze following the sword's movement. The tip of her sword met a different resistance, and she pushed it forward with all the strength she could muster. The smile faltered, and too observant eyes widened as he stumbled, grasping at the weapon protruding from him. After several inhalations, she realized the gurgling was not coming from her.

Rosealyn pulled the sword free, sidestepping his fall while shaking her head to fight the fingertips of darkness threatening to overtake her field of vision.

Blood dripped down her arms, crawling along until it fell from her elbows like raindrops. An intense throb radiated in her abdomen where warm liquid leaked, where the once perfect color of her dress frayed and darkened. She wasn't sure which stains would bother her more: the blood or the dirt.

Red streaks covered her hands. The lines of the hilt's leather handle dug into her palm, distracting her from the intensifying pain. She tumbled to her knees next to the dead soldier and retched. Rivers of blood continued to leak from the Hoclian's wound, staining the dirt beside her dead opponent. Rosealyn gripped the sword even tighter as more screams of pain escaped.

The discordant sounds of battle dissipated, replaced with an eerie stillness which sounded like the soft crackle of fire licking the wood in a fireplace. A gentle hand pried her fingers from the hilt, murmuring soft words. *Breathe, just breathe.*

The voice registered, and she relaxed into her father's sturdy grip. Above, the reddened sky burned brighter. It smelled like … *fire?*

He carried her inside the tent, laying her on what she thought was the ground. Her vision clouded, but she felt the scream escape when her father pressed a cloth to her side. Rosealyn clutched his arm, gasping for air.

"I should've known those screams were yours," he whispered, increasing the pressure against her side. She moaned, biting her lip to prevent another scream.

"I-I'm fine," she said. The unnamed soldier's face swam in her vision as though he still stood before her with his blade raised. But his face was lifeless. She flinched at the pressure and turned away from her father, not wanting to witness the concern etched into his face. "I took care of myself. That was the point of my training."

"Sire, uh—"

Rosealyn turned toward the voice, surprised at the mixture of hope and relief Charles was not standing there instead of Banner-Captain Preston.

"Speak." That was anger in her father's voice.

The soldier wet his lips and stood taller. "General Azeiah sends word. The Hoclian general is ready to talk."

"Good," her father said. The pressure eased a little. "Pasea?"

"Not lost, but there is significant damage, Your Majesty," Preston explained. His next words were hesitant. "Princess Rosealyn … is she all right, Your Majesty?"

"She will be."

Rosealyn knew her father looked at her, but she stared at the tent's entrance instead. An ache almost as strong as the throbbing wound spread in her chest. Charles. He stopped short, one hand holding the tent flap while the other flexed at his side. Hair slick with sweat and black coat unbuttoned, he stared at her. After a mere second, she saw the muscles of his jaw clench.

"It wasn't—"

"I know, my darling Rose," her father interrupted. "I'm surprised it's taken this long for you to follow me again."

The wound throbbed, and she moved her father's hand aside to lift the cloth. Seeing it confirmed what she thought—the blade had torn through the beige fabric and sliced along her skin, same as the minor cuts which had stopped dripping blood down her arms. *Was he trying to kill me with a thousand cuts?*

"Charles will get you home safe."

Rosealyn thought of arguing, but her head throbbed, and soon all she could hear was a high-pitched ringing reverberating inside her skull. A chill slithered over every inch of her, and she succumbed to the beckoning darkness.

7

Charles clenched the tent flap in one hand, frozen in place. She was alive but injured.

"How?" Phillippe's voice was gravelly, calloused, angrier than Charles had ever heard the king speak.

"I followed as soon as I knew, Sire." Charles winced. "She went to speak with her mother and—"

At the king's raised hand, Charles paused and flexed his fist at his side. Phillippe turned back to Rosealyn, brushing a stray strand of hair from her face. He lifted the cloth pressed against the wound on her abdomen; it trickled blood, marring the beige dress. Though shallow, the wound was deep enough to cause concern, especially given Hoclians often laced their blades with potions which could make soldiers delirious for days or sometimes kill them.

Charles searched through his memories of training the princess. Had he ever told her how to identify a poisoned blade? He had taught her how to block strikes to her midsection and knew she could. His jaw ached from clenching his teeth and from the speed of following once he'd realized she'd left the castle. Focused on the unconscious princess, Charles reprimanded himself, wishing he had found a reasonable way to add the same level of fear which occurred in a real fight to her training. But he'd never wanted her to experience that fear, the worry that another's blade could be the last thing she saw.

"Take her back to Vandyl with haste, direct to Doctor Alvin." Anger, weariness, perhaps even a hint of fear. "And Blazes help you if she follows me like that again."

"Yes, Your Majesty." Charles released his hold on the tent flap and moved forward. Closer, he could see dozens of slight cuts covering her arms, and he grimaced. One arm tucked beneath her knees, the other beneath her shoulders, he uttered a silent apology as he lifted her.

Back outside the tent, they found a red-rimmed sky. Whirl-winds of orange, yellow, and red licked the encampment. The colors danced from tent to tent, engulfing each in quick succession and encroaching on the nearby town.

"Preston, smother the fires and see what fields have survived," the king called.

"Yes, Sire," the Banner-Captain said, and he raced toward the other soldiers to shout orders.

Charles followed Phillippe's gaze to the sky. Against the deepening orange of the burning camp, a faint outline flitted above the clouds, nearly hidden by their obscure surfaces. He turned back to the king, whose light skin had become pale. Charles wished he had another option aside from returning to Vandyl by horse. With effort, he stabilized an unconscious Rosealyn and swung into the saddle behind her.

"Keep her safe, Captain," the king said, and he smacked the horse's backside.

Charles rode almost as fast as he had once he'd realized Rosealyn had left the castle. After aiding the townspeople, she'd been so distraught, so angry, he imagined he'd find her having a shouting match with her mother. But the queen hadn't seen her. He knew how it grated on her to be told to stay. To feel stuck and surrounded inside massive walls. One thing was certain—Charles would have a very serious conversation with Moss and Daniel when he returned to Vandyl.

The heat of the flames engulfing the king's camp no longer nipped at his back, so he slowed to a trot. Limp before him, Rosealyn groaned. Her entire body swayed with the horse's movement, kept atop the mare only by his arm. An arm whose sleeve was sticky with her blood. A smarter bodyguard would have grabbed an additional cloth from the camp. But between the encroaching flames and the king's stern voice, Charles had neglected the simple item. He continued to use the same cloth Phillippe had until no dry spot remained, substituting with his sleeve and a silent prayer the bleeding would stop soon.

Jaw clenched, Charles glanced behind and ahead. He knew exhaustion, combined with blood loss and potential poison, had rendered the princess unconscious. When one rode foolishly fast as she had, the journey to Pasea took three days. Charles didn't know if she would have three days. The gelding was exhausted, too. As was he.

Another moan from Rosealyn made Charles tighten his grip, steadying her. Had she not been wounded, he might have enjoyed the closeness of riding together. He berated himself for even thinking about it.

Pressure from the pain of grinding his teeth together increased. His job, his role, was to protect her. Nothing more, nothing less. Any other thoughts would be wrong. Foolish, really. He had only one reason to grow closer to her, as Phillippe had said. He would aid her in one day ruling Orda'an well, if not better than her father did.

He leaned forward, listening to her steady, slow breathing. If the Hoclian soldier had fought with others before her, the poison lining the blade's edge would have been gone. He knew what else could help, though he questioned how long the healing liquids remained viable.

Rosealyn's gasp pulled Charles from his thoughts and made hope spark—consciousness so soon after the wound reduced the possibility of poison. A hiss of air through her teeth came next. She was definitely awake. Hand gripping his forearm, she leaned into him and whispered, "Stop."

He stiffened, straightening his back and leaning away from her as he gave the gelding a gentle squeeze to signal a halt. Rosealyn followed his movement, using him as support. The mare flicked its tail, a slight lift of its rear a sign they should dismount. "How are you feeling, Princess?"

"Like a Blazing idiot who should've trained harder." Her grip on his arm tightened.

"Vision blurry? Strange tastes? Clammy skin? Anything that's different, Princess?"

"Well, it's almost dusk, my tongue is dry, and my stomach has a gash in it," came the dry response. "Your turn."

"His Majesty wanted you back home with haste, Princess," Charles explained. Would it be wrong to check the wound again? No, and yes. Why was it easier to spar with Rosealyn than be her caretaker?

"Figures," she grumbled, straining to sit without assistance. She glanced down and hissed again as she shifted the material of her dress to inspect the wound. "We, and this horse, need proper rest. How far to the nearest town?"

"We passed one a half mile back, Princess," he said, dismounting. "Think you can walk?"

"I'm afraid to find out." She pinned him with an accusatory glare. "You never told me it might feel like this. Like everything is on fire, like I'd be thirsty enough to drain the Guadelaide River." She pressed a hand against the wound, grimacing.

"Pain tolerance," he mumbled, turning away to survey the area. "Shall we backtrack or find the next town, Princess?"

"Continue." Air whistled through her teeth when she shifted in the saddle. "Have you never been injured before?"

He couldn't look up into her twinkling brown eyes, not when they were likely dulled by the pain he could have prevented. Should have prevented. Nor did he know how to answer. Many of his wounds were not physical, and many were. The jagged scar along his jawbone he'd earned the week prior to meeting Phillippe. The other, less visible, scars had occurred from wounds received while fighting at Phillippe's side until, eventually, the king had chosen *him* to protect *her*. Hundreds of soldiers at the castle and Phillippe chose him. Even without the agreement, he could not have declined.

"You've seen most of my scars, Princess." He knew how distracted she became when he removed the restrictive high-buttoned coat. Every time he removed it while sparring was for two reasons—easier for him to spar and forced Rosealyn to focus.

Rosealyn cleared her throat. "Right, well. Food, rest, and why didn't someone bandage my wound?"

"His Majesty cleaned it and then…" What would Phil-lippe want her to know? What should she know? The flames engulfing the king's camp were not from a few torches. Nor were they set by men.

"Tell me," she said through gritted teeth. Exhaustion would not combine well with anger.

"They lost the camp to flame. And some of Pasea. Thus the rush *away* from danger, Princess."

Charles dared a glance up and forced himself not to smile when he found a familiar scowl. She wasn't delirious, which meant no poison. She inhaled slowly through her nose and released a ragged exhale. Ahead, several buildings glimmered on the horizon.

"We shouldn't stay more than one night, Princess." Charles studied the town ahead. It was small, only a few buildings.

They moved forward in amicable silence—Rosealyn gripping the pommel of the saddle and Charles holding the reins—until shouts rang out from the townspeople. Perhaps it was his uniform or Rosealyn's braids, but he heard her name on their lips, heard their concern. Sole heir to their country's throne, wounded. What would become of them, this country, these people, if Rosealyn died? Others in the LeNoir line lived. Her cousin, even her aunt and uncles. But the heir, the future ruling monarch, was meant to receive the LeNoir Gift. What would happen when its current wielder had no heirs?

8

Charles sat opposite Banner-Captain Rake and waited as the commanding officer read another report, observing every visible inch. The two soldiers sat on the wooden porch outside the general's command center at Charles's request. Days had turned to weeks since the flames had destroyed much of Pasea.

Though Moss, Daniel, or Charles followed her everywhere, Charles worried the princess would escape them again. They were smart, but so was she. A cool breeze whistled around them, disguising the sounds of the trainees and giving way to the musky-sweet scent of fall. Crisp air lingered, a sign the first snows approached.

"Damn, more burned fields," Banner-Captain Rake muttered. After setting the rolled paper aside, he pulled out a small pipe. Rake looked over at the cylindrical stone wall which led to the castle's underused dungeons. "And no culprit to prevent more fields from being destroyed."

"Where?" Charles held out the map they had been marking. Every day, Charles and Rake marked which fields flourished and which demolished. Too many bore lines through their names.

"Demir and Lobelia." Rake scanned the map and scratched at his untrimmed beard. "We're lucky the Shendaran Forest didn't catch fire. And no casualties. This time."

Charles nodded, marking a line through the fields outside Demir. *We won't survive through the next winter at this rate.*

"No word from the scouts sent to Jearnia." Rake rifled through the papers again and puffed a ring of smoke from his pipe.

"How long since those scouts left?" Charles asked without meeting Rake's gaze.

Rake grunted, shuffling back through papers to find a calendar with random notations. "They left the week before His Majesty," Rake said. "Almost six weeks now. Do you think—"

"No," Charles was quick to interrupt, studying the training grounds before them. "Surely Jearnia is no longer petty enough to have captured mere scouts. King Phillippe sent them to learn if Jearnia suffers the same as the rest of Ebios. No other reason."

The Banner-Captain harrumphed. "And how has that stopped Jearnians in the past, Captain? Have you forgotten what happened to King Phillippe's father?"

"There are two sides to every story, sir," Charles muttered, returning to his study of the map. With Demir's last field gone, Orda'an had little left for crops. Many regrew, but as soon as the plants were visible, the field burned again. Charles shifted the collar of his coat away from his neck, contemplating undoing the button despite Rake's presence. *At least, that's what the scouts say happened to these blighted fields. I wish I could have stayed long enough to see for myself.*

"Two sides, yes, but only one truth, Captain," Rake said, glaring.

Charles shrugged, biting back a retort, and returned to the topic before them.

"Troops have been placed at each border town. Yet the fields continue to burn. And why only the borders?"

"Nothing more to say on Jearnia, Captain?" A small tendril of smoke drifted from the pipe in the officer's hand.

Charles followed it for a moment, choosing his next words carefully, with a reminder to moderate his inflections. "Until we hear from the scouts, or Jearnia itself, there is no need to dwell on that issue when we have villages under constant threat, sir." After a pause, he added, "Besides, if I recall, Jearnians were once Orda'anian."

"And they've tried to take it over ever since the civil war, Captain," Rake said, the tinge of a threat coloring his usually even temperament. "King Phillippe is the first monarch they've respected enough to let us live our own lives. It's been strange sending so many troops north rather than east."

Charles set the map down, eager to transition from the discussion of Jearnia and its tumultuous past with Orda'an. Another scan of the training grounds showed nothing changed—men sparred, the cool wind blew, and Rosealyn was nowhere in sight. *And Daniel better keep close watch.*

"But what of the northern towns, sir?" Charles asked as Rake puffed more smoke from his pipe. "If the troops cannot find and eliminate the threats, what commands do we send? What message do we send His Majesty? What do we tell Queen Roseanne and Princess Rosealyn at tomorrow's briefing?"

Instead of answering, Banner-Captain Rake stood and bowed, fist to heart against his high-collared and buttoned coat. Rather than the white cuffs Charles's coat showed, Rake's had a white collar. The rest was solid black, even the buttons. *Thank goodness we don't wear these uniforms into battle; we'd never stand a chance.*

Charles also stood and dropped into a full bow, berating himself for not noticing the queen. He was positive she had not been approaching when he last scanned the grounds, but she stood before them with that regal hollow stare.

"My Queen," Rake said, lifting from the bow while keeping his fist firm against his chest, just above his heart. "We did not expect a visit. How can we assist, Your Majesty?"

"Banner-Captain Rake, Captain Charles," she said. Her stare lingered on Charles and shifted back to Rake. "Reeve is droll in his description of the status of Orda'an. What news from my husband?"

"His Majesty remains at Pasea, my Queen." Rake repeated the news he and Charles had discussed. The queen's expression remained unreadable.

"Maintain the current trade routes for delivery of goods," she said. As usual, she kept her voice terse and short. "Remember your duties, Captain Charles. I know she grows restless and wishes to help, but she is safest here."

"Understood, Your Majesty," Charles said with a simple bow, finding it ironic Phillippe asked him to train the princess only to keep her sequestered to the castle.

The queen walked away as silently as she had arrived. Rake resumed his seat, but Charles scanned for the princess again. Seeing neither Princess Rosealyn nor Daniel, and knowing the queen was well out of earshot, Charles spoke first. "How do we tell King Phillippe his wife is making such foolish decisions with what little food we can send?"

The Banner-Captain shrugged, scratching at his beard and puffing his pipe. "Knowing His Majesty, he may already know. For now, we follow orders."

9

Rosealyn turned, auburn hair catching beneath her arm, to watch the trainees below. The palace garden balcony offered the perfect view. Moss whirled in circles, his quarterstaff a blur in his hands, knocking his fellow soldier to the ground in seconds. No matter how often Moss taught her the motions, Rosealyn knew she would never move the staff with the same grace it had in his hands.

Though her wound had been superficial, Charles—who stood stiffly at her side—insisted she ease back into training. So rather than daily, she trained every other day. Even so, sparring felt different than it had prior to her injury. She devised new tricks, but they seemed contrived and childish.

Soldiers returned from Pasea in small groups. Some burned beyond recognition. Her father, however, insisted on waiting until Pasea recovered, if such was possible. Each city with burned fields produced plants which withered and died, if the plants regrew at all.

As usual as winter approached, the black roses were the only blooms in the garden. Before those bushes, she sat with Gailin's journal open on her lap. A green-tinged black petal floated on the chilling wind, coming to rest at her side atop the white stone bench.

Reading her country's history brought solace, an avenue to direct her thoughts away from what she had raced toward. The tales of battle left much unsaid.

"But what was Gailin's reality? What was his truth?" Rosealyn asked aloud. Charles did not move nor speak at her side; he had to be used to her monologues. She ran a finger along the embossed white rose stitched onto the edge of her deep green bodice. Needle and thread, she had witnessed in the past weeks, were useful for more than pretty additions to clothing. Thankfully, Doctor Alvin had not found it necessary to stitch her skin together as he did many of the returning soldiers.

The more Rosealyn listened to the soldiers' stories, the more she wondered if history could repeat itself. She turned the page and read aloud, "'I thought I would write down answers, but all I have are more questions.'"

A breeze picked the petal up, blowing it onto the pages from which she read. The wind shifted the pages of the journal and hid the black rose petal within its midst. "Is the Lost Prince a story?"

She held her hair so it did not swirl around her face and flipped to the last page. "'Xannan had evil in his heart long before touching this blade. The blade … enhanced his dark, malicious intentions. Why else would he attempt to kill our father?'"

A click of a hilt against its belt and Charles's movement in her periphery provided a small warning. She closed the journal, one finger marking her place, and braced for whatever her mother thought she should be doing instead.

"Reading that entry again?"

She snapped her head up and froze, wondering if she had fallen asleep. She could be dreaming. He could be an illusion. But the tired smile was as real as his voice. That and Azeiah stood beside her father. As much as she liked the general, she doubted he would be present in her dreams. Both the general and her father wore clothes showing the lines where armor had rested. Swords remained at their sides. No different from any other time. Except, if they were home, Pasea must have recovered. Her father would not have left the city otherwise. Nor would the general.

"I've told you before, the words will not change no matter how many times you read it."

Her father moved to sit next to her, but she jumped up and embraced him, burying her face in his chest. Her heart felt like it might burst and tears formed. He was home. Safe and home. His arms wrapped around her, pinching her hair. Not wanting to let go, she squeezed harder despite the smell of his dried sweat mingling with the earthiness of dirt and grime. It was the hug she'd missed, the one she'd been denied. By the time she'd awoken after Pasea, she was already on her way home.

"Is it over?" she asked. She felt his shoulders slump and stepped back to look up at him. He offered a sympathetic smile that could not mask the weary red streaks of his eyes. Her question fell into silence as the general and her father exchanged glances.

Rosealyn stepped backward, out of her father's embrace, and glanced at each of them. "It isn't. You don't want to tell me." Her grip on the journal tightened, pressing the pages against the finger which marked her place. "But I know something's wrong because your faces are too grim for me to believe otherwise."

"Rose—"

"No, enough of that." Rosealyn straightened to her full height and rounded her shoulders. Gailin's journal gripped in her left hand, she demanded, "Tell me what happened."

Another exchange of glances. Her father's words came with a level of resignation and pity she never wanted to hear again. "We lost Pasea." He swallowed, tone hollowing. "Destroyed."

The backs of her knees met the stone bench, and she collapsed into a seated position. "But … Preston said when…" Rosealyn swallowed. White stone was bright when illuminated by the noonday sun, and she could find nowhere to fix her gaze, so she glanced from one dying plant to the next. Anywhere except at those forlorn, melancholy expressions.

"The people?"

"A few refugees." Her father sat beside her, leaning forward to rest his elbows on his knees with his hands held together before him. "They returned with us once we could do nothing more."

Breathe in, breathe out. The destruction of fields was one thing, but an entire town… Why? What purpose did such annihilation serve? She counted her breaths, focusing on a singular bloom. It was halfway open, as though straining for more light to reach it so it could grow into its full beauty.

"How? How did it happen?"

"Myths come to life," her father mumbled, and Azeiah grunted his agreement.

"Sire?"

Rosealyn jolted when Charles spoke, nearly forgetting he had been standing at her side for the past hour.

Her father shook his head and buried his face in his hands. Myths, he claimed. He called only one creature a myth. Dwarves, fairies, even elves, he claimed, were extinct. Dragons, however, he called a myth. Few stories surrounded the idea of the dragons and one of them intertwined with their own family history—two great dragons, Eilon and Magna, crafted a magical blade to gift to Orda'an's founder, King Seth. Lore claimed the singular blade split in two, creating powerful Twin Blades that none had ever found.

"Myths as in dragons?" Rosealyn asked while wondering if the reddening sky she had witnessed at Pasea was from fire rather than the sun.

"Just one attacked, though two were present." Her father spoke into his hands, rubbing his face and jolting slightly when he closed his eyes.

"You both saw them, Sire? General?" Charles asked. He moved so he no longer stood in her periphery, and she swore the grip on his sword hilt was tighter than normal.

Before either could respond, Rosealyn's mother marched into the palace gardens with a harried soldier at her heels. The queen's initial scowl transitioned to a stare of regal hollowness once she realized who was present.

"Glad to know you came home." The queen's words were bitter and made Rosealyn wish she was anywhere else in the castle.

"Not long ago, yes." The earlier weariness of her father's voice had a tension to it, one which arose from her parents' most common argument. "My apologies for not sending a forward scout to announce our approach. We had few to spare after Pasea's destruction." Her father's statement was met with her mother's silence, and he sighed. "Any news from Tenoa?"

It was not difficult for Rosealyn to envision her mother's disapproving stare at being asked such a question, so Rosealyn decided being blinded by the white stone balcony bathed in sunlight would be better.

"Duty before family, as always." Her mother's tone made Rosealyn's chest feel hollow and cold.

"I am responsible for the fate of more than our own family, Roseanne." Her father seemed to growl in response, and he moved to the balcony's railing.

Rosealyn glanced up to look at each parent and gripped her dress-skirts with her free hand, clenching tighter as her father spoke.

"Pasea, gone. Demir, Verbera, Asyir, all once bustling economies that provided goods, and now?" A heavy thud of his hand against the railing created a sharp ringing sound. "Soldiers missing, fields burning, people disappearing, mixed messages from *all* of the scouts. And the Gift?"

He shook his head, and a chill ran down Rosealyn's spine; he rarely spoke of the Gift. "The Gift is useless, stuck on…"

Rosealyn took advantage of the pause. "What did it show you?"

"A finality I do not wish to discuss," he mumbled so softly Rosealyn wasn't sure anyone but her had heard him, especially since no one else reacted to the statement. *A finality? What does that mean?*

Mouth dry, Rosealyn released her skirts and gripped the edge of the bench. Several heartbeats passed in tense silence.

"It's been too long since I've visited the other border towns." Her father continued to face away from them. "I may not be able to regrow the crops, but kind words often help."

Charles cleared his throat and spoke cautiously once her father's attention was on him. "With all due respect, Your Majesty, you are safest here in the castle."

"Rose, how would you respond to the captain's advice?"

Rosealyn glanced behind her to find her father's forced smile and hesitated. Desperate to hold onto a token of normalcy, she set the journal aside. Such a question was also a test. With muscles tenser than she cared to admit, Rosealyn joined her father at the railing and surveyed the training grounds below them.

There was Moss, opposite Daniel—her other two guards who could be needed elsewhere if Hoclia's attacks continued. And if they left, they might never return. Many soldiers hadn't. Those who did were not the same.

She rubbed her hands together, remembering how long it had taken to wash the blood off.

"I agree," Rosealyn said with a soft grin as Moss knocked Daniel down. "It is vital the people know their monarch fights for them and does not hide from danger. A ruler is a leader first. You cannot ask others to sacrifice what you yourself would not give."

It was the same speech he had given her throughout her childhood. Words she relished and despised. They meant she would one day do as her father did now—leave her home and her family to protect her people. They also meant her father would be leaving. Again.

"We all want you to stay home and *safe*," Rosealyn added. "But I know you will go where you are needed. You always do."

One of his arms wrapped around her shoulders and squeezed gently. "You've listened well, Rose." He turned to lean against the railing, one hand rubbing his chin. "Roseanne?"

"No point in arguing anymore. My advice to you is rarely considered, but it seems we know not what we are even fighting against."

Rosealyn turned around. "Father said a dragon destroyed Pasea."

Based on the tilt of her mother's head and the crossed arms, it was doubtful the woman believed such a statement.

"Then visit the waterfalls of Lycene to see if the beast still haunts them," her mother retorted. "Dragons are myths."

"Thought to be myths," her father corrected, and he directed his next question to the soldiers. "How does Lycene fare? Few wished to live near those supposedly haunted falls, but refugees are often desperate. Could it be where some of our soldiers have gone?"

"A possibility, Sire," Azeiah said in a way that made Rosealyn confident they had already discussed this during their journey home. "But our priority should be to speak with Hoclia and Alkaan again. Perhaps proper discussions can occur, given the losses on all sides."

Her father grunted. "I do not wish to continue the blame game between us, though it is worth the attempt. Azeiah, have Reeve draft the messages for me to review come morning. Hopefully the next meeting in Violet Grove will be more beneficial than the last."

Rosealyn stepped away from the railing. "I'm coming with you. A meeting with the other monarchs and leaders is something I can definitely help—"

She halted at her father's raised hand. "Lycene first," he said. "And no, you are not coming with me to Lycene. I insisted on your training so you can protect yourself *if* needed."

"Captain Charles can come with us, or all of my guards if it'd make you feel better, but I refuse to sit around and wait. That's not the type of leader you taught me to be, Father."

He winced. "I'll join you for the evening meal in a few hours." He paused at Charles's side and whispered something too softly for Rosealyn to hear. Fear and understanding warred with each other on Charles's face, but her bodyguard said nothing in response.

Azeiah at his side, her father walked back into the castle proper. Rosealyn considered following after him or screaming or hitting something, but she refused to act so childishly. A few hours would give her enough time to craft a better argument, one he could not refute no matter how hard he tried.

10

One hallway after another, Phillippe walked to where a bath and change of clothes awaited him in his rooms. At his side, Azeiah kept pace. Miraculously, Rosealyn did not follow. His instructions to Charles were quite specific: protect her and prepare. He closed his eyes and froze in the middle of the hallway. A solid black blade. So familiar and yet so strange.

"With all due respect, Phillippe," Azeiah said. "You should side with Captain Charles. I fear what could happen. And that's without a unique gift hinting at what's coming."

"I won't hide in this castle while my people are dying, Azeiah. You know that." He continued walking while making a mental note to never close his eyes unnecessarily again. Though it wasn't there, he could sense the rim of his solid gold crown weighing him down. Pressure upon pressure. No matter how he shifted his thoughts, or the adornment, everything grated against him. "Do you remember our last visit to Lycene?"

"Of course, Sire," Azeiah acknowledged. "We lost good men. And returned with an orphan. You never told me the boy's full history. And I know the last name he gave is false."

"I worried you would not trust him. But he's saved your life enough to overlook that now, hasn't he?"

"True, Sire," Azeiah said. At the honorifics, Phillippe felt a pain of nostalgia. He missed his youth, when the Gift was just an idea, when ruling was a fantasy. *Such a simplicity to the past.*

"The dark blade returned," Phillippe said, changing the subject. "It's not random. Not anymore."

"The same as you saw in Lycene ten years ago?"

"Unfortunately," Phillippe mumbled. They were at his rooms. He frowned when he entered; none of Roseanne's items occupied his quarters anymore. Thoughts of his wife created an unfillable hole inside him, and he sank into a chair by the fireplace, vaguely hearing Azeiah say something to a servant he had not noticed in the room. *Too tired and too distracted.*

"It's returned with such a vengeance."

"Your understanding of the Gift is surely better than mine, Phillippe," Azeiah said as he filled the fireplace with wood.

A moment later the servant, Leila he believed her name was, returned with matches to light the flame. Phillippe flinched. Fire was beautiful, warming, but also incredibly thorough in its destruction.

"Besides, all you ever mentioned of *that* image is how you believe it signifies your demise. You never described it to me as you have the others."

Phillippe buried his face in his hands, staring through the slits created by his fingers. The growth of stubble along his cheeks and chin itched. The fire licked at the logs, slowly consuming them like the sensation of calm dread had been consuming him. "Because who wants to admit they see a black blade plunging into them every time they close their eyes?"

Azeiah shifted on his feet, nimble enough despite the girth he'd gained with age. "Perhaps you should listen to your wife for once. Let me check on the border towns."

"If I don't go, it may happen closer to home. I dare not put my daughter through such torment."

"Phillippe." Azeiah stepped closer, his dirt-covered boots invading Phillippe's study of the floor. "I remember when the Passing happened to you. It matters not if she physically sees your death. Rosealyn will receive the Gift, you've told me so, which means she will experience the Passing same as you did."

Phillippe sank deeper into the chair, arms limp at his sides. "She desires to understand, to know, but my father and grandfather accepted what it shared rather than utilizing it. We do not know how it works. Images appear when I least expect them, and more often than not, they are illogical. Choppy, confusing, misunderstood. Rosealyn will want answers to questions I never thought to ask."

Phillippe listened to the crackle of the fire, thankful the general knew when to remain silent. Even though he forced his eyes to remain open, he could see the weapon. Silence continued, even when Phillippe moved to the desk tucked into a corner of his room. Bathing would have to wait. He pulled three blank pages and wrote, hardly pausing to think. After concluding the third, he mouthed a silent curse and pulled out a fourth paper. Once the pages were folded and sealed, he returned to his seat by the fireplace and handed them to the general. "I trust you can deliver each discreetly and at the proper time?"

"As I always have, Your Majesty," Azeiah said with a nod. He shifted the letters to see the names of the recipients, and a low curse slipped from his lips. "I had my suspicions, but you should have told me you were *letting* a spy into the army."

"I'm aware," Phillippe said, smirking. The general shook his head, mumbling more curses that only deepened Phillippe's smirk until the image of the black blade reappeared.

"One other thing, Azeiah." Phillippe waited for his friend turned commander to meet his gaze. "Be wary of the queen."

"What do you mean, Phillippe?"

"A feeling, nothing more." He pressed his palms into his eyes, as though such pressure could wipe away the vision. "And prepare a group of ten to accompany me to Lycene. We'll leave two days from now."

11

Though Roseanne considered joining her husband, she decided arguing with him truly was a waste of breath. Instead, she walked through the almost empty hallways of the castle, reminiscing on her first visit to Vandyl with her sister.

It was hard not to compare Orda'an to her home country. Every few feet, velvety purple tapestries brushed against the many windows lining both sides of the hallway, leading her gaze to the marbled stone floor. The red sun had begun its descent along the rolling hills to the south, casting an eerie glow against the lengthening fields to the north. Roseanne wished all the castle's stones were the deep black of dragon-stone that reminded her of home rather than the simple gray that so easily captured the colors of the sky.

The walls themselves were bare. Before Roseanne had arrived as Phillippe's betrothed, he had moved the exquisitely crafted tapestries of his family's past to the depths of the library. Most were immaculate portraits of the LeNoir line, using colors she had never seen outside nature before arriving in Orda'an. Each was a reminder of what Phillippe did not wish to be.

One tapestry showcased the Battle at the Cliff of Lycene, the end of Orda'an's Civil War which led to the formation of

Jearnia. That mesmerizing tapestry depicted a sea of mangled bodies darkened by the Cliff of Lycene's rocky palisade. On the matted green bluff above stood a minuscule King Gailin and Lord Edmund Tremaine, forming the tenuous agreement that Lord Edmund's son, Jonathan, refused to honor. Behind the pair jutted the Jearnian Hills, with the snow-topped Mountains of Ingoria shimmering amid dismal clouds in the background. The Guadelaide River surged along the tapestry's lower edge, flowing through the hills into the lands King Gailin had forfeited, opposite the evergreen Shendaran Forest.

Phillippe was home, but she bypassed their shared quarters without hesitation. No need to argue when his decision was already made. She gestured for her guard to remain in the hallway and entered her own rooms. While searching for her servant, Leila, she pulled at the strings of her dress. *Probably in Phillippe's room.*

After changing into her loose-flowing ruby red Tenoan dress, Roseanne began to remove her crown but stopped. It often helped her think. A half-filled paper full of scratched out words she had been writing sat on her desk. All the words she tried to write to her sister were wrong.

She tossed the useless letter aside. Even if she could write to her sister, Roseanne was not sure where she would send the letter. Neither Phillippe nor Ramon knew where Catarina was, but the man speaking through the black speck of a cloud hovering in her room almost every night offered a glimmer of news. Catarina was alive. Not only could he help solve the growing conflict, but he could reunite her with Catarina. Glimmers of hope surfaced each time the voice reminded her of such, but Roseanne stamped them down. Hope could make one do foolish things.

She bent over to retrieve the paper and froze. The overbearing sensation, like a thousand grains of sand coating every inch of her skin, created by such a small odd black cloud was undeniable. With her sweating hand pressed to her chest, it pained her how he knew when she was in her quarters. Weeks had passed since their first encounter, and his recommendations became more logical. Promises of reunions, though she was positive no one could keep Phillippe at the castle for longer than a week.

Larger and larger it grew until she had to step backward to stay out of its path. Soon she collapsed into her chair, almost tipping it over as the cloud continued its growth. The crumpled paper fell from her clammy hands to rest atop a solid black rug, and she focused on it to avoid the growing black cloud in front of her.

A gloved hand appeared in the mist, slightly cupped, as though awaiting hers. She shied away, trying to recede deeper into the chair, but the hand reached out farther, searching for her. She had no reason to distrust Ramon. He had always been there for her. Roseanne would never tell him the truth of why her relationship with Catarina had fractured or why it was vital she reunite with her sister even after all these years, but he'd offered comfort without question. All her parents had given was a command: marry the king of Orda'an.

Trust had formed between this man and her cousin, so trust could form between herself and this man as well.

As if impatient, the hand hovering in thin air motioned for her. No voice floated from the cloud tonight. She steadied her crown and closed her eyes. Whoever this was, he claimed he was helping. Trade routes rearranged, and so often to Lycene. Perhaps this man was caring for the refugees of the northern borders. She studied the hand, questioning what would happen if she allowed this hand to guide her through the cloud.

The hand continued searching, as though whoever belonged to it could not walk through this cloud themselves. The messages her cousin sent and the man offering advice on an almost nightly basis through this dark cloud had to be connected. With a glance around her rooms to confirm their emptiness, she grasped the outstretched hand and muttered, "You better not get me killed, Ramon."

She gasped when the hovering hand took hers and tugged her into the ominous mist. Absence of air, of heat or cold, of any indication of up or down, overwhelmed her. Before she could wriggle her hand free of the man's hold, she flinched against the sky's brilliant red glow to see matted grass beneath her feet. Mountains reflected the fading sun far in the distance to her right, and she heard the Guadelaide River's soft whisper far below. Water flowed over the edge of the cliff nearby and she strained to look, trying to pull her hand free, missing the intoxication of those sounds. Far below, the Guadelaide River whispered.

Roseanne thought the Mountains of Ingoria would be more imposing, but they were farther from the cliff than she expected given the tapestry's depiction. As was the castle. The young man whose hand had pulled her through the mist gave a tug, and they continued their walk along the grassy bluff.

"The Cliff of Lycene," she breathed. The tapestry seemed plain compared to the reality. Lush green grass tickled her ankles and the soles of her feet, shimmering in the luscious fading sunlight. The horizon was like a mesmerizing fire dancing safely inside its stony alcove. For a moment, she forgot about the young man guiding her. Though her hair was taut against her scalp, she imagined how it would feel to have the cool wind rippling through it, tumbling the strands until they tangled into knots. Here, atop this cliff, the wind would not coat her hair with a fine layer of sand.

"His lordship would like you to dine with him today." The high-pitched voice brought her attention back to the firm grip as they approached a singular large tent occupying the bluff. Below were the small dots of campfires, intermingled with buildings of the city of Lycene she'd believed to be abandoned.

"How did I come here?" she asked, wishing the youth would stop dragging her along. The Cliff was more than a day's ride from the castle and she had arrived with a single step.

"Eilon's abilities, my lady." The young man stopped in front of the tent and nudged her inside. *It's not him. The voice is wrong.*

A lantern pulsed in the middle of a small table, shadows dancing over properly full plates of food. She surveyed the sea of bread, fruit, and meat until her gaze fell upon the man sitting at the opposite end. He held a bone between his hands, inspecting it for the last traces of meat. A grumbling she could not control sounded deep in the pit of her stomach as she watched the man take a bite. He set the bone down and tossed a small, round black grape into his mouth. His broad shoulders shifted backward, the flame of the lantern flickering against pale bare arms as he lifted his chin. Roseanne recoiled. The green eyes were too fierce for such a youthful face.

"Sit down, Queen Roseanne."

He gestured toward a second full plate as he dabbed at his lips with a napkin. Roseanne stood still, resisting the urge to reposition her crown. She knew the lilting tone, the musicality of it, the simplicity of it. His voice matched. Almost every evening, this man with shoulder-length blond hair spoke to her. As gentle as a breeze was his tone, as coarse as the sand were his instructions.

This was the man who spoke to her through the dark cloud. This was the man Ramon had led to her. This was the man who claimed he would solve all of their problems, who said he cared about the people of Orda'an, of all Ebios.

"I know you're hungry." He plucked a roll from a basket in the middle of the table. The lack of sleeves had to be purposeful, but she could not pull her gaze away as he stood.

He held himself in a mocking bow, pale blond locks brushing against high cheekbones and even paler skin. "I've quite enjoyed being the Lost Prince, though Xannan is the preferred name."

"You aren't real," she whispered, surveying the room quickly. Behind the man claiming to be Xannan stood a solitary servant with shaking arms, his hold on a brimming pitcher of wine precarious. The table by which Xannan stood matched the shade of the tent's walls with their solid, simple browns. The tent held no bed or desk, just the rectangular table which stood between her and Xannan. Were this man not standing before her, Roseanne would have thought she occupied Phillippe's tent. She eyed the full plate of food sitting alongside Xannan's, hunger gnawing at her, closed her eyes, and shook her head. *It's just a dream.*

The lithe blond man chuckled, and Roseanne opened her eyes again to meet his emerald green eyes. Her heart sank as one hand drifted to settle her crown in its proper place. *Not a dream. He is real.*

"You can't keep me here." Roseanne hoped it sounded more like a statement than a question.

Xannan pulled the second chair away from the table and made an elaborate motion with his arm. "Please, eat. It's quite delicious. Even Eilon appreciates the cuisine."

"Eilon?"

"My dragon," Xannan said, pushing her chair in after she reluctantly eased herself down.

Roseanne slumped and stared at the plate of colorful, well-grown food before her. Vibrant vegetables and the mouth-watering scent of fresh cooked meat made her hope the man was using the food wagons well. And offering the soldiers the same plates.

His words caught up to her, and her heart skipped a beat. "You said—"

"It's amazing what the distilleries and cooks have learned in the many years since my youth," Xannan interrupted with a wink and downed a full glass of wine.

Roseanne glanced at him and the food before her, wavering between hunger and nausea.

"Eat, drink, be merry, no one died today," Xannan announced with a flourish, snapping his fingers for the lone servant to fill his cup. The boy trembled, arms shuddering, and the liquid barely stayed inside the cup as he poured. She inhaled to speak, to inform Xannan of Pasea's destruction. His gaze met hers above the rim of his wine glass with a nefarious twinkle, and she could give no sound to her voice. Instead, Roseanne picked up the fork and forced down a bite of meat. Swallowing, she stared at the plate, scrutinizing every morsel of food before her.

"What now?" She rested the cutlery on the edges of her plate and dabbed at the corners of her lips with a napkin.

Instead of answering, Xannan tore off several more pieces of bread and continued his dinner, motioning for Roseanne to do the same. She resumed her hesitant, small bites. The meal was more enjoyable than those from the castle, considering she had rerouted the food wagons herself, but her thoughts kept returning to her husband. And daughter. And sister.

Each morsel calmed the grumbling of her stomach, though it flopped around like a fish out of water.

Roseanne waited for a response, only to spend the rest of the meal in silence. The few times she dared to look at him, Xannan's unwavering gaze sent shivers down her spine. It turned her core to ice, making her colder than the first Orda'anian winter she'd suffered. The sleeveless brown leather top held fast to his shoulders, hovering over his chest with a small gap.

Spending this much time in the same room became suffocating and the occasional smack of his lips as he ate infuriating. His light blond hair fell forward, floating over thinned cheeks, a perfect complement to his equally pale skin.

"Nothing new to tell me then? No news of my sister? What of Phillippe? The fields? The food?"

"I want you to meet Eilon," Xannan said, disregarding her diatribe. "Tonight."

Roseanne opened her mouth to ask more questions, but he silenced her with a shake of his head and pointed at her half-empty plate. Xannan waited to dismiss the lone servant until she had finished eating.

He stood and held a bare arm out to his side, beaming. Roseanne hesitated but laid her hand in the crook of his elbow, wishing the man's arms were properly covered. She blushed, glancing down at the less than ornate Tenoan garb she had donned, grateful for the cover of a darker hue.

The thought dwindled as Xannan pulled back the tent flap. In the glowing dusk, Roseanne noticed the largest bird she had ever seen flap wings as vast as clouds. Dark scales blended into the night sky. Its shape and form tickled at her memory, slowly forming a connection to the dragons emblazoned on the hilt of Phillippe's sword. The Orda'anian crest had done them justice.

Roseanne's jaw slacked. "They're—"

"Not a myth." Xannan laughed. A firm hand pressed hers deeper into his arm. The dragon spread its wings. Roseanne followed the ridges as they collapsed back into the dragon's side until her gaze fell on the beast's silver eyes. Those same eyes turned black, and her throat squeezed within. It rested lazily on the edge of the bluff, with spiked wings and feathered tail tucked close to its body.

"We're lucky they don't annihilate us," Xannan said with a haunted reverence. The pressure on her arm increased.

Xannan tugged her toward the edge of the cliff, toward the large beast resting there, too quickly to ask more questions. Prickles of pain arose in the bare soles of her feet as they caught against the tufts of grass. Roseanne had always imagined what it would feel like to look up the Cliff of Lycene's rocky palisade, not down. She gulped, threatened by the distance to the dwindling campfires below. And by the dragon shifting to face her and Xannan.

The ebony beast's outline shimmered in the moonlight. Even lowered to the ground, its nose rested above Xannan's head. Scaled wings created peaks against his sides, while a long feathered and spiked tail flicked along the grassy terrain behind him. Each soft scrape made Roseanne's breath hitch in her throat where her heart seemed to be lodged.

At the base of the dragon's lengthy neck pulsed an orange glow, providing just enough light for her to see spindle-like protrusions from the dragon's head. Its eyes briefly flashed to black and returned to their silver hue. She held her free hand against her stomach, urging her lungs to accept the air she tried to give them. One of these had attacked Phillippe at Pasea. One of these had destroyed that town.

Is this the dragon Phillippe saw attack Pasea? It makes the mountains look small.

"Eilon," Xannan said, saying the name as though for a deity, "shows me what will happen. I wanted you to see as well."

Roseanne withdrew her hand from Xannan's elbow and repositioned her crown. Stories said dragons were finicky and volatile. But they could also be kind, calm, and endearing. Just like Ramon.

"H—" Roseanne worked moisture back into her mouth. Curiosity had taken hold at the mention of witnessing the future. "How?"

"Kneel before him, and think of a blank slate to be filled," Xannan explained.

He pushed her down to her knees, hands tight on each of her shoulders. Roseanne winced at the grass stains that might never come out and smoothed her dress-skirts so they rested against her thighs. The wind whistled through the slit sleeves of her dress, and she rubbed her hands against her arms and looked up at the beast. His stare seemed ... critical.

The moisture disappeared again, her mind already shocked into emptiness. Eilon's eyes flickered to black again.

Nothing.

"Eyes closed," Xannan admonished when she glanced up at him.

She obliged and gripped the skirt of her dress to suppress a scream. Roseanne saw herself, tattered, bruised, and chained to a wall. Her eyes fluttered open, gasping for air. The dragon's eyes turned silver again. *Reality or a possibility?*

"Again." Xannan growled, forcing her eyes closed.

Armies clashing against one another in the middle of the Orda'anian plains. One group wore haphazard clothing. Xannan's, she assumed, locating him amid the battle with his black blade lifted. Another army wore a drab brown interspersed with greens, blending into the landscape. A third wore colors akin to the LeNoir crest.

Roseanne held her head with her hands, suppressing the urge to scream as her crown tumbled from its braided nest. The ground rumbled beneath her, and she looked up to see the orange glow reflected in Eilon's silver gaze.

"Beautiful, isn't it?" Xannan asked. She glanced over as he crossed his legs under him to sit next to her. "Your husband will finally be at rest."

Her head felt like it was being pounded by stones. *What does he mean? What does any of this mean? How will this help?*

Roseanne swallowed and braced. Mind blank, she welcomed the images despite the pain which accompanied them. Xannan appeared … older. The second army weaved throughout the battlefield, wounding but rarely killing. The third had to be Orda'anian.

The pain in her head increased, and Roseanne pressed her hands against her temples.

"Doesn't the future look grand?" he asked, offering his hand.

Roseanne took the offered hand and grabbed her crown with the other. "A battle will not assist," she whispered, wincing at the pain her own voice created. "Especially one of such magnitude."

"Magnitude?" Xannan laughed. "It's a mere skirmish between weary men and my well-fed mercenaries."

Which I paid for because you and Ramon told me to. Roseanne positioned the crown atop her head, swallowing more than her words. "Skirmish?"

"Aye." Moonlight danced on Xannan's pale, uncovered arms. "A simple skirmish will bring peace. It will bring your husband home. And your sister. You're doing well."

Xannan laid her arm back in the crook of his elbow. Such pressure helped relieve the pounding of her head, though she found it difficult to process anything.

Roseanne looked back at Eilon's silver eyes, wishing she could understand, but he closed them, resting his head on the grass. She turned forward to see the black cloud had reappeared, allowing Xannan to guide her through to her private quarters and lower her to the chair before her desk. She stared at the half-filled paper, unable to stomach Xannan's fiery demeanor any longer. By the time she spun around to confront him, to make demands before she continued to lend any support, he had vanished, leaving only the essence of his presence behind.

Roseanne removed her crown. The stones pounding against her head needed no help.

12

Back in the quarters he had once shared with his wife, Phil-lippe sat alone. Dinner had consisted of arguing with Rosealyn rather than Roseanne. His daughter was adamant she should join his next journey. Fortunately for him, the soldiers obeyed his command. *For now.*

One hand tapped against the hilt of the sheathed weapon resting atop his thighs. The blade had belonged to his father, passed down to every LeNoir since King Seth, Orda'an's founder, forged it six generations ago.

The family crest was bold on the hilt. To one side, a black dragon hovered above a black blade. To the other, a white dragon hovered above a white blade. Their feathered wings rested in peaks on their sides, spiked tails curled along behind.

Between the two dragons, the black and white colors forged onto the hilt faded into a deep gray. It reminded him of a rain cloud, eager to shed its tears. The dragons, depending on the viewing angle, held either the cloud in front of them or the blades below them. Gailin's last entry, the one Phillippe had hidden from his daughter, claimed the Twin Blades were a magical gift from the dragons. His father had once told him, along with his three siblings, how the sword was a family heirloom meant only for the recipient of the Gift. With a shake of his head, he set the sword aside and rubbed his face with his hands. The door opening without a knock made him look up.

"Where were you?" Phillippe asked, standing as Roseanne entered their shared quarters. Dark hair flowed in thick waves, swaying as she moved just inside. "You missed the evening meal."

Roseanne paused, one hand gripping the door's handle. Her crown no longer rested atop her head, and she wore her favorite deep red Tenoan dress. *So quick to change from the court dresses. I should have let her wear these more often.*

"My apologies," she whispered, voice hoarse and tense. It was not the tone he expected after their conversation in the garden earlier. "I did not wish to argue in front of Rosealyn. Not again."

She pulled the door shut behind her and flinched away from Phillippe's outstretched hand.

"There's more to your absence than that," he said. After so long in armor and travel clothes, it felt good to be clean and wear something less form-fitting. The shirt hung loose, and the once tight pants tried to fall off as he approached her again. "I can feel it."

"A finality you do not wish to discuss?" Roseanne repeated, her gaze more hollow than before, as though something was pulling her even further away from him. It matched the anger and despair billowing inside him. "What have you seen?"

He let the outstretched hand fall to his side when she took another step to her right, another step away from him. A faint scent which reminded Phillippe of the Orda'anian fields reached him, and he frowned. *When was she outdoors?*

"Answer the question, Phillippe," she said. The hollowness changed as slight lines etched across her forehead. "If you know what will happen in this inconsequential town, why do you insist on going?"

"Roseanne, please," he whispered, sinking into his seat and looking down. Her feet were bare and brushed with patches of dirt. "I do not wish to discuss it. As I've said."

"Not with your wife, not with your daughter, but I'm sure Azeiah knows," Roseanne blurted out, her voice crescendoing as she moved closer to him. "Why do you shut us out?"

Roseanne paced the front room of their shared quarters. Gray stone had become marbled with white from the years of her pacing, the years of her desperation to find some connection with Rosealyn after she gave up on finding Catarina.

"You know it is to protect you," he said, resting his chin in his hands. Soon, he would have bruises on his knees from his elbows. The screams no longer tormented him, replaced with an eerie suspicion. *Grass stains, dirt-covered feet, and her hair … unbraided. Where was she?*

Roseanne glared at him and continued her pacing, voice thunderous. "Send Azeiah, send Rake, send Preston! Or Charles! You have an entire army of men out there, willing and ready to do your bidding. If I recall, that Gift of yours has been wrong before."

Phillippe failed to prevent a grimace. *Not wrong, misunderstood.*

"I've seen my death for years," he finally admitted, and her pacing stopped. Roseanne approached him, stopping just out of arm's reach. "All I can see is the blade plunging into me. It's getting closer. I see it almost every time I close my eyes."

"By whose hand?" Roseanne asked, the tone of a regal queen returning.

Phillippe shrugged. It was strange, to be so accepting of his own death, to acknowledge its near arrival. "I can see nothing more than the blade itself, along with my inability to stop it."

"Did you really see dragons at Pasea?"

Phillippe jolted at the change of topic and asked, "No more questions about that image?"

"Our previous discussions tell me the images you see are brief and difficult to interpret. I think you should stay here." Roseanne's tone reminded him of his mother's overbearing protection.

Phillippe shook his head, leaning back with his arms crossed, grateful he had removed the weight of the crown for the day. "Nothing changes what I see. I don't want Rosealyn to both see my death and experience the Passing. I won't do that to her."

"Do you have a choice?" Roseanne retorted. "Didn't you see your father's death multiple times during the Passing?"

He grimaced, pushing away the images of his father's death which threatened to surface. It was why he had moved the portraits. Every time he happened upon an image of his ancestors, he saw their deaths. The final stabs and final breaths as they died would seep into him. One hand absently rubbed at his chest, above his heart, where the fatal stab had landed in his father's chest. The calm dread resurfaced. Phillippe could see only the blade, not where it might land.

"You did listen to me explain the Passing, then?"

After Roseanne's nod, Phillippe leaned forward and braced his forearms on his knees. "Just one dragon *attacked*, not multiple. A massive beast." He paused, failing to filter the cascade of emotions within. No matter how many times he pushed thoughts aside, the Gift forced specific ones to the surface time and time again. Phillippe cleared his throat, remembering how the sky burned orange at Pasea, how the Hoclian general he'd tried to communicate with became engulfed in flames which might have been meant for him. All while hoping Rosealyn and Charles did not see. Too soon, his daughter would have more than dragons to worry about. "Not sure how it hides, given its size. Both disappeared in a blink. I believe this dragon to be the reason for the burning fields. But then Hoclia and Alkaan broke their treaties and—"

"In the stories, the ones you always read with Rosealyn, are the dragons sentient?"

Phillippe studied her. The creased lines disappeared from her face as a hand drifted to settle an absent crown, flowing through her long unbraided black hair instead. It held soft waves from the tight braid. Phillippe remembered how it glinted with a slight red tint when the sunlight touched it at the right moment. *Just like Catarina's.*

"Only in the story of the Twin Blades," Phillippe said, frowning. Roseanne's lack of a cold shoulder at his decision to leave, yet again, intrigued him. "Why?"

"A sentient being can be reasoned with, talked to," she said as she moved the bulk of her hair to her back.

"Because discussions work so well," Phillippe mumbled beneath his breath, hoping his wife did not hear him lest he start a different argument. He stood, grasping her hands before she could step away from him again. It was a slight comfort when she did not resist. He had lost count of how many times she had torn her hands from his.

"We should try to find this dragon," she said, and Phillippe almost laughed until he met the seriousness of her light brown eyes.

For the first time in many years, it seemed she was looking up at him. It was strange to see her head tilted toward his without the disapproving stare. If he shifted just right, he could rest his chin atop her head. Phillippe pulled her closer, wrapping his arms around her. She shivered when his thumb caressed the skin bared by the slit of her sleeves. Burying her face into his chest, her next words were muffled but clear. "The ones who gifted the Twin Blades, what were their names?"

"Eilon, the dark one, and Magna, the ancient one." Phillippe stopped the gentle motion of his thumb when her shivering continued. Grasp gentle and firm on her arms, he shifted her a step backward to look her in the eyes. "Why the questions? You've never cared for the lore of dragons before."

"Before they were myths. Now you claim to have seen two." Roseanne's voice softened to a whisper. She pushed his hands from her arms, and he let her, watching as she hugged herself, hair tumbling over each shoulder when her chin sank to her chest. Even with the loose fit of her dress, he noticed the puffing of her chest followed by a shuddering exhale. "Could the one which attacked Pasea be Eilon? Or Magna?"

"Perhaps. The stories say Eilon and Magna were the oldest of their kind when they gifted the Twin Blades to King Seth, not long after Gailin's birth."

"And Xannan," she added, saying it as a statement, not a question.

"A creation of Gailin's imagination," Phillippe reminded her, brows furrowing with his frown. "The historians proved it."

She rubbed her hands along her arms and avoided looking at him. The distrust returned.

"The dragons were myths until you saw them," she stated with derision. "Could Xannan be no different?"

He sighed, eyes closing without a thought. The black blade flashed again, lingering until Phillippe found the hand holding the hilt, finding the same emblem embedded in the hilt of his sword. "It's been a long day, Roseanne. Will you be staying with me tonight?"

His insides tumbled within as she nodded. *What does it mean that the blade I see has the same crest?*

13

Charles stood to one side of the hallway with thinning patience as Rosealyn paced and listed all the reasons she should join her father on his journey to Lycene. "It's barely two days by horse. There will be plenty of soldiers there. It's what a leader should do." As her list grew longer, Charles wished he could travel with his comrades once more. He could not refute many of Rosealyn's reasons, but his command as her bodyguard took precedence. It was easier, though, to forget his past when outside the castle's walls. Somehow, the threat of a proper fight, the potential finality of it, was less tormenting than keeping the princess protected.

"Nothing new from the other scouts?" Rosealyn asked for the sixth time, and he shook his head. Dress-skirts clenched in each fist, she resumed her pacing. She'd demanded the same of her mother not an hour ago. The woman had said no and unnecessarily shifted the crown nestled atop her head. Every time she did, it made Charles's skin tingle with warning, just like the slur of drunken speech often would.

"Not going to leave me alone for a second anymore, are you?"

"Not when you may run off to Blazes knows where, Princess." His lips tightened when her smile faltered. It returned, a smidge weaker, while her hands flexed at her sides. Charles took a step toward her and asked, "Practice fields? It would be a good distraction, Princess."

Her brown eyes twinkled, and she smirked. *She's devised another new trick to try on me.*

With one hand gripping her dress-skirt, she pivoted to walk to her quarters. The dress hugged her torso, cinching at the waist before the wide flare he knew aggravated her. The strings lacing the back tightened until they rested in a loose bow between her shoulder blades. After realizing he was studying her, he fought to cool the heat rising in his cheeks by surveying the area they walked. It was unlikely a genuine threat would reach her inside the castle. Yet his gaze bounced from place to place.

Walking into the princess's quarters was like being blinded by bright bouquets of flowers. Everywhere she could add color, she did, regardless of how the new items clashed or complemented the existing ones. The front room amused him with its half dozen mismatched chairs of various sizes and hues. When Phillippe was home, she read her books in here, curling up inside one chair after another until she insisted they train again. The training had halted, briefly, after their return from Pasea. He knew what she saw when she first grasped the practice blade again, could see the guilt of killing creating soft lines on her smooth dark-hued skin. Even now, the mischievous glint had a level of distance.

"You still can't come into my bedroom," she said over her shoulder as she walked through the small hallway. A brief stop in her closet on one side of the hallway, she reappeared with her favorite style—a cross between the Orda'anian court attire and her mother's Tenoan dresses. It suited her well and had proved effective at allowing the movement necessary for the practice yards.

He gave a soft chuckle as she tugged the strings of the large bow at the top of her back, grunting with the effort to pull them loose and release the bodice's hold on her.

"You sure you don't need help, Princess?" he asked when the bow tightened further rather than loosen, receiving a glare in return.

"Just the bow," she said firmly, standing with her back to him. He tugged the strings with nimble fingers, careful not to brush against her skin, until the bow dissipated into two long strands draping from her back. As soon as it did, Rosealyn took a deep breath and walked toward her rooms again, the newly made beige dress draped across one arm.

14

Rosealyn swung her wooden practice sword at the bare-chested captain, but he ducked. Again. She clenched her teeth, glaring, and blew the wisps of hair from her face. The small string holding most of her hair always wriggled its way out long before the training session ended and made her wish she could wear a full braid.

She dug her boot into the dirt, faced Charles, and gripped the wooden sword with both hands. Anger made her tense. Too tense. Fear kept her from nearing the short, dark-colored wooden fence surrounding them. If she pressed against it, she would see the dead soldier's face. Again. She blinked away the image of the Hoclian's last moments to watch Charles's movement in front of her. *Focus on his feet. His shoulders. Not on his chest that's glistening from the sun.*

Charles's sturdy hands grasped a blade of his own in front of him. The laughter from his eyes had faded since her father's return, the corners almost always wrinkled, returning to the melancholic soldier she had first met.

Rosealyn followed the shuffling of his feet and tensed. A kick? A jab? She wasn't sure, especially since he forecasted his moves less now. The bruises to her shoulders and legs were a reminder Charles had also stopped pulling his strikes; the lack of bruises to her midsection were proof of improvement. "If I'm to survive in another fight, I need to know how to fight when in pain," she had told him not long after their return from Pasea.

When his foot moved forward, she moved hers to match, only to find herself on her butt with Charles holding her sword.

"So much for getting any better." She brushed the hairs from her face, and the sudden lack of air hit her without warning, breaths coming in shortening gasps. Clutching her side, remembering where the Hoclian's blade had sliced, she counted. Rosealyn stood and held her hand out for the blade.

"You are improving, Princess." Charles squinted at her as she wiped the dirt from the back of her light-colored dress. It was the same as her first training dress, but this one was new. The other had been torn beyond repair. And stained.

"It took much longer before I knocked you to the ground this time, Princess." Charles shifted the lightweight blades to one hand and spoke with the slightest hint of admiration.

Rosealyn grimaced and scanned the dirt ring for the small string to retie her hair. No matter how many times she replayed the fight with the Hoclian, she swore it was luck which had given her the opening rather than talent.

"It would be best if I kept to my feet when in battle." The string found and replaced, Rosealyn stood and held out a hand for her practice sword. "Again."

Charles obliged, turning the hilt of the practice blade back toward her. She grasped the wooden handle and lifted the blade into position, briefly remembering how little time she'd had to gather her wits before the soldier attacked. Lungs which already burned from exertion turned to ice when she heard the cacophony of voices, and she rounded on Charles. "Father's leaving *now*?"

Charles tensed and avoided her gaze.

"You should put that back on." Rosealyn gestured toward the high-buttoned coat draped over the low fence. She couldn't remember exactly when the coat came off, though she could remember how much harder it was to focus on his shoulders and feet once it did. Warmth flooded her cheeks, and she turned away to rest the practice sword against the circular fence before Charles noticed. Practice sword safely stowed, she made it several paces outside the ring and paused, expecting Charles to be at her side. He gathered the weapons they had used, his coat hanging loosely to each side.

Low voices, heated whispers between a tight-lipped general and his king drifted across the practice yards. Stable hands dispersed. Her father stood beside his mare, gloves tucked in his belt, stroking the horse's mane. The motion of his arm halted, and he reached to where his sword rested alongside the saddle. Something was wrong. And they'd hidden it from her. Hidden her from the truth like she was some child in need of protection.

Rosealyn refused to let them keep anything else a secret. Not when the air tasted worse than a sour grape. Each step quicker than the last. Her jaw ached from grinding her teeth. *I'm not some piece of glass about to drop; I'm the heir to the throne. The only heir. They have to tell me what is happening.*

The smell intensified, an unusual wind slowing her determined steps to a complete stop while she searched for the cart of rotten food most assuredly responsible. The agitation turned to a quick jolt of pain lacing from her stomach to her lower back. Air stuck in her throat, Rosealyn tugged at the material of her dress along her midriff. It was whole. Completely intact.

"Breathe through the pain." Rosealyn pressed her hand against her abdomen where the ache lingered with a faint rhythmic pulse. A shake of her head and she dismissed the sudden twinge as nothing more than overworked muscles.

The courtyard with its hushed voices grew distant around her. Everything turned black, darker than a starless night. Blaring sunlight returned just as quickly as it had engulfed her. A slight shake of her head. Between her left knee in the dirt and Charles's grip on her upper arm, she wondered how long she'd been plunged into darkness.

Sunlight glinted off metal in her periphery. A sword. Charles's sword. Not the thick chunk of wood used for sparring. A solid blade she had never seen outside the slightly curved sheath was in his other hand.

Her insides were on fire. She tugged her arm free of Charles's grasp, hands roaming to locate the cause. Something bubbled up from inside, coating the back of her tongue with an odd taste she didn't recognize.

"Princess?" Charles held his free hand out to her.

For a few breaths, she stared at clammy but otherwise clean hands. She had no blood on her. It was all inside, exactly where it should be.

"I'm fine." Rosealyn placed her hand in his and gripped firmly, trying to will away the spasm within. When her grip tightened, he took a step closer. Coiled tension radiated from him, and he released her hand. A second later, he was holding the tip of a dagger, its hilt facing her. Eyes widening, she wrapped her fingers so tightly around the weapon's hilt she feared they would soon be numb.

The courtyard glimmered like the chapel did beneath its colored windows in the ceiling when the sun was at its peak.

Naught but silver shone before disappearing into a solid black cloud occupying the same space her father just held.

Fingers limp, the dagger clattered to the stone path, forgotten. Head shaking, the edges of her vision blurring, she knew whatever the soldiers flooding the courtyard would do was useless. A sound loud enough to rattle her bones emanated from the fading mist, and Charles motioned for her to stand behind him.

"A dragon?" Charles said so softly Rosealyn wasn't sure she had heard him say anything at all.

"Wh—" Another wave of pain pierced through her midriff. A weird taste—blood?—coated her throat. Another flicker into the darkness and this time her father was there, sprawled on the ground with a sword protruding from him. *No, it can't be. It's not him. This isn't happening. He's safe.*

Rosealyn shook her head so fast her hair lashed her cheeks. Frozen, she stared at the shimmering darkness sucking in light. When she opened her mouth to speak, the cloud winked out of existence and the muscles of her side spasmed with a renewed vigor. Shrill screams echoed in her ears and her knees buckled. Charles caught her and eased her to the ground. Slices of agony dug into each palm as though she'd run her hand along the edge of a sword. Or the dagger. But there was no blood.

She'd read about it time and time again. But it couldn't be. Not now. He was home; he was *safe.*

Teeth gritted, she fought to remain conscious. Her organs shifted inside her, and she clamped her jaw shut to stop another scream from escaping.

She shared his pain. Not sharing, came a fleeting logical reminder, experiencing.

Pressure from within eased without warning and turned to overwhelming cold. Tears streamed down each cheek while shivers sluiced along every inch of her.

Rosealyn succumbed to the Passing of the LeNoir Gift.

15

After rushing to the alcove beneath the garden balcony, Charles gently lowered Rosealyn to the stone walkway. With one hand, he cradled her head, the small string where her braids met digging into his palm as she tossed and turned. His other hand hovered above her chest, and he released a breath of his own when the fine cloth of her dress brushed it. Shouts of warning gave way to a sudden hush. Several soldiers approached with cautious steps, eyes darting about in expectation of another attack, stopping short at General Azeiah's singular raised hand.

Metal which usually gleamed in the noonday sun hid beneath sweaty palms gripping sword hilts. Moments before, chaos had consumed the training grounds. It lingered in agonized silence. The shift in the wind brought the smell of fear, adding to the ever-present musk which lingered around the well-used practice rings and their accompanying weapons.

Rosealyn shivered and squirmed in his arms. Her lips moved as though she was speaking, and he leaned closer to make out the words, frowning at the repetition of two words, until a singular shadow approached. Looking up, he found a face laced with pained stoicism. Occasional dark flashes flitted across the general's stone-like features. Despite what Azeiah believed, Charles could read the man's shift in emotions. Even such a small change was enough for Charles's throat to constrict. Azeiah kneeled next to them, surveying the princess and closing his eyes with a soft sigh.

"No, don't." Another gut-wrenching scream tore from her, piercing his soul. He searched. No wound on her, but the pain was real.

"Is it—" Charles's constricting throat swallowed the rest. It had to be what he thought; he wasn't ready for what came next. *For me, or for her.*

"The Passing," Azeiah finished for him, though it sounded like a question. The general's stoic features grew more quizzical as Rosealyn continued to lose her grasp on consciousness and the mutterings turned incoherent. "It has to be." When Charles looked up at the general, the man was frowning. "But it's different this time."

For the first time in several years, Charles struggled to inhale any useful air. His gaze darted about the courtyard, at all the faces staring at the unconscious Rosealyn writhing in his arms.

"How could the king disappear?" Each face Charles studied showed a greater level of dismal shock than the last. When the general remained silent, Charles asked, "What should we do now?"

Another prolonged scream halted their conversation, and Charles grimaced and exchanged another worrisome glance with the general.

"To her rooms, quickly." Azeiah glanced back to where he had been standing next to the king and shook his head slightly. "This is … different."

Charles tucked one arm beneath Rosealyn's knees, using the other to grasp her shoulders and hold her close to his chest.

Her screams faded to anguished murmurings, and her body grew limp as he stood. The movement of her head whipping back and forth reminded Charles he had never finished buttoning his coat.

"You there," came Azeiah's voice from behind him. "Find Queen Roseanne and the doctor. Send them to Princess Rosealyn's chambers. The rest of you—close the gates and double the guard. Lock down this castle until I say otherwise."

The scurry of feet faded as Charles quickened his pace to Rosealyn's room. She was no longer trying to hold onto him, her weight settling into his arms instead. A sheen of sweat formed on her brow, and the inaudible mumbles continued. Her hair rubbed against his chest, fraying into more loose strands with each turn of her head. *This is not what I expected of the Passing. Why does she keep saying those two names?*

Soon he was in front of her door, kicking at the handle to gain entrance. He bypassed the familiar patches of color of the large front room to enter her bedroom. Wide swaths of alternating solid black and white cloth hung between the posts, but the blankets on the bed were a deep green. Almost, but not quite, black. He moved until the lone window was at his back and lowered her atop the covers.

An interminable moment passed. Rosealyn trembled. Charles held the back of his hand to her forehead, expecting her to be cold. She was warm, much warmer than she had been while he was carrying her. She ground her teeth so loudly he could hear it, and he tensed, anticipating another soul-wrenching wail. Instead, she clutched the covers, and he leaned in closer, trying to make out what she was whispering. *Xannan isn't real. And Lycene is deserted—why does she keep repeating those names?*

"Move aside," the doctor said with a loud tsk, shoving Charles away. Charles continued the backward movement until the ledge of the windowsill dug into his lower back. Immediately behind the doctor were the queen and Azeiah. Queen Roseanne stood straight and tense, her hair in that obnoxiously impeccable braided crown. But her eyes were wide, and one hand held the side of the gleaming golden metal circle resting amid that braid. Next to her, Azeiah stood with each thumb hooked into his belt. His lips were tight, and his shoulders drooped.

"There's nothing more we can do for her now but keep her comfortable." Doctor Alvin gestured for the others to follow him to the door. "I will stay with her, but she does not need an audience."

The doctor waited until all three stood on the opposite threshold and shoved the princess's bedroom door closed. Roseanne rounded on the two soldiers, eyes narrowing at Charles as he buttoned the coat that hung loose against him. His already tightened throat protested at the last button on the collar, but he fastened it as well.

"What happened?" she asked, fiery gaze turning to Azeiah for an answer.

"It has to be the Passing," Azeiah said, but he sounded hesitant.

Charles stared in wonder at the general; the man was always confident in what he said. And yet, there it was, the slight lilt of uncertainty, the question of whether or not the words he said were true.

Queen Roseanne harrumphed. "Or that one took their training too far and harmed her."

Charles bristled when the woman's stare met his again. It was hard to hide his disdain at the accusation. "Certainly not, Your Majesty. She asked me to stop pulling punches, and I did. But this is not my doing. No simple practice weapon could cause this ... this reaction. My Queen."

"Remind me," Roseanne demanded, shifting that icy glare to the general again. Charles stifled the desire to roll his eyes, lips tightening when the woman tensed her shoulders. "What happened when Phillippe received the Passing of this gift?"

"Phillippe became unsteady and could see and feel his father's death," Azeiah explained with the same hint of disbelief. *Because it's happening? Or … because it's different?*

"Feel it?" Charles asked, curiosity getting the better of him. He tugged at the collar of his buttoned coat, swallowing. He didn't need the reminder of how Phillippe's father had died, but Azeiah gave it anyway.

"Aye, felt it. Every stab that maniacal Claude gave Thaddeus, Phillippe felt," Azeiah muttered.

Charles shifted, reaching for his sword hilt only to realize it wasn't there; it sat in the training grounds where he'd dropped it to catch Rosealyn when she collapsed. Azeiah's words made his own scars twinge, wondering what such a sensation would be like—to feel a weapon's fatal wound when there was none.

After a moment, Azeiah added, "No strange cloud, and he didn't pass out. Pain, of course, but not … not screams like those."

"So we need to check on him?" Roseanne said, crossing her arms with a poignant stare leveled at them both. "This is not the same. Whatever ails Rosealyn is different; therefore, Phillippe may be alive."

Azeiah's mouth worked to form words, and Charles's insides plummeted. The disbelief had turned to shock. Though he did not want to voice it aloud, Charles knew what this was, knew that what Rosealyn experienced could only be explained by the Passing of the LeNoir Gift. Where the king had gone was of little consequence to what had happened to Phillippe.

Based on the princess's condition, her father had likely been murdered.

"Where do you think he could be, Your Majesty?" Charles asked when Azeiah stayed silent. He watched the general as he spoke, understanding what even this small show of emotion meant. The solid rock had fractured, only a small one, but a fracture nonetheless. "I will go and see what I can find."

"No, Captain, you are needed—"

"I accept his offer," Queen Roseanne interrupted, the words coming out as one. "Lycene. That's what Rosealyn keeps muttering in there, yes?"

Charles nodded, meeting the queen's regal stare. The princess's ramblings were mostly incoherent, but Lycene and Xannan, those names rang clear.

"Then you will go there." She snapped the words at him as she turned toward the princess's bedroom door and knocked. "Blazes help you if you return empty-handed, Captain."

"Yes, Your Majesty," Charles said through gritted teeth and a slight bow of his head. The door shut behind the queen, and Charles tugged at his collar, studying the not-so-stoic-anymore general standing beside him. "General?"

"Rake will accompany you," Azeiah said. The general's chin rested on his chest, thumbs hooked into his belt, and his skin had paled.

"Yes, sir." Charles chewed on his tongue to prevent asking another question. He stared at the wooden door, wincing when another muffled scream came from just beyond it. In his periphery, Azeiah's features turned somber.

"Moss and I will watch over her," Azeiah said. "Learn what you can and come back safe."

"Yes, sir." Charles's heartbeat thundered in his ears. Several moments passed, and no more screams sounded.

"It's best you go now," Azeiah whispered. "She will be safe here. As safe as we can make her here, that is."

"It came from nowhere, sir," Charles said, voice barely louder than the general's. It was too similar to what he had read in the withering book of his mother's handwriting. The sudden suffocating silence followed by the sound shaking the stones, but he asked anyway. "One second he was there, the next … he—His Majesty disappeared. How?"

"Myths come to life. Again." Azeiah rubbed his face with a tanned hand.

Charles fought to keep his jaw from dropping at the display of emotion.

"Blazes keep you safe, Captain. I fear you need that blessing. For more than this journey."

Charles's teeth clicked together. "Thank you, sir. We will return as soon as we can."

When he reached the door to the hallway, Charles glanced over his shoulder to find General Azeiah slumped in one of the random chairs, face buried in his hands.

16

Rosealyn's mind drifted. She didn't understand the movement or the process; her father had been stingy with the grittier details. As had all the LeNoirs who came before.

And now she was in his body. He was still alive, and she moved as he moved. For a moment, she looked down from above, resisting the urge to gag. Sweat was familiar to her, almost comforting, until… Rosealyn felt her father's shoulders slump, eyes shut tight against the scene, his breathing steadying. She had no command over his body but felt an emptiness inside her—no, him—as the vision solidified.

She tried to move, but no matter what she did, she felt what her father felt, moved only when and how her father moved.

"It's generational," she remembered her father explaining once. "I experienced the Passing when your grandfather Thaddeus got himself killed in Jearnia."

His thoughts were like muddied water. She knew he was … thinking? Planning? Yet there was … *acceptance?*

A man in an unblemished plain brown leather vest and simple dark-colored pants provided a stark contrast to the bloodied and burned bodies. Given the similarities, and her father's thoughts, she labeled him the Lost Prince. *Strange. How is he still alive?*

Nearby sat an enormous beast, resting on its haunches, lazily blowing the occasional wide swath of fire just above the already burned homes. Rosealyn tried to take in the beast's magnificence and identify it, but all she saw were her father's hands fumbling for his sword. The sword he kept hooked on the saddle when he rode. It wasn't with him.

Every time she, no, her father, tried to move, the dragon roared.

Heat seared her face and…

The stone beneath her became soft bedding. She gripped the sheets in her hands, glimpsing a hand dabbing at her forehead. A groan escaped her, eyelids fluttering. Rosealyn tried to open them wide, annoyed they refused the command. *My bed?*

She was on the ground, trying to reach for her sword and stand at the same time. No, not her, she was back inside her father's body. The man, the one her father's thoughts called Xannan, caressed his black blade, an eagerness…

A damp towel patted against her forehead, voices humming above her. "Father?" she whispered. It stung to speak. Her mouth was so dry. She wondered if this was what sand tasted like. A rough tongue tried to wet cracked lips, and cool liquid fell into her mouth. Coughing and sputtering, Rosealyn tried to open her eyes again.

Pay attention, daughter. That was his voice. She was back in his mind. *Remember what I have taught you. I'm sorry, my darling Rose.*

The blade plunged into him, same as her invisible wound. She screamed. Aloud or within, she didn't know. She couldn't tell the difference anymore. Her father seemed to shout. "Dangerous, avoid the repetition. Pull away!"

She felt her … no, her father's anger, a lump forming in his throat as thoughts coalesced. The words forming in his mind were indignant. But he never got to say them. Xannan had already plunged the black blade through her father's midriff.

Then came Xannan's malicious smile. A glance to the left revealed a frightened child hiding in blackened rubble. A pang of guilt and regret surfaced as the wide-eyed boy ran.

Xannan twisted the blade.

Rosealyn screamed, pain flaring within as though she had just received the stab herself. She pulled away from the pain, and it lessened. Some.

The sheets were wet beneath her. *Soiled?*

"Father, make it stop," she mumbled, breathless, hair tangling with each turn of her head. This time she did not try to open her eyes. She did not want to meet the gaze of whoever stood above her with that distracting cloth. "I don't want this gift."

Even after his last breath, Rosealyn could still see through his eyes. She watched, horrified, as Xannan peered down at his work and wiped the bloodied black blade on her father's clothes.

The connection severed.

Her father was gone. Killed by the Lost Prince every historian had told her did not exist. Killed by the man who was supposed to be a figment of King Gailin's imagination. The pain was real. Too real. The Gift had still passed to her.

It beckoned for her though she could not see it. The Gift was like a person, an entity, a breeze which pushed her along the path it wished for her to follow. Rosealyn expected to wake in her room. But she was at her father's coronation. Then Grandfather Thaddeus's … not his coronation. A flash of Gailin writing in his journal.

The damn damp cloth again. She shoved it away, wiping her own sweat from her brow. "Gailin's journal," she mumbled, hoping to return to the scene.

King Gailin's wedding. His son's birth announcement. And so on down the lineage. She kept a view from above, unable to move as they moved. *Weird. This is not what Gailin wrote, nor what Father explained…*

Her father arguing with the priests. Then with her mother. Everything blurred together. She fumbled for control but found none, within or without. Rosealyn tried to think of her father again, only to scream. Her throat was raw, as though she had swallowed thorns. Thoughts edged toward her father again, and the pain returned. It was less, not quite screamworthy, but the ache was there. Agony, discomfort, and misery tortured her until she relinquished control, knowing she would never be without pain again.

A white dragon.

A shimmering sword.

She faded into a restless sleep.

17

Ten steps. That was all Roseanne could pace before the raging hearth. A mere ten steps to try to collect her thoughts. Her cousin's latest letter clutched in one hand, Roseanne considered ripping it to shreds. Or tossing it into the fire that barely persuaded the chill of night to stay away.

Ramon couldn't know what had happened, could he? So why was he telling her to return to Tenoa? After his foolish instructions to listen to a voice from a cloud, Roseanne found it difficult to trust any of her cousin's words.

She read the letter again. The youngest councilman, and newest addition to their group, had gone missing and, supposedly, the other members had removed Ramon as Praetor while allowing him to stay on the council. Whatever Ramon was doing, he had mixed her up in it as well. Ramon's words made little sense, especially since Roseanne was trying to wrap her head around what she had witnessed in the courtyard two days before. She'd seen it all from the garden balcony. One second he stroked the mare's mane after clasping his sword to the saddle. The next second, gone. Her attention had swayed from Rosealyn sparring with the captain to the cloud engulfing Phillippe with no warning. It was the same shade as the one which had not appeared in her room since the attack—the one she continuously expected to steal her away as it had her husband. But the one which often visited her had been, on all but one occasion, small. No larger than a rock one could hold in their hand.

Rest was what Xannan had promised. Had she misunderstood his implication? Rest and aid. Not death. Despite Rosealyn's murmurings, Roseanne decided something else was at play. Perhaps something greater than even a Lost Prince could orchestrate.

Roseanne paused in her pacing and shuddered. That roar. So similar to those vicious desert creatures. She closed her eyes, replaying the scene. Chaos. Soldiers drew their swords and ran. Then paused in uncertainty. *How does one fight what they cannot see?*

All except Charles and Azeiah. The captain had pulled his sword free like all the others but remained at Rosealyn's side. And Roseanne swore he had recognized that strange roar.

Azeiah had been closer than anyone. Perhaps he saw where Phillippe had been taken.

Roseanne crumpled the letter from Ramon and tossed it into the fire as someone knocked.

Pressing her lips together and rounding her shoulders, she opened her door to find the three whose presence she had demanded: General Azeiah, Doctor Alvin, and Elder Matthias. All men who had Phillippe's trust, who would follow her husband to wherever he requested of them. She hoped such trust would extend to her as well.

She motioned toward the table to one side of her room, the same table the black cloud usually floated above while Xannan spoke to her. Her heartbeat spiked, and she berated herself for inviting the men here. Could Xannan tell when she was alone? Or would he appear tonight?

"Princess Rosealyn remains unconscious." Alvin took a seat at the small table. He ran a finger through the sand, circling one of the potted plants as he spoke. "There's nothing more I can do for her. None of the potions which force wakefulness have worked. So we must wait."

"Daniel, Flynn, and Lori are with the princess," Azeiah said before she could ask as he and Elder Matthias sat down.

She followed but did not sit. She couldn't. "Tell me more about how Phillippe experienced the Passing."

"There is little more to tell than I already did, Your Majesty," Azeiah replied. His voice was too somber for Roseanne's liking, too believing that what her daughter was experiencing meant her husband was gone. Not for weeks or a month. Forever. Though Phillippe often aggravated her to no end, she had not wanted his death. *I wanted to help, not get anyone killed.*

"Then tell me what happened that day," Roseanne amended. "Did Phillippe feel anything *before* his father died? Any indication? A way to prevent the Passing?"

"My understanding of the Passing is that it occurs at the moment the previous recipient dies." That was the voice of a hardened general rather than her husband's friend. "We were not with Thaddeus while he spoke with Claude, but one moment Phillippe, his brothers, and I were talking. The next, Phillippe pressed a hand against his chest while claiming something felt lodged inside. He felt the sensation several more times, and after the third or fourth stab, he knew his father was dead. It was hours before those who attended Thaddeus returned. Much too long for Phillippe's liking."

An expression of understanding flickered across the general's face so quickly Roseanne wasn't sure she had seen it.

"And then?" Roseanne asked, wondering what details the general was leaving out.

"Phillippe had the Gift and insisted we return home before more died that day."

"Rosealyn is not conscious, but we cannot find a wound on her. There is no reason for her current state. If this is the Passing, why would Rosealyn's experience be different?"

All three men shrugged, and Roseanne ground her teeth together. "Based on that description, I think this may be something else," Roseanne announced. Three sets of eyes stared at her in shock. "Rosealyn keeps mumbling about Xannan and Lycene, so we sent Charles and—"

She paused and looked at Azeiah, who offered a simple "and Rake."

"Charles and Rake went to Lycene. Why Lycene, though? Phillippe intended to travel there before this…" She pursed her lips together, trying to decide how to label her husband's sudden disappearance. "This attack?"

"Correct, Your Majesty," Azeiah said. "A theory that refugees may gather there."

Not refugees, the mercenaries. She should have told Phillippe the truth. If she had been honest about what she had seen and the conversation she'd had with Xannan, then perhaps Phillippe would not have left the castle. But she doubted he would have done anything except let that family Gift of his guide his actions. Not to mention he would have thought her insane. The Twin Blades were a story. Perhaps her meeting with the man truly had been a dream. Albeit a much too realistic one.

"Perhaps they can help us learn the cause of the famine? Help us determine *what* is destroying cities and fields? Once we know the culprit, we can stop it from happening again, yes?"

"That is the idea, Your Majesty," Azeiah mumbled. He rubbed his face with the palms of his hands. Despite his age, the general was often vibrant and full of life. His current despondency rivaled that of the blank-faced Elder Matthias who sat to the general's left.

Roseanne resisted the urge to reach up, especially since she was not wearing her crown.

"Elder Matthias," she began, worried the tremor of her hands would sound in her voice. "What proof is needed to know the Passing has occurred?"

The elder squinted and tilted his head, nose scrunched in thought. "No one has ever questioned the Passing before, Your Majesty."

"What ails Rosealyn may or may not be the Passing." Roseanne's clenched fists did not help to stop the shaking. "Until Phillippe's fate is certain, there will be no coronation. Especially since she is in no state to become queen. She must recover first."

Only the crackling of the fire behind her broke the silence. Roseanne refused to allow others to control her actions. Not now, not anymore.

"I will speak with the other priests. For now, I am inclined to agree." Elder Matthias stood, straightening his white coat lined with gold thread and offered a small bow to her. "I will return with our decision."

Given what little the Orda'anian laws provided, the elder's response planted a seedling of hope. A small seedling Roseanne worried would be crushed and killed before it could sprout. Rest, apparently, could have more than one meaning.

Doctor Alvin stood, bowed, and added, "I will send word once she's awake, Your Majesty."

Once the door closed, Roseanne turned her attention to the general who remained in his seat. They stared at each other until Roseanne turned her back to him, staring into the flickering flames within the hearth.

"We should annihilate the threat Hoclia poses before they attack again," Roseanne said. "Send our army to their capital, to Hazael, and take it as ours. That will stop the destruction of what few resources remain before winter is truly upon us."

"Your Majesty, I dis—"

"Go." Roseanne's hands trembled. "You have your orders."

The door did not close gently. Alone, she braced for a dark cloud hovering above the table.

Nothing. She was on her own.

18

Dress. Sheets. Thick covers. All clung to Rosealyn's sweat-soaked frame as she blinked multiple times to adjust to the onslaught of light streaming through her lone window. She tried to push herself up, only to collapse when her left side protested. Blinking several more times, she propped herself up with her right elbow and groggily surveyed the room. Everything blurred before her, swimming in her field of vision. She closed her eyes again, a hand searching for the broken skin of her abdomen. It burned and ached, and she emitted a soft groan when she touched it. Her hand felt the faded line of her scar but no new unbroken skin. *I swear that weapon is still sitting inside me. Blazes. It hurts.*

"Finally," Lori breathed and raced out of her room.

"Figures." Rosealyn covered her eyes with her arm and peeked out from under it to look for a glass of water nearby. Nothing. She shifted her arm to prevent the light from further aiding the pounding of her head. Her stomach ached, desperate to receive sustenance it had not had in what had to have been several days, and she blew the loose hairs from her face only for them to cling to her drenched skin.

Her vision smoothed as she glanced around the room, finding comfort in the plain, unadorned walls and the long black velvet curtains drawn to the sides of the window. The simple blue sky showed it was midday, but the empty chairs around her bed brought questions. Rosealyn's cheeks flushed, gracious for the cover of her blankets.

Doctor Alvin followed Lori back in, carrying a bowl, brows furrowed. Lori resumed her seat at Rosealyn's bedside, looking as though she were trying to pry the skin from her aging fingers. Despite seeing the bowl of food she knew her body needed, Rosealyn wished she could return to blissful sleep instead. To sleep where she could not feel the throb in her side, the ache in her head, nor the scratchiness of her throat each time she swallowed.

"The fever has broken," Alvin declared with a hand resting on Rosealyn's forehead. *Probably the same hand responsible for that damn damp towel.*

"You've been unconscious, Your Highness," Alvin said but corrected himself. "Mostly unconscious, for just over three days."

"Father?" Rosealyn's voice sounded deep, and it hurt to speak. The physician sat next to her, holding a bowl of cold broth to her lips. Rosealyn didn't mind the cold liquid, even knowing it would have tasted better warm. It smelled of old fish and tasted bitter, but it cooled the raw muscles of her throat.

"You're awake," came her mother's regal voice from the doorway. "You kept mumbling about Lycene and Xannan." Her mother folded her arms across her chest, but she did not move from the doorway. "General Azeiah and I discussed the matter. Banner-Captain Rake and Captain Charles are on their way there now."

Rosealyn choked on the broth and bolted upright, sputtering liquid as a combined cough and scream escaped. Alvin set the bowl on the table at her bedside, reaching to inspect what she knew was not there.

"The wound isn't on me," Rosealyn said through gritted teeth, wincing and shoving the physician's hand away and pressing into her abdomen herself with a scowl. "Mother, why did you let Charles go? It's too dangerous!"

Her mother stood in the doorway and shifted the crown nestled within the miraculously perfect braid atop her head. Rosealyn could tell her own hair was in shambles. The fraying of her auburn locks dotted the edges of her eyesight. *Lori is going to love taming that nightmare.*

"I'm glad you're awake, Rosealyn. Doctor, please keep me apprised of her condition, and make sure she gets the rest she needs."

"Yes, Your Majesty," the doctor said, tipping the bowl to Rosealyn's lips again. It was almost empty, tasting more bitter with each gulp. She contemplated tossing the bowl after her mother, but she was too hungry.

The bowl empty, Alvin laid a hand against her forehead again and nodded. "True rest will do you good," he said, standing. "Your father had a much different reaction to the Passing. He resumed normal activities about a day after King Thaddeus's death."

"And the lingering pain? It feels like someone whacked me with a practice sword a thousand times in the front, then the back, and then inside. Father never told me about this part," Rosealyn said, grimacing at the slightest movement.

"King Phillippe never told me of any lingering pain," the silver-haired doctor said, eyes barely widening behind the small circles of his spectacles. "He was conscious between the … visions, I believe he called them. He could speak to us and had no fever."

"Any theories?" Rosealyn asked, fighting to keep her eyes open. *Everything feels so heavy.*

"Simple," the physician shrugged, pushing the spectacles back up the bridge of his nose. "No female LeNoir descendant has inherited the Gift before."

Rosealyn shook her head and held her side. "Nonsense. I don't believe my gender causes the difference. It must have something to do with the Lost Prince, with Xannan. It was his hand holding the—"

She grimaced when the pain flared inside at the thought of how her father met his end. Lori and the physician shared a concerned glance.

"You kept mumbling many things, Xannan's name among them, but…"

She glared at him, confident in what she had seen.

"He's nothing more than a creation of King Gailin's imagination," the doctor said. A note of condescension hung there while Rosealyn concentrated on not screaming again, this time out of emotional, not physical, pain.

Rosealyn avoided closing her eyes, afraid she would feel the blade plunging into her again. "Others were there," she reminded them. "Charles heard the dragon. Xannan hasn't aged a day."

She stifled a yawn. "Father—"

"Rest, Your Highness." Alvin patted the bed, stood, and turned to Lori. "Make sure she stays in bed."

Rosealyn laughed and whimpered. "A thousand practice swords would have hurt less."

Alvin smiled apologetically as he turned to leave. Rosealyn followed his movement to find her mother standing in the doorway again. The impeccable braid was betrayed by the woman's streaked cheeks. Queen Roseanne entered, Alvin left, and Rosealyn felt her eyes burning.

Rosealyn turned to Lori. "Leave us, please."

Lori stood and bowed, hands wringing. *Seriously, how does that woman still have skin on those fingers?*

Her mother stood next to her bed with a hand hovering above Rosealyn's abdomen.

"I know he's gone," Rosealyn whispered. She tilted her head, feeling the small droplets run down her face. The streaks on her mother's face filled with fresh tears.

A clammy hand wrapped around Rosealyn's own, and her mother whispered, "I should have made him stay. Insisted on another—"

Rosealyn laid her hand on top, tasting her tears as they fell to her lips. "Neither of us could have stopped this, Mother," she said, surprised to see such emotion from the immaculate queen.

She welcomed her mother's presence next to her, relaxing and giving in to another yawn as the queen's soft hand brushed the hair from her face. It was a comfort she had not felt from her mother in years. Rosealyn was not sure she had ever seen such emotion from the woman. Her eyes grew heavier, and as she drifted to a true sleep, she heard her father's disembodied voice whisper: *I'm sorry.*

19

Representative Catarina of Izari, written within the past year.

My dear ~~Jaida~~ Rosealyn,

Ebios is far from the peace Phillippe desired. Izari is unaware of the impending war on Ebios—the fear would be too much for their quiet lives. Naomi, Ruth, and I continue to settle disputes successfully. Except if I should stay or go to you.

I feel for you, knowing what Phillippe saw. I wish he still wrote to me about you. Writing to you helps clear my thoughts.

~~Naomi~~

I asked Naomi and Ruth if I should go home. Of course, they contradict one another. The boats between Ebios and Izari travel frequently enough. Yet I fear it. I fear what I might find when I arrive. Roseanne may have me killed or forgive me.

Not even my love for your father could keep me amid that chaos and disorder.

The people I represent on Izari need me. My voice on the council allows them to be heard. Please keep your father safe.

Love,
Your Mother

Catarina leaned back against her chair, rubbing the back of her neck. She blew on the ink to help it dry, annoyed the council had refused her "experiments." Placing the single paper inside a drawer, she ruffled through the hundreds of pages she had written since leaving Ebios. Her daughter had been barely two years old when she left.

Catarina found it difficult to think of her precious Jaida as Rosealyn. She knew Roseanne and Phillippe had chosen the name to protect the girl. And so she had eventually addressed the letters accordingly, with the occasional slip.

A glance out her window showed the setting sun illuminating the sea of trees which spread out from their growing city. Odd how the trees were so tall and skinny, their leaves mostly protruding from the tops of their trunks. They built most homes around the trees, raised high above the ground. And they made everything from wood. Even the most renowned buildings of their small town were made of dull wood. The nearby ocean was beautiful but problematic. Catarina suggested building with stone, but as was typical, the natives of Izari refused any change which came from Ebios.

Her neighbor's homes were hard to see through the enormous deep green leaves of the trees, but Catarina knew a sunset against the wooden homes would disappoint. She remembered Orda'an, remembered how dragonstone sparkled with the morning rays as she stared at her favorite painting decorating the wall opposite her desk.

Catarina released a disappointed sigh, pushing the drawer closed, setting the ink-filled pen back on her desk, and covering the ink jar. She hated how frugal she had to be with the ink; it was not cheap to make here. Her desk properly rearranged, she snuffed out her lantern. Lying on her bed, she stared at the ceiling and wondered if her dear Jaida-Rosealyn listened to the same trivial complaints.

PART TWO:
A CHALLENGE

20

A cooling wind tickled the hairs of Xannan's almost bare chest beneath the vest. An iciness, combined with the scent of burning wood permeated the air where he sat at the edge of a clearing near the town of Lycene. Plus burnt flesh. He stretched his neck from side to side to push away the remnants of that visual.

Day faded until the last embers of the sun cast an eerie red glow on the simple crown dangling from his hand. A vague memory. Do not step into or speak through the portal. Just stab. So he did. No more remained except a crown and a broken promise.

Remembrance. Fear. Adoration. All accolades he wanted for himself. None of which had come to fruition. The girl should be dead, too. But the king's sword was not on his person.

Somewhere above the canopy of trees floated the beast who claimed his flame and magic grew too weak. One swatch of flame, and Eilon had consumed all of Pasea. It wasn't the first city they'd torched. And now that Xannan held the last remaining evidence he had, according to Eilon, killed the king of Orda'an? Obnoxious silence.

The road to Lycene was strange to observe. Overgrown, yet decaying. Mostly dirt. Hidden by patches of grass and shrubs no higher than Charles's ankles. After several days of riding toward the supposedly abandoned city, Rake signaled for them to slow and dismount. Smoke rose in the distance. Campfires indicated a not-so-abandoned city.

At a small cusp of trees, they tied the horses and continued their approach on foot. Food. He could smell food drifting along the breeze. Seasoned, cooked, mouth-watering, though with a twinge of something … odd. Even living in the main castle of the country, proper sustenance was scarce.

"Keep a low profile and report back what you see. Return here in an hour."

"I don't think it wise to split up, sir," Charles said. His hand rested on his leather-bound sword hilt.

"We'll cover more ground, Captain. The sooner we assess Lycene, the sooner we can return to the castle."

"I'd be happy to accept more soldiers." The distinct ringing of a weapon leaving its sheath followed the words. "But I get the sense you are not here to join me."

Charles locked his gaze with Rake's and waited for the order. His commanding officer drew his sword and positioned his shield.

They turned as one, and Charles froze. Same as the tapestry Rosealyn had once found. Same chin-length blond hair. Same piercing green eyes. Same high angular cheekbones. Pale skin. Bare arms. Brown vest. The Lost Prince. Xannan.

"Sir?"

Charles could say little more. He'd listened to Rosealyn recite the stories. Listened to her read Gailin's journal aloud time and time again. The similarities crashed into one another between how the Lost Prince had disappeared and how it had happened to Phillippe only days prior. Black cloud. Then gone. Charles's grip tightened on his sword hilt.

Rake shuffled forward in silence. Tiny swirls of dirt lifted around their feet from an intense gust of wind, and Charles looked up, expecting to discover what he had seen once before. The light of the moon fought to pierce the cloud-filled night sky. One cloud moved differently than the rest, blotting out the others with its darker hue. If he could make out the dragon's outline from its current height… Charles stopped the thought and worked moisture back into his mouth.

"Rake," Charles said a tad louder than before. "That's Xannan."

Xannan tilted his head and shifted his sable blade. The deep color sucked in more of the fading sunlight. Mesmerized and terrified, Charles drew his sword.

"Tell the princess I'll see her soon, if she still lives." Xannan tossed the crown he held aside. "Maybe she'll provide more of a challenge for me than her father did."

"That's His Majesty's crown." Rake growled the words. "He killed King Phillippe."

Charles could feel his commanding officer's anger radiating but made no move to attack Xannan first. If what Rosealyn read in those journals were true, fighting Xannan would not work in their favor.

"True on both accounts; he had something we need." Xannan waited for them, blade held loose in his hand.

Charles jerked and lifted a brow, grip on his sword hilt tightening. *We?*

Before Charles could ask, Rake charged with his sword steady atop the shield and ready to plunge, but Xannan stepped to the side and slashed the back of Rake's thigh as the older soldier raced past.

Lines of blood soaked Rake's pants, and the Banner-Captain collapsed to the ground. Xannan approached the felled soldier with a cold, calculated expression.

Charles rushed forward to block Xannan's fatal downward strike and was met with a sound like deafening thunder. The moment their swords met, an invisible force pushed him backward until he lay prostrate on his back.

Disoriented and trembling, Charles lifted his sword arm, surprised to note the absence of the weapon's weight. He reached around him, desperate to control his breaths to prevent the onset of shock. Grateful the sword had not fallen far from him, he grasped it and hissed through clenched teeth. It was like grabbing a burning log.

Jaw clenched to ignore the pain, Charles surveyed the area around them and almost forgot how hot the hilt of his sword burned. Sprawled several yards away, Xannan sat on the ground, unmoving, peering down with the slight hint of curiosity and shock. One of his hands hovered precariously above the weapon whose crystalline facade writhed like the tendrils of flame hidden on Charles's sword's hilt.

Wind swirled around them, an unnaturally strong breeze that made Charles's breath hitch. He almost shifted the sword but remembered its heat. With his sword held before him, Charles blinked and Xannan disappeared.

No sign of the Lost Prince's presence remained, aside from the crown he had tossed aside. Nearby, Rake grumbled something about taking the crown back to Vandyl, as some indication of proof. It was the most they could do considering Xannan's attack and Rake's injury.

Another canvas of their darkening surroundings, another tense moment, and then Charles sheathed his sword, hooked the crown onto his belt, and moved to aid Rake. Proper care meant the older bearded soldier would have another scar to show off while telling stories to the new recruits. Before helping Rake stand, Charles checked the wound and grimaced. Spiderwebs of black and gray flowed from the gash on Rake's leg.

"Time to go, sir." Charles pulled Rake's arm over his shoulders.

Confusion and fear made Charles tense, especially as Rake relinquished more and more of his weight to Charles. Every time Rake attempted to put weight on his leg, he groaned. Half-dragging, half-carrying his commanding officer, Charles surveyed the open plains. They were well outside the view of Lycene, and Charles muttered a curse for leaving the horses behind.

"We'll need to rest here." Charles grunted with the effort of lowering Rake to the ground close to the road they had followed into Lycene. His muscles trembled too much to consider continuing. His sword hand stung, too, the skin growing more tender as it cooled.

Whatever words Rake wanted to say turned into a rasping cough followed by low moans. Next to him, Charles lowered to his knees and situated Rake in a prone position to inspect the man's wound again. Pale skin which rarely found the light of day was rank, unseemly. It smelled worse than the mostly rotten food he'd helped Rosealyn feed to the children. That no longer churned his insides while this threatened to upend them.

"I think it poisoned you." Charles steadied his voice. "We need to get you help, sir."

Rake took shuddering breaths between each word. "We can rest here for tonight. Help tomorrow."

Color drained from Rake's face with each passing second. Whatever ailed the man had already spread too far. Frantic, Charles removed Rake's breastplate to check his abdomen, only to observe more discolored and haggard skin.

Charles fell back into a seated position on the dirt, burying his face in his hands. Something sharp and hard poked beneath him, and he tugged at the item. The king's crown was all he had left to offer the princess and queen as confirmation that their beloved King Phillippe was gone. He wanted more concrete proof. Though Phillippe's death would not hurt him in the same manner it would Rosealyn, the Orda'anian king had treated him almost like a son. Albeit a son who had to follow a strict set of rules.

The princess's condition told them Phillippe was dead. Nothing else could explain the phantom pain she experienced or her unconscious state when he left. He replayed the words Xannan had spoken before the clashing … before the fighting. "If she lives," Xannan had said.

Rake's hand found Charles's and squeezed as though the motion could alleviate his pain.

"I'm not sure you'll survive the night, sir," Charles whispered, praying his words drifted away into the sky. Rake didn't respond; he had fallen into the rhythmic yet gravelly breathing of sleep. *Or unconsciousness. What did Xannan mean "if"?*

After a gentle, reassuring squeeze, Charles laid the man's arm at his side. When the chill air of night nipped at his cheeks, he collected wood. He created a small fire that offered a struggling source of light and a pinch of heat.

He frowned, sitting next to Rake again and wiping his palms against his pant legs only to wince. His palm stung like a thousand tiny needles had attacked it at the same time. With his other hand, he massaged the tender skin, knowing it would appear reddened. Rake groaned and shivered.

"I'm sorry there's nothing more I can do." Charles lay down next to the unconscious man, praying to the mountains and convincing himself Rake would wake in the morning. "It's too dark for me to see right now. Sleep will help your strength, make it easier for us—" He paused to glance over at Rake and cleared his throat. "For us to walk home."

He expected exhaustion to help him sleep. But the image of Xannan and himself flying backward when their blades met played in his mind. His sword had a slight curve that most Orda'anian blades did not, and though he had wrapped the hilt with multiple rounds of leather strips, Charles was certain others had somehow seen the insignia hidden underneath. Charles gripped his sword, tapping it against the ground in time with his beating heart, replaying the details of the agreement.

The late king had taken his sword; Phillippe knew what others could learn from it. The sword was a remnant from home, given to Charles by his mother. The dagger his father wanted him to use had been returned to his home. The sword, though, his mother had told him to protect and keep close. Thankfully, he'd gained Phillippe's trust to earn the sword back within two years of his arrival to Vandyl. He held the blade still, wondering what secrets his mother may have hidden within, listening to the critters of the night scurry around them while Rake's breath turned raspier and shallower. He flexed his hand and wished for some way to cool the heat of his palm. Despite the burned palm, Charles tightened his grip on the leather-bound hilt, and the image of the concussion replayed again.

"He won't survive the night. Not without proper care."

Charles bolted upright, cringing as his burned palm gripped his sword hilt. White robes formed the silhouette of a man who hovered over Rake, surveying him. Before he bared an inch of steel, the midnight visitor spoke again.

"Here, put this on your palm. It'll help the burn. I'm here to help you both. Let go of the sword."

No fear, just concern laced with annoyance. His hand released its hold, though Charles swore he chose to continue holding the weapon. A stranger was too odd a coincidence after encountering Xannan a few hours prior.

The white robes the man wore helped Charles see the outline of his extended arm, holding a bottle no larger than the man's hand. Charles hesitated, appraising the situation. The robes struck him as odd, even for an Orda'anian. Not even the Orda'anian priests wore robes. Try as he might, Charles could not resist the urge to grasp the bottle of liquid. So he did.

"I am Arjun, an occupant of Violet Grove inside the Shendaran Forest," he said, and Charles clamped his lips together. "I am loyal to King Phillippe, may he rest in peace. Now put that on your palm."

How would he know? The thought did not last long, distracted by the bottle full of liquid in his hand. A simple pull of the stopper and the bottle was open. His palm needed the relief if he were to properly hold his sword, so he dabbed a small portion of liquid onto his aching flesh. The tender skin smarted briefly and the pain eased. It tickled rather than prickled like before, like drifting his hand through cold water in the middle of winter. He flexed his fingers a few times and passed the bottle back to Arjun, who studied Rake's leg.

"I am not familiar with this poison," Arjun muttered while pocketing the bottle somewhere in his cumbersome robes. After lifting Rake's shirt, the concern from earlier turned somber. "Damn. I will try, but I fear it is too late."

"As I suspected," Charles said, settling back on his heels, hand resting on his sword's hilt. A claim to friendship did not a genuine friend make. His heart sank though, defeat swirling inside. Helplessness was not a feeling he wanted to become accustomed to, but it was there, settling deeper inside him as Rake deteriorated.

"Ah, you speak," Arjun said.

The small fire flickered and died, plunging the surrounding area into moonlit darkness. Clouds filtered the moon's rays and, thankfully, no dragon-like silhouette appeared.

"He is too weak to travel to Violet Grove." A pause as glass clinked together. "Here, help me get him to drink this."

First, Charles tensed, questioning the liquid. After a shake of his head and a muttered curse, he moved to hold Rake's head while Arjun poured the liquid. The Banner-Captain coughed and spluttered but drank most of the vial. Arjun's outline sat back. "Now we wait."

"Arjun—"

"I gave you my name, soldier. Now tell me who you are, and why you're even here, just the two of you," Arjun interrupted.

"Charles Tremaine." He paused and swallowed, wishing he could see this newcomer with proper lighting. *Why am I giving this man my full name?*

Despite his attempt not to, words tumbled forth as if he had no control over his own tongue. "I typically serve as Princess Rosealyn's personal bodyguard. Queen Roseanne wanted proof of Phillippe's death."

The strange desire to speak disappeared, and Charles returned his attention to Rake. Steady, albeit labored, breathing. Satisfied, Charles turned to Arjun, trying to decipher the man's features. A portion of him sensed he could trust Arjun, but he refused to release the hilt of his sword. "You only gave me your name."

"The people of Violet Grove are your friends," Arjun said.

It was matter-of-fact, monotone. The robes bothered Charles. But the throbbing in his burned hand had dissipated, and Rake was improving. *For now.*

"Sleep, I will watch over him," Arjun added with one hand resting on Rake's chest.

"I'd rather stay awake," Charles said, shifting to a better position on the ground, one where he could transition to standing much more quickly if needed.

His mind wandered again to the brief tap of blades, the sudden concussion, and his sword's unusual heat, but he forced the questions away. Throughout the night, Arjun checked Rake's wounds and muttered tsk-like sounds, applying various substances. Bottles kept appearing from the folds of the robes, one after the other. Some he poured down Rake's throat, others he rubbed against the initial wound and wherever the discoloration appeared. The smell turned rotten; Rake continued to deteriorate.

"I don't even know if he has a family," Charles muttered after several hours, more to himself than the midnight visitor. The beginning rays of dawn touched the horizon, casting their usual red-orange glow. He was used to seeing the rays light up the castle's outer walls during his morning walks. Instead, he saw the wide open, once breathtaking fields of Orda'an. Occasional spots of color broke the simplicity of tall grass, but most were pure decay.

The Shendaran Forest was closer than he realized, the coverage which its perpetually green trees offered mocking him. Above the tree line, a few clouds flared as though on fire, hiding the golden-red sun. Bold colors slid upwards, softly shifting the twinkling speckles on a black canvas into a blinding blue. Charles leaned back to stare at the sky, unable to ignore Rake's labored breaths. The higher the sun climbed, the fewer breaths Rake took.

"How did you know we were here?"

Arjun leaned over Rake, inspecting the wound on his leg again, and looked askance at Charles. "While looking for herbs at the edge of the forest, I saw your fire. And heard you."

Saw that dismal little fire? How?

"But the burn?" Charles asked. At some point in the night, he had released the sword's hilt.

"You winced when you gripped the sword's hilt. I made an assumption. An accurate one," Arjun said. "We are—were close friends to King Phillippe."

"We?"

"My people," Arjun said, tone matter-of-fact and simple. "Elves."

"First Xannan, maybe even Eilon, now elves." Charles avoided rubbing the palms of his hands against his eyes and subdued a weary sigh. "Don't tell me there's a fairy hiding in your pocket?"

Arjun shook his head of tawny-colored hair, red eyes glowing faintly in the sunrise as he stared down at Rake. Charles heard it too. Rake's chest struggled to rise, exhaled, and then ceased to move. Nothing had worked.

"May the Blaze of your ancestors carry you home," Charles whispered, same as he had to many other soldiers who had died at his side since Hoclia broke the first treaty. It still felt strange to say it.

"You may tell Princess Rosealyn of our meeting, no one else." Arjun stood and shifted the folds of his robes. The next came softer. "I am sorry I could not do more for your comrade."

When Charles looked up to thank the elf, Arjun was halfway to the tree line. What he thought were white robes were a lighter shade of brown, and the elf's tawny-colored straight hair was gathered in a small knot at the nape of his neck.

He could follow, ask more questions, but he would not leave his comrade out in the open. Charles shook his head at the oddity of the night and turned to Rake's lifeless form. He could not carry the man, so he removed the rest of Rake's armor, tossing it into a haphazard pile. The sword he set aside, and he tended to the man's body as best he knew how.

By the time he looked to the sky again, it was a noonday sun staring back at him. Charles wondered how many more noonday suns he would see along the Orda'anian fields before the castle's dragonstone walls greeted him.

He hovered his hand over the blade at his side, palm tingling as a reminder of the heat. Charles positioned the king's crown and Rake's weapon on his belt, and though he was not close enough to see the landmarks, he glanced toward *his* home. The debate of which direction to turn was quick, barely more than a moment's hesitation, before he continued on the dirt path to Vandyl. *Azeiah and Rosealyn need to know. Most of it, at least.*

21

Charles stood stiffly before the closed gates of the castle, staring at the iron rods Phillippe kept hidden inside the stone walls. He lingered, fingers clenching and unclenching on his sword's hilt, imagining the emotions he would find in each face as they read his expression. He spent the rest of the journey to Vandyl reciting the story in his head. No matter how he tried to explain Xannan's and Eilon's disappearance, it seemed … wrong. Showing the king's crown and Rake's sword would be enough; there was no need to say more.

The door near the closed gates opened, and a familiar face peeked through the sliver of an opening. Moss opened the door wider, his smile at Charles's return quickly fading amid the glare of the morning sun bronzing the young soldier's tanned cheeks. His expression fell as he studied Charles, and he said, "I'll get General Azeiah, sir."

"I'll go to him," Charles said, voice monotone, watching the dirt transition to stone beneath his feet. "Queen Roseanne will wish to be there. How is Princess Rosealyn?"

"She did wake once since you left, Captain," Moss said as they began their slow and steady walk toward the general's quarters. Charles stared down at the well-worn simple stone beneath his feet, allowing his peripheral view of Moss to guide him. "Sleeps a lot, especially during my time as her guard. Even during the day. Daniel is there now, and the doctor."

"Good, good." Charles cleared his throat, realizing his mind-wandering murmur was likely not the appropriate response. Those screams as she collapsed, when nothing visible attacked her. He straightened, shoulders tensing. "I never realized the Passing of the Gift could affect the receiver so much."

"Nor I, Captain." Moss knocked on the general's cabin door.

The two heard grumblings and movement within, and a disheveled Azeiah greeted them. "Why in … oh, come in."

"Sir, Queen Roseanne will…"

"Me first, then the queen. I believe we each have news to tell the other, Captain. Where is Banner-Captain Rake?"

Charles removed Rake's weapon from his belt and held it out to the general, eyes downcast. He looked up when General Azeiah's hand touched his shoulder, the weathered man's disheveled appearance no damper to his demeanor.

"Moss, gather Banner-Captain Rake's belongings. His family lives in town. I will visit them today."

Mountains be cursed. Lieutenant-Captain Moss saluted and left. Charles was alone with the general.

"Tea?"

"Please," Charles said, standing beside the general's small table. He pulled the crown from its position on his belt next and set it in the middle of the table with a gentle reverence, without a word.

Azeiah cleared his throat, hooking his thumbs into his belt. "Was he…"

"I've returned what we found, sir. Xannan attacked us on the outskirts of Lycene. Admitted to killing His Majesty." Charles rubbed a hand over his face. "I couldn't save Rake. I'm sorry."

"Did Xannan have a black blade?"

At the mention of the weapon, Charles's grip on his sword hilt tightened, and he nodded. The whistle of the steam created by the boiling water sliced through the silence.

"As Phillippe said." The general removed the boiling water from the stove. He paused and glanced back at Charles. "And Xannan?"

Charles swallowed, debating how much to explain while wondering what Phillippe might have told Azeiah.

"Disappeared, sir."

Azeiah arched his brow. "Odd, though I doubt that is the last any of us will see of the Lost Prince."

Shaking his head, Azeiah reached into his coat pocket, pulled out a sealed envelope, and tossed it onto the table before Charles. King Phillippe's seal was prominent in the letter's center. As was his full name. Charles did not move to retrieve it, settling into the chair instead.

"Do you—" Charles cleared his throat, remembering the agreement with a slight dread. All of him ached. Armor that was once clean dug into his sides. He *knew* what the letter would say. There would be no rest for him. "Do you know what it says?"

The general grunted and gestured. "Sealed, see?" He found two cups, pouring boiling water over the leaves pressed into the bottom. Azeiah carried the cups back to the table, setting them each down, and sat directly opposite the captain. "Though I have my suspicions."

Charles nodded, holding the sealed letter. He tucked it behind his musty armor with a whispered, "I'll read it later."

General Azeiah watched without remark as Charles took a sip of the offered drink and winced. "That is not tea, sir." Whatever it was, it warmed his chilled bones. After another sip, and a pronounced wince, Charles asked, "What news to discuss?"

"Her Majesty, Queen Roseanne, delayed Princess Rosealyn's coronation. The priests agreed. And the queen wishes to attack Hoclia."

Despite the warm, albeit much too bitter tea in his hands, Charles's mouth went dry.

22

Rosealyn struggled to open her eyes, as though keeping them closed could alleviate how her body ached. Pain, an incessant throbbing in her side, overwhelmed while she stared at the ceiling. "Perhaps a thousand whacks with a practice sword would have been better."

"I doubt that, Princess."

Surprised to hear Charles speak so dejectedly, Rosealyn shifted upright, but his firm hand pressed her back down.

"You're back," she whispered, surprised to feel the sting of tears. *Not the first time I've cried from the pain.*

He nodded and sat back in the chair beside her bed, but she wished he'd move closer. It might be wrong, considering he was only one of her bodyguards, but she wanted to hug him. She wanted proof she wasn't dreaming, though she imagined in her dream he would be less stiff.

"And I'm right, the practice swords would be better." Rosealyn attempted to sit up and blushed. He'd never seen her wear anything besides court attire or her training dress, and she was wearing a simple nightgown. She pressed her hand against her side and glanced down, remembering how the sword had protruded from her father. She swallowed and met Charles's gaze. "I felt him die. Not just the wound … everything. From the moment it—"

She gasped at the onslaught, as though the weapon had pierced her abdomen again. Unabated tears spilled from the agony.

"This differs from what you've read, doesn't it, Princess?"

After sinking back into her pillows so she could use the sheets to wipe away her tears, she grimaced. "Yes and no. Some of it is the same. But neither Gailin's journals nor my father ever mentioned this level of pain."

Another solemn nod and Charles held that dreadful broth she'd received all too often.

"At least it's warm," she said as she sat up and took the bowl from his hands.

"Doctor Alvin claims it will ease the pain, Princess."

"Claims is different than does." She tipped the contents of the bowl into her mouth. It tasted and smelled like week-old fish. "Maybe this time it will *actually* help."

A hint of a forced smile appeared on Charles's features. Bowl resting on her lap, she surveyed her room. Only one chair. Her gaze snagged on where Azeiah had placed her father's sword by her bedside. No explanation for why he'd brought her the sword or if he would obey her mother's most recent requests.

She returned her attention to Charles, who appeared not to be truly seeing anything despite his roaming gaze. "What happened in Lycene?"

His gaze halted on a spot on the floor and his tone was absent of any emotion. "General Azeiah knows. He also informed me of your mother's plans." Charles looked up again, brows knitted together. "You need to rest, Princess."

After huffing a laugh, she winced and rested a hand on her side. "All I've been doing is *resting*. Mother tells me nothing, just stands in the doorway and stares at me as though I'm some foreign object she doesn't understand. Azeiah visited once and left my father's sword. Daniel or Moss stands at my door and stares at me like I'm dying until Lori or Alvin come and insist I walk at least a few paces. After about five minutes, Alvin claims I need more of this ridiculous broth and then I'm *resting*. Again."

Charles leaned forward as though he might reach out to her but didn't. A muscle in his jaw twitched, making the scraggly white scar along his chin more obvious, but he said nothing as he motioned for her to drink from the bowl.

One sip and she asked, "Do you trust my mother?"

He reached forward and grasped the bowl to move it to her bedside table. "Do you, Princess?"

While waiting for her answer, he resumed his rigid posture.

"No," she said. "But I have no reason not to other than a strange feeling she knew Xannan existed before he … gah, stupid throbbing nonsense!"

His gaze softened into one of pity, but he did not lean forward again. "Her Majesty requested additional food wagons be sent to smaller towns bordering Lycene. She may have known Lycene housed someone. Perhaps the missing men and soldiers?" Charles shook his head, as though dismissing the idea. "I will help you however I am able, Princess."

His words were sincere and soothing, but between rising anger and pain, her tears began anew. After crossing her legs beneath her and sitting up, she wondered whether Charles or Azeiah was leaving anything out. It wouldn't be the first time they tried to *protect* her by offering half-truths. "What does Azeiah say about Mother?"

"He is wary of her decisions, Princess." Charles rested his forearms on his legs and added, "And rest will probably help you recover faster."

"I must regain my strength, and I can't do that by lying in this bed." Rosealyn shifted the blankets and swung her legs to the side of the mattress. Slow and cautious, she stood and took a single step, only to stumble and end up in Charles's arms as he prevented her from falling. Warmth flooded her as she whisked her hand away from him and almost collapsed to the floor again.

"Sorry," she whispered, and the heat increased when she remembered she wasn't properly dressed. With both hands wringing the fabric of the simple nightgown, she inched back toward the bed and sat. "I lost my balance. That's all."

At his arched brow, she sighed. "I'd like to, um, get dressed and take a walk beyond my rooms today. Or at the very least try."

Charles squinted and his lips twisted into a frown, but he nodded and held out a hand. Though she wanted to confront her mother, she would be content seeing something besides the four walls and one window of her bedroom.

23

Rosealyn sat on the edge of her bed, steeling herself with a deep breath as she pushed to standing. The invisible wound groaned in protest. Her left hand strayed to her side, but she pushed it down, grimacing. Lori stood nearby, a hand ready.

When Rosealyn took a tentative step forward, she grasped Lori's outstretched hand, cursing at her own inadequacy. She looked down at Lori's near permanently wrinkled forehead.

"It's merely a throbbing ache today. I can't feel the blade inside anymore," Rosealyn lied with a half-hearted attempt at a proper smile. Lori twisted the fingers of her empty hand and the wrinkles darkened.

"We must get you dressed, Princess." Lori's grip tightened. "Don't worry. Captain Charles will escort you to the funeral."

Rosealyn leaned into the woman's support as an emptiness returned. Her lady-in-waiting moved Rosealyn about as necessary, shifting her into a darkened court dress befitting a funeral procession. She stayed silent, mind blank, biting her tongue with each tug of the strings as they laced up her back. The dull ache became a present throb, the bodice cinching her together until she imagined her lungs were as thin as needles. At the last pull, she gasped, pressing a hand to her side. Thinking of him made the pain inside increase, and, at times, the piercing of the blade itself returned. Since the Passing, her family's Gift had only been more confusing. And painful.

Lori finished the last touches of Rosealyn's hair, connecting the two braids woven along the sides of her head in the back before brushing the rest of her long auburn locks. Task completed, Lori inhaled to say something but turned away at a gentle knock to let Charles enter.

"Her Majesty waits for you at the tombs." Charles's voice was soft but dry. So solemn, so reminiscent of the adolescent boy she'd first met a decade past. No matter how many times she asked, he did not explain Lycene or Banner-Captain Rake's death.

She gripped Lori's arm, biting her lower lip as she stood to stop the gasp from escaping. Wells formed. Pain and grief intertwined so frequently she did not know which caused her tears. Charles moved forward to hold her other arm. When her eyes fluttered closed for a second, Rosealyn saw herself in a different outfit, similar to the one she had spent hours deciding on for her first training session with Charles. But it was not the same. If the person she'd seen in the brief vision was even herself.

Rosealyn stumbled, eyes fluttering again before a brief vision of her father's study flickered. A man she did not recognize sat at his desk. Papers were strewn about, fluttering on the breeze toward the disheveled books filling the shelves on the wall. Her grip on both Lori's and Charles's hands tightened though it did nothing to alleviate her pain.

"Princess?" Charles wrapped his free arm around her shoulders. "Say the word and we will have them delay the ceremony again."

"No, I'm fine." Rosealyn forced herself to smile, meeting Charles's soft blue eyes. "Like I told Lori, it's merely a throbbing ache today."

Charles gave an absent nod, but his arm lowered to support her waist. She winced as his fingers grazed against the invisible wound. Rosealyn swallowed hard. *Dismiss the pain, push it aside.*

With a final squeeze, she released her hold of Lori's hand. "I'm ready," she whispered. "If one can ever be ready for a funeral, that is."

"Not when it's for those you love, Princess."

As they walked through the castle hallways, Charles kept a firm hold on her waist, shifting to grasp just her arm once they were in view of the small procession. Rosealyn studied everything around her *except* the other attendees. Long faces with tight sympathetic smiles would be too much, even from her family. Her Aunt Adela and Uncles Theo and Alan had arrived. Even Jacin, her cousin she'd not seen for several years, was there. But she couldn't look at them. Not when their appearance reminded her too much of her father. So she continued to study the stones beneath wobbly but strengthening legs. Despite Alvin's persistence she walk the hallways multiple times a day for lengthening stretches, her muscles burned at the effort it took to walk down the hill toward the tombs and the priests' residence.

Rosealyn passed the ceremony in a daze. The tombs were cave-like and housed many of her ancestors. The ceremony itself was simple. Repetitive, really. And final. She said her parts, not letting them sink in lest she collapse again. One by one, others left the tombs. Once alone, she lowered to her knees, vision blurring as the torches lit by the Orda'anian Blaze glinted across her father's name etched in the stone.

"I … I don't know what to say." The gentle echo of her voice sent chills down each arm. Rosealyn shivered, lowering her chin to her chest. "This Gift … I don't understand what I am to do with it, or why I keep reliving your…"

No reason to say it aloud. Not when those final thoughts and feelings reared too often. She wrapped her arms around her, desperate for one more hug. Even one more admonishment to stay safe.

The sobs slowed when footsteps sounded behind her. Rosealyn wiped her tears and looked up to find Charles's outstretched hand. "I'll take you back to your room, Princess."

Rosealyn squinted at him, noting the slight thickness to his voice. "No, the gardens." She gripped his outstretched hand so he could pull her up from the dusty ground. "I tire of being cooped up in my rooms."

"As you wish, Princess."

Her feet betrayed her, and Charles wrapped his arm around her waist again. This time she pushed his hand up just enough for his grip to rest above the throbbing and released a slow and steadying breath. At her nod, Charles led her to the garden, shortening the path by ambling through the training grounds she so desperately missed.

Charles guided her to the bench within the gardens, releasing his hold as she sat. Rosealyn studied the rows of color supported by tufts of green speckled against the aging white stone. Most of the black rose petals littered the dirt beneath the bushes, displaying the fascinatingly odd shimmer of green with ebony. She closed her eyes to inhale the last remnants of their summer sweetness and recalled running from flower to flower as a carefree child. Many more leaves would fall in the coming weeks. Refreshing breezes would become cold and the occasional bouts of rain would turn to ice and eventually blanket the world in coats of white snow. She smiled, small and brief. Snow often reminded her of Charles since he'd first arrived in the midst of winter.

She sighed, pushing away the visual of the day her father had returned with Charles ten years ago and instead thought of the garden in full bloom. No tears remained to fall. The garden shimmered with its intoxicating array of color and then shriveled. The brilliant blooms withered into nothingness, leaving naught but glimmering stone. A bird's-eye view offered a brief scan of the lands, showing only more decay. She opened her eyes, finding the flowers still in the last stages of their summer blooms, cursing how mindlessly her hand drifted. *Is that truly our future? How am I supposed to know?*

"'The most beautiful rose may have the worst thorns.'" Rosealyn whispered with a moan. "I thought it was his favorite joke."

"Princess Rosealyn?" Charles turned toward her, appraising her to see if she needed help.

Rosealyn shifted, rubbing her arms as she stared at the bare limbs of her father's favorite flower. "Please, call me Rose."

When he cleared his throat, she glanced up to see his cheeks had flushed. With a soft smile, she patted the bench next to her. He surveyed the gardens, obviously worried someone might be watching, and sat down at her side. Stiffly.

"You'll hold my side to keep me from falling on my face, you'll spar with me and knock me to the ground a dozen times in a row, but you're worried about sitting next to me in the gardens?" she asked, thinking of how she used to mock him when the curls appeared and about his strict rule-following personality. She sidled closer, only for a groan to escape when her side endured the awkward motion. His hands lifted as though to catch her, squinting when she batted them away.

"Sorry," she whispered, studying the bare rose bushes again. "Just a sudden cramp. From the walk."

Charles gave one of his distant, linger-worrying nods. He ignored her question and inched to the edge of the seat, likely so he could spring at a second's notice to catch her. Carefully, she rested her shoulders on the back of the bench, sighing.

"Thank you," she breathed into the lingering silence. The captain's presence was comforting. He sat close enough for her to feel the warmth of his body, and she could smell the faint scent of snow that always lingered around him. Sitting there, side by side, even with his rigid posture, soothed her. For a moment, a brief moment, she forgot the pain. Forgot how each time she tried to sleep, she saw through her father's lifeless eyes. Forgot, until an invisible crushing pressure reminded her life would never be the same.

"For what?" Charles asked.

Rosealyn stifled a laugh, worried it would cause a spike of pain. It was the first time he'd failed to use the honorifics when speaking directly to her.

"For taking care of me," she said, turning toward him with a smile.

"It is my job, Princess," he said with a slight dip of his chin and a suppressed sigh. He wasn't looking at her anymore, seeming to study the ground before him as she had been. The stark white outline of the small scar on his chin sent her mind wandering, and she worked her lips, thinking, contemplating. Emotions already surged through her, crashing into one another without warning, but she wanted to know. She *needed* to know.

"Because of the agreement?" she asked. His head snapped to hers, eyes widening at the words.

For an immeasurable length of time, he stared, wide eyes studying her. Rosealyn could see his mind working to form words, working to decide what, precisely, she knew. Eventually his light blue eyes softened in their intensity, the fear flickering away to the ever-present worry as he gave her a singular nod. Standing, he held out his hand, and she grasped it, pulling up with a grunt at the strain.

"Your father was beyond kind to me." The words were cautious, selective. She followed Charles's gaze to where her hand rested in his. For a long breath, Rosealyn waited. As his hand shifted away from hers, she tightened her hold. It was not the enveloping comfort of her father's arms around her, but she didn't want to let go.

"Why?" Rosealyn swallowed to strengthen her voice. "Protection … or guilt? He found you alone…"

He shook his head with a tight smile. After a slight squeeze of her hand, he let go. "I will be forever grateful for what he gave me by keeping me here."

24

Rosealyn had to hold her stupid practice sword in one spot for endless minutes all over again. It reminded her of the first day she'd stood inside the fence with Charles, but it was nowhere near the same. Then she could count to at least thirty before *lowering* the sword and switching arms. It was only the second day either Charles or Moss even considered letting her hold a weapon, and she could barely count to ten before the ache in her side turned unbearable and whatever she was holding fell to the ground. Or clamored to the fence's railing with a thud.

All of her muscles throbbed. Almost three weeks had passed since she'd earned a wound none could see. Two weeks since Charles had returned. One week since they had lit the torches on either side of the plaque bearing her father's name. Moss moved forward to help but retreated at the fierce gaze she shot toward him. Charles stood with arms crossed just outside the fence. Since an attack had occurred within the castle, Charles claimed it would be best for her to have more guards around at all times. Not that it mattered.

Beads of sweat rolled down each temple, hair clinging to the back of her neck, breaths shallow as she stared at the blade resting atop the wooden fence as though she had meant to strike it there. She hadn't.

Both arms protested as she lifted the sword, and the foot she shifted betrayed her. She pressed her swaying heel back into the ground with a low growl, lifting the sword high enough to attempt a weak strike upon the fence. The reverberation of the impact through her arms made her lose her hold, and she frowned, fumbling to catch the blade before it clattered to the ground. "Blaze of a fool," she mumbled, inhaling the brisk air.

"You shouldn't be using a weapon yet, Princess," Charles said, verbatim to his previous day's words. "Not for the forms, at least. Your muscles need to be reacquainted with the movements."

She bit back a retort. Years of training and coming so close to knocking Charles down had all come to naught. When it mattered most, she could do nothing. Nothing. Gailin's journal offered no answers. The story of the Twin Blades sounded more convoluted, and the dragons … those were real. Had she not blacked out in Pasea, she might have seen one.

Two soldiers approached, a small paper handed back and forth with obvious fervent whispers, all while avoiding her gaze and directing their attention to Charles. His stoic face betrayed nothing, and she loosed a long breath.

A quick twist of the sword so the point faced the ground, she rested the weapon against the fence and latched the belt holding her father's blade around her waist. The buckle bumped over the spot he had usually hooked it, but she had to tighten it much further. Despite being right-hand dominant, she kept the weapon against her right side. Between the sword's weight and the thump of its hilt against her invisible wound, the pain had been too much. A sword on her left hip lasted barely an hour before the pain overcame all other senses.

"Sir," the corporal said after a quick salute that Charles did not return. No more white buttons or white cuffs for him; Azeiah had promoted him to Banner-Captain. Charles seemed to hate every second with how often his absent stare became a frown, just as it deepened further at that moment. "From General Azeiah."

By the time Charles glanced over his shoulder at her, she was by his side. Blank blue eyes met hers. "The general requests you there as well, Princess," he said, folding the small paper.

"Why?" Rosealyn inquired with a shrug she immediately regretted. Sore muscles pulled taut were not a pleasant experience, especially over the invisible wound. She worked to stifle the pain from her voice as she exhaled slowly. "Unless Mother changed her mind, again."

"That's possible," Charles said with a tight grimace. His gaze drifted to her left side and she muttered an internal curse. Her left hand was clutching her side. That invisible wound made her mother claim Rosealyn was not ready for the crown. Supposedly, she was not yet "recovered" enough to take command. He kept his gaze on her, frowning, as he said, "Thank you, Corporal. You're dismissed."

Both soldiers bowed to her, saluted Charles, and hurried back to the barracks. She envied their simple life compared to what she was about to do. She needed to do it. There was no other way. Hand clenched against her side again, she faced Charles.

"General Azeiah's been trying to delay all of your mother's military-centric orders, fearful it's grief, not logic," Charles explained. He uttered a tiny hollow chuckle. "I figured we'd be arguing with you about these matters, not her."

Rosealyn narrowed her eyes at him, but the flicker of a shadow from above distracted her. Her mother stared down at them, hands resting on the railing of the garden balcony, her loose red Tenoan dress floating to one side in the breeze. Rosealyn tensed and shifted to hope it looked like her hand was propped on her side rather than clenching it to suppress the pain. She walked with swift determined steps toward the general's office, not bothering to glance behind to see if Charles followed. His footsteps soon hit the stone walkway in time with her own.

"The dragon," Rosealyn mused aloud, not for the first time in the past week. "That cloud was identical to what Gailin describes from Xannan's disappearance. Which means Xannan has one of the last dragon-wrought blades, one of the two King Seth had. The Twin Blades? Might explain the color…"

She swallowed. The few times she had voiced how the black sword killed her father, she'd nearly fainted. Even thinking about the weapon made her side screech in protest. A sidelong glance at Charles met a distant expression. Attentive to his surroundings, eyes never stilling on one spot for more than a few seconds, he obliged her curiosity by listening to her incessant repeating of the histories and myths she knew.

"So his black blade must be from a dragon? Made by one? A black dragon? Would the blade blessed by a dragon take on the beast's color?" she continued. All questions she'd pondered. All questions with no answers.

"A task force was created after the second blade disappeared," she added. A new tidbit she had learned during her sleepless nights as she rifled through mostly boring court documents.

Charles met her glance with a sidelong stare of his own. Ever the resolute soldier, his face gave away naught but stiff stoicism.

"Father didn't disband it. If they're alive, men are searching for the Twin Blades."

Still no change in his features. A lingering question surfaced, one Rosealyn was positive would generate a reaction. "How did you recognize the dragon's roar?"

Charles's forward momentum stopped, and she turned to face him. His usual distant gaze was replaced with a fierceness she'd only seen once before, when she questioned whatever that "agreement" had been.

"A past I do not wish to relive, Princess," he muttered and walked ahead.

"The stories say dragons hide underground," Rosealyn continued, following close on his heels. "But Gailin desired to look above, to search within the mountains, to go beyond the Cliff of Lycene, to go beyond the Jearnian Hills. Granted, this was before the civil war—"

Words halted when she nearly slammed into his back. Since the Passing, since Rake's death, Charles had retreated as far as possible back into his unbreakable shell. "We're here," Charles said, one arm gesturing toward the already open door of Azeiah's office, the other offering her assistance up the few stairs of the command center's outer porch.

Lips pursed, she walked past without comment. And without assistance. Her air of annoyance must have gotten to the general too—he stood so quickly he bumped the desk littered with paper, knocking several pages onto the floor. "Speak," she said with a wave of her right hand. The left hadn't moved from where she had planted it on her left side before walking.

The general handed her the order with the queen's broken seal, sitting as he explained, "Her Majesty wishes us to leave by morning to attack Hoclia, straight to Hazael. Full army."

"They hold little responsibility for the destruction of our fields, or we of theirs." Charles leaned his head and shoulders against the wall beside her.

"She's asking you to leave Vandyl defenseless," Rosealyn muttered. After a quick perusal of the paper, confirming Azeiah's words, she squinted at the man who insisted on watching her every move. Where Charles had once never forgotten the honorifics, he now often did. Yet no matter how long she spent trying to decipher him, she came no closer to understanding what had changed. "How will attacking them fix anything? It won't heal the land. Or bring Father back. So what is her goal here?"

"My lady, Her Majesty must still grieve," General Azeiah said, as though grief could explain the command to attack another country's capital.

"I know you do not trust her, Azeiah. I don't either." Rosealyn lifted her gaze to Azeiah's, hoping her voice did not betray her conflicted emotions battling each other inside. She wanted to trust her mother, but what had to be sensations from the Gift made her wary when thinking of the woman.

Azeiah nodded, a muscle in his lower jaw flexing rhythmically as he rested his elbows atop the paper-filled desk. "Phill—His Majesty wished to speak with them again; Her Majesty should do the same, but..." He shrugged.

Rosealyn surveyed the small room. Even at midday, lamps were lit in each corner despite sunlight trailing in through multiple windows. A chilling breeze brushed its way through, floating between them with the first of the fallen tree leaves, the crisp scent of colder days on its edge. "Could you arrange a meeting between me and the leaders of Hoclia and Alkaan?"

"I can, Your Highness."

To her side, Charles lifted his back and shoulders from the wall. "Princess, you've barely recovered—"

Her glare stopped Charles's words short. "I am recovering. Another week, maybe two, and I will be able to travel. Until then, General, ask both Hoclia and Alkaan to reconsider the treaties implemented by my father several years ago and arrange a meeting at a location where you feel comfortable escorting me. If Mother asks, remind her that words can have power just as much as wielding a blade."

Azeiah stood, offering a proper bow. "As you command, Your Majesty."

She clamped her lips together. Some might consider it treason to go against the queen's orders. But her mother should no longer be the queen. The Passing of the Gift ensured its recipient became the next monarch. It was why her father, as the third-born of her grandparents, had become king. Not Theo, not Alan, but her father had received the crown when the Passing happened to him. Unlike her, he had not had to fight for the crown.

Rosealyn stood, stifling the groan which threatened to escape, and grasped Charles's arm to drag him toward the door. "I need to speak with the priests. Today."

Charles didn't budge from his place despite her tug. "And if Queen Roseanne questions—"

"Tell her I requested it," Rosealyn said with a dismissive wave of her hand. "She can be mad at me all she wants. I can handle Mother. I can't handle the deaths of soldiers for no reason."

If the two soldiers exchanged a glance, Rosealyn didn't know. She was already out the door, bracing for the steep path leading to the chapel and knowing it would strain muscles that refused to respond in the manner she wanted them to.

"Why must you see the priests today?" came Charles's voice at her side.

"For my coronation, before Xannan attacks again," Rosealyn said in a tone she hoped left no room for arguing. She tired of everyone coddling her as though she were some naïve clueless child. "I think Xannan … I don't know how to explain it. There is this feeling. This urge."

It was the Gift. She knew that, but she didn't understand how it worked. Though she wanted to destroy Xannan, she felt something else. A tug urging her to find him.

She stopped and turned to Charles, using that same tone of expectancy she'd learned from her father. "Tell me about the dragons."

Skin crinkling around his eyes, he looked down at her and dropped his gaze to the stone beneath their feet. Charles had called the beast by its known name that day in the courtyard. The soldier was hiding more than some ironclad agreement with her father. One that, despite searching her father's study, she'd found no written record of.

"As a young child, I was told they were extinct, like everyone else on the continent of Ebios, but…" Charles shook his head, cheeks red and chapped from the onslaught of the morning and afternoon winds. "I'd heard a dragon's roar before. My mother—"

"Mother?" Rosealyn interrupted. That singular word was like a punch to the gut. In the ten years she'd known him, Charles had never once mentioned his own family. "You-your family … where are they?"

Another dismissive shake of the head. "A dragon-wrought blade and a dragon likely makes Xannan unstoppable."

"All that which lives must die," she said, squinting. He knew more but wasn't saying. She could see it in his posture, hear it in his voice. "And we could find our own dragon-wrought blade. If the journey takes us beyond our neighbors, we will go. I believe I need that weapon to annihilate Xannan. And the dragon."

"You, Princess?" Charles moved closer, a hand reaching for her, but it fell back to his side before she could place her hand in his. "None have found either sword in a hundred years. The Twin Blades are just a story. Perhaps you can negotia—"

"With Hoclia and Alkaan, yes. With Xannan?" She shook her head emphatically. She couldn't shake the image of him plunging his black blade into her father. Head held high, she reiterated her plan aloud, "First, the crown. Then meet with the other leaders, probably in Violet Grove. Father visited there often enough they must know something. Whoever they are. He never took me."

Somehow, Charles stood even more stiffly. In response to her raised brow, he whispered, "I met one of them. He tried to save Rake."

"Them?" she countered, wondering why he referred to the inhabitants of the forest town in the tone he did.

"An elf, Arjun," Charles said in such a serious manner that Rosealyn forced herself not to laugh.

"The elves are extinct."

"So were the dragons." His blank stare returned, as though he'd done more than hear its roar.

Her chest and throat clenched. "I'm sorry," she whispered. "About Rake. And your family."

That sharp iciness returned to his gaze. "None of what has happened was your fault, Princess. Not to Rake and definitely not what happened to my brothers."

Rosealyn mouthed the word "brothers" with wide eyes and studied him a moment, wondering when his secrets would surface. "You lost them, didn't you?" she breathed, glancing up at a bold blue sky whose sun was just past its peak.

"Some of my family will always be lost, even if they're still alive." His boots scuffed against the steep stone path leading to the temple and the tombs.

She walked past the tombs she had visited once since her father's funeral, mulling over Charles's cryptic non-answers to her questions. Such responses were as infuriating as the throbbing of the invisible wound any time she thought of her father.

Soon they stood before the chapel. The garden beds to either side of the large double doors contained the shriveled and darkened remnants of past blooms, though a few of the faded petals clung to the limbs of bushes and stems. Halfway up the dull gray stone of the chapel's outer walls was a rectangular box large enough for their swords. She laid her father's sword reverently inside, frowning at the plain blade Charles rested next to it. That was not the same sword her father had given him two years after he joined their army. No slight curve, no leather binding the hilt. A simple sword like any soldier of the army would carry.

Rosealyn stared at the door and spoke softly once Charles stood by her side. "Father always said I could trust you, despite your past." When she turned to look at him, he looked away, and her gaze lingered on his scarred chin. "What did he mean?"

"A story for another time, Princess." Charles swallowed and rounded his shoulders. "I'll wait here."

"You're coming with me," she commanded. When he raised one brow, her heart fell a smidgen. Fists clenched at either side, she whispered even more softly than before. "I need you. Just in case."

Charles nodded and held the door open for her. She entered an expansive room crisscrossed with rays of light changing color as they danced through the windows far above. It was like a rainbow-filled, never-ending sunset. Rows of benches lined the floor, separated by spaces just wide enough to walk. Four priests gathered around a quaint circular table, wearing the common castle garb of a simple shirt and pants, were finishing the last of their evening meal.

Lighthearted conversation fell to silence as she approached. Rosealyn avoided glancing up at the thin cylinders of varying lengths behind them. Those golden pipes often filled this room with sounds that tugged at her soul. Every song contained the same theme the priests taught: keep the world balanced or it will betray all.

Standing mere feet from their table, she held her chin high but not too high. She wanted to be commanding, not haughty. If she could sway Elder Matthias to her side, she could control both the army and the country. A private audience with him, not all the priests, was what she needed today.

The ancient priest studied her down his long narrow nose, pushing a set of dulled spectacles up and gesturing toward the side of the vast room. Rosealyn, with Charles poised at her side as though she might fall, followed Matthias into a quaint office. When he moved to close the door before Charles had entered, she halted his motion with a firm hand and a fierce stare.

"He's a part of this conversation too and already aware of some of what I will discuss," she said, her voice much steadier than her muscles or her heart. Elder Matthias obliged, allowing Charles to enter, then closing the door before easing himself into the rickety wooden chair behind his desk. Two chairs sat opposite the desk, and Rosealyn lowered herself into one. A quick glance over her shoulder found Charles resting his upper back against the wall with arms crossed.

"With all due respect, Your Highness," Elder Matthias said before she could speak. "You must wait for Her Majesty. She is the ruling monarch. It is her decision."

Rosealyn scowled. "Wrong. After the Gift passed to Gailin's second-born son, the laws were adjusted so the recipient of the Gift would always inherit the throne. The Gift has passed to me as the only heir. I should *already* be queen."

Elder Matthias leaned forward, hands positioned like the tops of the trees, spectacles falling as his gaze met hers. "Laws have, once again, been adjusted. Her Majesty does not believe you are fit—"

"Mother is not to be trusted," Rosealyn interrupted with the sharpest tone she could muster.

"You know what the law allows, my lady." The priest spoke with a dry aloofness, fingertips resting together.

A painful silence stretched as Rosealyn replayed every conversation she'd had with the immovable elder in the past week. *Only one option left.*

"Then I formally charge her with treason and the intent to hire another to kill my Father to take his crown."

Behind her, Charles's cough did not hide his muttered curse that made her eyes widen, but she held Elder Matthias's blank stare.

"Present proof and a council will be convened, as the laws require."

She stood and took a step toward the aging priest. Left hand gripping her side, her breaths shortened. Daylight faded and she had not taken her new customary break in the middle of the afternoon. Sometimes the bed beckoned her, other times ancient texts kept her company. Today she had done neither.

"Princess," came Charles's cautionary tone from behind. "You need rest."

"I'm fine." She dropped her left hand into a fist and stood tall, speaking with the commanding tone she'd learned from her father. "Convene the council, Elder. Proof will not be difficult to find."

Elder Matthias cleared his throat, "As you wish, my lady." He pressed his fingers against each other, desk creaking below the weight of his frail form as he stood. A deep frown. The priest left. *He better do as I ask.*

"Feelings are not proof, Princess," Charles said.

Her stance wavered, the room with paintings of landscapes and previous LeNoir monarchs blurred in her periphery. A groan escaped and a second later Charles's arm wrapped around her shoulders to guide her back to her seat. Rosealyn relinquished a portion of her weight to him, relying on his strength to keep her steady even while seated.

"This Gift, the pain," she bemoaned, head rolling from side to side. "Why can't I do more than feel or see—"

She inhaled sharply at the sudden piercing pang of pain. Charles released his hold of her shoulders and shifted away, but she grasped his arm with her right hand so tightly she thought her nails might pierce his skin through the solid black sleeve.

"If she is colluding with him, we will find proof," Charles said as he lowered into the seat next to her and tried to pull his arm away again. Her grip tightened, and she winced and released a shuddering sigh. Her side had not ached this badly since the funeral.

"Help me find the lost blade. It could provide the proof we need," Rosealyn whispered, resting her head on Charles's shoulder. "Leave with me."

The shoulder beneath her temple tensed. "Your place is here."

"She has spoken to Xannan. I don't understand how I know, but I do. And I know I—" She paused, taking a deep breath and letting the Gift guide her next words. "We will not stay here. Neither of us."

"There are others whom you can trust, others you can send to the east mountains."

Rosealyn straightened in her seat, but all Charles's face revealed was shock he had even mentioned the mountains. "What's in the east mountains?"

Charles's lips tightened. "My job is to protect you, in more ways than even you know. When the time is right—"

"No, now." Rosealyn shoved him with more strength than she thought she could muster. "You *can* tell me about the agreement, your family, everything."

Charles turned away. For the millionth time, she cursed the illogical invisible pain; otherwise, she would have stood and stared down at the soldier with a hidden past.

"You already know everything—"

Rosealyn huffed a laugh. "Everything? That's a lie and you—"

"Your Highness, sir," a voice interrupted from the doorway. A soldier with his sword buckled around the waist despite the priests' persistent and adamant requests that weapons not enter their chapel. "Her Majesty sends for you. The messengers His Majesty sent have returned."

Rosealyn frowned and grumbled, "So much for answers. Or rest."

"Lieutenant?" Charles asked. "Which scouts? From where?"

"Everywhere, sir," the young soldier replied.

"I really hope they bring good news," Rosealyn muttered while using Charles's leg as leverage to push herself to standing. Charles's steady hands caught her outstretched arm to stabilize her.

25

"Tell me, child," King Claude of Jearnia droned with his favorite wine glass held loosely in his left hand. Plush cushions absorbed his weight, though wine stains dotted the material. Such failure at proper cleaning soured the last vestige of his iconic and pleasant demeanor. "Will I be sending you to the fields or the execution block?"

Two young men, barely more than boys, kneeled before him and his wife. The beautiful and fierce Queen Nerida sat to his right, clad in a bold red dress with an untouched glass of wine held in both hands. Shoulder-length curly hair prevented him from making out all of her expressions, though she often kept those blank as he questioned men once they returned from their tasks.

Filth from the scouts' journey covered them, and the one to Claude's left swallowed and shivered before rounding his shoulders. A drab brown shirt clung to his arms and chest, sticking with darkening patches. The young man straightened his fingers against soiled black pants while beads of sweat rolled down his temples. A feeble, hesitant, choppy, though reverent voice filled the gilded room. "I … heard … saw."

He glanced at his comrade, who did not meet his gaze, and swallowed again, staring down at the floor as drops of sweat hit the decorative stone below him. Golden walls surrounded them, glittering in the rays of the sun streaming through the windows high above. A second drop followed the first, and his words came in a slow cadence; he'd rehearsed these lines before his return.

"There was a funeral procession in Vandyl last week. I believe King Phillippe of Orda'an is dead. I heard talk in the streets of a … uh, a Captain Charles protecting the princess."

The scout inhaled, face contorting, chest puffing with the added air. He released his next words in a single breath. "I believe him to be your eldest son, Your Majesty."

Claude methodically lowered his cup and prowled toward the scout. His hand wrapped around the scout's neck and lifted him so his feet no longer touched the ground. Claude's arm shook with the effort of not crushing the man's neck for such a blatant lie. "My son? My *eldest*? The one who gave his *life* for his country? Hiding in plain sight with our *enemy*?"

The scout started to move his hands, and Claude tightened his grip.

"Yes, Your Majesty," he wheezed. Claude studied the boy, studied the set determination, recognizing the scout believed what he said to be true.

Curiosity piqued, Claude released the boy and shoved him back to his kneeling position. The scout's hands strayed halfway to his neck and, after a brief pause, fell limp atop his thighs. At his side, the second scout tensed.

"My dear Nerida." Claude lowered himself back into his seat and snapped his fingers for more wine. His gaze never left the scout, watching the young man's mannerisms. It was easy to make others fear him; he'd killed plenty who brought unsatisfactory news from across the hills. None ever returned from their journey to the opposite side of the mountains, though. But this claim was beyond what Claude could allow, even if it intrigued him. He forced the simmering pot of rage to cool inside him, doing his best to lace his tone with a curious kindness. One could not question the dead. "What say you of this scout's revelation?"

"I recognize this one. He has always been honest, my dear. I see no reason to doubt him; however, I would seek additional proof of this information. No other scouts returned with this news. Tell me, child, what else did you see?" Nerida asked. She set the glass of wine aside and rested her arms to each side, chin held high. The epitome of a queen whose smooth regal demeanor could turn as fierce as a raging beast at a moment's notice.

"Heard more than saw, Your Majesties." The scout winced, as though waiting for the admonishment. Claude sipped his wine and gestured for the scout to continue speaking. "Rumors of a dragon attacking one of their towns. Little else was discussed aside from King Phillippe's death, Your Majesties," the scout whispered, hands fidgeting in his lap while his face turned ashen. His eyes darted from the floor to the man kneeling next to him, with quick flashes toward Claude.

After a pause, Claude released a boisterous laugh, wincing when wine sloshed onto his hand. "A dragon?" He transferred the cup and held out the other to be wiped dry. "You must be delusional, child. The dragons died long ago, same as my eldest. Only stories remain, meant to scare you as a child so you didn't escape into the Mountains of Ingoria."

The scout flexed his fingers, hands back atop his thighs, waiting to be addressed before speaking.

"What did this 'dragon' look like, child?" Nerida asked in that intonation of curiosity Claude found intoxicating. She was like the river, ebbing and flowing with him, but she was also like the fire, flaring at his side when he least expected it.

"I'm sorry, my Queen, I do not know." The scout grimaced as Claude stood from his seat. The young man hastily glanced at his companion, avoiding watching Claude's approach. "But I am sure others will soon corrobor—"

Claude's back-handed slap cut the scout short, a thin line of blood sprouting along the boy's cheek from Claude's solitary silver-plated ring. "You do not speak for others," he said through a clamped jaw, inspecting the golden-yellow stone inside his ring with a frown and studying the two scouts before him again.

The injured man's lower lip trembled. Sweat mingled with blood and tears as he pushed off the floor, resuming his kneel and waiting. The second shifted, worn shoes rubbing against the stone with a squeak, but neither dared to meet Claude's gaze.

Claude turned toward Nerida once again. "Do you still believe this fool? Claiming he saw a dragon! Lies—all of it!"

Claude downed another glass of wine, sitting as he observed Nerida, analytical in his study of the woman who sat beside him. She straightened in her throne, a note of disapproval dashing across her face when he snapped his fingers for the cup to be refilled.

In a soft whisper, she told him, "I have heard rumors of others seeing these dragons, of shifting shadows in the moonlit nights, of loud roars which could not otherwise be explained. This young man believes he is telling the truth."

Claude's nostrils flared wide, fighting to keep the simmering pot roiling inside him from boiling over. His thumb rubbed along the ring while the other hand brought the sweet liquid back to his lips. *Such careful words!*

Seated on her throne, arms resting to each side, Nerida appeared relaxed. Hidden beneath the calm was a raging storm which could rival his own. He soaked in her presence, appreciating how the subtle hints of her cheekbones accentuated her features, especially those pale blue eyes all of their sons had inherited. All framed by her perfect curls, resting ever so enticingly against her cheeks. After another slow sip, Claude dipped his chin as permission for Nerida to continue her own line of questioning first.

"Fear of death ensures our scouts always speak the truth, but the smartest among them always come with proof." Nerida shifted her penetrating blue-eyed gaze to the boy. The scout shook as though bare steel already rested against his neck. "What proof have you to offer that Phillippe is dead and a dragon attacked?"

"None, my Queen, save what I heard," the scout admitted. Claude slapped him down to the floor again.

"You have failed your country, *child.*" Claude pressed the heel of his shined boots into the fallen scout's neck and took another lazy sip of wine. His free hand twitched, unwittingly, toward the dagger gleaming from his black belt. A bold red ruby sat in its hilt's center, mirroring the mingling colors of his jacket, both shining with vivid exuberance atop plain black pants. Daggers were not cumbersome like swords, and sometimes they could be a touch less messy. Sometimes.

Claude's hand drifted, thick fingers wrapping around the hilt, covering the glint of the ruby. But then he might spill his drink, and Nerida's disapproving stare would no longer hide. Claude savored the smooth sheen of the gem against his palm as he loosened the blade in its sheath, rolling his eyes when the boy's body shook uncontrollably beneath him. Less than a second was all it took for the dagger's sharp edge to cut the boy's flesh. The wine spilled, of course, mingling with the blood as it drained from the boy's neck to create a widening puddle. *Such a pity. Today's pitcher has been quite enjoyable.*

With a frown, Claude followed the edges of the pool of blood until it touched the second messenger's pants. Dagger still poised, he shifted his attention. A cold slim hand wrapped around his, and he turned to meet the one face that could calm him—Nerida's.

"What good are servants if you kill them all, my dear?"

Beautiful soothing voice, incredibly logical question. His shoulders fell a smidge as he studied the still-breathing man kneeling at his feet; he would question this messenger. Later. As Claude wiped the blade clean, he snapped a quick and menacing, "Guards, take him to the fields. If we learn this story has been falsified, child, your life is forfeit. Off with you!"

Two guards dragged the sobbing messenger away while others carted away the corpse. Claude returned to his throne with a loud sigh. "What kind of insanity was he speaking? Our Charles is dead. And the dragons died with Magna. Otherwise we would have one of those blades by now."

"My dear." Nerida sat beside him and placed a gentle hand on his arm while blue eyes as deep as the river stared up at him. "We create stories based on reality. These blades may exist and are simply waiting to be discovered. We never found our eldest dead, and you obliged my request to never stop looking for him. Deep down, I know you have that same hope. That out there, somewhere, is our Charles. The messenger claimed this captain may be the same as our eldest—why should we not believe him?"

"Nerida, we've discussed this before. The child's been gone for ten years. I'm positive the Orda'anians killed him long ago and hid the body. Payback for Thaddeus, I'm certain. There's no way our son would have colluded with *them*. We must have proof to believe otherwise."

He slouched back in his seat, grabbing another glass of wine from the table, and glaring at his wife. Her gaze rivaled his own, as usual. He took a sip and waited. *I have always adored that feisty demeanor.*

As he tipped the glass to capture the last drops of wine, Nerida whispered, "I have seen dragons before."

His grip tightened on his cup, and he choked on the liquid. "Nerida?" he coughed, eyebrows raised.

"Do not demean me." His wife's whisper was fierce and tentative. "I know your looks and moods better than anyone. Believe me, I know how that sounds. Shall I continue? Or would you like to slit my throat too?"

Claude stared at her, eyebrows rising, lips tight, and his hand twitched toward the dagger again. But he said nothing. So Nerida continued, studying the servants cleaning the pool of blood before them as she spoke with a cautious hush. "As a young girl, before my family rose in nobility far enough for me to become your bride, we lived on the eastern range. The Mountains of Ingoria, as you call them. To myself and my family, we referred to the highest of these mountains as the Dragon's Shield. There are markers in those mountains that my kinsmen have passed along for generations—the markers which we dare not pass for beyond them await the dragons.

"Curiosity once got the best of me, and I ventured beyond the markers until I heard a loud roar from within the mountains. My father found me first, thankfully, but this did not satiate the curiosity welling within. I continued to test my limits, venturing farther beyond the markers each time. I saw one, face to face. At night, the week before my family finalized a deal which allowed us to move to the valley. It let me be, but his size … or hers, was awe-inspiring.

"I did not fear the dragon's presence; I felt a desire to live."

Claude listened without comment, wishing he had another glass of wine, but his pitcher was empty. A familiar fuzziness warmed him, and he itched to tip further into its abyss. "So the stories are true? My parents spoke of this Dragon's Shield, claiming the Mountains of Ingoria are haunted by them. My parents must not have known that part of your family's history, or we would probably not have been wed. But … how does this relate to some Captain Charles guarding the Orda'anian princess? The only reason Charles would not complete his task is because he is dead."

Nerida shrugged. "I merely wanted you to know the messenger likely spoke true. Although it is strange for a dragon to venture from the Shield and to attack alone. We certainly need more information." She paused, hands resting lazily atop the armrests.

A pained look flitted across her features, so quick Claude wondered if he had consumed more wine than he thought. Then it hit him; the bloodied floor always made memories of their deceased sons arise within her.

"Christopher's mission is to be decided soon. Have you thought about it?"

Her voice rang clear, steady, though the hint of a frown lingered as her gaze studied the servants who scrubbed against the stone too loudly. Soon the stone would be pristine again, displaying fine veins of gold which shimmered with the rays of sunlight through the clear glass ceiling high above.

Claude grunted and shook his head, staring dismally into his empty cup. "The council recommends a mission similar to the one on which Charles embarked. I have refused it. I understand the necessity of the mission, but I cannot sentence another son to his doom. Where will my lineage be when—if Christopher fails?"

Nerida took her first sip from her own glass of wine, ignorant of Claude's jealousy. "We sent Charles to infiltrate Orda'an and destroy them from within—which he may have truly accomplished." She paused, chest expanding with a deep breath while Claude wondered if she knew what he had told the boy to do instead. Eyes glistening, Nerida continued, "We need to hear from this man, this Captain Charles. Send Christopher with orders to speak with King Phillippe, or Queen Roseanne if Phillippe is truly dead. Send him with a banner of peace and some soldiers as support. Surely no harm will come to him should he arrive peacefully?"

Claude shook his head, one finger following the rim of his wine glass. His golden-yellow gemstone flared with each pass under the ray of sun casting its glow from the windows in the ceiling high above along his throne's armrest. *Five. Five sons, and he's all that's left.*

"What happens if Christopher is killed? He is our last, our only son left to continue *my* lineage."

"You cannot break custom," Nerida replied, though it sounded forced. "Failure to send Christopher on his own mission would bring into question if he is fit to take the throne. I'm surprised, Claude. It is unlike you to suggest breaking tradition."

"I'm surprised you do not agree with me, as he is your only child left."

"Perhaps it's time to let Christopher decide for himself." Nerida nodded at the entrance.

Christopher stood at the door with a hollow gaze, a gift from the trauma his eighteen years had brought him. Though he stood only to Claude's shoulders, his presence demanded obedience. His shoulder-length unkempt curly hair was reminiscent of his mother's, though his once-dimpled cheeks had hardened with each brother's death. Claude missed the boy's smile.

"Mother, Father," he said with a brief nod to each, eyeing the servants scrubbing at the recent spillage of blood and turning his attention back to his parents. "I heard the guards dragging out another messenger. And … saw the other. What news did this one fail to provide?"

"Christopher!" Nerida admonished.

"Really, Mother?" he asked, rummaging through the plate of food on the table beside her. "Guards dragged the man out of here. Father killed the other, I presume? Will the screaming one be executed, too?"

"No, Christopher, I sent him to the fields for claiming to have seen a dragon," Claude explained, reaching for his glass of wine only to curse its emptiness. Nerida tried to limit the amount of wine near him each day, but his thirst had not been quenched. Not even close. "The other claimed to have found Charles."

Christopher paused in his rummaging, hand hovering over a small round blue fruit before plucking it from the plate. "And did he?"

"It's unclear," Claude said, glaring at Nerida as she sipped her glass of wine. "The messenger offered us no proof. It has, however, given us an idea for your royal mission."

"Sounds eerily similar to the one which Charles failed to achieve. Where did he claim this Charles is? Or must I learn that myself as part of the *mission*?" Christopher popped the small fruit into his mouth and folded too skinny arms across his chest, glaring at Claude with his usual disdain.

The King of Jearnia had been hard on his sons. A condescending stare did not cause Christopher to look away. Claude studied his last surviving son's posture, recognizing the weight he already had, and looked to his wife. Emotionless, withdrawn, but no argument. Not in this moment. *Maybe this son will prove his worth.*

"I believe you will succeed in this mission, son. You are the last hope for my lineage to remain on this throne. You must not fail. You will not fail. Discover the truth of this Captain Charles. Either he is your older brother returned from the grave or he is not."

"I was a child, barely eight years old, when he left. I have naught but the tapestries drawn of him at almost fifteen. Surely he has grown and changed since then. What proof will you desire, Father?"

"You must bring this Captain Charles here." The words escaped before Claude could change his mind, recognizing the near-impossible task he had just gifted to his only living heir. *And if this Charles is my son, he will pay for such silence.*

"So we may question him and ascertain if he is your long-lost brother fulfilling the longest mission of Jearnian history or a valuable prisoner in the fight to regain Orda'an."

"Of course, Father." Christopher half-laughed, grabbing a handful of fruit. "Nothing easier than kidnapping the bodyguard of the Crown Princess of our rival to the west. Does Mother agree with this mission?"

Empty cup in hand, Claude turned to his wife. Nerida remained resolute, arms at her sides, the slight hint of a frown crinkling her smooth alabaster skin. When she made no move to speak, Claude returned his attention to Christopher, who continued to nonchalantly pop one fruit after another into his mouth.

"You will do as I command. Nasir will attend you with fifty soldiers." Claude looked to his right and discovered the lines marring his wife's skin deepening from her scowl. "Leave us, Christopher."

Christopher walked out without a word to either parent. Guards by the doors opened and closed them without Christopher so much as gesturing for it to happen. When those two heavy unadorned slabs of wood thudded shut with a reverberating echo, Claude crushed his wine cup. "I would rather lose all of my children than see our beloved country lost to the traitorous Orda'anians."

26

A day after his father told him his mission, Christopher shifted atop his chestnut stallion, trying to alleviate the pressure growing in his legs. An entire troop of soldiers, his parents had insisted, rode behind him. *Not the entire army, just one battalion of fifty men. Charles had had only Nasir.*

Beside him, the Guadelaide River flowed from its namesake lake into the Jearnian Hills. The maps he studied showed the river sweeping through the entire Orda'anian plains before emptying into a larger body of water—the Vadamon Sea. One day, he decided, he would see that massive expanse. He tried to imagine what a never-ending lake would look like, and the visualization shimmered before him, shattered by the surrounding jangle of soldiers atop their horses. And Nasir.

He heard Nasir's shouts behind him but didn't listen. Christopher had not seen the hills this close since his childhood. He had never gone beyond them, spending most of his adolescent life hidden inside the castle walls. Not quite two years had passed since his brother Caedmon's death. And that *accident* occurred less than a year after Silas challenged Zane. Both died that day. Less than three years ago, he'd had three older brothers. Even before then, his parents were protective. At least his mother had been at one point, but even she could do little.

This mission, however, this rite of passage that none of his older brothers achieved, was one not even his overly attached mother could change. Nor would his father have even listened to such an egregious idea. Christopher didn't mind. It provided an excuse to escape the castle and enjoy the countryside.

The Jearnian Hills sang to him with their slow rising and falling, the trickling Guadelaide lending a sinuous beat. Christopher thought of his favorite poems and how their words, which helped him understand his lot in life, seemed to create music. These bright green rolling hills made a song out of land. Looking either way, he saw the occasional tree standing tall and strong, unyielding despite the powerful winds they endured.

Best of all was their unabandoned nature. The hills continued for miles around him, separated only by the Guadelaide River. They could grow, could nurture themselves, could bask in the open air of freedom. An openness not even Caedmon's death provided the last heir of the Jearnian throne. Neither the rising nor the setting of the sun, nor even the downfalls of water from the sky, could dampen nature's beauty. He savored the imminent danger of intense storms, delighted in nature's ability to give in to its whims, wondering how and when he could do the same.

Hooves stomped behind him, reminding Christopher he was not alone. Less than a day's ride had brought them to the eastern side of the lake, the furthest he'd been from the dank, dark castle. At least another week of travel awaited him before arriving in Orda'anian territory, if his judgment of the map's distances was correct. He visualized the map without opening it, lips turning down in a frown at the storm clouds darkening the horizon. If those traveled quickly, his journey would take longer than a week.

He chuckled, thinking of the storms gathering in the distance, unsure if they would bring white flakes or heavy drops. Perhaps a unique combination of both. The claps of thunder such storms wrought reminded him of his father. The man had impeccable timing in reminding Christopher he was not their only child. Some days, the king believed his eldest would revive and return victorious, reuniting the two lands under a Jearnian family. The next day he would claim the Orda'anians had killed Charles, as Christopher long ago decided, and plan an attack. His mother, ever calm and ever present, turned the thunderous storm into a gentle rain as often as she was able. With a soft grimace, Christopher remembered how often she had saved him from the barrage of anger his father could summon over the past ten years.

"But she could not stop this. Father would never allow that," Christopher muttered, surveying the intoxicating landscape before him.

"My lord?"

"Nothing, Nasir," Christopher said, easily recognizing the aging soldier turned mentor's voice without looking at him. "We will rest here for the evening."

"But, my lord, it is barely past midday and we have—"

"I wish to rest here for the remainder, Nasir." Christopher dismounted and almost stumbled out of the saddle. It had been several months since he'd ridden, and his thighs ached from the strange seat one must keep atop their mount. The chestnut stallion pranced at his side, calming when he ran a gentle hand along its neck.

"Yes, my lord." Nasir's voice was gruff and tense, but he hollered back for the remaining soldiers to make camp.

Christopher handed Nasir the reins to his stallion and watched as the aging man held both sets in his one remaining hand. Failure, regardless of by whom, required punishment. Neither spoke as Christopher removed a select few of his belongings from the saddle. He grabbed two wrapped packages and set both near the edge of the river, sitting down on the soft ground. He removed his boots and rolled up the legs of his pants to sink his feet into the cool current. A soft hiss escaped his lips when his feet met the chilled water. Colder months would be upon them soon. In the distance, he studied the darkening storm clouds, frowning and cursing his inability to determine what misery awaited.

From the smallest sack, he pulled multiple clumps of paper which had once created a bound book. Wasteful to some, a treasure to him. It held writings from his mother's family. Pages filled with descriptions and stories which seemed too fantastical to be true. Stories of journeys throughout the Mountains of Ingoria. *But never beyond them. No one ever returns from going beyond them.*

He glanced over his shoulder to look at the distant mountains. To Christopher, the mountains were as frightful as the hills were intoxicating. Every time his mother spoke of the mountains, and of her family, she would mention her journey there with Charles. And every time she did, Christopher's heart would clench inside his chest. He did everything they asked and more. Yet they still compared him to his elder brothers.

Christopher never knew how to explain what hearing his brothers' names did inside him, nor had any of the poems he read truly described it. The strange strangulation of his heart, the rising angry heat which flushed his cheeks, the slack jawed shock. He hated the comparisons, the constant reminders he was not his brothers. There had been no room for Christopher as a prince of Jearnia until he was the only prince left.

"My lord." Nasir stood above him and spoke with the tone of a mentor who disapproved of his charge's decisions.

Christopher glanced up and, seeing the soldier's face upside down, smiled. "I know you suggest continuing at a steady pace, Nasir, but … this place was too beautiful to march past. I want to watch the sunset along the hills."

"His Maje—"

"I am well aware of my father's *wishes*." Christopher enunciated the word and resumed watching the trickling water of the river. He wondered how long he could listen to its melody. "We made it to the Guadelaide Lake before nightfall. I see no reason to rush."

Christopher heard a huff behind him and chose not to watch Nasir leave. *Last remaining prince and I can't do what I want when I damn well please.*

The piled clumps of paper rested in his lap, but his eyes strayed to the larger sword-shaped bundle his mother had gifted him upon his leave-taking. He did not understand why she had given it to him—he had already chosen his weapon. A dagger, just like his father. As he unwrapped the package, a tiny paper floated down until it rested atop the others. Three simple words stared up at him, an oozing black ink dotting a dull parchment with his mother's handwriting: "Use it wisely."

With the blade free of its scabbard, Christopher wondered if it was a relic of his father's line or his mother's. The slight curve of the metal shimmered as he turned it. Lightweight yet sturdy. He sheathed the sword and set it next to the weapon of his childhood. Delrich, he had named the dagger. *She knows the dagger serves well enough. Why give me a sword?*

Christopher sighed upon hearing footsteps behind him once more. "What now, Nasir?"

"Your Highness." It was not Nasir who spoke behind him, but one of the soldiers. "The camp is set."

Christopher cursed himself for not learning the names of all the men with him, nodding rather than speaking. Footsteps faded behind as something thin and slimy flitted against the soles of his feet. He jolted, withdrawing his feet to investigate the clear water. Within the river was a swarm of tiny fish. Christopher grinned and resubmerged his feet into the icy water, eager to enjoy the journey despite his wariness of the destination.

As the fish continued to tickle his feet, his grin faded to a frown. He studied the thin animals, envious. "How do I convince this Charles to return with me?" He wiggled his toes. "And if he is actually my eldest brother, the true heir, and my only surviving brother? What do I do then?"

Though he knew the fish could not provide an answer, Christopher continued to stare into the river, mulling over answers to his questions as the changing colors of the sky reflected in the water's ripples. Nasir checked on him again, reminding Christopher of his father's words. The king wished for them to have a quick journey. *Probably too eager for another battlefield. Though he could order an attack if that's what he wanted, rather than send me on this ridiculous quest.*

When the colorful sky had turned to the same dull darkness which surrounded him inside the castle, Nasir brought a plate of flame-roasted rabbit and sat by his side. Christopher sat cross-legged after withdrawing his feet from the cool water and donned his jacket to block out as much of the night's chilly wind as he could. Warm plate in his lap, Christopher picked at the pieces in contemplative silence.

"Was it your choice to join me or Father's?" Christopher asked, breaking the common silence between them. Besides mentoring and brief training, Nasir and Christopher had little in common, save their fear of failing the king.

"Both." Nasir crossed his arms in a way that gave Christopher a poignant reminder of the man's missing hand. Lips tightening into a thin line, Christopher glanced back toward Volante. Would he return, even in failure, as Nasir had? Two days ago, his father had sliced open a man's neck for claiming to have *heard* about Charles. *What will he do if I return* with *Charles?*

"Bring this Captain Charles home is what Father told me." Christopher paused, savoring the taste of well-cooked meat. It wasn't what the castle cooks could concoct throughout the course of the day, but it satisfied the slight ache of hunger. "How do you think this will go?"

"I live to serve the crown, my lord," Nasir said. Christopher glanced over to find Nasir staring into the river. But he wasn't reveling in its movement as Christopher had been; it seemed to take Nasir elsewhere.

Christopher swallowed again and cleared his throat, wondering if Nasir had suffered more than his lost hand. "Charles certainly had more of a chance to kill Phillippe. They were still occasionally fighting, and Phillippe was on those front lines. Was my brother not a good enough fighter to best him?"

Nasir's glare met Christopher's, eyes shining with a ferocity akin to the king's. "I am…" Nasir shifted his arms so his hand covered the stump. "Was one of the best."

"And if Charles didn't stand a chance, then I am doomed, no?"

Nasir's gaze didn't flinch, nor did Christopher's when the mentor's furrowed chin dipped slightly.

"Do you think this man we go to collect is *my* brother? Could he be the one *you* claimed was dead ten years ago?"

"If His Majesty wishes for the man to be brought before him, then that is what I will help you do, my lord," Nasir said as the muscles of his jaw pulsed.

"If it is Charles, I doubt Father will stop at a hand upon your return." Christopher studied the near-ancient soldier at his side.

Nasir's back stiffened, shoulders rounding, and Christopher could not stop his smirk. "All these years and you're still afraid of Father."

"Your tent is ready, my lord." Nasir stood and brushed his pants.

When Christopher reached for another bite, he realized the plate was empty and handed it to Nasir. Neither said more, though Christopher believed Nasir wished to admonish him for the afternoon of rest. Christopher lay back in the grass to stare at a cloudless evening sky that would soon be dotted with roiling dark clouds.

When Nasir's footsteps had faded and all he could hear was the river's inspirational current, Christopher whispered, "I'm afraid of him, too."

27

Words converged in a mass of black ink as Roseanne stared at the papers lying on the table before her. Thoughts came and went as Reeve, the court organizer, continued his steady, monotonous discourse while standing behind her. To one side sat a stone-faced and grizzled General Azeiah. Next to him was Banner-Captain Charles, who rarely left Rosealyn's side. Opposite the soldiers sat a withering Elder Matthias who, thankfully, continued to agree with her.

When Roseanne dared a brief glance to the opposite end of the table, she found her daughter's fierce brown-eyed gaze. Two braids adorned each side of Rosealyn's head, and her deep green dress made Roseanne feel somewhat foolish for wearing such a bold red. Rosealyn grimaced, one finger tapping on the table in an impatient rhythm. Roseanne resumed her study of the paper she held—all it did was explain how the famine had only continued to worsen after Pasea's destruction. Logical, since that city had been their largest producer of grains. As retaliation, they needed to claim Hoclia to use their enemy's resources. What little food they had stored did not keep. It was as if the Orda'anian fields had given up.

She laid the report down and nudged it aside, listening as Reeve listed each city's exports and imports. Trade routes, which she'd changed per Xannan's recommendation, were not helping. Over the past several weeks, Roseanne had wondered if such recommendations were to help the citizens or him.

While drawing in a slow, deep breath, Roseanne glanced over at the thrones aligned along one wall. The priests accepted her role as widowed queen. They had to. She had insisted she was their ruling monarch. But sitting on her throne, without Phillippe at her side, made it impossible to focus. Despite the arranged marriage, she had grown to care for him, even if she spent most of her time frustrated by his actions.

A quick glance up found Rosealyn's unwavering stare once more. Heat blazed forth from her glare. And the incessant tapping. Soft but persistent. The younger woman's chin lifted when their gazes met. Roseanne recognized that look of decisiveness; Roseanne could do little when her daughter became so determined. *Just as strong-willed as my sister.*

Roseanne grimaced, gaze flicking from one person to the next as Reeve continued to drone in his usually soothing monotone. She could not relinquish control, not until she understood both Ramon's and Xannan's goals. Or how they had met. *Why does it feel as though the mercenaries will only bring me more pain?*

Pain like the burning inside Roseanne's chest and at the back of her throat. Pain like that which made Rosealyn's hand continue to stray without her realizing it, making Roseanne believe the Passing either incomplete or too much for her daughter to bear on top of the country's condition. Pain like the unanswered question of who she was without the title her parents had insisted she take.

She relaxed the muscles of her jaw and cheeks, resisting the urge to reposition her crown. Every line of possibilities she entertained reminded her of being trapped by those endless laces of the proper court dresses as Reeve's droning voice once again came into focus.

"Lobelia and Demir have requested more grain. All they harvested this month decayed within a day, Your Majesty."

She grimaced at the statement. Little could be done. No other food remained to be shared. Lack of proper stores would test the renowned resilience of the Orda'anian citizens, especially since they had no explanation for why it did not keep. Unless the decaying food had a connection with the enormous dragon somehow hiding near the Cliff of Lycene. Probably beneath that waterfall.

"What news from the messages sent to our neighbors, Reeve?" Roseanne maintained eye contact with Rosealyn while trying to ignore the rhythmic tapping. Despite her command to attack Hoclia's capital of Hazael, General Azeiah had insisted on reopening the lines of communication between them.

"They will meet with Princess Rosealyn," Reeve said.

Her daughter leaned forward against the table, hand gripping her side, while Roseanne mentally recited the court organizer's words. Either their neighbors had willingly chosen this route or Rosealyn had sent a message of her own.

"Rosealyn is not well enough to travel yet." Roseanne shifted her crown, and her daughter's indignant stare intensified.

"I can speak for myself, Mother." Rosealyn straightened in her seat, though she continued to tap against the table as if she were maintaining the beat for a song. "I am Orda'an's voice in all except ceremony. The Passing is complete, and I am its recipient. That is all it takes, yes, Elder Matthias?"

Roseanne's gaze shifted to the elder who leaned back in his seat, hands held with fingertips resting against each other.

A pristine white coat with golden trim made his sagging skin appear paler than the light-toned Charles.

"You have not fully recovered, Princess." Elder Matthias cleared his throat. "It would not do to have you collapse during the journey."

A slight loosening of Roseanne's chest. Not completely. Roseanne steadied her crown again, recalling the elder had only agreed to delay the ceremony rather than change the laws completely. *Phillippe could convince him. How do I change his mind?*

"With Banner-Captain Charles and my other bodyguards as escort, I will be more than fine." Rosealyn did not break eye contact. "I can take care of myself."

"Princess," Charles said with soft caution, giving Roseanne an excuse to shift her glare to find the Banner-Captain was studying his lap. "Elder Matthias is right. You have barely resumed simple training. I fear what a journey might do."

Smart man. A quick glance, a barely noticeable grimace, and Roseanne steeled herself to meet that glare which had been staring her down the entire time Reeve spoke. Dependent on how light hit them, her daughter's eyes wavered between a light brown or a green hue—a mixture of her parentage. The green claimed the gaze today, as resolute as the princess's tone.

"Father never mentioned trouble with finances, just food. We set the trade lines decades ago with all of our neighbors save Jearnia. By speaking with Hoclia and Alkaan, we allow those routes to resume. What of our trade routes with Tenoa? Last I was aware, the fields of your home remain fruitful, right, Mother?"

Roseanne pursed her lips, shifting the papers in front of her with one hand, the pen Reeve had given her fluttering back and forth in the other. "Ramon has been trying to settle the matter of a dead councilman. As Reeve stated, Hoclia and Alkaan do not wish to speak with us."

"With you, Mother," her daughter did not hesitate to correct. "They will speak with me." She spoke with her father's demeanor, making it even more difficult for Roseanne to look at her. "But what of the finances?"

Roseanne continued beating the pen against the air in time with her daughter's tapping against the table. When Reeve uttered a word, Roseanne held up a hand to halt him. She'd lied on those reports to hide the truth of where the money had gone. No one else dared say a word.

"Last Father and I spoke…" Rosealyn paused, her grip tightening on the paper she held. "Where has the money gone?"

Roseanne set the pen down and interlaced her fingers atop the growing pile, meeting her daughter's leveled stare. She worried what the princess might try to do, worried what would happen to her if she had no purpose in Orda'an anymore.

"General, Banner-Captain, resume preparations to attack Hazael. They will not encroach on our lands again." The two men glanced at the princess and back at Roseanne, and she grimaced. "That was not a suggestion." Both men nodded but remained seated while she turned her attention to Elder Matthias. "Draft amendments to the laws regarding the Passing—"

"Elder Matthias, you will continue to meet with the council as requested. If they agree I am to remain an incapacitated heir—which I am not—then you may amend the laws." Rosealyn's sharp tone made Roseanne jolt. "Until then, I will prepare to meet with the leaders of our neighbors in hopes to use words to settle conflicts."

Hands clasped together in front of her, Roseanne focused on the center of the table. "Leave us." Roseanne glanced at the others surrounding the table, avoiding her daughter's icy stare. "I wish to speak with my daughter alone now."

Elder Matthias stood first, leaving after a quick bow to both her and her daughter. Azeiah and Charles studied both women for a moment, standing only after the princess gave them a slight nod. Roseanne gritted her teeth. *I am nothing to them. To any of them.*

Roseanne studied her daughter as the hinges of the throne room doors creaked open and closed. The princess's unwavering gaze rivaled Phillippe's.

"Mercenaries," Roseanne said without fanfare. "Protection from Jearnia."

Rosealyn's face scrunched in confusion. "Mercenaries? Soldiers for hire? When we have an army of our own to protect us? And we've heard *nothing* from Jearnia for the last decade." She shook her head and finally stopped tapping against the table to cross her arms. "General Azeiah will not approve."

"Mercenaries are both necessary and expensive. I can't expect you to understand, protected as you are in the castle. An attack is imminent. Mercenaries on our side outside the castle; Orda'anian soldiers within."

Rosealyn's gaze turned quizzical, studying the table and allowing Roseanne to breathe. Then her shoulders fell, remembering the battle her daughter had run off to join. Neither Phillippe nor Rosealyn had told her anything. *Naïve, sheltered … but how many did she kill?*

Rosealyn half-laughed after a moment's hush. "There's a reason General Azeiah refused your command to attack."

"You should not undermine my orders, Rosealyn."

The young woman tilted her head. "Stop paying the mercenaries. Or sending any provisions. If they join the army, then we pay them." The tone, the stance, every aspect of Rosealyn's demeanor radiated the expectation to be obeyed. "And what of their leader?"

Roseanne's heart leaped to her throat, berating herself for allowing even half the truth to escape her lips. She chewed on her tongue, letting the silence between them linger, hoping her daughter would tire of the wait and leave. That was how these stare downs usually ended, but the princess maintained the leveled glare.

"None of your concern." Roseanne searched the empty table as though it could provide answers. "You must stay here. We cannot risk you leaving the castle. Not after what happened to Phillippe."

Rosealyn stood, hands pressed against the table. "Father disappeared from the castle courtyard!" A brief pause led to a sharp inhale. "I may not have concrete proof yet, but I know you have been lying. Or at the very least providing half-truths. All of you do it, thinking you can protect me."

Air stuck somewhere between her lungs and her throat, Roseanne scrunched her brows and grimaced. "Once you can prevent your hand from straying, we will speak of your coronation."

"This persistence on delaying my coronation could be construed as treason, Mother."

Roseanne's body flushed with warmth reminiscent of being stranded amid the Tenoan sand dunes. "I have done what I believe best for Orda'an."

"Best for Orda'an?" Rosealyn stood to her full height, auburn hair shifting over the slit sleeves of her deep green dress as she shook her head and whispered, "Or best for you?"

28

Fists held tight at her sides, Rosealyn swallowed a frustrated scream when footsteps sounded immediately behind her. She wanted to think. Alone. Just one moment with no one in arm's reach.

Nails digging into her palms helped distract from the ever-present throbbing. Cool winds whistled through the hallways, bringing the intoxicating scent of first snow. The footsteps slowed to match her pace, and the soft scent of snow lingered long after the open windows had transitioned into solid stone walls.

"Princess?" came Charles's voice at her side when she stopped walking. It was his job, one he had never done with any malicious intent. No matter what agreement or secrets he hid, he would protect her. But she'd prefer to be alone.

"I'm fine," she whispered, though her fingers ached. Eyes closed for a brief second, she turned to face him. Hand on his plain sword hilt, lips in a tight line, brows furrowed, Charles tensed.

"Are you?" he asked, gaze flicking down to her clenched fists and back to her face.

Rosealyn bit her lower lip to stop it from trembling. Several blinks helped the tears dissipate but couldn't prevent the shouting. "Everyone wants to control what I can or cannot do. I'm not some stumbling drunken fool or willing to pay mercenaries. Nor am I too young. Inexperienced perhaps, but whose fault is that? Not mine!"

Arms shaking, Rosealyn tried to look away, but Charles gripped her arms, forcing her to stand still and face him. "You've done nothing wrong," he reminded her, and the burning started again.

Not knowing what else to do or say, Rosealyn wrapped her arms around him. As she knew he would, her bodyguard for the past several years stood stiff, hands awkwardly gripping both of her arms. Tilting her head back, she looked up at him and chuckled. The often furrowed brows raised, and the thin line of his lips had parted.

"Why are you always so stiff?" The question slipped out of her. "If we aren't sparring, it's like you're afraid someone will throw you in the dungeon if you're too close."

He grunted in response, releasing his grip, gently removing her arms from around him, and taking a step back. He slipped a finger behind his collar to loosen the topmost button while avoiding her gaze.

She wanted answers about his past, but she was also furious with her mother and needed to become the rightful ruler she already was first. Neither moved, so Rosealyn pressed her luck with getting a less cryptic answer than usual.

"Well? What is with the stiffness? Something to do with Father." She pursed her lips together and added, "Or perhaps that agreement."

"Better to follow the rules, even the unspoken ones," he said, resuming his common stance around her as his gaze turned distant. "As you are well aware."

"Always so vague," she said, propping one hand on her hip and grimacing. So illogical to feel pain for a wound she never received. "Besides, I should make the rules now."

"Some rules should not be broken, Princess." Then, softer, an addition she didn't expect. "And others should be."

When he looked away, Rosealyn reached out to grasp his free hand and gave him a comforting squeeze. "You can tell me," she said, stepping closer to him. "Father trusted you at my side so I can think of no one else to continue protecting me. But he knew everything. How am I to trust you with my life if I think you're hiding *anything* from me?"

His calloused hand went limp and fell from hers. Every time she thought she'd gained ground, another cavern opened for Charles to fall into. She could see him forming the cryptic non-answer again, knew he'd repeat words verbatim to what he said several hours earlier. In his mind, she already knew what he believed she needed to know. She had to find a way. Rosealyn refused to allow others to decide what she could handle knowing. Working through the emotions of the truth would be better than the anger of all the secrecy. All of them had told her lies. Harmful, dangerous, ridiculous secrets.

"Before you give me a half-truth again, I have a suggestion." Rosealyn crossed her arms, one finger tapping in a rhythm she couldn't shake. "The next time I best you in the sparring ring, you tell me everything. About you, your family, the agreement. Everything about you."

"Next time?" Charles graced her with a rare, slight quirk of his lips. "When was the first?"

Rosealyn pinned him with a stare, trying not to smile at the twinkle in his eyes. "Yes or no? I win, you talk. The next time I best you by either knocking you to the ground or disarming you."

"I wasn't aware disarming me counted as winning," he said, this time with a full grin.

She glowered at him and waited, finger continuing to tap its steady beat. He was her guard on duty today, so he couldn't walk away and leave her alone. In fact, he must have been waiting just outside the throne room doors. Rosealyn wondered if he had eavesdropped on what she and her mother had discussed. Not that it mattered since she would tell him about it soon. Wind whistled through the open windows beyond them, and the faint click of shoes against stone sounded behind her.

Charles rounded his shoulders, standing even straighter than usual, the plain leather sword belt creaking as his hand gripped the hilt tighter. "You won't accept a no. Not with that look on your face."

Try as she might, Rosealyn could not withhold her grin. He'd agreed. It wasn't an answer, but it was progress. Breathless, she wrapped her arms around him again. Her cheeks flushed as she thought about how she wanted more than to simply hug him.

Firm yet gentle hands gripped her shoulders and guided her several steps backward. Charles stood stiff as the walls of stone surrounding them. Perhaps once he answered her questions, she would understand why the man was always so tense. It was strange, witnessing his shocked expression, but his brief reaction made her grin. *At least he hasn't changed much in the past month.*

"Good, I look forward to holding you to this promise." Her smile grew, finger resuming its tapping against her arm. "We'll go as soon as I've changed out of this constricting nightmare of a dress."

She turned on her heel and almost walked into Azeiah.

"The training will have to wait." He pulled a sealed envelope from inside the solid black coat of his rank. "From Phil—His Majesty." Clearing his throat, Azeiah held the letter out to her. This letter meant her father knew what would happen. All with the Gift knew when their death was imminent. It was a comfort her own fatal vision had not yet surfaced.

"I feared giving it to you earlier, lest the difficulty with the Passing worsen," he added. "It's good to see you smiling again."

Rosealyn nodded, breaths coming in shallow gasps as she gripped the skirts of her dress to dry the sweat from her palms. An unbroken seal. Black wax formed a perfect circle, meaning he'd used his ring to seal it. Hands clammy, fingers tremulous, Rosealyn held the envelope and wet her lips. "Thank you, Azeiah."

In her periphery, the hint of a grin flashed across the general's features. After a singular nod, he walked away. All thoughts of sparring with Charles today fled as she stared, riveted by the blurring seal. Today, now, she would read it. She reached for the handle of her door and jolted when Charles's hand enveloped hers, halting her before she could open the door. With a roll of her eyes, she muttered, "Since you always insist."

What was likely seconds felt like hours as Charles searched her rooms. Satisfied no dangers lurked for her, he reopened the door and gestured for her to enter. Face lined with slight creases of worry, he watched her every move.

"I'll be fine." Rosealyn sank into a chair in the middle of her colorful room, the one where she'd left her father's sword resting against its edge. Wearing it into the throne room with her mother could have gone badly. Perhaps she should have, but her father had always taught her to defend herself rather than be the instigator.

Charles closed the door but didn't leave. Instead, he sat in a chair within arm's reach. "You look like you're about to faint, Princess."

"I really hope I don't," she murmured, staring at the envelope. "But I'd prefer to read this alone."

Brows knitted together, he nodded and stood, hand resuming its hold of his sword hilt. "As you wish, Princess." Charles bowed his head and approached the door, hesitating at the threshold. "If I hear anything out of the ordinary, I'm coming back in."

Without waiting for her response, he left. Door shut, she was alone. Walls of color made the room seem smaller than a closet while her chest ached for a proper breath.

"Please, please, don't make me pass out," she whispered, eyes flicking up to the door, where she knew Charles stood just outside. If she dropped to the carpeted stone floor, he'd be by her side in a blink. Inhale. Hold. Exhale. She broke the seal and willed shaking hands to still.

My darling Rose,

The Gift, I am sure, has frustrated you. For many generations, the LeNoir line continued through male heirs, but as you are my only child… I've always known you would inherit the Gift. From the first moment I held you in my arms, I knew.

Keep my sword close; you will need it. The pain, the obnoxious invisible pain, should decrease when you wear the sword. I pray the sword finds its way to you quickly—that wait was a nuisance when I endured the Passing.

Letter resting in her lap, Rosealyn glanced at her father's words and down at the weapon. No more than a normal sword. It weighed more than the wooden practice blades but gleamed silver when unsheathed. She pulled it a few inches from the scabbard, frowning. Metal sharpened to slice and maim greeted her. Blade returned to its sheath, she laid it across her lap and picked up the letter again. A noise to her left made her frown deepen. Had one chair moved? No, she was alone. Not even Lori was in her quarters. Charles knocked once. Loud enough for him to hear, she said, "I'm conscious."

He must have cracked the door open because the handle moved. Or maybe that had been her imagination. Information, truths from her father, beckoned her.

There are more entries to Gailin's journal hidden in my study which may provide answers or more questions. Perhaps with your affinity for studying our histories, Gailin's words will make more sense to you than they did to me. The Gift is so much more than an ability beyond your control. I never desired to understand, not until it was too late. In my desire to protect you, I neglected to share all you needed to know. I hoped that not telling you meant your experience would be different.

Warm air swirled around her. Beads of sweat popped up along her temples. A breeze must have caught heat from the fire. Two lines left. Such a brief letter.

As I've said before, trust Charles. One day, I'm sure he'll help you understand why. But remember, my darling Rose: beauty is brilliant at masking thorns.

Rosealyn scanned the single page again, hunting for hidden words, hidden meanings. Nothing else. No second page. No explanation of where to find the rest of Gailin's journals. And to end with his most common phrase. Who was he warning her about? If not Charles and his hidden past, then her mother?

Another rush of warmth came from above. She crinkled the letter in her right hand while gripping the sword hilt with her left. "I told you I wanted to be alone." Rosealyn lifted her gaze, but the eyes staring into hers were not Charles's pale blue.

Air disappeared from her lungs, and her heart stopped for a mere second before racing faster than she believed possible. Purple eyes, white scales like leather, and a long snout. Identical to the family crest but life-size. Petrified, she stared, afraid to blink. A dragon stood in front of her. How long had it been there? Could dragons be invisible? Wings spread out from its sides, knocking over several chairs. Rosealyn's gaze followed the length of the scaled and feathered wings. Akin to clouds, or perhaps the softest bed, the wings folded back into the white dragon's sides and it huffed, sending another rush of warmth onto Rosealyn's skin.

Its purple eyes stared into hers, unblinking as the color switched to a solid white. An image of herself sheltered beneath the beast's feathered wing appeared in her mind. A knock—second, third time? The dragon's long thin snout craned toward the door. She could hear Charles's voice, knew he'd heard the chairs falling over.

Its head swiveled back to her, occupying her vision. Hands gripping the letter, Rosealyn swallowed hard. She could draw the sword, but the thing could eat her head before she moved her arm. None had ever taught her how to defeat a dragon. Nor had the Gift provided any warning of its appearance.

Another knock. Rosealyn didn't respond. She had no air in her lungs for speech.

The image, the exact same image, reappeared with a hint of urgency. Eyes white, the dragon moved forward. Fighting the sudden onslaught of a throbbing head, Rosealyn cowered back in the chair, knuckles aching from the grip on her father's sword. The letter fell to the floor. She'd need both hands to fight.

Charles shouted her name at the same moment the dragon's snout touched her forehead. Lost in a whirlwind of darkness,

Charles's voice faded away. Blacks and grays and flashes of white, spinning, circling, encasing. The too familiar movement ceased. Caked mud rubbed against her cheek. Stale air coated her lungs. Eyes opened or closed didn't matter. Rosealyn reached out with a hand and met smooth, damp stone. "A cave?"

Her voice echoed off the wall-like rocks, providing a sense of depth she had not known since her father had taken her to the edge of the Vadamon Sea. The cave seemed larger.

Rosealyn stood, hand trailing the smooth wall while her vision acclimated to the darkness. A cool breeze whispered around her, creating goosebumps along her arms beneath the thin material of the court dress. After a few steps, a faint swath of sunlight filtered through an opening. She approached, looking out at the land beyond. Past the cave's entrance, the land dropped into nothing but sky. Stretches of forests occupied a valley far below. A valley which transitioned into rolling hills. She was in a cave in the only known mountains on the continent, those which created Jearnia's eastern border. *How in the name of my forefathers am I in the Jearnian mountains?*

Rocks crunched behind her, accompanied by a low, reverberating grumble. Distracted by the darkness, Rosealyn had forgotten to listen to her surroundings, had somehow forgotten about the dragon. She inhaled deeply and reached for her sword, but it wasn't at her waist. It had been in her hands when the dragon's snout touched her forehead. Chest heaving against the barricade of her dress, Rosealyn turned slowly, tensing for an attack.

Purple eyes glowed like a lantern. Wings with small tufts of feathers clumped atop scales tucked in close to its body. It paused, head tilting and then lowering to rest atop inordinately large paws compared to the rest of the dragon's proportions. Claws peeked between the nubs of its toes, and slight ridges were flowing down the beast's tail. The ruffle of feathers partially covered its paws. Her father's sword rested between her and the dragon. One step forward, and the dragon's tail flitted across the mud-caked dirt.

Heart racing, Rosealyn bent to retrieve the sword. The imprint of the LeNoir crest rubbed against her palm. Voice cracking, Rosealyn stated the obvious. "You're a dragon."

The dragon blinked once and shifted its gaze beyond her. Muscles tensed, Rosealyn drew the sword as she turned.

"No need for that, Princess Rosealyn."

Rosealyn tilted her head and observed the woman who spoke with a strange musical lilt she'd never heard before. Dark pants, a loose brown shirt. The newcomer maneuvered through the cave with ease. Red. Her eyes had red irises. White hair stopped short at her jawline, framing high cheekbones. Despite the frown, no creases adorned the woman's enviable features. "I'm surprised Phillippe did not tell you more about us or the dragons. How connected you are to them. He certainly asked enough questions each time he visited."

Her father's letter had mentioned nothing about a connection to the dragons. Grip faltering, Rosealyn's eyes narrowed at the woman, wincing as she steadied the sword with both hands. *Charles was right. I'm not ready for the weight.*

"Who are you?" Rosealyn demanded, voice tremulous.

"A friend, Celena by name," she said, red irises studying the shaking sword. "The dragon is Synda. Despite Magna's many warnings, young Synda disobeyed and brought you here anyway."

29

Charles opened the door as he knocked a third time. A brief flash and the seat she had occupied was empty. Without thinking, he shouted, "Rose!"

He ran inside her rooms, turning about as he gripped his sword's hilt and cursed himself for leaving his preferred blade in his quarters. And for thinking it would help him find the princess. Several chairs had been knocked to the ground, but everything else remained the same. No colored swatches had moved. The fireplace crackled to one side. With each second, his heart raced faster. He tossed cloth and chair aside as though he might find her unconscious or hiding beneath one of them.

Realization dawned, and he sprinted in the direction of General Azeiah's office, shouting for people to move and shoving them out of the way as he did. Dozens of questions formed in his mind as he ran, questions he hoped the general could answer. Aside from Rose, he would be the only one to understand the Gift.

The soldiers in the practice yards stopped their sparring as he sped past, but he didn't slow to hear Lieutenant-Captain Moss's shouted question. He flung the door wide into the unsuspecting general's quarters, forcing himself to speak in as level a voice as he could manage. "She's gone."

"Gone?" Azeiah looked up from his seat at the small table. "Who's gone?"

Heart racing, Charles forced himself to stand still. His initial attempts to even his breathing faltered when he remembered the general placing the letter Charles had not yet read in the center of that table. A chill breeze swept over him, making the hairs on the back of his neck stand on end as he remembered what the king had said about winter's arrival.

"Ro-Princess Rosealyn." Charles found it difficult to keep his voice from rising. "He's taken her."

"He who?" Azeiah said, and Charles let out an exasperated sigh. "The Lost Prince? What rea—"

"She disappeared from her quarters just as Phillippe did in the courtyard. I thought he…" Charles remembered the detail he had neglected to tell Azeiah when they spoke of his trip to Lycene. "It makes sense Xannan would do the same to her. Too easy. I never should have left her alone." He raked a hand through his hair, halting when his palm reached his scalp. "The queen! She must be in on it."

"Slow down, Captain." Azeiah glanced down at a half-full plate of pathetic-looking food. The general took a generous bite, and Charles watched the man think. Without enough space, especially given the amount of furniture in the general's quarters, to pace, Charles gripped the hilt of his sword.

Anger and annoyance coated each word more heavily than the previous one, and he spoke the last through gritted teeth. "Apologies, sir, for the interruption, but Princess Rosealyn is missing."

"Your calm surprises me, Captain." An unusual twinkle lit the general's eyes and made Charles continue to grind his teeth. Azeiah sighed. "You said she was in her quarters? Not the throne room. So perhaps Her Majesty is less involved than we assumed?" The general scratched at the neglected hairs of his chin. "Read that letter yet, Captain?"

Charles's heart skipped a beat, and his grip on the hilt tightened, wondering if Phillippe had ever shared his true history with the general.

"No, sir. Why?"

"Curious what message Phillippe had for you, that's all." Azeiah resumed scratching his chin, with a frown. "What did you see? Be precise."

"She was sitting in one of her chairs one moment and the next, gone. We have to find her, help her—"

Azeiah cleared his throat. "Precise, Captain."

Charles grimaced, and the muscles of his jaw ached. Eyes closed, Charles recalled what he'd witnessed. A few soft thuds, her simple albeit annoyed announcement she was conscious, then the crashing of chairs to floor. He shook his head, berating himself for agreeing to let her read the letter alone. Charles's shoulders fell. "That's it. One moment there, the next gone."

"No black cloud like when Phillippe disappeared?"

"No cloud at all." Charles shook his head. "None that I saw, at least."

Azeiah nodded and took another bite. The general's features turned thoughtful, almost quizzical as he chewed and swallowed with a slight grimace. "I wonder if she has the letter with her or if she read it yet."

Charles wanted to scream, yell, berate the general for his calm demeanor and was mustering the courage to calm his tone when the general spoke again. "I understand your need to protect Princess Rosealyn. Phillippe put me in similar situations many times, including one near identical to this. The lack of a colored cloud is good, Charles. I believe the princess is safe. Though, I am surprised Xannan did not try what you assumed. Odd. To wait around all this time."

Charles's jaw opened and closed, but no words came out. Of everyone in the castle, Azeiah would understand the frustration of the LeNoir Gift. Rosealyn had barely spoken about the Gift throughout the past few weeks. Instead, she'd hugged him and made him nearly forget he was only her protector. A bodyguard tasked to keep her safe. A task he had failed at miserably. Between the hugs and her demanding to know about the agreement, Charles had been distracted. Sometimes he wished he'd never made that agreement. Not that he had a choice.

"Relax, Captain. I imagine she'll be back soon. Go read his letter to you."

He tried to relax his muscles, but his fear of reading Phillippe's letter to him and his worry for Rosealyn warred with one another and kept him tense. Charles pulled out the second chair at Azeiah's table and sat on its edge, mind racing. "Why did Xannan wait?"

Azeiah shrugged, shoving dilapidated morsels around with his fork. "I am certain Phillippe did not share all he saw. I will search the princess's quarters to learn if Phillippe's letter is there or with her. Now, Captain, did I not give you an order? Or a semblance of one at least?"

The general piled the last vestiges of his plate onto his fork and glanced at Charles with a raised eyebrow and a slight inclination of his head at the door. Charles took several deep breaths, stood, and gave a brief salute, turning on his heel and walking as swiftly as he could without running.

Once inside his quarters, Charles fumbled for the book on his bed, breaking the letter's seal as soon as he pulled it out. It was a single page, filled with the tight lines of the king's hand. Charles scanned the words, enraptured and in awe. Several lines made him pause and reread the king's words—it was odd to see their agreement in writing. The last sentences felt like a kick to the chest. "Rose is safe with the young white dragon. Do not go after her. I fear what your father will set in motion once he learns of my demise. See to it my darling Rose does not return home to more trouble than she left."

He tossed the letter on top of his small desk, glanced up at the sword hanging from its belt on the hook, and sighed. He pulled it down, unraveling the leather bound around its hilt to reveal the insignia beneath. The insignia Phillippe had helped him hide. Where the Orda'anian crest used the dragons and the swords its people denied existed for so long, the Jearnian insignia showcased that which the dragons created: fire. The hilt itself was a deep gray, allowing the billowing flame which emblazoned the pommel to appear like it glowed.

It was the last gift from his mother, a remnant of home he could not part with no matter how often he tried. After the concussion between the two blades at Lycene, he had racked his brain for answers within the stories his mother often told of her youth. He'd even reread the book from his mother. Tales of ancient dragons. Myths and legends of where dragons lived, what they provided, and what they took. Phillippe's letter had only added to those questions; that man's past was not as uneventful as he claimed.

"Don't go after Rose because she's safe, he says," Charles said aloud, holding the sword out in front of him as though it would tell him its secrets. "Make sure she doesn't come home to more trouble."

He glanced about the small room that had become his home for a decade. Simple. Plain. No elegance. No unnecessary vastness. Years of waiting had made him complacent. He sighed and allowed the tendrils of flame on his sword's hilt to overcome his vision. "Meaning go home and 'take care' of Father. Meaning give Rose an ally, not another enemy. That was always the plan. To make our countries allies instead of enemies."

He mulled over the words, wondering if his father had changed for the better. Or worse.

The blade buzzed in his hands, and he stood to sheath the weapon and wrap the belt around his waist. Charles shut his eyes tightly, mentally reciting the speech he had prepared for when Phillippe would request he honor their agreement. *I feel little for those who once called me son, for I no longer call them parents. One of my brothers can have the title. I have no need of it.*

"I am no longer Jearnian." Charles finished the recitation aloud, opening his eyes. "But that is a lie I cannot continue to live."

He counted, as he had taught Rosealyn to do, inhaling slowly and exhaling even more slowly. Phillippe had honored his portion of the agreement. The fighting between their countries had stopped. Charles realized, as he continued counting slow and steady breaths, he must honor his portion.

Charles undid the topmost button of his coat, shifting it away from his neck, and took a deep breath. One hand on the door handle, he glanced back at his mother's book and over to the letter. He shook his head, positive the general already knew what secrets Phillippe had kept for him. Charles took a step outside and hesitated. The book had the written copies of his mother's stories. Stories which might lead him to answers. He shoved the book inside his coat and stepped outside. *Wherever in this world you are, Rose, please be alive.*

30

The sword was heavier than Rosealyn remembered. Her arms shook with the effort to hold the sword poised. "Why should I trust you?"

"Synda can show you, Princess Rosealyn." Celena gestured at the large animal behind Rosealyn who lay there, long tail flicking across the dirt. Rosealyn's eyes narrowed, questioning how this strange-looking woman could know her name and title.

Unable to hold the sword poised any longer, Rosealyn lowered the point to the ground. She held the pommel with both hands to avoid clutching her side and paced her breathing to slow her racing heart.

Shifting her grip on the sword and dismissing the idea of holding it at waist height, Rosealyn turned back to the white dragon. Its purple eyes met hers, and when they flashed white, she saw Charles standing within the palace gardens. Her father's favorite black roses had been replaced by more natural hues, creating a rainbow of color spreading around Charles.

"Where is he?" Rosealyn took a faltering step toward Synda. The sword fell from her grip, its drop muffled by the soft ground beneath her. As Rosealyn bent to retrieve it, she kept her focus on Synda. When she picked up her sword, the hilt was damp from the cave's moisture.

Synda tilted her head and sent the same image. It brought Rosealyn a sense of comfort, but seeing Charles safe was not enough. "What about Mother? Azeiah? Was the castle attacked? Why did you bring me here? What—"

"Synda can only show you one image at a time, Rosealyn," Celena said. "And Synda is too young to have proper control of her magic."

"Too young? Magic?"

"Dragons live for generations, same as us elves," Celena explained.

Rosealyn bit back the laughter. The strange white-haired, red-eyed woman in front of her was not joking, Rosealyn could hear it in the woman's, the elf-woman's, voice.

"Synda does not yet have her flame despite her forty years of life."

Rosealyn looked around them, the cave walls glistening in the fading light. She tugged at her lower lip, trying to decide what was most important to know. The way her father wrote of the sword bubbled to the surface. After taking another step toward Synda, she grimaced and lifted the sword to her line of sight. Simple silver. No adornment other than the LeNoir crest on the hilt. Shoulders falling, she sheathed the sword and glanced between the elf and the dragon. "Why am I here?"

The next image lingered longer than the last, and Rosealyn saw another dragon. An older dragon. An ancient dragon. Where Synda's wings reminded Rosealyn of soft white clouds in a bright sky, this dragon's wings were like the near barren limbs of a tree as they prepared for colder months. Spikes peaked at the tips of its wings, their sturdiness an odd contrast to the thinning leathery brown skin. And its eyes—Synda's were a bold purple, but this dragon's eyes were a pale white. A faded white, tired from the generations such an ancient creature must have witnessed, tired from watching the world alternate between chaos and tentative peace.

Rosealyn recalled the story her father had told her often during her childhood, the legend of the Twin Blades. That story involved a white dragon. Not brown. "Dragons aren't—" She paused, frowning. *Blazes of an idiot. You are talking to a dragon.*

"That one can answer my questions?"

Synda blinked and huffed as her wings flexed until they brushed the walls to either side of the small cavern in which they stood.

Rosealyn stepped closer to Synda, tensing to prepare for the whirlwind which had occurred when Synda's snout had touched her forehead and made her disappear from her quarters. "Take me to her."

Synda stood and walked deeper into the cave. Rosealyn looked to Celena, confused.

"It takes months, sometimes years, to gather the strength Synda used to bring you here." Celena spoke as though such should be common knowledge. "As I said, Synda is young."

Gripping her sword hilt, Rosealyn shifted the belt around her waist. A young dragon. Not the renowned Magna. Or even Eilon. Perhaps those two ancient dragons were actually a myth. She looked over her shoulder at the entrance which allowed a view of the Jearnian landscape. Either way she traveled, danger could await. Grip tightening on her sword hilt, she breathed deeply and followed the cloud-like white dragon deeper into the cave.

The three walked without speaking, listening to the plodding of Synda's feet against the caked mud. Fading light made it difficult to avoid tripping against the divots of the cave floor, increased by the steady scraping of Synda's drifting spiked tail.

"Meeting Magna will be different." Celena walked in time with Synda's plodding steps, making Rosealyn forget the elf-woman was there. At the confirmation of which dragon they approached, Rosealyn's heart raced anew. "She may choose to show you entire scenes, not just images. It will be painful. Possibly more painful than what your family now refers to as the Passing."

"More painful?" Rosealyn swallowed hard. Her days of unconsciousness had left a lingering confusion, an inability to understand the random images she believed were of the Gift. A thump against her leg brought her attention to the weapon hanging from the belt struggling to stay in place around her too thin waist.

A faint light greeted them from beyond Synda's form as her wings brushed along the walls of the narrowing cave. After several more steps, the path widened into a large cavern over-looking a vast land thriving with foliage. She gasped. Green. Vibrant, luscious green. Mystified by its beauty while simultaneously riddled with the guilt of not having the same to offer her own people, Rosealyn gulped down the forming lump in her throat. The famine continued to worsen, the damage to the fields nearly too great to survive the winter months. *And I'm lost in the mountains. With a dragon. And an elf.*

Rosealyn's gaze fell on the withering dragon lying to one side of the great cavern. It looked no different than the image Synda had shown her, and Rosealyn understood what her father had once meant by a "calm dread." A level of trust welled inside in addition to a worry, a concern that whatever she asked would not provide the answers she truly needed.

Magna's dull white eyes watched her closely. Rosealyn flexed her hand, mentally reminding herself not to grasp the weapon. But the orange orb pulsing at the base of Magna's neck made her wish to pull the weapon free from its scabbard. One step at a time, Rosealyn approached. Celena's hand pulled hers away from the hilt.

Mind racing, Rosealyn flexed her hand and tried to dismiss the constant throb in her side. Steady breaths would help calm her erratic heartbeat. She hoped. Caked mud became small chunks of rocks vibrating with the rumble coming from Magna.

Rosealyn chewed on her tongue to work enough moisture into her mouth to speak. "What next?"

Celena sat with her legs crisscrossed and patted the ground next to her, red irises illumined by a fading sunset. "Brace yourself. Stay calm. Don't fight it."

Rosealyn scrunched her nose, unbuckling the sword belt and sitting with the blade resting atop her crossed legs. *Brace? Don't fight what?*

"What do I do?"

"Close your eyes." Celena waited for Rosealyn to oblige. "Do not fight what Magna shows you."

Rosealyn gripped the sheathed sword, the edges of the knitted leather digging into her palms. And she became like a bird in the sky, watching people from above.

Tendrils of darkness culminated around Xannan, enveloping him piece by piece. Near him stood Gailin, holding a sword whose essence reminded Rosealyn of the blade she now gripped. But both Gailin and Xannan's blades were a clear crystal.

"No, Xannan." Gailin gripped his brother's arm. "Whatever you're about to do, don't."

The shadows surrounding Xannan strengthened.

Rosealyn tried to pull away. The vision was identical to what she'd read in Gailin's journal, though with far less despair. The scene carried her along, and she watched as Xannan's blade turned from clear, to murky, to shadowed clouds, to a deep ebony. When the sword and dark cloud matched in shade, both Xannan and the shadows blinked out of existence. Her chest clenched, remembering how that same magic had stolen her father away from the castle grounds.

"I know this part." Rosealyn's fingers ached and her head throbbed in time with the invisible wound in her side. "Why are you showing me this? Why not send me home so I can take care of my country?"

A huff of breath came from the great dragon as she laid her head atop her paws. Synda walked toward them. The younger dragon clawed at the ground, kneading the dirt.

"Magna has been reserving her strength to fight Eilon," Celena said. "Did you show her what will happen if the blades merge?"

"Blades merge?" Rosealyn wondered if she had actually fallen unconscious while reading her father's letter. "There is—"

"Ah, he did not tell you that piece of its history then." Celena's lips twisted in a cross between a frown and a grimace. "You are Gailin's descendant and the bearer of one of the Twin Blades."

"You mean to say that this—" Rosealyn lifted the sheathed weapon. "Is one of the Twin Blades?"

Celena nodded. "I helped craft its original design before Magna gave it the finishing breath. That event was … unique."

"But the Gift…" Rosealyn's head was pounding again. She gripped the sword's sheath tighter, gasping. Celena was wrong; the Passing hurt worse.

Gailin stood in front of Magna, inside the same cavern. The sword was a faint white, the hilt unadorned.

"Take it back," he whimpered. "Make it stop tormenting me with the unknown."

Magna filled the cave, standing with solid wings spread. A gentle nudge pushed the weapon to Gailin, but he kicked it back. A growl intensified the glowing orb inside her neck, and Gailin fell to his knees.

"It's useless." His voice echoed against the cavern's walls. "Everyone, my entire family, dead. Father said this gift you and Eilon gave would help us. But it didn't. It's done nothing more than hurt us time and time again."

The low rumble stopped when Magna touched her snout to the blade's hilt. It turned crystalline, and Gailin collapsed to his side, hands clutching his chest. He writhed on the cave's floor and Magna's eyes flickered between a bolder white and a solid purple. The blade turned a shimmering silver when she touched it.

A desperate gasp escaped Gailin, his hand pressed against his chest. He lay there, staring at the ceiling, shaking with sobs.

Rosealyn set the sword on the ground and rubbed her temples while shaking her head. "It was a mistake," she said to the floor. "The Gift is because of the LeNoirs' connection to this sword?"

No new images. No response from the elf-woman. Rosealyn sighed. Whatever Gailin had asked Magna to do had nearly killed him. *That explains why it helps to keep it close, I suppose.*

"Without this sword…" Rosealyn hovered one hand above the blade. "Would I die?"

Rosealyn looked to Celena, who offered a singular nod.

She picked up the sword, pulling it from its scabbard and shaking her head. They had to be wrong. But she couldn't fathom letting another have it. Keeping the blade on her person calmed her, eased the emotions warring within, and quieted the Gift's often persistent roaring.

Rosealyn shoved the sword back into its scabbard. "This doesn't tell me why Xannan killed my father. Or what role Eilon played in my father's death. And what of the other Twin Blade? I assume Xannan has it?"

The elf-woman's hair shifted forward as she nodded. "A portion of Magna's magic resides in your blade. It protects you from the creature which created it, meaning neither you nor Magna could kill the other. Same with Eilon and Xannan. Naught but a dragon-wrought blade can kill Xannan now considering the length of his connection with Eilon's magic. Especially since Eilon continues to gather strength."

Celena paused, red-irised eyes seeming to glow brighter for a moment, as though the elf was eager to discuss these weapons.

"So now I must learn how to defeat a dragon in addition to killing my father's murderer?"

"Your sword, Futurae, could annihilate Xannan. As could Prince Charles's. Or, I suppose, Prince Christopher's. But Futurae and Praeteritum must return to Praesidio for Eilon to be killed."

Rosealyn's jaw slacked, hung up on a detail the elf-woman likely thought unimportant. "Prince Charles?"

Celena stood and held a hand out for Rosealyn. "I will guide you to Violet Grove and explain more on the way."

She did not take the outstretched hand. Tugging at her bottom lip, Rosealyn met Magna's gaze again. "What of the pain within which torments me? Father said it will decrease the longer I wear the sword…"

Synda moved forward and lowered her snout to Rosealyn's forehead. A huff came from Magna, and Rosealyn shuddered. Despite the warmth of Synda's breath, a chill ran down her entire body. It tingled from shoulders to arms to fingertips and shot down to her toes, culminating in the invisible wound at her side. A gasp escaped Rosealyn as the pain dissipated, along with the strange chill. When Magna huffed again, Synda's wings flicked out and back in.

Rosealyn's mouth went dry, both hands rubbing against her side. The pain was gone. Tears welled, overwhelmed at feeling empty and complete at the same time. It was like the last piece of her father had been ripped away from her, but she could fill her lungs without fear of wincing.

She let herself breathe deep, a slight twinge of fear that the pain might reappear, but the movement of her body did not hurt. Rosealyn's eyes darted, trying to find a place to concentrate, trying to decide what question to ask next. "If we merge the blades…"

She paused, confused. The stories never spoke of the blades merging, only the creation of them. As she thought about what could occur when the weapons became whole again, the faint tapping she'd heard since receiving that invisible wound crescendoed. It came from her sword. And from somewhere else.

Synda approached, tail flicking in quick, anxious movements. Rocks slid when Magna emitted a deep rumble. It was a warning, one which faded when the two dragons exchanged a glance.

"Come." Celena offered her hand again. "You will be needed in Violet Grove soon. Arjun organized a summit between the countries there, which begins in ten days' time. Or, at least, that was the agreed upon date."

A knot formed in Rosealyn's stomach, and the calm dread returned. While discussing the Twin Blades, Rosealyn had forgotten that war was about to break out between countries, all struggling to provide food for their people. And would if her mother got her way. Rosealyn accepted Celena's hand and situated her sword belt.

"Wait." Rosealyn lifted her chin to look at the magnificent ancient beast. "What about my mother?"

A flash of purple faded into the image of a woman who shared similar features with her mother. But whoever this woman was, it was not Rosealyn's mother.

Christopher studied the map in his hands, annoyed at the stallion shifting beneath him as he rode.

"Nasir, you're taking us too far south." He looked up and realized the soldier was several yards ahead. Christopher nudged the stallion forward.

"Better to go further south than follow directly behind those mercenaries, my lord," Nasir said as Christopher approached.

A gust of wind tried to snatch the map from his grasp, so Christopher folded it. "We should have stayed there longer, spoken with their leader, and determined their purpose."

"No need, my lord. Mercenaries lie."

"I understand that." Christopher scowled at nothing in particular. The journey should be relatively simple. Visit Vandyl, find this Charles, and take him home. He was curious about the group of mercenaries. A strange combination of Orda'anians, Hoclians, and Alkaanians. Since encountering the group two days ago, Christopher had been trying to decide what could bring those three countries together. Christopher had no answer because he continued debating if the man they went to retrieve was truly his eldest brother. "We are inside Orda'an now, are we not?"

Nasir nodded, and Christopher surveyed the surrounding land. Open plains, no intoxicating ripple of the river, no overbearing yet comforting presence of looming mountains. His mother had never taken him to those mountains as she had his older brother. He tucked the folded map into his bag and wrapped his cloak closer around himself. Ahead, Christopher thought a city loomed, but he could not make out any distinct walls. He stifled a yawn, shifting his inordinately tired legs as a cramp crept into his thigh.

"How much further?"

"Hard to say for sure, my lord, given we are not taking the roads which lead straight to Vandyl. We cannot turn back, though. I'm sure the men you left near the cliff will return home soon and update His Majesty."

"I'm well aware of my task, Nasir." Christopher clenched teeth which threatened to shatter in the cold. "It's simple, really. We march straight to the castle gates and demand entrance. Once inside, we ask to see Charles and take him home with us. Nothing more to it."

Nasir grunted, glaring at Christopher with wariness. "My lord, if you believe this task is simple, you forget our destination. I pray to the mountains that band of mercenaries does not beat us to Vandyl."

Every muscle tensed; he had not considered the implication of the mercenaries traveling to the castle. "And if they have?"

"An issue to answer if it becomes our reality, my lord."

Christopher pulled his mount to a stop and all the soldiers accompanying him halted as well. Tails swishing, hooves stamping, and wind whistling added to Christopher's tumbling thoughts. Nasir heard the shift, turning his mount around to face Christopher.

"What happened, Nasir? When you escorted Charles to these lands?"

"I took him no further than the border. Prodded him to go, as he had been instructed. The next morning, I found Charles's ripped clothing and his dagger—which His Majesty now wears. Losing my hand was punishment for failing to train the boy properly. A punishment I do not wish to repeat."

A pit opened inside Christopher, fearful what his father might do if he failed this mission. "I wonder, if this man is my brother, if he still works toward the mission Father gave him."

"If Charles is alive, I believe he would have informed His Majesty long before now. A decade is a long time to remain silent, my lord." Nasir frowned and glanced at his stump. "Besides, Orda'anians do not take prisoners."

"How would we know?" Christopher looked westward at lands he'd only ever read about. If one continued long enough, they would encounter the Vadamon Sea. A body of water too large to cross without a boat. He'd never seen one of those, and the idea of being stuck on slats of joined wood with naught but water all around both intrigued and frightened him. Between where he sat atop his stallion and the sea, however, was not a thriving land. Occasional patches of green appeared, but most was an ugly combination of brown and black. "I've read the details. After you returned home without Charles, all fighting stopped. Father stopped pressing for land, and Orda'an did not retaliate. Why?"

"A king need not explain his commands to his soldiers, my lord."

He has a point. Christopher nudged his stallion forward to follow Nasir. Methodical thumping, leather creaking, even stronger wind gusts. He would prefer sitting at the river's edge where he could soak his feet in the cool water and laugh as fish tickled his skin. Nasir gestured for Christopher to move closer. When Christopher rode alongside the aging soldier, the pit inside him deepened into a cavern. He'd read about Vandyl's appearance, how the walls of the castle were unlike any other. The stone mirrored the sunlight one second and then soaked it in the next. Dragonstone.

"Vandyl," he whispered. At Nasir's nod, Christopher straightened and pulled his shoulders back. "Might as well get this over with."

32

Charles stepped outside his quarters and straight into General Azeiah. "Sir?"

Azeiah squinted and tucked both thumbs into his belt. "You read that letter."

Charles nodded. "I will ensure Rosealyn does not return home to more trouble than she left."

"You never even tried to leave." Azeiah crossed his arms, one hand scratching at his chin. "Why not?"

Despite the turmoil raging within, despite his constant indecision at how to think of himself, Charles smiled. It was probably the most genuine smile he had ever let himself display, warming his insides as he spoke the truth of his heart. "Sir, Orda'an became my home. A home that, no matter what wrath I dreamed my father might subject me to, I could never fathom destroying. My father raised me to believe those beyond that cliff were unkind, petty, and ruthless. Phillippe offered the opposite. All of that, and the agreement."

Azeiah nodded, returning Charles's smile with a tight one of his own as his gaze landed on the uncovered hilt of Charles's sword, and he chuckled. "That crest looks better on the flag, I'd say. How many men do you need?"

"None." Charles replaced his content smile with grim determination. "Leave Jearnia to me."

The general nodded, hands hooking into his belt loops as they typically did when he became pensive. An unspoken understanding passed between them, broken by a shout from across the bustling training yards.

"Sirs!"

Charles glanced over Azeiah's shoulder to see a young private running and waving his hand as though it would help him move faster, but it only helped the boy trip over his own feet. He stumbled back upright, shouting "sirs" several more times as he reached them.

"Mercenaries." The private struggled to catch his breath. "They approach, sirs."

Azeiah let loose a string of curses. "You better be right about not needing help, Captain. Looks like we have trouble of our own."

Charles held out his hand, but Azeiah embraced him instead. He returned the hug, allowing the warmth of friendship and camaraderie to renew his vigor for the task ahead.

Before Azeiah released the embrace, he whispered. "Here is the letter Phillippe wrote to Rosealyn, and that final entry of which it speaks. I suspect you will find her before she can return here. Try to be quick about becoming king over there, will ya?"

Air rushed out of Charles, and he swore his rib cage would collapse when Azeiah gave him another squeeze around the middle. "You knew? For how long?"

"Once Phillippe asked me to give you that letter." Azeiah released his hold and stepped back, smirking. "But your technique gave away your Jearnian training from day one."

"Of course it did," Charles said with a small laugh. Behind the general, the confused soldier remained with hands on knees, waiting. Shoulders tensing, Charles met Azeiah's gaze again and brought his fist to heart. "May the Blaze of your ancestors protect you until we meet again." He lowered his hand to grasp his sword hilt and looked to the eastern sky, toward Jearnia. "While I pray to the mountains my father doesn't try to kill me. And, if he does, hopefully you trained me better than Father's men trained him."

Azeiah's tense chuckle became lost in the wind as he leaned forward in a slight bow. "I wonder what Princess Rosealyn will say when she learns?"

Charles grimaced, unsure how he felt about his commanding officer bowing to him, and even more unsure of how to tell Rose. He left the question unanswered, leaving the general to speak with the young soldier as he walked away.

He entered the stables and went through the motions of preparation. Soft murmurs, scratching at each horse's ears to gain a sense for which would be most receptive to him. The mare he had grown accustomed to since arriving in Vandyl had not returned with him from Lycene, and he had ridden little since then.

"Brown mare, last stall," said a voice Charles remembered all too well. He wished he had kept the man's cooling liquid to further aid his burned palm, though it had long since healed.

"Arjun?" Charles turned about, trying to locate the mysterious elf. "What are you doing here?"

"We elves have been close friends of Phillippe's for a while. We helped with—" There was a soft chuckle amid the jangle of reins. "Well, the details surrounding the princess's birth." Arjun walked forward, leading his own mount. "I've been here, watching, since the funeral. Best get her saddled."

Charles continued through the motions of saddling the horse, glancing over at Arjun occasionally. When they had first met amid darkness, Charles had barely noticed the man's unsettling red-irised eyes. He wore the same drab brown robes, and Charles wondered how many vials hid within those folds. The horse saddled, Charles led them both from the stables to the kitchens where he could scrounge up dilapidated scraps of food for the four-day journey.

"Why are you coming with me?" Charles tied the pack to the saddle, leading the mount toward the castle gates. A quick word with the guard and the gates creaked open wide enough for him and Arjun to exit.

"I'm not following you, Prince Charles." Arjun smiled when Charles paused in his walk, confused how this elf he had met once before knew the secret he had kept safe for a decade. Arjun continued walking, unfazed. "I'm making sure you take the path Phillippe intended for you to take. Rosealyn will visit us soon. Do not fear for her safety; fear for your own."

"Fear for my own?" Charles half-laughed, following at an even slower walk and pointing at the scar along his lower jaw. "I'm well aware of my father's whims."

"You've been gone from Jearnia a long time." Arjun mounted, red-irised eyes reflecting the fading sunlight. "Be cautious, be calm, be diligent. Head south. You will find your youngest brother."

Charles shook his head and mounted, idly wondering how Arjun knew so much about them. He urged his mount forward, trotting around the edge of the city to head south. A single glance over his shoulder. Arjun had disappeared. The castle gates closed. His gaze lingered on the sprawling city stretching along either side of the castle, and he grimaced, wondering if he should have told Rosealyn the truth about his past. Eventually, she would learn everything, and he feared her reaction.

The elf was right; it wasn't long before he saw the group of Jearnian soldiers ahead of him. They wore armor such a deep red it was almost black atop a variety of stallions and mares. Two rode at the front. A grizzled soldier with a missing hand and a hardened youth not wearing ranked armor. Charles reminded himself to breathe and ignore the thudding of his heart inside his chest. He didn't have to wonder if the younger man was his youngest brother. The resemblance was too strong. But it was difficult to imagine Christopher like this. The version of his little brother he remembered was a carefree child, one obsessed with spinning one tale after another, constantly following each sibling. Christopher reminded Charles of himself during his younger years. Except his younger brother had kept his hair long. It was almost as curly as their mother's. Even Christopher's eyes were the same bold blue as his own. A twinge of guilt surfaced, wondering how his brothers' lives would have been different had he done as their father requested.

Though he wanted to look behind, to return to Vandyl, Charles forced himself to watch their approach. His study of the men transitioned to the soldier next to his brother, and he slowed his mount. For a second, the man's appearance didn't register. Age had not been kind to Charles's mentor. Wrinkles etched the man's forehead and lines bracketed his lips. Charles sank back in his saddle, loosening his grip of the reigns with a slight shake of his head. It was unlike his father to leave men alive if they failed in their assigned task.

Charles nudged his mount into a simple walk. Shoulders pulled back, sitting as tall as possible in the saddle, Charles kept his face void of emotion. Once they were within shouting distance, Christopher held up a fist for his group to halt.

Charles continued the ambling walk for a few paces, stopping when he was close enough to speak without raising his voice. He studied the young man beside Nasir, seeing himself in his younger brother. Phillippe's letter confirmed the rumors Charles had heard of his other brothers. *Did Christopher witness those deaths? Or have any part in them?*

"You cost me a hand," Nasir said, breaking the silence. Charles flinched inwardly, maintaining as much outward calm as he could muster.

"Is that Charles?" Christopher glanced between Charles and Nasir, mouth slightly agape. Nasir stared at Charles, nodding once. His younger brother tilted his head, nearly losing his balance when the stallion pranced to one side. After resuming a proper posture, Christopher asked, "Did you know I would be here?"

"I do not wish to fight you, Christopher," Charles said. "What mission did Father give you?"

Christopher glanced between Charles and Nasir, eyes wide. The younger man shook his head, reins held loosely in his hands.

"To bring you home. Though I expected it to be … difficult." Christopher's voice was a soft whisper, almost overpowered by the occasional stamping of the horse's hooves around them. Charles nodded, wondering what his father might have planned.

"My time in Orda'an is over." Charles chose his words carefully. Christopher relaxed while Nasir pulled shackles from a pack. Despite his resolve, Charles flinched at the jingling of the metal. The grizzled mentor, whose ranked clothing showed he'd been demoted in Charles's absence, tossed the linked shackles over his shoulder, holding the pommel of his saddle with his good hand as he dismounted.

Nasir's brows furrowed as he approached Charles. "My lord, this man is a flight risk. How do you wish to proceed?"

Great. Treated like a prisoner. Charles dismounted and unbuckled his sword from his waist to lay it on the ground. He took several steps away, unbuttoned his coat to show no other weapons hidden on his person, and held his hands out to his sides. He could have avoided them, taken a different route to Jearnia, but Charles would not risk the lives of those inside Vandyl. Not when he could prevent harm from coming to them.

"I am unarmed and willing to return home." Charles glanced askance at Nasir, who looked much too eager to snap the metal around Charles's wrists.

Christopher did not respond as he stared at the weapon Charles had laid down. "I suppose a claim of willingness is not enough proof, given your history of disappearing." A brief, wary glance up. "But it should be."

An attempt to read his younger brother's thoughts as if they were his own was useless. He seemed to hold a tinge of agreement toward Nasir but also some toward Charles.

"My lord, do you wish to risk the man escaping in the middle of the night while we journey home?" Nasir approached, tensing as though he expected Charles to run away. "He broke his promise once before—"

"A promise I did not intend to break, Nasir." Charles lowered his hands and rounded his shoulders. He would have little possibility of talking sense into the aged mentor, especially since it seemed the years had only hardened Nasir's resolve rather than softened it. His lips tightened together, wary; the same could be said of his father's temperament. Either way, Nasir's presence was not helpful; he was positive his father would have at the very least demoted Nasir to a life of servitude in the Jearnian fields. "Place chains on my wrists if it makes you feel better, but I am returning home either way."

Christopher dismounted and walked several steps, stooping to pick Charles's sword up from the ground. He tested its weight, frowning at the curvature, at the hilt, and even the gleaming metal itself. After sheathing the weapon and tucking it into his saddle, Christopher folded his arms and tilted his head. "Did Mother give that sword to you? Right before leaving on this mission Father insists on keeping?"

"I had to earn it back." Charles paused, debating whether to explain what control Phillippe had held over his life. The clink of approaching chains brought him back to the present. "Mae gave that to me, with a message to use it wisely."

A subtle parting of the lips followed by a sharp inhale, Christopher mounted his stallion. "Do as you wish, Nasir. My brother may be here of his own volition, but that doesn't mean he may change his mind." His younger brother's gaze searched his own, but Christopher's blue eyes had none of the spark Charles remembered.

A small part of Charles's tension eased when Christopher referred to him as his brother until his once almost friend snapped the shackles around his wrists. Nasir's smug smile made Charles grit his teeth, especially as the man tugged the chain leading from the center of the combined metal locks. He could fight back. Even chained as he was, Charles knew he would give them a decent show. But that was not the goal. And returning with his brother offered an opportunity.

The chain became taut as Nasir approached his mount, and Charles sighed. With a fleeting glance back at his own mare, he asked, "Do you plan to make me walk, Nasir?"

"Let him ride." Christopher sounded distracted while his gaze drifted between the two swords. "It'll take long enough to get home without dragging him beside a horse."

"As you wish, my lord," Nasir said through tight lips, pulling Charles back toward his mare. He held onto the chains, and Charles doubted the man would ever release his hold.

"Why so long?" Christopher asked as Nasir mounted his own horse. "Why now? After ten years?"

Charles shifted, trying to calm the mare with pressure from his knees. It had been a question he asked himself daily for a while. "Part of the plan Phillippe created. There is much I learned from him." Charles glanced down at his shackled wrists and pursed his lips. "I wonder if he knew about the chains." He shook his head, dismissing the idea that the Gift was so visual. Charles looked up to meet his brother's gaze and offered a tense smile. "Time to go home."

33

Rosealyn walked back through the cave's narrow passage in silence with Celena by her side. Synda guided them, flicking spiked tail creating lines in the dirt. Every few steps, Rosealyn felt her side and breathed deeply. She had grown accustomed to the ever-present throb over the past few weeks. With it gone, she shifted her sword belt so the hilt rested on the proper side. She wrapped her hand around the hilt, tracing the emblem of the LeNoir crest as they continued walking. Her father's sword, her sword now. A legendary blade capable of killing a dragon.

Rosealyn gripped her dress-skirt with her free hand, wringing the material as they continued to walk. Her fear at Synda's appearance had dissipated into anxiousness. Rosealyn wanted to return home and, if needed, protect her people. She also wanted to see Charles and tell him what she'd seen. He'd listen, mostly in silence, but she enjoyed talking to him. She frowned, remembering Celena's mention of a Prince Charles and a Prince Christopher. Both names together tugged at her memory. As far as she was aware, Prince Charles of Jearnia had died in battle.

Back in the smaller cavern where Synda had first brought her, Rosealyn paused. She tapped one finger against the top of her sword hilt. The rhythm continued to grow stronger, becoming an incessant hum which refused to be ignored.

"Did she really use all of her strength to bring me here? Could she not send me back home in the same manner as I arrived?" Rosealyn nodded toward Synda, smiling as the fluffy white dragon turned about in a quick circle and settled onto her haunches, resting her snout on her front paws. She flexed her wings as her tail continued to drag across the mud-caked dirt floor.

Celena placed a hand on the dragon's snout, and Synda purred in response. Wings tucked into her sides, Synda nestled her head into the elf-woman's hand. "As I said, Princess, it can take decades to gather such strength." The tone was so matter-of-fact and simple. "Good thing humans can regain strength much quicker."

At Rosealyn's raised brow, Celena chuckled. "You could barely hold your sword upright for more than a few seconds. If we had meant you harm, I doubt you would remain standing."

Rosealyn swallowed, grip tightening on her sword. She hated to admit the elf-woman was right. But Celena spoke true; she'd be worthless in a true fight until more of her strength returned. She glanced at the cave's opening, noting the golden glow of the sun against the damp stone walls. "The summit is not for ten days. We're in a cave in the Mountains of Ingoria, yes? The far eastern side of Jearnia?"

"You are correct." Celena nodded, red-irised eyes twinkling with what Rosealyn could only assume was amusement. "It will take us three days by mount to travel from Andalova to Violet Grove. A better question to ask yourself, however, is what you feel you should do next."

A string came loose from Rosealyn's wringing of the dress-skirts and she tugged at it, thinking. All of her thoughts blurred together as she attempted to make sense of what she had learned and seen. Rosealyn grimaced and pulled the string free. "I need a change of clothes." She smoothed the skirts, frowning at the marred line running down its length. "And I should regain my strength. Especially now the pain is gone. I can go home—"

Words halted short as an icy sensation spread over her skin, accompanied by a frightful vision she refused to acknowledge. "My home is in danger," she whispered. "And there is nothing I can do."

Celena glanced over while continuing to stroke Synda's snout. "I will travel with you wherever you feel you need to go. However, I prefer to be on time to meetings, especially since Arjun likes to start them early."

"Arjun?"

Celena tucked chin-length white hair behind one ear. "My centuries-old friend. You'll like him."

The elf-woman patted Synda's snout one last time and met Rosealyn's gaze with those strange red eyes. It was the only truly distinctive feature Rosealyn noticed about Celena. Though her hair was an odd color, it was not an unfathomable one. "The mountain path is dangerous by day and worse by moonlight."

As Celena strode toward the cave's opening, Rosealyn approached Synda and held out her hand until it hovered above the dragon's snout. Synda lifted her head, nudging her nose against Rosealyn's palm. A deep rumble emanated from the dragon, providing an odd calm for Rosealyn.

"Follow me," Celena said from the entrance. A deep breath, Rosealyn let her hand fall from Synda's snout and obliged the elf-woman.

The path appeared more dangerous than the elf-woman claimed. Often, Celena waited for Rosealyn. It was a series of selective positioning of her soft-heeled shoes. Orda'anian court attire made the process more difficult. The bodice constricted her chest and the laces caught on stray branches. Worse than the occasional snag of those strings, the material was thin. Much too thin to provide any warmth against the winter mountain winds. Those were worse than the gusts of the Orda'anian plains. Not that she'd been allowed to experience those in several years. If she hadn't been conserving her breath for the arduous task of not falling off the mountain, Rosealyn would have laughed. Her father had spent so much effort keeping her safe, and a simple touch of a dragon's snout had whisked her away before she could blink.

Rosealyn's foot dislodged a slew of rocks, but she steadied herself with a hand on the mountain's rocky side. Wind whistled in her ears, whipping her wider dress-skirts about and causing her balance to shift. "I don't understand why Xannan waited for my father," she said in short bursts, trying to speak over the howling wind while searching for grips with aching fingers. Training on flat ground was nothing like descending a mountainside.

Celena held out a hand to help Rosealyn steady herself further. "I suggest we talk once we reach the village."

Rosealyn rested a hand on her abdomen. "You're not even out of breath."

A tilt of her head, the elf-woman chuckled. "I've traveled this path many times. As I said, I'll explain more when you are not avoiding falling off the mountain and have had proper sustenance. I imagine you won't say no to a proper meal?"

"A proper meal?" Rosealyn gasped and contemplated loosening the strings of her bodice at the effort to fill her lungs. "As in, not half rotten?"

Celena nodded once. "Jearnia and its plantations have, either fortunately or unfortunately, been blessed with Magna's protection."

34

Sounds of battle crescendoed within the walls of Vandyl's castle, and Xannan sheathed his weapon. The longer he held the blade, the more he wanted to satiate his own blood lust, wanted to release the pent-up anger welling deep inside. Pieces of his past, snippets he should remember kept surfacing and disappearing. Every attempt to relive them was almost as painful as receiving images from Eilon. Sometimes more so.

He shoved thoughts of his past aside to survey the unfamiliar castle. To his right were the training rings and barracks. An aging man with a solid black coat stood in front of the largest building, barking orders Xannan could hear from his place at the door. To his left was the castle proper. He visualized the path Eilon had shared as the blue sky glowed orange again. Screams of dying men made Xannan's skin tingle as flames flickered above the castle walls.

The dragon was near; Eilon was always near.

With each stride, Xannan heard the growing hum. The sound tickled at the edges of his memory. Eilon's response to any question over the past month had been the same. Seek the princess; reclaim the weapon. It made little sense. Based on his sword's reaction on the outskirts of Lycene, he had no need for another weapon. Yet Eilon persisted. That was his promise. Retrieve the sword and Xannan could resume his place as Orda'an's leader.

A month of occupying an abandoned city which lay empty once more. A month without visiting the queen. A month wondering how the princess had survived the attack on her father.

No need for fanfare or clever attacks. Not with a dragon on his side, a creature whose breath caused destruction of cities and fields with ease.

It had been too easy, really. Once inside the castle gates, a successive ring of weapons from sheaths met the pure terror of the Orda'anian army. Skirmishes initiated by the mercenaries he'd already paid thanks to the queen's generous contribution abounded. He avoided most of those, hunting for the one person he needed to find. Soldiers wearing black coats with white buttons and cuffs surrounded him, halting his forward movement. Xannan craned his neck from one side to the other. He pulled the sword free, admiring the color as deep a black as Eilon's scales.

A spear plummeted, and Xannan sliced its tip with a deft motion. Another sword met his, the bearer cowering behind a shield. A second spear neared the flesh of Xannan's bare shoulder, and this time he sliced through the man's arm rather than the weapon's base. Black lines spread up the man's skin as the poison embedded in Xannan's sword spread.

When a grunt came from behind, Xannan ducked, narrowly avoiding a heavy battle ax. He smiled, reveling in the sensation of blade meeting flesh. It had been far too long since he'd enjoyed a proper fight.

From his vest pocket he took a knife, thrusting it into the meaty leg of the ax-wielder as he wondered how long it had truly been. His brother shouting. Eilon's black cloud. A lost connection.

The other sword-bearer approached again, standing a little taller, weapon resting atop his shield. Xannan tilted his head, knife and sword resting at his sides. Small footsteps inched the soldier forward, halting when the commanding officer arrived. Blood lust threatened to take him, but Eilon intruded upon his thoughts.

The bladeless spear, now just a staff, approached him from the right. A quick stab with the clouded blade and Xannan looked over to see a young soldier gasping, clutching at his abdomen. Weapon withdrawn, Xannan turned to the older officer poised with sword and shield.

Sword held loose at his side, Xannan studied the grizzled soldier. A commanding aura radiated from him along with a resolve so determined Xannan knew it would only dissipate with a fatal blow. Another piercing reminder, strong enough to make Xannan wince.

Power or death were the only options he had left. With the other blade, he'd be unstoppable. His gaze lingered on the bold blue sky above. Not him. It was Eilon who wished for the other blade to be in their possession. Two blades of such power, blessed by dragons and forged by elves. But in the past few months, Xannan had not seen a single elf. Nor more dragons than Eilon.

"All I need is the princess's sword," Xannan said in a monotone voice.

Sweat. More death screams. Metal clanging against metal.

Shield raised, the officer lunged with his sword and grazed Xannan's leg. Xannan stepped backward and raised his sword to meet the second blow. He stepped forward, grinding his sword against the soldier's weapon until he was close enough to plunge his knife into the side of the officer's shield-bearing shoulder.

The soldier grunted, and Xannan twisted the knife. "Take me to Princess Rosealyn. Now."

"She's not here." The soldier lifted the sword with his good arm. Xannan twisted the knife, and the sword fell from the officer's hand before finishing its arc.

More Orda'anian soldiers approached, weapons raised, and Xannan looked to the sky, searching. The ground rumbled beneath them, but no more orange flame came to Xannan's aid. He ripped the knife from the soldier's arm, glancing toward the sound of a crescendoing hum. "I'll find her myself."

An additional group of soldiers approached, but Xannan did not play with them as he did the others. Quick strikes made quick, uneventful kills.

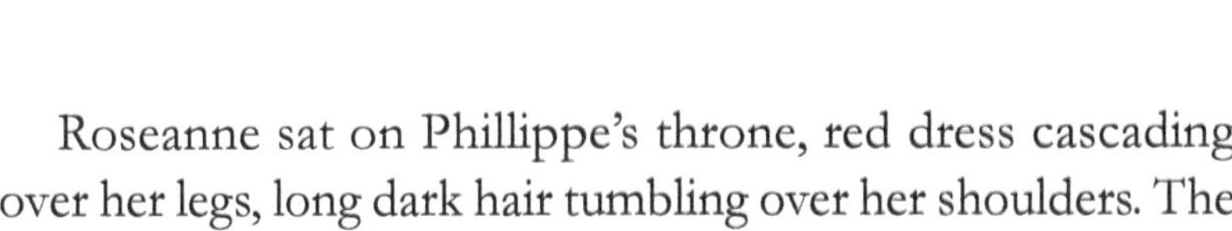

35

Roseanne sat on Phillippe's throne, red dress cascading over her legs, long dark hair tumbling over her shoulders. The room was dull. Almost empty. A pair of small, well-worn boots invaded her study of the solid stone floor.

"My Queen." She glanced up to find a frightened, youthful face covered in sweat. "General Azeiah sent me with a message. Princess Rosealyn is missing, and the mercenaries are upon Vandyl."

She had nothing to say. Nothing to do. She had been wrong. So incredibly foolish and wrong. Neither her cousin Ramon nor Xannan had ever meant to help her. They wouldn't protect the country from their northern neighbors. Instead, they were about to topple the country into their hands. And she had warned no one.

"My Queen?" Soft voice, meek, untested by years of trials and tribulations. Muffled shouts sounded, and Roseanne exhaled. Mercenaries approached, and she doubted any of them would let her live. Not when she had a semblance of claim to ruling what they so obviously wanted. Silence stretched, and the young boy's boots did not move.

"I would tell Azeiah to protect our city, but I fear Xannan is already within." She took a deep breath, grateful for the loose dress. Stray hairs clung to her neck, wrapping around her arms as a reminder she had not cut her hair since her sister had disappeared. Rosealyn had been so young when Catarina left in the middle of the night. Not even a letter of explanation. A singular green-tinged black rose sat in the center of her bed. Nothing else. Like a fool, Roseanne had blamed the girl for the tension between herself and her husband. It was not Roseanne's fault the Tenoan council had made the ruling they did. Though Phillippe did his best, that tension had always been there. From the moment they had all met, she'd known.

A second set of footsteps, heavier than the last, pulled Roseanne from thoughts of the past. From a desire to return to moments which could have changed where she had ended up in life.

A sword slid from its sheath, and gurgles precipitated the young soldier's lifeless thud to the ground. Roseanne looked up to meet the green-eyed monster her cousin had convinced her to trust. The tip of his blade was cold against her chest.

Azeiah entered the throne room seconds later. Blood trickled from a puncture near his shoulder, spurting as he lifted his sword and advanced toward Xannan. The weapon wavered. His movements were weak, the strained grunt too loud.

As Xannan stepped away from the lackluster swing, he retrieved a bloodied knife from inside his vest and plunged it into the same wound on Azeiah's upper arm. The blade's cold tip barely moved from her chest, even as Xannan wrenched his knife free of the general and returned his piercing gaze back to her. No flinch as Azeiah crumpled to the floor beneath her, groaning and cursing. Roseanne bit back tears as she shared a glance with the general. He'd tried to protect her.

"Where is she?" Calm, breath unhindered. Anger in Xannan's voice would have been less menacing.

Roseanne shrugged. She had followed her daughter, watched Azeiah give her the envelope, then returned to the throne room. A ridiculous thought that sitting in those seats could help her think. Now, even with a sword resting against her chest, it empowered her. Her fingers gripped the stone edges until her nails ached. "You can have the kingdom but not my daughter."

He barked a singular abrupt laugh. "Take me to her."

"No." She leaned forward until the pressure of his blade against her chest was almost too much to bear. The neckline of her dress shifted, and the sleeves clung to her arms. Despite the danger, Roseanne laughed. Boisterous, unabated as the realization settled. "You need me. More than I ever needed you."

Xannan snapped his fingers, gesturing toward her. But the odd-clothed men who had trickled in after Xannan and Azeiah stood dumbfounded.

Roseanne quieted her uncouth laughter and eyed the soldiers. Weapons drawn. Streaked with blood. Chests desperate for air.

"Eilon here?" She pursed her lips and leaned away from the murky blade. *Eilon's vision ... the chains.*

"Close." Xannan pressed the blade against her chest. It wasn't as cold this time.

"Eilon didn't show you where to look?"

He took another step, pressing until she wondered if it would cut skin. "Limitations."

The terseness confused her, as did his persistence on finding Rosealyn. If Eilon couldn't see her, then she had to be safe. Wherever the young, determined Rosealyn was, she would not rest until she knew her family, her friends, her entire country was safe.

Lieutenant-Captain Moss entered, shouting, "The mercenaries…"

He raised his staff and paused. Dark eyes shifted between her and Azeiah with an unspoken question. Azeiah's hand pressed against the wound, blood oozing through his fingers at an alarming rate. One nod.

"No." Her whisper meant nothing as the tip of Xannan's sword left her chest and seemed to float in slow motion. Black, white, and gray mingled within the blade. Azeiah couldn't move, not with the amount of blood he had lost. When the sword sliced along the general's abdomen, she gasped, surprised at how much blood could come from one man.

Tears clouded her vision. Phillippe's best friend, the man he had trusted more than any other. And she had lost him, too. Her gaze met Moss's, his expression a mixture of grief and anger. Roseanne shook her head, and Moss's staff fell to the floor with a deafening clatter.

"I give the orders now." Xannan calmly pressed the weapon against her once more. Warm blood trickled from the tip of the blade and down her bosom. Eyes closed, she took a deep breath, finding her love of the red hue fading. Pressure increased, and she swallowed the forming lump climbing up her throat as Xannan said, "Take me to her."

"Never." Roseanne met Xannan's gaze with a firmness of her own, though her fingers trembled in their grip on the edges of the throne. Her crown moved more without its braided nest.

"Ramon insisted on your survival, and your sister's." Xannan's words sent her heart racing. Several questions rose to the surface, but she had no desire to provoke him. He tilted his head and several strands of shoulder-length blond hair fell from their hold at the nape of his neck. "Fortunately for you, he has not confirmed completion of his last task."

"Lucky for me." Roseanne forced herself not to recoil from Xannan's appraisal of her. "What task?"

Pressure increased, and her chest heaved. *To provoke … the dead councilman. Was Ramon responsible?*

She shifted the blade away and stood. Xannan let it fall to his side, sheathed the weapon, and grabbed her arm. When she first met Xannan, his grip had been firm yet kind. Now it was immovable. He pulled, leading her from the throne room, out of the castle, and beyond the grand walls of dragonstone. Eilon sat there, eyes black. A small cloud floated in front of the dragon, the smallest she had seen of the few times it had appeared. Xannan pulled her toward it, his nails pinching her skin. Tugging against him was useless.

"Remind Ramon of his task." Xannan jerked her forward.

Unable to pull away in time, she stumbled into the dark cloud. It was like being tossed into the sea during a storm but without the cascades of water drenching her.

When it stopped, her cousin's broad smile stared down at her. Skin as dark as her own wrinkled by too many hours in the sun, black hair barely visible on his scalp. She reached to straighten her crown, but it was gone. A frantic search of Ramon's room, on whose floor she likely lay, proved useless.

"What task?" Roseanne stood and shifted her skirts.

His lips curled as he licked them. The stench registered first, and Roseanne could not stop the bile she'd trapped from escaping. Adrenaline, which had kept her resolute before Xannan, disappeared; the culmination of the deaths she'd witnessed with the deaths she saw now became too much to bear. It was not Ramon's quarters in which she stood, but the makeshift council room within the Tenoan castle at Delphi. The bodies of the council members lay around her. Lifeless.

"Welcome home." Ramon wrapped his arms around her in an awkward hug.

Roseanne shied away, staring at the dead Lord Asa, Lady Jalinda, and Lady Helen. Their vote had confirmed her marriage to Phillippe to settle the tensions their countries once had. Now she felt guilty for ever wishing them ill.

Swallowing, she held a hand to her stomach as though she could stop herself from retching. "You … he…"

Roseanne's foot slipped in blood, and she fell into one of the chairs forming a small circle around the bodies. Another swallow helped work the moisture back to her mouth. Despite the dryness, the whisper was quick to turn to a shout. "Phillippe was handling Hoclia and Alkaan well enough until you brought Xannan into the mix. Now Rosealyn's missing, too."

Ramon shrugged. "Xannan wanted Phillippe's blade; I wished to rule. And she's not missing. I have a message from Violet Grove to meet the other leaders. Her name was among those summoned. There was a debate about who should go and, well."

He paused, surveying the room appreciatively. "No more debate. Unless—"

Roseanne shook her head, unable to move any other part of her body.

"Good." Ramon placed his hands on his hips and frowned. "Time to ensure you don't mess anything up."

Roseanne stared, petrified. No amount of swallowing could stop her heaving.

36

Beside Christopher, Charles rode with a stiff back. Anger at his brother mingled with curiosity of what their father had planned. Each time he chose to watch his brother's expression, it transitioned between set determination and a softness Christopher had only seen from his mother. Their mother, he corrected, glancing down at the sword Charles had relinquished. The weapon appeared identical to the one she had gifted him. With a flame emblazoned on the cross guard and its slight curve, he knew their mother had designed both.

"Know what you're going to say to King Claude yet, boy?" Nasir asked. Every time he spoke to Charles, his tone became more degrading. Christopher didn't mind. Many of Nasir's questions were the same as those he wished to ask.

"I'm not a boy anymore, Sage." Charles glanced at Christopher, holding himself as though they were his escort. "And neither are you. I know what happened between Silas and Zane. But Caedmon?"

"An accident." Christopher shrugged. He had been there when it happened; he blamed himself for Caedmon's death. "But no need to worry about our dead brothers."

Monotonous plodding of the horse's hooves around them did little to cover the clinking of the chains connecting Charles's wrists. Christopher should have expected Nasir's reaction and wondered if he should have been quicker to consider doing the same. Even shackled, Charles remained resolute.

"You remind me of Mae," Charles said.

Christopher winced at the use of the term of endearment she had never let him use. The softness sounded strange to Christopher. His brother's voice was so similar to their father's in all ways except tone.

"Tender at heart but hardened by your lot in life."

"Watching your brothers die at each other's hands has an impact," Christopher grumbled. He sat straighter in the saddle and, having grown more accustomed to the stallion's movement, found it easier to look at their surroundings. An hour's ride, maybe two, would bring the Jearnian Hills into view. "Not that you would know," he added. He kept his voice plain and dry, watching for his brother's reaction. "Your leaving led to their deaths."

Charles didn't even flinch.

"And now—" Christopher waved his arms carelessly. "I'll probably be forced to watch another brother die." If Charles felt anything at Christopher's words, he didn't show it. So Christopher pressed further. "Father's angry you never sent word."

Charles shook his head. "I have no plans to die, Christopher. Certainly not at Father's hands or yours."

It was a simple acknowledgment of what could happen when they both returned. Hands clammy, breath short, the landscape around Christopher blurred. Panic welled in a way it had not since his youth. He had developed a mental thickness against his father's wrath, had worked to perfect those invisible callouses. Years of comparisons reared with ugly memories as he debated if his father had sent him to fetch the man who might kill him. He ground his teeth together, determined to prove his competency.

"You should think beyond Jearnia. I know Father doesn't. All of his actions lead to one goal: retake Orda'an." Charles paused and gave a slight shake of his head. "But it was never Jearnia's to claim." While Charles continued speaking about the status of the continent, Christopher shifted atop his stallion. His gaze roamed the countryside as he summoned his resilience, nudging his stallion to ride alongside Charles and Nasir once more.

"We shouldn't go back together," Christopher said. His mind raced, doing his best to place the details before he spoke. "If we both return, Father will have us fight each other for the crown. And he will not back down. It would mean death for either of us. Maybe both."

Nasir cleared his throat. "My lord, that is—"

"Foolish, reckless, unexpected, I know." Christopher smiled as he met Charles's incredulous expression. "I know I'm right."

Charles nodded once, and Nasir yanked on the chains connecting the shackles, almost pulling him off the horse. "I'd like to keep my other hand." Nasir's glower rivaled the king's. "You are both coming home. I doubt His Majesty will force another trial by combat between sons."

Christopher chuckled. "And if I left camp tonight, Nasir, would you go after me and risk losing Charles? He is the king's eldest, the son he's always wanted to have back home."

Nasir's glower darkened, spurring Christopher to continue outlining his plan. "Say it was an exchange? Tell Father that Phillippe—"

"Phillippe?" Charles's voice sounded too loud compared to his other words, and he raised his hands slightly to prevent

Nasir's pull, brows furrowing. "Phillippe died almost a month ago. Murdered by, according to Princess Rosealyn, a man known as the Lost Prince."

Christopher looked at Nasir and back at Charles, and his mouth went dry. "Once Father knows—"

"He'll send the army to take Orda'an," Charles finished with a knowing nod. "There's no reason he should. Father is foolish to want their land. Besides, there is also Xannan and the dragon—"

"Dragon?" The reins slipped from Christopher's hands. "Mother's stories…"

Charles tilted his head and nodded. "Definitely not just stories."

Nasir pulled the chains, jerking Charles to the side again. "Stop feeding him with lies, boy. Next time I'll make sure you land on the ground."

"Why would he lie about dragons? Or Phillippe's death?" Christopher gathered the reins in his hands, legs tensing to halt his stallion while wondering if Charles had been responsible for their rival king's death. No matter how much Christopher studied his older brother's expression, he could not discover the answer to his question. "No wonder you came so willingly."

"The ambush was not by my design," Charles said, seeming to read Christopher's mind while holding out raised palms. "I couldn't hurt him. Not after he gave me a place to call home."

Christopher's thoughts continued racing, trying to form a plan that would both appease his father and prevent him from having to fight his brother. He turned toward the horizon where Vandyl was no longer visible. "I'm going to take Vandyl and its castle with these men," Christopher decided. "Nasir, take Charles home and inform Father I have taken the Orda'anian castle."

Nasir spat an angry curse while Charles said, "That's an awful plan. What did you teach him, Nasir?"

Nasir ignored the question and met Christopher's defiant gaze with one of his own. "If you want to get yourself killed, my lord, go to Vandyl and take your chances. Or did you forget about the mercenaries we encountered?"

"I don't appreciate the mockery, Nasir." Christopher rolled his shoulders to straighten his back, jaw set. The demoted soldier had not been the one to train him. "I made my decision."

He turned his mount to face the group of soldiers, none of whom he knew by name. A grunt, then two thuds, followed by chains clinking. He counted his brother's steps, looking down when the clinking stopped. *How can he look so similar and sound so different?*

"I won't fight you, Christopher," Charles reminded him. "I wish no more bloodshed. Besides, I recall Father prefers when people do precisely as asked. Was it your mission to bring me home or Nasir's?"

Christopher looked behind him to see Nasir was brushing dirt from his pants. "Mine," he said with a dejected sigh. "Nasir," he called and waited until the man stood at his side. "Return to Vandyl, and take it as His Majesty, my father, has always wanted. I am aware fifty men are not the full army, but I'm sure Charles could share a map of the castle grounds which would assist?"

Though Christopher expected a reaction, his older brother kept his features neutral. "The patrol routes change often, and the throne room is well fortified." Charles did not look away from Christopher. No emotions flitted across his older brother's expression as he continued speaking. "Most of the Orda'anian army lives within the castle walls. Your fifty won't—"

"A map, boy, not a threat." Nasir crossed his arms with the stump visible.

"The outer wall is solid. Dragonstone. No way inside except the front gates." Charles shrugged. "Adept at keeping citizens inside, and even better at keeping enemy soldiers out."

"My lord," Nasir said, turning back to Christopher. "Are you sure this is how you wish to proceed?"

Christopher nodded, studying Charles as he did. *If it comes down to the two of us… If Father forces trial by combat… Can I kill…?*

37

Hours after Xannan had tossed the queen into that black whirlwind, nervous sweat permeated the hallways filled with chaos. A tickle of awareness made the hairs on Xannan's neck rise as he marched down one corridor after another, marbled black blade in hand. With each room torn asunder, he realized they had all spoken true. Princess Rosealyn was gone. He ground his teeth, shoving aside soldiers and servants alike as he continued his search. His connection to the blade waned, but the weapon itself remained effective.

A pallid groan led Xannan's gaze to the blood-soaked floor as a mercenary fell. The feisty lieutenant from the throne room met his gaze, turned on his heel, and ran. Xannan grunted and stretched his neck to each side, fingers curling around his sword's hilt.

Bare walls surrounded him. Battle cries sounded and faded. Men cried, yelled, shouted, slashed. And died. Xannan stared at his sword as the solid black transitioned to swirling ebony clouds.

"My … lord?"

Xannan recognized Blake's gruff voice and chose not to let his vision stray from studying his weapon. It was there. A faint hum. The other half. His other half. It yearned for him. Beckoned him as it had the moment he and his brother first held the swords in their hands.

He heard the ring of weapons, felt the rush of wind caused by their swings. But Xannan had vowed long ago to never let another blade pierce his skin. A thrust here, a duck beneath a forecast swing, a kick behind him—Orda'anian soldiers were less of an opponent than he had imagined. With each death blow Xannan delivered, he wondered why Eilon had spent years tormenting him with the image of his own death. *Years? Decades? Longer?*

The castle's defenders lay dead or dying around them. Xannan cleaned his blade and lifted his chin. "Problem, Blake?"

"It's Moss," Blake whispered, speaking with a touch of familiarity of the Orda'anian soldier. "He's—"

"Take care of him." Xannan sheathed his weapon and walked out of the castle proper to the training grounds. A castle like this needed at least a hundred servants and as many soldiers. He planned to question each of them until he learned where that weapon was hidden.

Shouts surrounded him, screaming about a group of soldiers outside the gates. He ran up the stairs, Blake at his heels, and studied the arrivals.

"Jearnia?" Blake said in a whispered shout. Xannan frowned at Blake and resumed his survey of the men below. Fifty mount soldiers in deep red armor, led by a one-handed man, approached the gates.

With a shake of his head, Xannan motioned for the gates to be opened. The crank worked its slow tune as Xannan marched down the stairs and through the gates. He cared little for the numbers or for the mere soldiers. It was an idle wonder if any would claim surrender, knowing he would kill them regardless.

"They won't hesitate to kill you," Blake yelled after him.

"Then come help." Xannan continued his steady walk toward the group of Jearnian soldiers. A country whose name he barely recognized. *He never mentioned it, which means there must be a connection between Jearnia and Magna. Otherwise we would have torched Jearnia's fields as well.*

He itched to pull his sword. Hack, maim, careless of who these men were or why they'd arrived. None drew weapons as he approached. Horses pranced in place, tails swishing in a beat asynchronous to the one drumming in his ears. The marbling colors of his sword brought questions he dared not ask the dragon, lest he see his own death again. But the other blade beckoned; he could feel its pull, could hear it begging to be reunited. After years of silence, he could point in its direction again. East. He needed to travel east.

The one-handed man looked confused as he contemplated what words he might say to keep himself alive, while Xannan contemplated if the Jearnians should have slow or quick deaths.

"Who are you to Orda'an?" The Jearnian's clear voice rang out like a musician's first note.

With a slight roll of his eyes, Xannan said, "None of your business." He eyed the Jearnian up and down, head tilted. "Who are you to Orda'an?"

"Their rival to the east, come to claim Orda'an for the renowned King Claude."

Xannan barked a laugh, squinting as the one-handed Jearnian dismounted and drew his sword. "Rival? Jearnia is the youngest country of this land and no threat to mine."

The Jearnian soldier rushed forward. Xannan sidestepped the blade with ease, and the force of the soldier's forward movement made him stumble and fall to his knees. A shadow hovered over them as Xannan's sword made one smooth motion from its sheath and through the soldier's good wrist. He stood above the injured Jearnian, sword point pressed against the man's neck.

The soldier stared at the bleeding blackening stump which remained, shivering as shock set in from losing another limb. Leather creaked behind Xannan, and he turned to witness the remaining Jearnian soldiers shifting in their saddles.

"You can join me and be paid." Xannan lifted his blade so all could see its hue and smiled as the deep gray clouds within darkened. "Or die the same death your lackluster commander now faces."

The handless soldier's shout for his men to attack stopped short when Xannan pointed his sword at the man's chest and explained, "Imbued with poison. A remnant of the dragon's kin that is now extinct. There is no antidote."

Several dismounted and approached with hesitant steps. Xannan wondered if the pulsing of his blade was faster or slower than his heartbeat. Soldiers encroached, and his men arrived from behind, slowing the Jearnian soldiers' steps even further. Their commander, stump bleeding, lay on the ground shouting orders, demanding those mounted ride forward in an attack. But none moved. The Jearnian soldiers watched as their commanding officer's severed arm turned rank. Blake stood next to Xannan, a tension emanating from him Xannan had not expected.

Several soldiers inched forward, holding sword hilts as though waiting for the right moment to draw and attack. Xannan did not give them the chance, and each soldier fell to the ground before they could pull their weapons free.

"Blake, take care of the rest. I could use more men. Useful men, not … these." Xannan gestured to the fresh corpses littering the surrounding ground. The blade wiped, he sheathed it, noticing the murkiness reappearing. Shaking his head did nothing to dismiss the obnoxious yet somehow comforting hum of the other half.

He did not wait for Blake's response, turning so none could see his hands trembling. The murkier the blade became, the more his muscles shook, the more he fought to cull the blood lust always raging within, and the less he succeeded. Not knowing where else to go, he walked back to the castle and renewed his search.

The army would be a distraction, Eilon decided. Xannan had enough distractions to last all the lifetimes Eilon had kept him quiet. Hiding above the clouds, Eilon beat his wings in a languid motion. The more he pulled from the land, from the men he encouraged Xannan to kill, the less it sustained him. He wanted it back. Needed it. Soon, he would reclaim his full power.

As usual, humans grew too scared, too fearful of the un-known. Xannan had failed in destroying the weapons. Not that he would remember the attempt. Eilon let the flame coalesce at his neck's base, allowing thoughts of Magna's trick to fan the heat. It was time for Eilon to return the favor. His island, his home, demolished. A desperate plea for aid. She could only trick him so once. He would not fall for it again.

The mass of flame grew within his neck as he glided below the cover of the dense clouds. Sometimes it stung afterward. The give and take of Eilon's aging magic was alive in fire. A whole castle full of men and women. Destroyed with a single breath. Eilon basked in the growing well from which he could pull.

The flame tingled in his neck, heat warming him from the inside, and it singed the back of his throat and tongue. The castle in view, he released a flame which grew stronger with every scream of death. Wider, farther, the flame grew. Only the man he'd named the Lost Prince could survive it. The blade kept Eilon's own magic locked within, protecting the man. No matter how hot Eilon's flame grew, not even Xannan's clothes would catch fire.

He knew. He had tried.

Orange flame turned a bold, harsh white. A distraction, the image he tormented Xannan with faltered. Changed. New futures awaited them all.

Eilon's growl rumbled deep in his chest. Even dragonstone could burn when the flames grew hot enough.

38

Find an area to rest, dismount, chain his ankles, eat, then attempt to sleep until the sun met the horizon. Another simple meal, remove the ankle chains, mount, and continue. Days blurred together and the bonds which never left Charles's wrists chafed, providing a constant reminder there was no turning back.

He'd forgotten bits and pieces of what Volante looked like and soaked in the view as they approached. The rolling Jearnian Hills had transitioned into the plentiful valley surrounding the city of Volante, backed by the imposing, snow-capped Mountains of Ingoria. Charles imagined how, from above, Volante would have colored squares, one for each small plantation families often fought over. The larger the plantation, the greater their impact.

A frigid breeze whispered around them, nipping at his raw skin. Following the well-worn path winding its way through city streets at a steady climb, they rode in silence, watching as men home for the midday meal ventured outside at the sound of horses' clopping hooves. Houses lining the streets were barely large enough for one man, let alone a family, to live in.

Beyond them stood sprawling mansions, filled with extravagant empty spaces which served no purpose other than to impress. Charles knew his cousins lived in those homes and wondered how many of them survived. He gripped the pommel of the saddle, trying to silence the clinking of the chains.

Charles sat straighter, meeting the people's gaze rather than shying away from it. He wondered how many staring through those tiny windows had been tasked with finding him, only to be demoted to slavery upon their return. If they got to live. Hushed voices filled with dark tones threatened to dampen his resolve.

The small homes of the city fell away to the castle walls. Tall, extravagant, unnecessarily overwhelming. Just like everything else in his home country. Beauty resided in Vandyl's simplicity.

Christopher grabbed the reins of Charles's mare, leading them inside the gates. Memories Charles had spent years suppressing flooded to the surface. He saw the wall where he and Silas once stood to drop eggs on unsuspecting servants, followed by the ledge Zane had often challenged him to run along and the training ring where Nasir had beat him, even after he had fallen to the ground. Charles took a shaky breath, staring at that ring. Nasir never stopped. Even if Charles bled or could barely move from unhealed bruises, Nasir never relented. They had trained daily as soon as he could hold a proper sword without falling over. In some ways, Nasir had been more ruthless than his father.

Thinking about his father made his last moment with the man resurface. The day he learned what his mission would be, what it would take to prove himself capable of assuming the throne. Followed by memories of trips into the mountains with his mother.

Christopher dismounted, motioning to the approaching soldiers. Gauntleted hands gripped Charles's arms. Teeth close to grinding together, Charles remained silent as the guards guided him toward his father.

Nerida sat on the throne next to her husband, stitching white cloth with red thread, weaving it in and out, each stab more fierce than the last as Claude snapped his fingers for his cup to be refilled. Nerida continued to stab the taut cloth, no pattern yet apparent as the thread moved along, each piercing leaving a piece behind. An image of her five sons floated through her mind, a scene she could never recreate.

She glanced askance at her husband, having lost count of the cups he had drained today. He lounged haphazardly in his throne, barely listening to the reports before sending some to the fields and others to the stocks. When a servant brought another pitcher of wine, Nerida motioned for the young lad to set it on her table instead. She placed the needle and cloth aside, poured herself a glass, and sipped, listening to a scout claim mercenaries occupied a city on the border.

"A week of hard labor ought to sober you up, child," Claude drawled, and a guard grabbed the scout's arm and dragged him out of the room.

The man's face fell in dismay, eyes darting to her in a desperate plea. She looked into the cup instead, flinching at her appearance. The large crown Claude insisted she wear slipped, and she winced as it tugged on a strand of hair. The scout began screaming. Screaming there had been a dragon and they weren't safe.

"When was Nasir's last message received?" Nerida asked quietly, staring at her reflection, dismayed at her sunken eyes and sallow skin.

Claude stifled a hiccup. "Why's it matter?"

Nerida bit back a retort. His drunkenness was a coping mechanism, a way to disregard any thoughts of whether they'd lost all of their children. She studied his lackadaisical stature, wrinkling her nose at the putrid smell of wine wafting from Claude's glass. Age had been kind to his grizzled features, but the more gray streaks appeared in his flowing dark locks, the more wild his moods became. And the more his thirst for wine disgusted her. "You're drunk, dear husband."

"I'm no less sober than an hour ago, Nerida," he snapped. "Send in the next scout. Surely one of them can tell me what is happening around us."

"That is what they've spent all morning doing, Claude, and you haven't listened to any of them. Surely the reports of the ten you already condemned saying the same should be enough proof. If you don't believe them, perhaps it is time you see for yourself?"

Claude sighed obnoxiously, waved the cup under his nose, and inhaled before sipping. "Let's not shout today, my dear."

Her simmering storm of anger and despair surged, but she veiled it with a whisper. "Why did you send all of our boys to their deaths?"

He snapped his fingers again, and Nerida replaced her cup with the needle and cloth. The sea of red grew, spreading the same as Zane's and Silas's blood had when they stabbed each other in this gilded room. The same as Caedmon's must have, after the supposed accident. No apology for pitting sons against one another. No explanation for not seeking answers.

Her times with Charles tugged at her as she pulled the thread, thoughts roaming to the last time she had spoken to him, the last time she had laid eyes on her eldest. Nerida remembered the fear and determination and the wavering drive to please his father. Tears dripped, darkening a section of the red circles as the thread tangled and halted her pull with the needle. She set the cloth aside and quickly wiped each of her cheeks with a silent wish that Magna's magic would protect them both.

Exasperated at Claude's uncharacteristic silence, she curled her hand around the cool metal of her cup of wine and glanced over in hopes to see him passed out from drinking. But he stared straight ahead. Muscles along his jawline twitched. Head moving slowly, Nerida turned to the doors. Gaze on the floor, ribcage near to bursting with the increase of her heartbeat, she chewed on her tongue until she could muster the courage to look up. She expected a body, another of her children dead. Limp, lifeless, void of color and warmth.

Red liquid spilled from her cup like a thin line of blood down her white skirts when she lifted her head. Seconds passed before the racing of her heart began anew. Eyes of pale blue, light skin tanned from days in the sun, and dark brown hair stopped at his temples, about to curl.

As her gaze roamed, she frowned at the chains upon his wrists and the hands holding firm to his arms. A brief survey of Christopher showed him unscathed and resting against the wall with his hands shoved in his pockets, so she returned her attention to her firstborn. Charles had grown taller, more mature and, despite the chains, stood as though he belonged, as though he were not burdened by anything.

Before she could stand and take a step, Claude's arm shoved her back to her seat. Cup tossed aside without a thought to the liquid within, Claude stood and drew his dagger. Legs useless when she attempted to stand, Nerida sank back into the throne.

Claude marched toward their eldest and did not hesitate in releasing a swift back-handed slap. Chains jangled and the thud of Charles's knees reverberated through the room. He steadied, wiping his mouth with a solid black sleeve. She stood then, willing her muscles to propel her forward. But she froze. Claude's mood was too unpredictable today, even for her.

"That's unfortunate." Charles rested his chained hands on his knees. "And here I thought I might have a decent conversation with my father for once."

"I am not your father." No sway marked Claude's stance, and he held his dagger much too close to Charles's neck.

Head tilting to meet his father's stare, Charles laughed once. Short and clipped. No show of fear etched his features, despite the sharp weapon resting against his skin. "If I recall correctly, threatening the life of a Jearnian royal is akin to treason. Unless it's a formal trial."

Claude's shoulders rounded, and Nerida braced for the quick slash. Dagger pressed against Charles's skin, Claude crouched in front of their eldest son. "There will be a trial, boy." Claude's breath hissed through clenched teeth. Charles did not look down at the blade, even when a small well of blood appeared along its edge.

"Dear husband—" Nerida's chest heaved, and her words lodged behind a lump crawling its way up her chest and into her throat. Vicious dark eyes rounded on her, but the dagger returned to its sheath, followed by a smack and another thud. She winced, forcing the lump back down and blinking away the impending barrage of tears. It was a miracle Charles's blood did not coat the floor beneath his feet.

"You have no sway in this, Nerida." Claude sauntered back to his seat. Behind him, Charles pushed to standing, acting as though the chains were invisible. "If he wishes to have my throne, then he can take it through trial by combat."

"Claude!" Nerida seethed, an arm outstretched. "Look at him! That is our son, our Charles, returned to us."

"He came willingly." Christopher walked toward his parents. "The chains were Nasir's idea, a precaution."

"Nasir didn't return with you?" Nerida asked, studying Christopher's calm walk.

"Once Charles told us of Phillippe's death, I sent Nasir to take Vandyl." Christopher shrugged and picked up the cup Claude had dropped. "He likely needs reinforcements."

"If they claimed the castle." Charles also approached, holding his hands so the chains connecting his wrists remained silent. "And, as the rightful crown prince of Jearnia, I formally challenge you for the throne, Father."

"Tomorrow, after the morning meal." Claude turned to her, a challenge in his gaze that to provoke would likely end in her own death. "The trial will decide."

Grimacing, Nerida stood in front of Claude and braced her arms on his throne. Heat rose to her chest and cheeks, anger scaring away her tears. "You will regret this," she whispered. "I cannot go through more … more death!"

Christopher moved closer, refilling Nerida's cup and drinking from it himself. "If anyone has the right to challenge another in this room, it would be me."

Nerida's shoulders dropped, and her eyes shuttered. "Mountains be cursed."

Claude glowered, and words darker than storm clouds came forth. "You wish to challenge me?"

"No." Christopher shrugged, leaning against the table. "It was a question and a thought. And perhaps a discussion to have when you aren't drunk, Father."

"Go," Claude said. The pressure of Nerida's crown tilting forward as she sank lower in her seat made her wince, listening to her husband's drunken insanity continue. "Prepare to join General Ashtar in the journey to Vandyl to assist Nasir."

"But my—"

"The king has spoken," Claude roared, wine sloshing over his hand as he pointed at the door. "Do as you are told, Christopher."

Nerida tensed. *They had to show up now, of all times.*

"Custom allows both challengers to have a proper night's rest and a proper meal," Charles said. For a moment, Nerida thought it was Claude who had spoken, the voices were so similar. But Charles's voice did not carry the slur of drunkenness. His words were crisp, untainted, and careful. "Which means it's time for these damn chains to come off. Set guards by the door if you must. I will be here either way."

Charles visibly relaxed as the chains were removed, gently rubbing his wrists and pulling the solid black sleeves down to hide the redness as best he could. Nerida etched him into her memory, amazed at how much he looked like his father. And the level of calm he expressed.

"I will stay with him until the evening comes." She approached Charles before Claude's arm could stop her again. Pity shone in her son's eyes, and glancing back at her husband, Nerida saw the anger with which Claude looked at his son.

"Perhaps we can find another way." She wrapped Charles's arm around her own. She wanted to embrace him, to fix him into her memory before he, too, was lost to her.

"I doubt that." Charles placed his hand atop hers and squeezed. Her heart beat a thousand times faster as they left the gilded room behind and entered the dark hallways. Charles was home; Magna had not lied to her.

39

On occasion during their silent walk, Nerida scowled at the two guards who followed them. Arm still wrapped around his, she guided Charles through the hallways until they reached his room. She'd made sure it remained as it always was, but Charles seemed not to register the simple stone nor the untouched furniture. If anything in the room dredged up years past, he didn't allow it to show. Not on his face nor in how he held himself. Once they sat at the table near the hearth, Nerida snapped at one guard to bring several plates of food. When she requested the doctor as well, Charles interrupted, claiming such a visit would be unnecessary.

After food arrived, she urged him to eat. "All you need to do is refuse trial by combat, insist your aunt and uncle come and determine your fate." Charles pushed his empty plate aside, and she filled another with pasta and covered it with sauce, setting in front of him. "Many will recognize you, will stand by you even. It may be possible to—"

"I appreciate what you are trying to do." Charles pushed the plate away again. He moved to rest his arms on the table, but the sleeves moved up to reveal reddened skin, and he tugged them back down, hiding his hands beneath the table. He was more than the son she remembered.

"Mae," he whispered, and she forced the sobs back down her throat at hearing the term of endearment leave his lips. "You've known no other life besides this one, and for that I cannot fault you. But do you know what's happening beyond the Hills?"

She embraced him, unable to find comfort in his mere appearance anymore. When he gently pushed her away, she said, "Some. Claude listens selectively. As always."

"Rose." He cleared his throat and spoke more levelly than he had initially said her name. "Princess Rosealyn is missing. Queen Roseanne—" His jaw clenched for a second before smoothing. "I'm not sure what she's up to, but something. Xannan killed Phillippe, and I worry he has Rose."

Nerida embraced him again. She wanted reassurance he was real, that she wasn't dreaming, so she tightened her arms around him and relinquished her hold. "A battle approaches. I'm aware." She glanced around the room. "The sword I gave you, where is it?"

"Christopher has it." He surveyed the room as well, stone-like features softening as he did. "Why?"

"I'll have it for you tomorrow." Nerida hugged Charles again, and this time he returned the embrace.

After a reassurance from Charles that he could take care of himself, Nerida exited the room. It had been only an hour of being in his presence, being reminded he was real, but she cherished every moment. He had survived. Not just survived. He had thrived while living with the Orda'anians. Although haggard from the journey home, he had taken care of himself, maintained his physique and training, like any soldier would.

Outside stood several guards, sword arms eager and ready. She looked at each disapprovingly and ventured to Christopher. *He has no need for both weapons.*

One knock and she entered her youngest's room, surprised to see him lying on the bed, staring at the ceiling. No packed bags near him. Clad in simple travel garb, Christopher didn't move when Nerida entered. Light from the flickering lamps around his room of crisscrossed wooden beams danced against the bared swords lying to either side of Christopher.

"Chains?" She rummaged through his drawers and packed a small bag for him. "What were you, or Nasir, thinking?"

Christopher huffed and sat up in his bed. "Why didn't you take the rest of us, Mother?"

Nerida tossed several more items of clothing into his bag, cinching it shut and tossing it onto his bed. "Magna's instructions were explicit." Nerida tightened her hands into fists. "You must meet with Celena. Which means you are leaving. Tonight."

Christopher undid the bag she had packed, shaking his head with a slight tsk. "You forget I've grown, Mother." He stood and replaced several items. "And Father told me to attend—"

"Your father is a drunken idiot," Nerida interrupted, and Christopher's eyes widened to the size of small saucer plates. It was unusual for her to be less than kind when speaking of Claude, but his ignorance over the past several days had worn down every nerve she could muster. "Willingly fighting his…"

She could not finish the sentence, could not acknowledge it. "If I—"

"Don't you dare say it aloud." At Nerida's heated whisper, her youngest's features softened. Barely. Moving to the bed, she sheathed each sword, handing one to Christopher while gripping the other.

Christopher grasped the sword and set it beside his bag, pulling out a set of plain travel clothes which did not bear the royal insignia. As he changed, he asked, "How will I know where to go? You never took me there yourself."

A smile tugged at the edges of Nerida's lips, a cross between disapproval and appreciation. Her youngest was more wily than she had given him credit for. "Follow the path at the mountain's edge. You know the way. You've been on it before."

A slight hesitation and he pulled his plain shirt on, gingerly tucking its expansive length into his pants. "You knew?"

"A mother is more observant than her children believe." Nerida decided against mentioning the accident which had occurred on the same path. "Now, go, before your Father comes. Tell Celena, the elf who will help lead you to Magna, that Ebios has succumbed to the chaos."

Christopher studied her for a moment and gave a simple nod. "Are you sending me away because you need me to give this message or to save me from the same trial which killed Zane and Silas?"

"Go, now, please," Nerida whispered. "And for all the curses the mountains could tumble down upon us, please be safe."

Christopher chuckled, gave his mother a brief hug, and left her holding a sheathed sword. It was a short walk to her private quarters; she refused to face Claude again until morning.

40

Moonlight succumbed to daylight, and Nerida had not slept. The inevitable occupied every lengthening wakeful moment, knowing Claude was not likely to change his mind. She had missed her opportunity to say or do anything. Not that he would listen. Her servants arrived, bearing several of her dresses. She surveyed each, choosing the one she liked the least.

"Quicker," she urged the servant, watching the lengthening rays of the sun crawl along the floor and holding her curls out of the way. The servant finished the buttons which ran up the back of Nerida's dress, the last one nearly choking her. She grabbed the necklace she often wore, positioning the winged pendant so it rested in the center of her bosom.

The necklace set, the dress placed, Nerida grabbed the blade and gathered her skirts to head to Charles. One soldier remained as guard and was quick to allow her entrance, but the room was empty. The many plates of food she had requested for him sat uneaten upon the table.

"Where is he?"

The guard pointed in the direction of the throne room, and Nerida hurried to its entrance, slowing as she came upon the open doors. Golden walls sparkled with the morning rays floating in from the windows in the ceiling high above, nearly blinding her with its intensity. One hand gripped her skirts, the other kept a tenuous grip on the sheathed sword. Around her were fully armored soldiers standing guard at intervals throughout the room.

Nerida approached the thrones, which had been shifted to one side of the room, and sat poised on its edge. Waiting. Her husband stood, unarmored, at the opposite end of the room. Glass of wine in one hand, Claude surveyed the rack of weapons. Though he inspected each one, she knew he would settle on his sword and the ever-present dagger tucked into his belt. She wondered if another hid up his sleeve.

The thud of the throne room doors shifted her attention to her eldest son, walking in surrounded by guards. Clad in the same solid black coat as the previous day, Charles pulled his sleeves down, but they were too short to hide the raw skin of his wrists. Nerida stood and met Charles halfway, handing him the sword. When she opened her mouth to speak, Charles gave her an understanding nod, and she clamped her jaw shut.

Where Claude would choose a blade which shone and glittered, Charles had a blade of efficiency. Custom allowed him the same perusal of weaponry, the same selection of armor. Charles chose a shield and helmet. Nothing more.

Nerida pitied them both and was about to speak when the doors opened once more, giving entrance to Claude's siblings. Her husband's younger brother and his family of four were followed by the elder sister's family of six. Claude had spared no custom. So far.

When she realized her lower lip was tucked between her teeth, Nerida released a lengthy breath. Cordial greetings passed between the siblings. Lukas, who was half Claude's age and whose children all stood below his waist, listened with wide eyes. Marsha, less than two years older than Claude, offered subtle nods. Her children stood along one wall, joined shortly by their mother, cousins, and uncle. Even Marsha's eldest was several years younger than Christopher.

"The noble families agree." Claude spoke in a tone that made Nerida scowl. He was already drunk, or extremely close to it. That was if he had sobered up after the incessant drinking yesterday. Or rested. "Trial by combat."

Threats must have been made. Nerida moved without thinking, whisking away Claude's wine and downing it before he could blink.

"You must fight with clarity, dear husband." She kissed him on each cheek and offered a tense smile. Claude returned the gesture by grasping her chin and kissing her firmly. She melted into him for a mere second and pulled away as quickly as he had pulled her to him. A step toward Charles was halted by Claude's tight grip on her arm, shifting the trajectory of her walk to return to the thrones.

After climbing the few steps, Nerida faced the wall. With no one watching, she wiped the drops which had escaped down her cheeks, dampening the few stray curls blocking her vision.

Cheeks dried, curls tucked back behind her ears, Nerida faced the open room and sat. Charles strapped the shield to his arm and lowered the helmet's visor. The blade sheathed at his waist really was simple, unadorned, and sturdy. *And more powerful than he knows.*

"Be careful." An almost voiceless whisper, Nerida was unsure to whom she spoke. "Please."

41

Brows furrowed, Claude stared at Nerida's back. When he had visited Christopher that morning, both his son and General Ashtar had already left. With Phillippe dead, no reason remained not to venture beyond the hills. He'd been a fool to let the smooth-talking, manipulative Phillippe strong-arm him into a decade of silence with a promise that any additional attacks on Orda'anian lands would mean the utter destruction of Jearnia. Like an idiot, Claude had believed him. Four of his five sons had been alive then. In his despair at losing his eldest, Claude had agreed to Phillippe's terms.

But a trial for his throne had been issued and would be met. And won. The boy, whose appearance reminded Claude a little of himself, stood too calmly in the middle of the throne room to be his eldest. Their son had never portrayed this level of poise; their Charles had been quick to anger. Despite Nerida's belief of the boy's words, Claude knew the truth: their Charles had been killed by Phillippe ten years ago. A decade of silence Claude had coped with only through one drink after another. Numbing his emotions with wine was preferable.

No reason to wait. Before Marsha could announce the proper proceedings, Claude lunged forward, sword aiming for the boy's unprotected legs. This Charles jumped back, but Claude pressed forward. He alternated the swings, but Charles blocked, sidestepped, or ducked out of the way of every strike until his back pressed against the rich golden wall. Claude paused.

After the flurry of blows, Claude's heart beat faster, blood warmed by a morning glass of wine pumping through his veins. He stepped back, pacing and monitoring the boy. Charles's sword remained sheathed at his waist. A sword Nerida had given him. Claude needed to annihilate this threat to his throne, to his kingdom. He glanced over his shoulder to see Lukas's youngest children hiding their faces while Marsha's children were mirrors of her icy demeanor. Claude hadn't asked their recommendations—if any were to rule Jearnia, it would be him. His sons were obviously incapable of leading. All of them.

Given enough time, and if he pressed hard enough, Claude could splinter Charles's resolve. He was certain of it. As he turned his attention back to the boy, he swung his sword and met the resistance of the boy's shield pressing back against him. The force of the push knocked the wind from his lungs and made him stumble backward. Charles finally drew his sword. He balanced it atop the fracturing wooden shield.

No reason to stop now.

Though the boy's sword was out, Charles continued blocking with the shield. Wood splintered with each blow until Claude used the hilt of his blade for one final thrust, which shattered the shield. Behind him, Nerida gasped, and his triumphant grin faded into a scowl. She, apparently, had the audacity to be concerned about this impostor.

With his shield useless and tossed aside, the boy stood to his full height, shoulders tensing. Claude had rested long enough. Wear down this man's resolve. Taunt this Charles into injuring him. Murmured voices drifted from behind him, but he ignored them. He had a fight to win.

He expected Charles to lunge and slash, but he didn't. Instead, he waited. Patiently. Claude frowned, hefting the blade in his hand while contemplating his next move. He feinted left, waiting for Charles to follow and turning mid-strike to slice his sword against Charles's right arm. It was enough to cause the boy's black coat sleeve to tear, revealing a minor wound. Claude grinned, raising his arms in celebration for being the first to draw blood. Claude basked in his pride for several seconds, hoping he had cracked part of the boy's resolve by wounding him first.

Nothing.

Charles paced. One step to each side. When his pacing stopped, Charles lunged at Claude. The sword didn't go where Claude expected. Each blow jarred his bones more than the last, until a searing heat flashed along his leg and forced him down to one knee.

Warm blood drenched his pant leg, and Claude's lips tightened. The boy had deigned to harm *him*. Charles held his blade leveled at Claude's chest.

Slow and cautious, teeth grinding both at the effort and the boy's audacity, Claude dug the tip of his sword into the marbled stone and stood. Blood trickled down his thigh and into the crease of his knee. When he tried to place weight on it, his leg buckled, so he relied on the sword to keep him upright.

More than one weapon could kill. And this one, this dagger, was his favorite. Ruby hilt gripped tight, Claude pulled it from its sheath at his waist and, placing most of his weight on the sword, slashed forward.

Too late, he realized someone had invaded their space with arms raised. His dagger met clothing first and then the familiar resistance of skin before a sudden release. He had not found Charles's side to slice against but his wife's.

Nerida gasped, staring at him in horror and disbelief as she stumbled backward into Marsha's arms. While Marsha gently lowered Nerida to the floor, Claude's fingers flexed on the hilts of both weapons. Sticky liquid squelched through the fingers holding his dagger. His wife's blood.

The boy had not only harmed him but his wife as well. "Fetch the doctor." Claude growled the words and did not turn his attention away from the boy who held his sword at his side.

Claude gritted his teeth against the lightning bolts of irritation beneath his skin where his leg continued to leak blood, rising to a tenuous stance and readying to throw his dagger. If he could aim true…

"I will not let you kill me, Father." The boy's words forced Claude to pause. Even the boy believed it to be true. But it couldn't be. His Charles was dead, and this man would soon die too.

Claude repositioned his grip on the sword hilt, deciding where to target his dagger. Beneath him, his leg quivered, and he swayed as his vision blurred.

"Please do not force my hand."

No quiver to Charles's raised sword. The lace of a plea coated his words. As if this man cared. But those eyes. The same shade of blue as Nerida's. Even the same slight twinkle. And the voice. So similar yet so changed. Claude shook his head and clenched his jaw. The warm fuzziness of the wine was speaking. Once he could focus on one spot, he'd toss the dagger and hit true, then snap his fingers and be rid of this challenger. If anyone thought to appear claiming to be another dead child, they'd think twice.

"They won't trust you." Claude ground his teeth against the pain lacing down his leg and blinked to remove the fogginess encroaching on the edges of his vision.

No quiver, no shake, no flinch—Charles's sword remained poised.

In his periphery, he saw Marsha kneeling beside Nerida. No doctor present. Yet. Then Marsha's melodic voice gave an unnecessary reminder. "It is a trial by combat. One must die."

Claude's chest tightened and beads of sweat formed on his skin from the effort of staying upright, of tensing so his leg didn't tremble. This could not be his son. No attack when the time was ripe? No Jearnian would shy from the final blow.

"There has to be another way." Charles lowered his sword, both hands resting atop its pommel as he lifted the helmet's visor and his contemplative gaze raked over Claude. "This should not have to end in either of our deaths."

Claude surveyed his opponent, noted the readiness of the boy's tense muscles, and paused when he noticed the flame emblazoned on the sword's hilt. Not only had Nerida given this man a sword, she had given him a sword with the Tremaine family crest. None but the royal family could use that emblem.

His lips curled, his nostrils flared, and Claude lunged, hissing through his teeth at the sharp jolts surging in his leg. His ruby-hilted dagger faced forward, aiming for Charles's unarmored side. In his lunge, Claude lost his balance and time seemed to slow. As his dagger neared his opponent, Charles's sword lifted, pointing at an angle that would impale Claude as he fell. Claude's blade met flesh, which gave way to it, but not enough. Though the boy's blood oozed onto Claude's hand and mingled with that of his wife's, it would be no more than a flesh wound.

The pain of Claude's earlier wound faded, replaced with a new overwhelming sensation. It suffocated him, crowded his insides together, and all feeling to his legs was gone. Claude fell to his knees and grasped at the blade protruding from him. This was no stab wound. He had felt those before. This was more. His hands gripped the protruding sword and tugged weakly, but blackness crowded his vision. Claude couldn't shake it away, nor could he ignore the taste of blood on his tongue, on his lips, nor could he swallow.

"Fool." Every other word he tried to say came out as groans. Cold. He was cold. Like the raw, icy mountain air that made one shiver with such ferocity they thought their body might shatter. His body convulsed, and more blood gurgled up his throat.

As the last vestiges of consciousness left him, Claude noted the grim dismay on his eldest's face. Charles's voice was hardly more than a whisper and rife with weariness and melancholy, but he spoke the words Claude had instilled into all of his sons.

"Kill or be killed is the way of life."

Had he any life left in him, Claude might have laughed.

42

As the light faded from his father's eyes, Charles's gaze fell to his sword protruding from the man's abdomen. His last words to his father echoed the last words his father had spoken to him. And they left a bitter taste. Worse than bitter.

Charles took a deep, shuddering breath and winced when the dagger wound in his side smarted. Blood trickled through his fingers as he applied pressure. He flinched, but the grimace represented more than the twinge of pain the pressure brought. More death had come to his family. This time at his own hands. He'd agreed ten years ago to protect his family. To save his brothers from the illogical deaths others of their lineage had suffered. To protect all of Jearnia from full-scale war rather than the skirmishes his father once insisted he lead. One small part of his agreement with Phillippe. But not even the kind Orda'anian king could change Charles's father.

Breath hitching, Charles bent down and pulled his sword free. It was not how he had desired to "take care" of his father. Blade free, he let his chin droop to his chest. Killing his father had been inevitable but far from desirable.

An ache, a throb, and he remembered his mother suffered a similar wound. He removed the helmet and turned to where

Lukas and Marsha hovered over his mother. Young cousins he did not recognize stood with blank faces along one gold-plated wall, as though this was not the first time they had seen death. Charles pressed his lips together and studied the youthful faces again. Some would have been present when Zane and Silas fought. Others were, hopefully, too young to remember such an event.

Shoulders drooping, Charles turned his attention to his aunt and uncle, who kneeled on either side of his mother. Charles paused, waiting to see the slight movement of her chest, and sighed with relief when it lifted. With a grunt, he lowered himself beside the others. Nerida grabbed his wrist and pulled him closer. Tears pooled in her eyes, but she met his gaze with one of understanding, not fear. The wound on her side was bleeding worse than his own, and the hand wrapped around his wrist was clammy, the color of her already pale skin fading.

"The doctor?" Charles glanced between Lukas and Marsha. His aunt gave a brief nod, as if to confirm a doctor existed in the castle, but did not move. A small trickle of blood leaked from his wound as he pressed against it while staring at the puddle forming beneath his mother. "One of you, fetch him, quick."

When neither moved, Charles shouted at the guards surrounding them. "Someone fetch the doctor! Now!"

The guards shifted, and Charles grimaced. "The combat by trial is complete. My father, King Claude, is dead." His tone laced with more force than intended, he said, "I am your king now." He pointed at the guard closest to the door. "You, run, and Blazes help you if you don't return with the doctor before that door closes behind you."

The guard performed an awkward salute and ran out of the room. *Did they forget the rules of trial by combat? Father was the one who ignored them.*

"Keep that sword close." His mother whispered the words, and her grip on his wrist tightened, making his raw skin flare with pain. "I asked Magna to make it for you, to protect you. I once thought she lied to me. That you died."

His brows lifted at the explanation of his sword's creation, and he settled back on his heels. "We can talk about this later, Mae."

"The dragons—"

"I know. I've heard the stories and read them."

The doctor arrived, prodded forward by the guard Charles had sent. He had to have been close, but he was not the doctor Charles remembered. This man was frail, no more than skin and bones. He joined the others in kneeling beside the weakening Nerida, and Charles noticed goosebumps riddling the ancient man's skin. Charles wrinkled his nose, watching the elderly man feel along the unbroken skin immediately surrounding his mother's wound. A crooked gash spread along her stomach.

From his pocket, the doctor pulled a small case housing both needle and thread. He looked toward Charles, and the prominent red eyes made his jaw slack. *An elf? In the castle? After Father tried to kick them out of the country?*

The elf frowned at the small amount of blood staining Charles's fingers and retrieved several vials from his pockets. After pulling the stopper, he handed one to Charles. The other he poured down Nerida's throat. Charles gripped the vial, staring at the elf's pudgier nose and narrow facial features. He struggled not to let his jaw slack further at the sheer difference in age since their last encounter. "Arjun?"

"His father. Eonar." The elderly elf gestured at the vial Charles held. "Drink. It'll slow the bleeding and assist the recovery. The queen may yet survive. But she's battling poison. Perhaps by the blade which cut her?"

Poison? Arjun's father? Charles downed the liquid. A warming sensation spread through him, and the wound ached less. Brows knitted together, Charles asked, "What are you doing here?"

Eonar slit Nerida's dress to stitch the wound as he said, "Magna was always a good friend to us, despite the chaos which engulfed this continent over a century past."

His mother gritted her teeth but did not scream as the doctor sewed her skin back together. Charles clenched his jaw, wondering if the doctor would insist on stitching his wound, too. It throbbed, but it was not the worst wound he had received, and ignoring it was simple. He shifted, sitting on the floor instead of kneeling, one hand pressed against his side.

"What fool of a king insists on trial by combat against his own child?" Lukas's question pulled Charles's gaze from watching the doctor stitch his mother's wound. His uncle frowned at the floor, sitting in much the same position as Charles. Next to Charles was Marsha, whose sole focus remained on Nerida.

Charles laughed, soft and short. "You expected different? Though—" He shifted, vision flitting over his father's body. "I'm surprised he didn't pit me against Christopher."

"I sent Christopher away." At Nerida's whisper, all focused on her. "I could not watch my sons fight again. But Claude—"

Her gaze drifted to the man's body, and her eyes fluttered. Eonar paused in his stitching, nodding approvingly when she took a shallow breath.

"Let her rest." Eonar returned his attention to inspecting Charles's wound, and his frown deepened. "No poison, but you also need stitches. And must rest."

Charles shook his head and stood. "No stitches. And no time for rest." After a quick survey of the bright, gem-encrusted golden walls whose shimmering surface he'd once admired, he breathed deeply. Voice firm, yet kind, he said, "Guards, assist Eonar in moving my mother to her rooms."

The guards hesitated again. Charles gritted his teeth and walked over to grasp the crown which had fallen from his father's head, careful not to use his blood-soaked hand. It was more opulent than he remembered, encrusted with at least a hundred jewels. A piece of metal. An adornment one should not need. But he had agreed. Even if he had briefly hoped to have a future without it.

With a small sigh, Charles set the heavy crown on his head. Marsha rose to stand next to him, and her soft voice carried in the silent room. "He won the trial and is our king, which you should not question."

The guards around the room offered tentative bows, and Charles's chest clenched. If gaining the trust of the guards who witnessed the trial was this difficult, he feared the country's response. Charles shifted his gaze to the plush throne his father had designed but did not move toward it.

He pointed at guards—all of whom looked odd and yet familiar in their deep red coats—as he spoke. "You two, help the doctor. And you, find General Ashtar. If he's already left, ride after him and tell him to return. We do not need to start a war with Orda'an."

The men he pointed at lowered their heads and left to complete their tasks. "Lukas, stay with Mother—"

"I'll stay with her," Marsha whispered loud enough for him to hear. "Apologies, my King, but most of your mother's extended family remains in servitude to Lukas."

Charles glanced at Lukas standing amidst his children, the youngest of whom had buried their faces into him. "I'd forgotten," he mumbled.

Marsha nodded with a kindness he did not remember and followed alongside the guards carrying his mother's limp, but living, frame. He wanted to rub his eyes and wake up in the barracks, where following orders was his greatest worry. But his hands were sticky from his blood. And his father's.

"You two." His raised hand shifted his sleeve, revealing the raw skin of his wrists. "Take care of my father."

"My King." Lukas approached where Charles stood alone. Despite his resolve, Charles flinched as more memories surfaced. "You should rest. Marsha and I passed Ashtar as we arrived this morning. It will take some time for the guard to fetch him and convince him to return. I can escort you to the king's chamb—"

"No," Charles interrupted. The two guards he'd last spoken to struggled to lift his father's lifeless frame. "My own rooms will suffice. I know the way."

"As you wish, my King." Lukas bowed his head and walked back to the children to guide them out of the throne room.

Charles watched them leave, understanding why Phillippe had always hated the honorifics offered. Even alone, he swallowed the scream climbing its way up. Fists tight at his sides, eyes closed, Charles sank to his knees. Grabbing the idiotic crown from his head, he threw it at the gilded walls. Jewels scattered, broken from their plentiful placements on the circle of gold no king of Jearnia would ever wear again.

43

The small city of Andalova welcomed Rosealyn. And suffocated her. One sturdy wooden home after another lined paved streets, each coated with vibrant vines of green snaking up their edges. The evening they'd arrived, Rosealyn had gone in search of a horse. Had even saddled the mare and led her to the city's edge before Celena stopped her with one simple question: "What can you do by yourself?" A question Rosealyn still couldn't answer. Not without meeting with the other country's leaders first.

Instead, Celena recommended they remain in Andalova for several days. First, the elf fed her enough food Rosealyn swore she could have fed Vandyl for a week. Perhaps longer. Then, Celena helped her recoup her strength. Not by holding swords or moving through forms. No, Celena's idea of helping Rosealyn involved hiking through treacherous paths Rosealyn would have rather admired from below. Plus some running. She'd seen Charles and other soldiers run around the training yards or beyond the castle's gates but had rarely taken part. Now she remembered why.

After two days of Celena's training, Rosealyn wished to return to Vandyl and those she was accustomed to sparring with.

Though she worked with several of the soldiers, Rosealyn had learned their habits. She knew how Moss forecasted a swipe to the feet, always noted the subtle drop of Daniel's shoulder before he loosed a hesitant strike of his fist. Charles, no matter how often she watched him train with others or sparred against him herself, was the only one whose next move she could never anticipate.

Today, the fourth day since she'd arrived, Rosealyn stood in a small garden behind the home she assumed must be Celena's. She wore a dark shirt and pants akin to Celena's, along with boots the elf had provided. All of which allowed for an ease of movement Rosealyn adored.

Three swift strikes and Rosealyn fell to her knees with a blade held close to her neck. She scowled and whipped her head back as she grasped Celena's arm and pulled. The elf tensed, forcing Rosealyn to use all of her strength to topple Celena to the ground.

No sword. No dagger. No weapon of any kind, so Rosealyn stood and pressed her booted heel on Celena's chest and smiled. "Nice try."

"Proper sustenance helps, does it not?" Celena tapped Rosealyn's foot aside, and she obliged, allowing the elf to stand.

"True." Rosealyn crossed her arms and glanced up at the mountains towering over the small village. "I still want to return home."

"Synda was too afraid to get close. Eilon was there when she tried. You should be grateful Synda brought you when she did." Celena brushed the dirt from her pants and tilted her head. It was the motion she made whenever she seemed to listen. As Celena had claimed, and proven, she could communicate with the dragons as if holding a conversation with another elf. Or human. Nevertheless, the words of confirmation that her home was harmed grated on Rosealyn.

She grimaced and tapped a finger against her arm. "I should go home." She forced her finger to still and turned westward. Quaint homes blocked the view. Bushes, flower beds of vibrant color, and trees taller than she'd ever thought possible surrounded the thriving garden-like city of Andalova.

A chilling breeze nipped at her arms, and she sighed. "But, as discussed, returning home by myself would be foolish."

She closed her eyes and breathed deeply, allowing the visual she'd first denied to surface. Her home encased in fire. She swallowed, wondering how hot a dragon's flames must be if they could melt stone with such ease. Six days remained until the summit Arjun had organized at Violet Grove. Six days Rosealyn could use to travel home and see what had happened for herself. She released a long breath and shook her head. "You claimed both of the Twin Blades are needed to kill Eilon. I have one sword. And no soldiers to help me fight Xannan to take his." She scuffed the stones beneath her feet and frowned. "Every time I consider going, an icy dread overwhelms me. I don't see my death, but I don't see success either."

Before Celena responded, one knock sounded on the front door, followed by a voice calling out. "Celena?"

The elf squinted at her home, lips pursed as she gave a subtle shake of her head and walked back through small rooms filled with wooden figurines and plush furniture to open the front door. When Celena moved for the newcomer to enter, Rosealyn gasped, wondering if time had reversed. The color of his eyes, the bone structure. If she cut his dark, curly hair and scarred his chin, he'd be the spitting image of Charles from when he'd first arrived at Vandyl.

The newcomer took one step inside and surveyed the home, snagging for a second on Rosealyn. She bristled at the brief appraisal and retrieved her sword from its resting place beside the back door.

"Celena?" he asked. She offered a silent nod, and the young man tensed. "Mother said I should speak with Magna."

Celena closed the front door and leaned against it with arms crossed. "Did she not tell you of the path, Prince Christopher?"

His brows furrowed at Celena's question, and he shot Rosealyn another wary glance. "She did." Christopher placed his hands on his hips, jostling the sword at his side as though he rarely wore it, and shook his head full of shoulder-length curly hair. "She also said to tell you how Ebios has succumbed to the chaos. Whatever that means." He scoured the room again, squinting at Rosealyn as he asked, "So can I speak with Magna as my mother instructed?"

"Magna is resting. She will not speak with you." Celena lifted from the doorframe and tied her white hair back. Several strands loosened immediately, too short to be contained. "She took enough risk communicating with Princess Rosealyn."

When Christopher's gaze shot back to her, Rosealyn bit the inside of her cheek. He moved further inside the home and lounged in one of the plush chairs. "Will not speak with me?" He leaned forward and tapped a small wooden figurine resting on the table between the chairs. "Interesting."

Celena whisked the figurine away from him and set it on a ledge. "Nerida begged Magna for that sword of yours to be blessed, worried for your safety. Magna did not see fit to waste such effort on you; however, Synda could not refuse Nerida." She turned and frowned. A different figurine had made it to Christopher's hands. "Your brother is more trustworthy than you."

Christopher chuckled and set the figurine back on the table. "How can you say Charles, who lied to an entire kingdom for ten years, is more trustworthy than I?" He leaned back again, arms languid at his sides, though he flinched as the sword shifted. "Mother simply told me where to go and whom to seek. There was no explanation of why."

Ten years? Blazes. She inched her way to the seat opposite Christopher and sat with her sword atop her lap. It became difficult to meet Christopher's gaze; the resemblance was too similar. Instead, Rosealyn focused on the pale wooden floors as the feeling she had always reserved for her mother coalesced.

"Charles lied to me?" She meant it as a question, but all she managed was a whisper. Her grip of the sword tightened and her breaths shortened. "He lied to all of us."

"He's home now," Christopher said. She couldn't lift her chin, not when she was losing her tenuous hold on her emotions.

"Good." Celena's voice sounded closer. "You can join us on the journey to Violet Grove. We should leave—"

"What do you mean 'he's home now'?" Despite her concern she might fall from the edge of her seat, Rosealyn leaned forward and forced herself to lift her gaze.

"Father instructed I bring him home." Christopher shrugged. "So I did. Mother wanted to make sure Father didn't force us to fight." Another pause, this time accompanied by a flitting emotion Rosealyn couldn't place. "Perhaps she does like me more than Charles, unlike Father."

Rosealyn swallowed, and her shoulders tensed. She could not decide where to look or what to say or how to react.

"Dear princess." Celena's admonishing tone elicited another harsh swallow from her. "Did you never learn the names of the monarchs and their families of your surrounding kingdoms?"

She shifted, muscles shaking from tenseness. "A name can be held by more than one," Rosealyn whispered.

A sigh followed by a dismissive wave toward the young Charles look-alike, Celena announced, "Meet the youngest of the Jearnian princes. He and Charles are the last remaining heirs to that throne."

Christopher's jaw hardened at the statement, but he said nothing.

"You took him home?" Rosealyn loosened her hold of the sword as she remembered the singular image Synda had shown her of Charles and how her favorite black roses were missing. *Not missing. Because Charles isn't at Vandyl anymore.*

"That was the mission." Christopher crossed his arms. "Father also told me to attend General Ashtar to assist Captain Nasir with taking Vandyl, but Mother was quite persistent I come here instead."

"Mission?" She shook her head. It added up. The timeline, their uncanny resemblance. But she didn't want it to be true. "What would your father want with Charles? He's a Banner-Captain in the Orda'anian army and one of my bodyguards."

"And my brother." Christopher positioned himself on the edge of his seat and rubbed his hands. "So." He drew the word out and looked her way, but Rosealyn studied a unique wooden figurine to occupy her vision. Celena had many. Most were different sized dragons, all painted a rainbow of hues. With a hint of amusement, he said, "Either Charles or Father is dead, and the living man rules Jearnia."

Rosealyn tried to work moisture back into her mouth to no avail. Even with the loose shirt, her skin felt flushed. This young prince spoke as if he didn't care who survived. She chewed on her tongue and chose not to continue down that line of thought. "You were inside the castle at Vandyl?"

He grunted and shook his head. "Charles came to me. Outside the gates."

Celena cleared her throat. "We should—"

"I have to speak with Charles." At her outburst, Celena's brows rose and Christopher chuckled.

"There is no way to know he's alive." Christopher's nonchalant tone in discussing who lived and who died turned Rosealyn's stomach, but her resolve splintered when the young prince explained, "A challenge for the throne was issued. When done properly, only one lives."

One question dominated her thoughts, and she dared not ask it aloud. *He's killed in battle before, but his own father?*

"Either way, the threat posed by Eilon and Xannan affects Jearnia as well." Rosealyn's determination surged. She had enough time to visit both. She'd rather learn Charles's fate than continue hiking mountain trails. And if Charles had become king, she could ask him for help. Refusing to consider the young prince's other implication, Rosealyn stood and buckled the sword around her waist. "Take me to your capital city, to Volante."

While Celena muttered about distances, the time it could take to travel, and making the other leaders wait, Rosealyn proffered a poignant reminder the summit was six days away. Besides, she wouldn't budge. Not when the urge to know overwhelmed her.

"I should warn you." Christopher spoke in his same matter-of-fact tone when Celena acquiesced to Rosealyn's request. "Father does not hesitate to kill."

44

Rosealyn,

I usually write to you daily, but I received a letter from Phillippe the same day I learned of his death. If I can feel such grief after so many years apart, I cannot imagine the despair you must have experienced in the past month.

I made plans to return to Orda'an but could not keep them. The elves are angry. The few humans I represent are making ridiculous demands, and the other races act as though we have never considered their plights before.

Despite not being the first race to arrive on Izari, the elves (whom Naomi represents) get their way too often. Ruth has become our mediator as best she can.

I have little time now. Please take care of my sister, and stay safe yourself.

With love,

Catarina

She tapped the excess liquid on the quill into her tub of ink and covered it. With the amount of writing she had done for their meetings, only a thin layer coated the ink tub's bottom. Catarina moved the single paper aside, allowing it to dry away from the danger of her tears. This letter would join the hundreds she'd written to her daughter hidden within the bottom drawer of her small desk. Never to be sent or read.

A knock against the wooden frame brought her attention to the opening the people of Izari called a doorway. Naught but a flimsy sheet covered the entrance, and Naomi did not wait for an acknowledgment before entering.

The elf's shorter height never hindered the woman's aura, even in combination with Naomi's deceptively slight frame. She kept her hair short, the white strands barely touching the edges of her round face. Every day she wore the same style dress of varying solid colors. The dresses clung to her bodice and waist and flared out slightly at the knee. Even the sleeves looked too snug for Catarina's preference.

Today Naomi walked in wearing a deep green, the color rich enough to effortlessly hide in the depths of the jungle surrounding Izari. Colors of a setting sun danced along the sky, marking the time of day when Catarina preferred to be alone. Shouting in the streets meant the city had other plans.

"I thought you decided to return home," Naomi said.

"And leave my people with no representative?" Catarina looked out her one small window. In the muggy heat of Izari, she wore her dark red-tinged hair in a tight braid. Rather than pin the braid to the top of her head as she knew Roseanne would as Orda'an's queen, Catarina wore her braid down.

"Understandable." Naomi clasped her hands behind her. "Recent decisions have become lopsided."

Catarina harrumphed while etching the colors of the sky into her mind so she did not have to meet Naomi's prying red eyes. "All voices should be heard, Naomi. We cannot squander those who wish to speak."

"They spoke, we listened, we decided," Naomi said non-chalantly. "That is the process."

"They spoke, we listened, *you* decided," Catarina corrected, biting back the urge to admonish the elf further. "There is much unexplored land on the islands of Izari. This ruling body we created may be sufficient for our community, but we cannot force everyone to stay."

"You should return to Orda'an." Naomi turned away from the window to look at Catarina's paintings hanging on the wall above her bed. During her journey through Orda'an while pregnant with Jaida, she had imprinted the country's beauty onto paper. Her favorite image was that of the Guadelaide River weaving its way through Violet Grove under the cover of the Shendaran Forest. She had delivered her daughter as the leaves fell, and the soft differences between brown, orange, and deep green took her several weeks to perfect.

"Jai—" She grimaced, reminding herself to use the name by which the world knew the young woman. "Princess Rosealyn can certainly care for Orda'an as its rightful heir; she has no reason to need my assistance, not when I am needed here."

"You should go," Naomi reiterated. Catarina looked away first. Not until the elf's footsteps had dissipated did she dare shift her focus. As she listened, the shouting in the streets grew louder. No rest awaited Catarina that night.

PART THREE:
THE GIFT'S PRICE

As Christopher led the two women through the fading paths which once connected Andalova and Volante, he kept a close eye on the Orda'anian princess. Her facial expressions changed as quickly as the direction of the breeze during a valley storm. He could feel Celena's gaze on him, knew she didn't trust him. But what his mother told him to do, he would do. She had saved Christopher from his father's drunken tirades too many times to count, and he wondered if his father might have beaten her for it. He wouldn't put it past the man. Granted, his father did sometimes apologize. Not that those apologies changed anything. So when his mother insisted he leave, Christopher listened.

The horses made the journey back home swift. He thought of demanding to speak with Magna, but that argument seemed useless. He would not admit such out loud, but he feared Magna's reaction to meeting him if she had refused his mother's request to protect him.

As they crested a hill, Rosealyn asked, "Why is it all so—" She waved a hand at the valley spreading before them. "Uniform?"

"The plantations?" Christopher glanced over to see her confused expression as she nodded. "Each plantation is owned by relatives of the Tremaine royal family. Right now, that is my Aunt Marsha and Uncle Lukas. Higher nobles, those who have proven capable of the responsibility, serve as overseers of each major grouping, based on what they produce. The civilians live on the edges of the plantations."

"In those tiny cubes?" Rosealyn's voice had layers of emotions, shock and concern most prevalent.

Christopher scrunched his brows and nodded. "How else would one run a country?"

"With love, care, and affection, not some—" Rosealyn gestured with an arm. "Some strange organization scheme!"

A soft grunt escaped his lips. "Your people may be starving, but even those demoted to servitude are fed here."

Christopher did not think his tone unkind, given what she had already mentioned of her home, but Rosealyn's glare said otherwise. He rubbed his chin and said, "Welcome to the Jearnian capital, Princess Rosealyn. My home, and the once home of my four older brothers, Volante."

"Four?" Rosealyn's voice rose sharply, and he studied her as she looked at the castle, dismayed by her lack of awe.

With a sigh, he explained. "Charles, believed dead ten years past; Zane and Silas, challenged one another for the throne when Charles did not return, and neither survived; Caedmon's death was an accident."

"Why didn't Father tell me?" the princess whispered, glancing west, toward her home. It was a constant motion, one Christopher wondered if the princess realized she did.

Momentarily disappointed she did not ask more questions about his brothers' deaths, Christopher wondered if he could ever admit to his own actions. Rosealyn's surveying of the land seemed to skip the castle itself, avoiding its grandiose nature, awed instead by the simple beauty of nature. Christopher understood, and often felt the same about the dank castle, wishing he'd ventured outside its walls more often.

He turned back to Celena. "You should stay outs—"

"You do not command me, Christopher." Voice as sharp as her gaze, she sat taller. "My people may help yours, but our roles in this land do not give you the right to tell me if I can or cannot enter this castle. Without me, you would not have that protection around your waist."

Christopher glanced down at his sword belt, forehead scrunched, lips pursed. "Fine." He stared at the main path leading to the castle, unsure whom he wished to find. "But remember my warning, Princess. Father does not hesitate to kill."

He noticed the princess's swallow, the quickening breaths, the shifting of her gaze from one thing to the next, and her inability to stay focused. But her tone remained devoid of emotion. "Is that a threat to me?"

Her soft, simple words carried an edge to them. An acknowledgment of her own loyalties. Christopher glanced back at Celena and returned his attention to the princess. "Only on behalf of my father. For myself, I have no need of your lands."

He let the words linger, making it obvious he had not finished the thought. Uncomfortable silence followed them until they reached the castle gates. Guards posted atop the walls did not question his arrival, though he gripped the medallion hidden beneath his shirt as they entered. A quick glance at the fading silver metal revealed the same emblem of his sword gilded on its front. A dragon's head spouting fire. Every unique item he owned had that front and center: a dragon's head spouting fire. *And I haven't seen one. Yet.*

Once comfortable attire felt too plain when surrounded by the deep red of Jearnia's colors. His loose shirt and pants were a far cry from the fanciful outfits a Jearnian royal typically wore. Dark colors made it much easier to blend in than the bright red and orange coat his father always wore.

Releasing the medallion, Christopher halted his horse and said, "We can rest—"

"Rest?" Rosealyn interrupted with a vehement shake of her head. Long strands whipped from shoulder to shoulder, further loosening the faltering braids leading from her temples to the back of her head. The muscles of her arms tensed as she tightened her hands into fists. "I've done enough resting for the past month. Lead the way."

Christopher pursed his lips, handing the horse's reins off while Rosealyn and Celena did likewise. The princess's hand wrapped around her sword's hilt like she thought it might disappear if she wasn't gripping as tightly as her dainty fingers could.

He led while they trailed behind. Occasionally, he glanced back, hoping to see awe inscribed on their faces. His home was dank but beautiful. Decaying yet breathtaking. Footfalls reverberating against the dulling gray stone, Christopher recalled his favorite poet. An ancestor of his mother's, who wrote about loss, doubt, and fear. Those emotions only tipped the peak of what one would experience when standing before his father. A brief thought slithered from the depths, wondering if standing before Charles as their king would be better or worse than facing his father.

The echoes haunted him. How many times had his own feet sounded alone, praying to whatever invisible force could save him from his father's wrath? From his father's disappointment? From the comparisons? Unadorned walls juxtaposed by inordinately decorated doors. Wood with immaculate carvings, painted to the king's satisfaction. Destroyed by the king's own hand. Recreated with the trembling fingers of ones who feared a sudden unexpected death. The same which could await the princess trailing him if his father awaited within the golden-walled throne room.

Least decorative of all were the doors which identified the throne room. No guards stood by their side to push them open. So, without hesitation, Christopher did, wincing at the bright glint of the surrounding metallic walls which glimmered with the rays of sunlight filtering through the windows high above. A quick survey found a select few guards, and then Christopher's sweeping observation halted.

Both thrones sat empty, save for his father's almost jewel-less crown. He met his brother's pitiful, apologetic gaze from where Charles stood with hands resting against a table.

Christopher tightened his lips into a thin line, wondering if he should feel an ache of disappointment or a soothing calm enveloping him. He tilted his head. "Father must have been drunk during the fight."

Still wearing the clothing of Orda'anian soldiers, Charles bristled and tugged at each sleeve. "Father's fighting was pre-dictable. He did not back down when…"

Christopher glanced behind to see Rosealyn walk forward with one hand tight around her sword's hilt. This time it was Christopher who bristled.

"She insisted." Christopher gestured toward the princess and shoved both hands into his pockets. Recognition and con-fusion warred with each other across Rosealyn's dark-skinned visage. Christopher moved aside to allow both Rosealyn and Celena to enter the throne room and leaned against the wall.

In one way, he had been demoted; in another, he had been saved.

"I—" The princess straightened to her full height. Were it not for wearing the travel garb of the elves, Christopher might have described her posture as regal. She stood only one pace inside the doors, staring at Charles as she tried to speak again. "We—"

Charles tugged at both sleeves, failing to hide the fading red of his wrists. Emotions surged and faded inside Christopher, so he focused on his older brother and the Orda'anian princess while wondering precisely what their relationship had been.

While Charles and Rosealyn stared at each other with words evident on the tips of their tongues, Christopher surveyed the room and almost missed the general whose fanciful armor blended into the walls surrounding him. "General Ashtar, why—"

"Do not speak for me, Christopher," came a harsh command from his brother, though Charles's eyes lingered on the princess. Christopher followed that gaze to see Rosealyn's expression fall as Charles spoke, as though such a tone confirmed the suspicions she already had. *How naïve, to not know.*

"I told Ashtar to return home so Princess Rosealyn has a home to return to someday."

"My King, a reminder." Despite Charles's scowl, Ashtar continued. "Nasir will need aid at Vandyl."

His brother, now his king, scoured the documents before him and did not answer. Celena stood at the open doors, watching disapprovingly. Leather creaked as Rosealyn shifted her hold of her sword's hilt, appearing as if she felt trapped.

"Did Father know?" the princess asked, breaking the awkward silence.

Charles nodded, eyes darting toward her without lifting his gaze.

"So why not tell me?" She took one step forward. Tension radiated from her. From them both.

His older brother shrugged, but a muscle in his jaw ticked. "Fear, at first." Charles gripped the edges of the table with arms that seemed to tremble. "And Phillippe told me not to. Ordered me not to. Part of the agreement."

"Fear? The Orda'anians?" Christopher asked, surprised a laugh didn't escape. "They are nothing like Father was."

"'Kill or be killed is the way of life,'" Charles quoted, his voice eerily similar to their father's.

After pushing away from the wall, Christopher asked, "His last words?"

"The last he heard." Charles frowned and lifted to his full height, facing the princess who stood as though frozen in place. One of Rosealyn's hands held the sheath of her weapon, the other on the sword's hilt as though she might draw it and attack. If Charles worried she would, his face did not show it.

Brows furrowing so they wrinkled his forehead, Charles asked, "Why are you here, Ro—" Charles cleared his throat. "How are you here, Princess?"

46

Not only was the room too bright, Rosealyn could not meet Charles's gaze. Her throat parched at the reality of what stood in front of her. A king. He was a king while she was a fool of a princess. Naught but a clueless fool who should have known when her father returned with Charles ten years ago. She'd never met the Jearnian princes, only heard about them until skirmishes with their eastern neighbor simply stopped.

When she realized her grip on her sword's hilt had not loosened, Rosealyn forced her arms and shoulders to relax. The man standing before her, still wearing an Orda'anian soldier's uniform—though his coat hung loose to reveal a simple white shirt—was both a king and someone she'd known for years. Not a stranger she was about to ask for aid.

No crown adorned his head, no fancy clothes, no insignia-riddled jewelry. Same slight waves to his hair, same jagged scar along his chin, same person whose behavior now made sense. His tension, his incessant stiffness. One slip, and everyone would know. The difference was obvious in his tone, his inflection, his presence, and his sword. Without the strips of leather adorning its hilt, Rosealyn concentrated on how the Tremaine family crest, and Jearnia's emblem since its founding, glinted with the surrounding flickering torches.

Round shoulders, head held straight, Rosealyn tightened her hands into fists. She wanted to be overjoyed that someone from her home lived. But he wasn't from there. Not really. *Blazing idiot of a fool.*

His unanswered question hung between them. As did his near use of her name without any honorifics. Her palms stung from where each nail dug. Torches in every corner added to the sunlight streaming through from above, glinting off the metal crown sitting on the empty throne behind him. Both thrones were empty, and Charles avoided even looking at them. Answer his question, and then it would be her turn to demand answers.

One deep breath and Rosealyn spoke with as much calm as she could muster. "Synda, a dragon, took me from my rooms to the ancient dragon, Magna. They're in the Mountains of Ingoria, like you once said."

She paused, trying not to laugh at how crazy it sounded to say it aloud, but none reacted to her statement. *Dragons. Real dragons. Blazes. The stories are true.*

"I know Xannan attacked Vandyl. That I saw with the Gift." Rosealyn swallowed, nails digging deeper into her skin. "And you can help me. You can help me save my kingdom."

Jaw clenched, Charles looked to the general and asked, "Any word from Nasir?"

The general shook his head. Rosealyn frowned, both at the general's lack of respect and at Charles for not directly responding to her.

Charles raked a hand through his hair, halting when the sleeves of his coat revealed raw, chafed skin on his wrists. He lowered his arm, tugged at the sleeves, and tightened his lips into a thin line.

"I can assist." Charles turned to the table and spread his hand over the parchment. "One of—" After a small shake of his head, he cleared his throat and faced her. "One of my men, who was ordered by my brother to take Vandyl for our father, should be there."

Her brows lifted at the statement, and she realized she gripped her sword's hilt again. "You mean to say that *your* men also attacked my home?"

His gaze shifted, looking past her where she'd last seen Christopher leaning against the golden-plated walls. A strange tone, one Rosealyn had never heard before, laced Charles's words. "I pulled back most of the army, but the scout sent to bring Nasir home hasn't returned. Nor has Nasir sent word."

Rosealyn's grip tightened until her muscles trembled from the effort of not lashing out. "But you agreed in the first place? Allowed *your* men to attack the place you called home for so long?" She shook her head, surprised at the lack of angry tears. "Do you care so little for us, for me, now?"

His shoulders drooped, and he leaned back over the table as though to hide from her. "I had little choice at the time." A small shake of his head, Charles said, "Nor did I expect Nasir to attack."

"The man follows orders." Christopher chimed in from behind her. Nonchalant, callous. No other words could describe the young prince's tone and mannerisms. "Loyal to the crown to a fault."

Rosealyn recoiled from the gaze Charles leveled at his brother. "Nasir's orders came not from me, but from Christopher. Before I took the throne—"

"You actually killed your father?"

He winced at her question. An almost imperceptible motion. But he did not answer.

Rosealyn wanted to scream, lash out, or determine how the past week's events could fit together. She started to take a step forward but thought better of it. As she settled back onto her heels, the travel-worn boots squeaked, and she clenched her hands back into fists. She lifted her chin and pinned Charles with the fiercest stare she could. In his soft blue eyes, Rosealyn did not find anger or fear. Concern. She swallowed. Once. Worry knitted his brows together, creasing his forehead.

"I need *someone* in my life to be upfront and honest with me." Rosealyn struggled to keep her voice even. "Even Father kept secrets. He knew your past, allowed you—" She inhaled and forced her fingers straight. "The least you can do is speak true for once."

He lifted a hand, which lowered as soon as the sleeves shifted. "As the eldest, it was my birthright. That did not stop them—" Charles tossed another poignant stare at his brother and returned his attention to her. "From treating me like a prisoner. Father did not believe me to be his son, despite Mother's recognition." He paused, his gaze lingering at a spot on the floor while he took a deep, shuddering breath. "I won the trial. Now I must change what Father created."

The swallow Rosealyn attempted felt like a clump of dirt had buried itself inside her throat and chest. Little by little, the bodyguard she'd spent years failing to decipher came together.

"Start by helping me." Rosealyn grimaced at the scratchiness of her throat as she swallowed again. Hands flexing at her sides, she approached, halting when the map of the continent on the table beside Charles became visible. "You may not call it home anymore, but surely you will not deny this request."

The stretch of an awkward silence made her heart pound more heavily with every second.

"I will assist. And—" He leveled a dangerous stare at the general who appeared the exact opposite of Azeiah in both physical appearance and personality. "My men will listen."

Charles turned back to her, his soft voice laced with uncertain tension. "I wanted to tell you." Selective words precipitated the returning stiffness as the shadow of reliving the past blanketed his features. "This was always part of the plan. I've always known how Phillippe would die. And what he believed you would need."

Rosealyn gasped as Charles's lackluster explanation knocked loose information she had yet to share. "The blades! Xannan wants to combine them. And they can be. Blazes. I should have asked Magna more questions."

Charles raised a brow and grimaced. "The mercenaries—"

"I know." One tentative step, then another, until she stood beside the table as well. Rosealyn traced a finger along the map, stilling when it covered the dot representing Vandyl. "Every time I think of home, it's covered in fire and smoke." Words caught in her throat as she whispered, "Azeiah, Moss, Daniel, Lori." She paused, not wanting to voice any worry for her mother, who had likely allowed the mercenaries entrance. "I hope most found a way out. There's little I could have done alone. Not even the fastest horse would have gotten me there before Xannan attacked."

A stride she'd familiarized over several days approached and Celena said, "Now that King Charles has promised you aid, I should remind you of the summit Arjun organized. It's four days away. It will take at least two, perhaps three days to travel there." Given the elf's ever-present matter-of-fact tone, Celena's recommendation did little to calm Rosealyn's inner turmoil. "Hoclia and Alkaan may provide aid. I'm positive Tenoa will, given your connection to them. Hopefully Arjun will wait to begin discussions until your arrival."

Rosealyn mulled over the idea of asking those against whom she had recently fought for aid, tugging at her bottom lip. "I think I could handle—"

"You are listening to the weapon's call rather than logic, Princess Rosealyn."

She grimaced at the elf's words and looked up at Charles, who shrugged. "I've learned the elves know more than they say. What they do say, you should listen to. And do." He tilted his head toward Celena, whom Rosealyn realized she had never properly introduced, though she had a suspicion Charles knew more people in this world than she did. "If the elf says you are needed in Violet Grove, then go."

"You said you would come with me," Rosealyn reminded him. "Has that changed?"

"I said assist," Charles corrected as he turned to lean against the table. "I'll head to Vandyl. We can stop at Lycene and wait for you to send word." His lips twisted, and he turned his head just enough to get a visual of his younger brother. "Christopher can go with you to Violet Grove. I'm sure Mother has told him more of our own dragon lore than she did me."

"Your own dragon lore?" Rosealyn asked, tired of feeling like the last one to know pieces involving her own country. *And myself.*

"Everyone has their stories. Even dragons," Christopher said, reminding her he still stood nearby. "Charles once met them, but it appears Mother did not share all of their stories. Do you even know where your sword came from, Charles?"

"Considering the protection it provided, I have my suspicions," Charles said and turned back to Celena. "Rest here for the evening."

"This was a stop I did not intend to make." Celena kept the words terse and tense, clipping them short with an air of frustration. "And storms approach from the north that I would rather not traverse within."

After tilting her head back, Rosealyn said, "We arrived less than an hour ago, Celena." Exhaustion crept into her muscles, forming a tightness at her temples akin to when her braids had just been woven. "Another change of clothes. A meal?" She glanced at Charles and prayed it did not sound like pleading when she said, "I'd like to rest. Even if it's just for one night."

Celena pursed her lips and nodded. The elf turned to Charles and, after a slight bow, said, "Thank you, King Charles, for your hospitality. I look forward to your reign and the calm it can bring."

"Capt—" Rosealyn tugged at her bottom lip, listening as Celena's footsteps whispered along the floor. When she glanced at Charles, the corner of his lips made a slight tug. "Thank you," she whispered with a small incline of her head.

He returned the gesture and signaled a guard who had stood so silently to one side of the room Rosealyn had forgotten they'd been present. "The guest rooms." His features hardened as he looked over her shoulder toward his younger brother. "We can speak alone later."

Rosealyn followed the guard, glancing back before the throne room doors closed to find Charles and Christopher approaching one another. The doors thudded shut before she could determine if it was with friendship or hostility that the brothers would speak.

47

Both hands on his hips, Charles stared at his younger brother, who still had his hands shoved into his pockets. While Charles contemplated what to say, Ashtar's gravelly voice sounded behind them. "You should not have brought us back." He added a quick "my King" when Charles glanced over his shoulder.

One deep breath, Charles rubbed a hand over his face. He did not question the honorifics but the actions of his father.

"But why take Vandyl?" Charles scratched at his chin. "Why send you there only after my arrival here?" Though he voiced the questions, he knew their answers. His father had wanted Orda'an since before he could remember, as had several of his ancestors. Even the mission his father had sent him on was designed to tumble Orda'an from within. He grimaced at the irony that he had killed a king, just not the one his father had intended.

Ashtar stood with arms folded, frowning. "I await your orders, my King."

The words were a quick grumble. Charles shifted his sword belt, distracted by the bare hilt. Glimmers of light created by the ornate room made the typically dull image of a flame appear to be ablaze.

"No messages from Nasir?" It had been Charles's most repeated question since becoming king. Ashtar shook his head, and Charles sighed while watching Christopher's methodical movement through the room. His youngest brother's steps were slow. Calculated.

"I've been trying to sort out what Father was doing," Charles explained to Christopher, staring back at the table where Ashtar stood with arms crossed. "Seems people have issues trusting me, believing me to be their rightful king."

Ashtar grunted, shifting to rest one hand on the hilt of his sword. "Not every day the prodigal son returns and kills his father."

"We've been over this." Charles pressed his lips together and shoved the simmering anger back down. "Father kept you all blissfully unaware that Ebios is in chaos. Hoclia and Orda'an were at war before Xannan ambushed and killed Phillippe. Alkaan remained neutral, and last I knew, Tenoa sides with Orda'an. But considering Nasir has sent no word, it is safe to believe Xannan has taken Vandyl. And it is probable Nasir and his company are now dead."

Ashtar grunted. "My recommendation is to consult the heir who stayed."

Charles studied the general, noting the similarities to his father. Even down to his stature, Ashtar was too similar. The beast of a man tested what little patience Charles had remaining. He walked back to the table, brushing a hand over the map, and tapped a finger atop Vandyl's marker.

"I've spent the last decade as a soldier. And fifteen years before that as heir to Jearnia's throne." He met the general's gaze and wondered if speaking with the air of finality and authority was a skill monarchs had to practice. "You will do as I say."

"My men will listen to me." Ashtar folded his arms across his chest.

"Damn it, Ashtar!" Charles slammed his hand against the table. "If we do not help rid Orda'an of Xannan, he will come here next. If not him, his dragon will."

"Even dragons have limitations," Christopher reminded him. In response to Charles's glare, Christopher added, "You should know that better than I, considering you've met the beasts."

"Yes," Charles whispered. "Once. And if I feared the kind Magna, I'd rather not come face to face with Eilon."

Charles's gaze roamed the gilded room for a moment before settling on his youngest brother. A small pot of anger boiled beneath the surface of Charles's calm for how his sibling had treated him during the journey. But if their mother did not recover from whatever poison she battled, Christopher would be all he had left of his family. Brief thoughts of their mother reminded Charles she had wanted him to change his attire. A simple swap. One coat for another. He hadn't even deigned to try it on yet. Doing so represented a finality to one chapter he wasn't ready to close.

Christopher looked markedly more comfortable, resting his back and shoulders against the wall next to the closed throne room doors with little evidence of the travel-weary exhaustion Rosealyn displayed. Volante, the city, the castle—it wasn't his home anymore. It was Christopher's.

"I should have returned, for your sake," Charles said. "For all of our brothers, really."

A singular shrug in response.

Unable to discern his brother's demeanor, Charles sighed. "You claimed that if anyone had the right to challenge, it was you." His brother nodded once. "What did you mean by that?"

"Exactly what it sounds like." Christopher walked to the edge of the room, letting his hand glide over the metal-plated walls. "To go from being the last to bringing you back to claim what was so close to being mine?" He continued trailing his hand over the wall, long curls shifting as he shook his head. "I figured Father would pit us against each other, not fight you himself. I wish I had been here for the trial. Would have been the perfect opportunity for me."

"Then why not kill me on the journey home?" Charles assumed the stance he'd adopted after years as an Orda'anian soldier. "Call it an accident?"

Christopher's hand stilled on the wall, and he shoved it back into his pocket. "Even I could not get away with breaking Father's rules."

Charles tapped his thumb on the top of his sword's hilt. "I believe we can come to a compromise."

Christopher's eyebrows raised, and his head tilted with an acknowledgment of curiosity.

"I must journey with the army," Charles explained with a piercing stare leveled at Ashtar. The general grunted. After muttering a curse under his breath, Charles spoke to Christopher again. "You will journey with Rosealyn and Celena to Violet Grove, speak as Jearnia's liaison at the summit. And keep her safe. Show me you are not our father, and we will discuss how to lead this country. Perhaps we can work together, rather than against one another."

"Are you offering me the crown without a proper trial?" Christopher asked, brows furrowing. "You know how Fath—"

"No." Charles shook his head. When he heard the general's grunt, he glanced askance at the man.

"We'd rather follow Prince Christopher than you." Ashtar finished the statement with a mocking bow and added, "My King."

Charles ground his teeth together and gripped his sword's hilt tight enough that the etched flame scratched at his palm. "I am your rightful king now." He could feel the muscles along his jaw ticking. "Father would have killed you himself for such insolence as you've shown me."

At the statement, Ashtar bristled, showing more emotion than he had in the past several days. Charles flexed his hand, wondering if he would have become like his father had Phillippe not offered him something different. Something better.

"But I am not my father." The general's pent-up tension eased slightly until Charles added, "Remember your place, or I will have you stripped of your station."

An obvious swallow, a singular nod. Before Ashtar could speak, Christopher asked, "Then what do you propose?"

Charles studied the map as though he had never seen it before, despite having stared at it for several hours before Christopher showed up with Rosealyn. "Her safety first." It was the least he could offer, considering what her father had provided for him. "Once we defeat Eilon and Xannan and return home, we will discuss it further."

"And if you don't return?" Christopher asked, stepping toward their father's throne.

"Then, as per custom, the crown and the kingdom are yours." It sounded odd for his own sibling to be so quick to consider what awaited should he die in battle. "Ashtar, prepare the army. And for the sake of the mountains, obey your king. This is not some trick against the Orda'anians. Or any other country. We aid the good Princess of Orda'an. It's the least I owe her."

The general leaned forward in a proper bow—hand on hilt, gaze to the floor—and departed without another word. As Ashtar left, Charles wondered what the general remembered about him.

"Now that we're alone." Christopher sat on their father's throne and rotated the gaudy gold crown once embedded with a rainbow of gems in his hands. "Why shouldn't I challenge you for the throne? The only claim you have to it is because of birth order. You failed the mission Father gave you." The crown's movement paused as Christopher lifted his chin and lounged back in the throne, as if it were already his. "While I succeeded."

"I won the trial." Charles paused, watching his brother tip the crown end over end, its remaining jewels sparkling in the fading sunlight. "Would you have agreed to fight if Father insisted upon it?"

His brother flashed him a strange smile, and the rotation stopped. "Would you?"

"Father is dead." Charles placed his hands on his hips again. "We must not let his decisions color those we make." He rounded his shoulders. "Orda'an needs our aid. It no longer matters if our countries have been at odds. At first, there was a reason—land, yes? Let that idiotic rivalry die with Father."

Hope lifted at Christopher's simple nod. *Is this how hard Father had to work to make others trust him? Or Phillippe?*

"As you wish, my King," Christopher said with a half-hearted bow, but his face held little emotion, as though he could not decide if he would trust his older brother.

"And—" Charles snatched the crown from Christopher's grasp. "You need to stop threatening to challenge me for what is already mine." He lowered the damaged crown, wondering what he should do with it. "We must learn to work together, Christopher."

Christopher harrumphed, standing and snatching the crown from Charles. "Mother and Father only ever cared about you. They took little notice of the rest of us." He set the fractured crown back in the chair. "I tire of living in someone else's shadow."

"Let Father's sins die with him," Charles advised his brother. "Do not threaten me again. You may leave."

A mocking bow, a childish phrase, and soon Charles was alone in an overbearing, fanciful room. He rested his hands on the table, staring at the markings of the towns. It was an old map, and several Orda'anian cities were missing. He rubbed his eyes, wishing he didn't see his father's face when he did, and sighed. *Blazes. What will she think of me now? What do I think of myself now?*

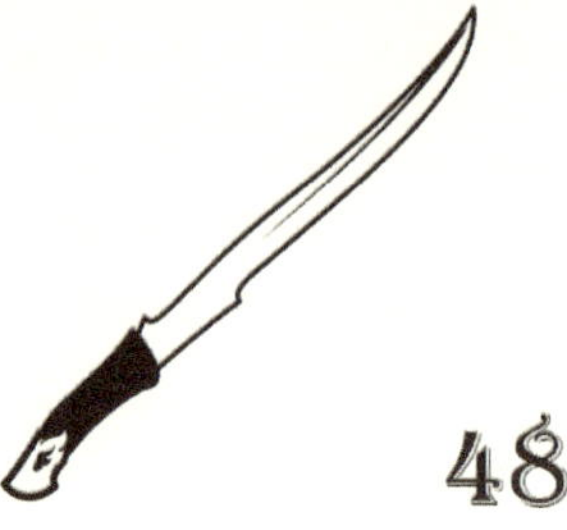

48

Charles sat at the table near the hearth in his boyhood rooms, staring absently at the seat his Aunt Marsha had recently vacated. Near him sat the Tremaine signet ring, a single flame engraved into it, meant to show prominently and quickly the station of the one who wore it. Typical royal garb would accentuate the colors of that flame with its red and orange hues, garb he had yet to don. Marsha's words lingered, a reminder that forming lines of trust with those around him would not come easy. Step one: accept the role.

He picked up the ring, the too short sleeves of the familiar coat falling as he inspected the crest staring back at him. His family crest. After setting the ring on the table, he rubbed his face with his palms. Despite his exhaustion, sleep remained elusive over the past week. The skin of his wrists no longer stung, though the redness had not dissipated. Where his father's dagger had pierced his side was tender, especially since Charles had later relented and allowed the doctor to stitch the wound. His focus alternated between the receding sunlight seeping in from the windows high above him, the table before him, and the door as he debated if he should go to her. *I thought I would find her before she found me.*

He wondered if she had already eaten and winced at the thought of enduring another meal with trembling servants. Evidence his father had gotten worse in his absence. Hesitant, cautious steps, wavering words, a consistent air of uncertainty when they spoke to him. Names became difficult to learn once he realized a new servant was showing up to his rooms each day in uniform dress which hid distinctive features. The boy from today's evening meal attempt was young and nervous, and Charles sent him away with kind words after the fourth plate broke. The fifth plate sat full, untouched. Full of vibrant color, foods not molding and decaying. Foods that beckoned to be consumed.

"King," he whispered into the suffocating air as he picked up the ring again with his free hand. With the fork held loose in his other hand, he flicked at the morsels of smoked meat around the dark-colored plate which made the green leaves almost too vibrant. The few bites he had consumed were tasteless. Rich, earthy tastes tickled suppressed memories, a desire to be enraptured at the textures and smells of his childhood. But everything around him was bland. "I returned. Now what?"

When the knock sounded, he pocketed the ring and stood to open the doors himself, finding Rosealyn standing on the opposite side with a servant. Bushy-haired, almost as tall as Rosealyn, the servant girl curtsied without lifting her chin and almost tripped over her feet when Charles told her to return to her quarters. He sighed, lips tight as he watched the girl disappear down the dark hallway. Everything was too dark. Except the coat.

Beyond the threshold of the door, Rosealyn stood tall, wearing what could be one of his mother's dresses. No laces cinched the bodice, making it looser and the skirts smaller. Its white color complemented her brown-tinged skin while perfumed soap replaced the earlier muskiness of horse and sweat. The forming smile faltered as he met her steeled determination and noticed the sword around her waist.

"What else have you not told me?" Rosealyn demanded. He stood at the door, one hand holding it open, the other gesturing inside. Hope, fleeting hope, swirled inside. *Maybe she'll treat me like me? But why wear the sword?*

The small table he'd occupied before she arrived was littered with plates of fruit and bread, but neither ate. After a cursory glance around his quarters, she marched to the table and sat. Without her left hand drifting to grasp her side. As he finally released his hold of the door, which remained open, he asked, "The pain? It's gone?"

Rosealyn rubbed a hand over her left side briefly and nodded. "Synda did something."

"Synda is one Mae did not tell me stories of." Charles sat on the opposite end of the bench. Too short sleeves rode up his arms, despite his unbuttoned coat. Hands shoved into his pockets, he fidgeted with the ring. "I knew of Magna, of her role in creating your ancestor's weapons, but little more. Mae took me to meet Magna. Once."

"Can I speak with her?" Rosealyn asked. She gripped the bench beneath her with each hand, loose hair not contained by her twin half-braids falling over her shoulders as she leaned forward. Each movement was jolting. Probably no different than his own. Seven years of training her, teaching her everything he had ever learned about weapons, and he questioned what dynamic could exist between them. "With your mother?"

"She won't turn me away." His chuckle ended with a grimace, worried his mother was still too weak to leave her bed. "Each time I visit she acts like she'll never see me again."

Rosealyn nodded. After wrapping her arms around herself, her shoulders drooped. It was like she tried to carry the weight of the world. Whatever strength she had mustered before visiting him was fading. He turned, facing her. But she didn't look up. Didn't react to his movement. One week. Only one week had passed since he had willingly met his brother in a field. One week since he had watched her disappear from view. Several questions formed: How much strength had she regained since the Passing? Was the invisible pain actually gone, or had she gotten better at hiding it? Would he need to train her before battling a legendary dragon?

"Tell me everything."

It was a fierce, fiery whisper. Bold light brown eyes bored into him. An unrelenting stare he could not hold. The wooden bench had several fine striations, and each became worthy of intense study. He braced for shouts, perhaps even a swift smack from her—though it'd be completely uncharacteristic. Even in sparring she was sometimes timid with her blows against him. But the demand and expectation rang clear.

"I have to know. And considering Father's hospitality, given what you came to do, you need to tell me."

Charles turned to rest both feet flat on the floor, elbows digging into his knees as he buried his face in his hands. "What is left to discuss?" he asked into his palms and sat back upright. His gaze roamed over the room before him. Vast. Open. Each piece of furniture exactly as he remembered. Not even dust coated their edges, as though he'd never left. With a deep breath, he forced himself to look her in the eyes. "I will take my army to Vandyl. Distract Xannan until you can bring more aid from the other countries. That is what the elves suggest, yes?"

Rosealyn tilted her head to one side, and the fiery sparks flared.

Charles continued. "I don't trust anyone to obey my orders without me there, else I would go with you to Violet Grove. Resume your training. For now, I hope I can trust Christopher to travel with you to the summit. Or at least trust your own abilities to keep you safe."

A twinkle of appreciation interrupted the simmering flame. "I understand all of that Cap—" She paused. At his dismissive wave, she continued. "It's hard to believe. An army at your command while I do not know who of my friends, or my people, are alive." She wrung the material of her dress with both hands. "I'm supposed to protect them."

A brief sniffle which could introduce tears sounded, but her voice. "I'm not sure when I'll see Vandyl again."

He whipped his head toward her. It was an odd combination of fiery softness. Acceptance. She believed the words.

"The Gift?" Charles dared ask, trying and failing to read what little emotion she was expressing.

She shrugged, and the following sigh quickly turned into a yawn. "For whatever that is worth, yes. It comes from the dragons. Magna showed me. And Father's letter said to keep this sword close."

"That sword?" Charles glanced down at the weapon wrapped around her waist. A small raised silver bubble of the two dragons and the weapons they had created adorned the hilt. Same as always. A masterpiece he would have preferred to inspect rather than battle against.

"It's one of the Twin Blades." Rosealyn leaned forward with her hands still gripping the bench below them, and Charles had to force his brows to stop climbing his forehead. All those years wondering if the Twin Blades were real, and he'd been within arm's reach of one on multiple occasions.

Rosealyn's voice softened. "Magna did not show me what happens when they combine, though Celena expected her to. That idea gives me a calm dread I cannot shake."

Awkward silence ensued. Charles tensed, unsure what he should do. Raise an arm or perhaps shift closer or sit stiff. Before he could decide, she spoke.

"Tell me about the agreement."

This time her bold gaze seemed to bore through him.

His back collapsed into the hard line of wood on which plates upon plates of food grew cold, and he fought not to scrunch his face. No more reason to lie. No more reason to hide the truth of his actions. No more reason to do anything except tell her everything. She would never think of him in the same way again. And he could not meet her gaze as he told her what had occurred. Rosealyn's bond with her father had been the opposite in every way of his own relationship with his—she would always mourn her father's death while Charles wasn't sure he cared his father was dead.

"It is Jearnian custom for the heir to be tasked with a mission to prove their competence." He cleared his throat. "Mae believed my mission was to become a spy inside Orda'an to topple its monarchy." One swallow. A second. His chest hollowed as he formed the words before speaking them. "Father instructed me to kill Phillippe during the next border skirmish."

Memories surfaced, reliving the moment which had changed his life's trajectory. "I tried. Snuck into his tent in the middle of the night. But Phillippe wrenched my sword from my hand like it was a twig from a child. And he could have ended me before my next breath. But he didn't." With each word, his mouth parched further and his tongue became like a stone weighing down his jaw as he tried to swallow again. "Phillippe offered me two choices. Continue fighting him and likely die trying. Or allow him to fake my death and use it as leverage to end the decades-long war between our countries with one caveat—return home and take my place after his death to provide you with an ally."

He wasn't sure if Rosealyn's silence eased his fears or renewed them, especially as her breaths became uneven. After shifting so his elbows dug into his thighs and his chin rested in his palms, he continued. "We weren't far from Lycene. That part was always true. He met me there. And Phillippe knew what to say, explained the future he saw for me. For him. For you. For us." An invisible weight lifted one word at a time, replaced with a new concern. "The agreement I made with your father allowed me to live along with so many others for both of our countries. When Phillippe convinced the Jearnians there with me I had died, he told them any subsequent attacks would be met with the same result. Unless the attacks on Orda'an stopped."

He filled his lungs and shifted to hold his hands together in hopes to stop his fingers from trembling as he exhaled. "I'm aware the Gift is not as specific as I once believed, but the message worked. The skirmishes stopped, and I became an almost nameless Orda'anian soldier."

Charles wanted to smile at the memories he'd made in Orda'an, but Rosealyn's uncharacteristic silence only caused the drumming of his heartbeat in his ears to increase its speed. "Your father offered something I *never* would have had with mine. Even if I had escaped Phillippe's tent with my life and returned here—" He paused and glanced around the room again, stopping before he encountered the shock and anger likely etched on her features. "As a failure? Father had four other sons to send at the time. He wouldn't have needed me."

A slow, deep breath in and out. "Father was always quick to kill." His hand strayed to his side, where the ridges of stitching could be felt through his shirt, a reminder his father would have landed the killing blow had he not done so first. "Although Christopher claims Father still spoke of me as his favorite. But I don't believe him. Not after the trial."

Charles cleared his throat again and glanced toward Rosealyn but hesitated. He didn't want to witness any fear in her eyes. He waited. She remained relatively close, but she didn't speak, so he continued, each word leaving more smoothly than the last.

Chin resting in his hands, he said, "I fought it at first. But everyone was so kind, so welcoming. Before Hoclia attacked, I believed, hoped I would spend the rest of my days there. As a simple soldier, following orders. A life as a protector of the beautiful princess and future monarch of Orda'an."

Courage swirled when he stopped talking. But as soon as he lifted his head, she stood much more quickly than he expected. Charles grimaced, waiting to incur a level of wrath he had likely never witnessed from her before.

Silence.

When he dared to look up, she was halfway to the open door, exiting without a glance back at him. Then the door stood wide, and he wondered if she remembered her way back to the guest rooms. He took a singular deep breath and buried his elbows into his knees and his face into his hands. *How does one understand such silence?*

Rosealyn reappeared in the open door less than a minute later. Angry tears, which he knew she despised, would have provided more comfort than the regal tone with which she spoke. "Thank you for the aid you have promised, King Charles."

Rosealyn walked away again, and Charles wished the silence had lingered. With a sigh, he stood and approached the doorway, knowing Celena had requested their mounts be prepared to leave before the day's end, despite Rosealyn's request for a night of rest. Storms in the valleys of Jearnia moved quickly.

Besides, it was not the first time he had suffered her wrath. At the threshold, he hesitated, glancing back at the brightly colored coat Marsha had laid across the bed.

"Might as well look the part." He pulled the ring from his pocket and slid it onto the first finger of his right hand. Cold metal sat snug against his skin, the burst of flame staring back at him when he flexed his fingers, and he wondered what had happened to the version of their signet ring which had given him the small scar along his chin. He shrugged off the solid black jacket he had insisted be repaired and draped it across the back of the chair at the head of the table. He walked to his bed and lifted the intricately woven red and orange coat. Its cut was so similar that, out of habit, he tugged each sleeve after clasping all but the topmost button. But this coat was a perfect fit.

With a quick shrug of his shoulders against the stiff unworn material, he stuffed the letter Phillippe had written to Rosealyn, along with Gailin's journal entries Azeiah had given him, into the coat and walked steadily until he found her standing at a crossroads in the intricate maze of hallways of Volante's castle, unsure of which direction to take.

"I'm not sure what to do next." A quick sniffle meant she was losing her battle against the angry tears, and when she faced him, her glistening eyes widened, likely at his change of attire. "Or, um, even where to go."

"Mae will be more than happy to speak with you." He turned down a hallway to the right. "Follow me."

49

Blanket resting atop her legs, Nerida shifted to sit further upright in the bed as her door opened, wishing she could walk without potentially tearing her stitches out of the jagged wound. White cloth with red stitching lay in her lap, though she had not added to it. When she heard neither Eonar's mutterings nor Marsha's admonishments, she lifted her gaze to see Charles enter. Stoic, pensive, almost to the point of appearing abrasive, he had donned the coat she'd demanded created for him. Living so long in a different world, with different customs, had changed him. How he spoke to others amazed her. A kindness which had been absent from her other children, even from Christopher, had grown in Charles during his years away. Behind Charles was the Orda'anian princess, tall, proud, holding herself like any noble. The pale white dress made her darker skin glow a deep gold. Nerida's smile faltered as she watched the two approach. An aura of tension wafted between them, which Nerida found odd given how fondly he had spoken of her.

When she lifted the blankets to stand, Charles shook his head. "Rest, Mae. Any update from the doctor?"

"I'm recovering," Nerida said, hoping he could not hear the lie. He should know the poison wasn't from his father's dagger; otherwise, Charles would suffer the same weakness as she. Who was poisoning her, or why, was a question she pushed away for later.

He squinted, studying her with his lips twisted in an almost frown, and pulled two chairs closer to her bedside.

"Rosealyn has questions, Mae." Charles sat and gestured toward her. "You know the stories better than I."

"You had the book, Charles," Nerida said with a weak smile, pocketing the idea to question their behavior later. "You came home with it."

"Rosealyn has questions which I cannot answer and little time as Celena wishes to beat the storms to Violet Grove." His sword knocked against the wooden chair as he sat back and crossed his arms.

"Who is Magna to you?" the princess asked before Nerida could turn to meet the princess's gaze.

"Straightforward this one." Nerida half-laughed, but it turned into a cough. She accepted the cup of water Charles offered. "Magna is the giver to the land, the protector of all we hold beautiful, the one who wanted to bring peace among all races. And she tried. You know that with your story of the Twin Blades. However, Magna had other concerns besides us."

Less than a heartbeat passed before Rosealyn asked, "Eilon?"

Nerida nodded, though Charles's crestfallen demeanor became more distracting. She studied her son as she spoke, hoping to decipher the emotions hiding beneath his smoothed visage. "Eilon lost his family, his own species of dragons, and came to Magna for help. She was in the midst of creating an alliance with us humans, with the elves' assistance." At every statement she expected a reaction from her son or an interruption from the princess, but neither came. When a cough snagged her chest, Charles refilled her cup. After a sip, Nerida said, "Magna wanted to test what Eilon would do. To help him was to share her magic, and Magna feared he would attempt to take what was hers."

Nerida ran a finger along the rim of the cup, grateful she could not see her reflection in the clear water. "Eilon failed that test. As Magna suspected he would." Nerida paused, wincing at the oncoming flurry of coughs. They racked her chest and made the ache of her wounded abdomen reignite.

Another sip of water cooled her throat. She set the glass aside and concentrated on her words rather than the pain. "Eilon takes. More than takes, he consumes. Magna saw what was happening and what could happen. So she trapped his magic—as much of it as she could—into the weapon meant to be a symbol of unity. The reason Xannan lives, if I'm to understand correctly, is because he subsists on Eilon's magic trapped within."

Rosealyn's nods were knowing, understanding, absorbing. Everything Nerida had said so far did not seem a surprise to the princess. "What of Synda? What role does she play in Magna and Eilon's story?"

"Synda is the youngest progeny of the dragons," Nerida answered. It felt good to speak of the dragons, of the stories she had learned, without fear of death surrounding her at a moment's notice. "The last born of any dragon for the last several generations. I know Synda is important since Magna insists on her protection, but Synda is—"

"Rash and young." Rosealyn chuckled, but her tone hardened with worry. "She brought me to Magna, pulled me from my rooms in Vandyl out of thin air."

Nerida gasped and held a hand to her chest as the action caused more coughing. "Then she is weak now. No flame?"

Rosealyn squinted and leaned forward. "Why not share what you knew of the dragons?" She almost looked at Charles, but the motion jerked to a halt. "Why not tell their stories to all who would listen?"

Nerida met Charles's gaze and in his blue eyes remembered all of her children, all she had lost throughout the years. Warmth swelled within her; Magna had protected him as promised.

"Magna showed me how most would react." She winced at the memory, at the pain of receiving what the dragons sometimes shared. "We fear what we do not understand, we fear the unknown, attack it with an unabated vengeance. Not even my own parents believed me when I said I saw a dragon. A very young Synda. Even then, her presence awed me. I believe your family gift came from them, considering their magic is so similar."

"Their magic?" Rosealyn tugged at her bottom lip for a moment. "Does all magic come from dragons?"

Nerida lifted a shoulder, an action she immediately regretted. "That is a question I cannot answer."

Rosealyn nodded, eyes moving around the room and chin jerking when she came close to looking at Charles. Eventually her gaze settled on her lap, and she wrung the material with both hands. "Do I need to be concerned about Eilon? Or do I just attack Xannan and take back my home?"

Nerida chuckled, winced, and took a deep breath, shaking her head at the princess's questions. "They are connected. I do not know how the blades work, perhaps Celena does. But Xannan and Eilon are connected. It's likely a similar, much weaker, connection exists between yourself and Magna." She shifted to sit taller with a silent prayer the doctor would not need to redo her stitches again. "Tell me, dear princess, what did Magna show you?"

At this, Rosealyn did look at Charles, who gestured toward Nerida again. "You asked to speak with her." He delivered the words in a dejected tone she did not expect given his choice to wear not only the coat, but the king's signet ring as well. Though Charles's words sounded cold, Nerida needed to discover the underlying emotion. He tilted his head. "If you wish to have questions answered, you will also need to answer questions."

Rosealyn gripped the material and rounded her shoulders. "As far as I can tell, my life depends on this sword. A portion of Magna's magic must lie within this blade." She released her hold of the material and smoothed the skirts. "The same must be true for Xannan."

Nerida watched Charles's eyes widen as the princess spoke and almost shook her head again. *Those two need to be more honest with each other.*

Instead, Nerida explained further what the Orda'anian and Jearnian history books had removed from their past. "Eilon wants more than just his magic back. He wants to revive his race of dragons. After Charles was born, I went to Magna directly, during the Harvest Feast. She, with Celena's assistance, made Charles's sword." She swallowed down the cough crawling its way up from her chest. "Magna denied my request for the others. Synda eventually took pity on me and made one for Christopher. I visited every year, hopeful. Only this year did Synda agree; she no longer listens well to Magna."

"Magna looked weary, weak, tired." Rosealyn twisted the fabric of her dress-skirts between both hands again. "How many dragons are left?"

"Few. I've not met any besides Magna and Synda, though I believe others live in the land beyond the mountains."

"What did Magna show you of the protection she gave Charles?" Rosealyn asked. The princess avoided looking at Charles, even sat as far away as possible from him without physically moving the chair he had offered.

"Magna gave of her own magic to his weapon when she blessed it. Not to the extent Eilon did to Xannan's, but enough to protect him from it."

"Thus the reaction," Charles muttered.

Nerida watched Rosealyn give her son another sidelong glance and met her eyes again. Those eyes held a question, a question the princess refused to ask. Nerida pursed her lips, wondering what had occurred between them. The Orda'anian princess's care for her son was obvious; otherwise, Rosealyn would never have come into enemy territory.

"The sword's protection worked?" Nerida reached for the cup of water, grimacing at how it stretched the wound.

"When I went to Lycene with Rake," Charles said in a deadpan dazed tone. "We fought Xannan. Briefly. He injured Rake, but when I blocked his next attack, the swords rebounded and forced both Xannan and me to our backs far from one another." He sat a little taller and rubbed his hand along one arm. "I burned my hand on the hilt, even through the leather strips. Xannan seemed confused, and by the time I moved to help Rake, Xannan was gone." The motion of his hand halted. "Xannan's blade poisoned Rake through a small gash on his leg. Arjun, the elf I met that same night, assisted but couldn't help."

Nerida took a deep, relieving sigh, realizing her request had been honored and fulfilled. Rosealyn's jaw slacked slightly, grasping her weapon's hilt as she shifted in the chair again and glanced between Nerida and Charles.

With a shake of her head, Nerida asked, "Now, the real question is if that weapon can do the same again?"

"What do you mean, Mae?" He sat up a little, eased back into the chair, and crossed his arms.

"Magna made the weapon, imbued it with her magic, but how much I do not know." Nerida shook her head again with a soft sigh. "The ancient dragon is cautious. Helpful but wary, fearful another may subvert her like Eilon attempted."

"There's more," Rosealyn said, finally truly looking at Charles, though she did not shift closer. "Celena said yours and Christopher's weapons can help kill a dragon, but we may need them all if Xannan takes the combined blade. I think I now understand the connection they have." Rosealyn intertwined her fingers, resting them on her knees. "If Eilon's magic is trapped inside that weapon, he has been using Xannan all this time, trying to get back what he lost. There's still one question to answer: how do I combine these blades without Xannan taking it from me?"

Nerida shrugged, and the princess fell back into much the same position as her son, without the crossed arms. "I'm sorry, Princess Rosealyn, that is a question I cannot answer. The dragons have shared much with me, trusted me to record their stories, though many did not believe them. Eilon will continue to take from what is around him, and the only way to stop it is to sever his connection to the blade which contains it."

"Kill Xannan, then kill the dragon," Rosealyn said with a firm nod of her head.

"If Xannan has spent generations beside the dragon—" Another cough took over. "Perhaps a conversation?"

The princess stood and gave Nerida a slight bow, the bow common between nobles. "Thank you, Your Majesty, for your time, and for the answers you have given. I can question Celena further during the journey. Surely someone knows how this ridiculous theory of combining two swords will work without speaking to my father's murderer."

Charles did not stand or react to the princess's ignoring him when she left. Naught but Nerida's occasional sips of water sounded in the room.

"I told her everything," Charles said when the silence must have become too much for him, and Nerida smiled behind her raised cup. The wooden chair creaked beneath him, and he rubbed sunken eyes, blinking several times and staring at the floor between his feet. "What I tried—"

"Everything?" Nerida interrupted and shook her head with a knowing smirk. "The truth of your past actions is different from the truth of your character. This deadpan unfeeling diatribe will get you nowhere but the role of lonely king. Go. Speak with her again before she leaves." She nodded at the doorway. "And don't you dare leave anything unsaid."

50

Distracted and overwhelmed, Rosealyn walked several steps outside the queen's rooms and realized she had no idea which path to take. Resting her back against the wall, she slid to the floor. Dark, windowless hallways. Torches lined the walls at intervals, casting shadows that flickered over the stone. Hands wrapped around her knees, head buried in her legs, she tried to quiet her racing thoughts, confusion becoming more rampant with each piece she gathered. She fought the tears which continuously threatened to fall. She refused to give in to the inner turmoil, concentrating on her breathing, fearful of no end to her crying once it began. A small lump formed in the back of her throat, tormenting her resolve.

She rubbed her face against her knees, certain such a movement had frayed the tight braids she insisted on keeping. The maid who helped her bathe offered several hairstyles, but it was a change she could not make. Those two braids itched to become a full one wrapped around her scalp. Someday she knew it would be. But it didn't feel right. Not yet.

The weapon at her hip was still a foreign aspect of her wardrobe. It often snagged her skirts at odd angles. The belt constantly rubbed against her waist until she scowled and shifted it to a more comfortable resting place, and the hilt obnoxiously clanged against the belt which held it.

For a brief second, Rosealyn lost control of the lump crawling its way up her throat. The jangling of metal made memories of walking through quiet hallways with Moss several steps behind flood her mind. Another whose fate she did not know. After a deep, shaky breath, she tilted her head back until the rough stone grated against her scalp and she could watch the shadows of flickering flames dance along the ceiling.

A scrape of shoes against stone sounded from the queen's door moments later, stopping when they reached her. What she'd always thought was a lingering scent of snow hovering around Charles was actually the crisp mountain air. He sat against the wall next to her.

For a long time, neither spoke. No banter, no tricks, no honorifics.

"You stopped calling me princess." Rosealyn's voice sliced through the tense silence. A chuckle almost accompanied it, but a cold shimmer blurred the bottom of her vision when she peeked at him. If she wasn't careful, laughter would descend into tears. Whispering, she added, "And I still tried to call you Captain."

"A logical slip," he said with a second intake of breath, as though he might add the honorifics again. "We do have names in addition to our titles."

"Our titles." Rosealyn shifted so her knees rested against the floor and she could face him. She turned the sword belt, released an aggravated sigh, and unbuckled the weapon to lay it on the floor instead. Then she studied Charles, his clothing, his expression. His coat made him look as though he were ablaze, a stark contrast to the solid black pants. The bright hues of orange and red mingled with one another in the same manner as a burning flame. Her eyes roamed over the colors, trying to figure out how the seamstresses had combined the two. It framed him better than the castle garb of the Orda'anian soldiers.

She leaned until the side of her head met the cold stone as Charles shifted so one leg stretched toward the middle of the hallway, drawing the other closer to him, head resting against the wall only inches from hers. "You did once tell me to call you Rose."

"Yes," Rosealyn whispered, heart skipping a beat when he said her name. Only her father had ever called her that. "Before I knew—"

"You know everything about me now." Charles shifted his head, but the motion stopped before their eyes met again. "What I've done, what I tried to do before fighting alongside your father." He paused, resting a hand atop his knee. "I've protected you."

"In more ways than even I knew?" Rosealyn asked, repeating the phrase he had once told her. She picked at the folds of the dress, layered on top of each other with the angle of her knees, fighting the mixture of laughter and tears. "I'm a fool. I thought I would be more upset with you, but I should have seen the signs of your past. I've always known you weren't Orda'anian. The color of your eyes and how you talked. But Father trusted you." She swiped at her eye before a tear could escape. "So I saw no reason to question you. Or him."

"And now, because of his trust in me, you have one less thing to worry about." Charles paused again, whether to say her name or honorifics, Rosealyn wasn't sure.

"Charles—" she said and stopped. She'd never called him by just his name before. And while it sounded wrong, it felt right. "Who am I if I lose my country? I've already failed to protect so many—"

She held a piece of the dress's fabric in her hand, rubbing it between two fingers, biting at her lower lip as though pain would prevent the brimming tears from spilling. In her periphery, she saw one of his hands reach for her, the flickering torches glinting off a silver ring adorning his right hand. His hand hovered for a few seconds, and he placed his palm on the floor between them, making the Jearnian royal insignia of the ring he wore clearly visible. It was not the voice of a protector, but of a fellow monarch, of one who understood her plight, which spoke to her. A calming, melodic, and smooth tone, laced with small threads of hesitation. "You've only failed if you've given up. You are still fighting. That's why you're here."

Rosealyn met his gaze, wiping away tears she could not stop to meet an odd, rare, and yet quite contagious warm smile softening his expression. The floodgates lessened, and a silent laugh shook her shoulders. "Dragons. They all think dragons extinct." Her hair snagged on the rough stone as she shook her head. "And here I am forming a plan to kill one."

Charles's eyebrows lifted, and he appeared to be fighting between staring her down and laughing at her. "Kill a dragon? I thought you wanted to take back Vandyl and annihilate Xannan first."

Rosealyn nodded, her laughter fading as she whispered a dejected, "That too."

Charles chuckled. "Always biting off more than you can chew, attacking something new with a vengeance, but you—" He cleared his throat. "We can't run into this blind." He hooked his arm around his raised knee. "I thought Xannan had taken you, like he did Phillippe. But it was Synda, right?"

She nodded, studying the fabric of her dress.

"When Synda did that, made you disappear, what did it feel like?"

"Like sparring with you," Rosealyn said with a slight smirk, continuing to pick at the dress. "One second I'm in one place, certain of my surroundings, the next I've face-planted into the dirt with no knowledge of how I got there."

"Though it's only been a week, I've missed that," Charles said as his disarming, contagious smile returned, stilling her wringing of the dress. A comfortable silence ensued, lingering as they sat in a dull hallway. The dim light of the torches flickered around them, casting odd shadows which Rosealyn studied until Charles shifted to sit straighter and broke the silence again.

"What exactly did Magna show you?" The concern returned, as did the hesitation and absent pauses at the end of each statement. "There was a hint of finality earlier, the same tone I heard in Phillippe."

Rosealyn breathed deeply, closing her eyes to visualize the brief scenes Magna had shared. "Gailin almost died when Magna removed the Gift as he requested. Would have killed him, had she not given the Gift back to him." She paused, letting the words linger, uncertain in its implication of her own survival, and opened her eyes. "And I saw you, Charles, sitting at my father's desk, in his study. Books strewn about in haphazard piles. And you looked older."

A series of nods occurred before Charles rested his head on the wall and turned to her again. At some point, he had shifted closer. With a simple movement on her part, or his, their foreheads would be touching.

"Swords imbued with the magic of dragons," he muttered. Despite the softness, his voice echoed in the silent hallway. But he didn't move, nor did she, as he asked another question.

"Who mentioned the combining of the Twin Blades again? The myth never mentioned such a phenomenon."

Rosealyn picked at the folds of her dress again. "Celena did." Her voice echoed too, somewhat softer than Charles's had. "Gailin hinted at it throughout his journals. I don't think it's been done before. I'm not sure I can trust what I've read in the history books, though. If Gailin lied about the dragons, what else is a false truth?"

"And there can only be one truth, Rose."

Her chest lurched in a way she never thought possible at him saying her name again, heart beating faster as his hand covered hers with a gentle squeeze, pausing her incessant wringing of the cloth. At the same time, she reminded herself, they had been this close before. Closer even. Sparring did not come without contact. Rosealyn swallowed, thinking about how natural it felt for her hand to be held with his. A deep breath in, an even slower breath out. The stone against her arm and cheek was no longer cold. Several more breaths passed, a question resting on the tip of her tongue for far too long.

She shifted her hands within his, and the bright orange and red coat drew the words from her. "What is your truth, Charles? Who are you?"

"Mae said to leave nothing unsaid," he mumbled with a half smile, glancing over her for a brief second and letting go of her hands. And then he stared at the ceiling. "I was your protector, a soldier in your father's army—"

"No, I know who you were." Rosealyn pulled herself toward him until her dress-skirts covered his outstretched leg. "Who are you now, Charles? What truth do you plan to follow now? You're more than my protector. You have your own people to consider. Your own kingdom to rule."

"And by protecting you, I protect them," he said, brows furrowing as if there were no other answer to give. "I'm not sure I would have returned had your father not asked me to."

"Perhaps." Rosealyn shifted to sit on her knees. Before she could begin toying with the folds of her skirts, his gentle, though slightly calloused, hands wrapped around hers once more. Rosealyn considered whisking her hands away until Charles offered another comforting squeeze and pulled her hands to him. His hands shifted, moving so their fingers intertwined. The cool silver band she could no longer see brought shivers as he moved his hands within hers. She flexed her fingers and considered pulling away again until she realized the lingering dread resting in the pit of her stomach for days had all but disappeared. Leaning back on her heels, Rosealyn said, "I can protect myself, Charles."

"You have the tools, yes, but you have always had help." The hesitation almost gone from his voice, he did not break away from her watchful gaze. "My truth now—" She could see him forming the words, could see the belief with which he would say them. "As king of Jearnia, I promise to be an ally to Orda'an. An ally to you and your people."

"And if I—" Rosealyn shuddered, remembering how quickly Gailin had fallen to his side, and she tugged both of her hands free to fidget with the folds of her dress. One of his hands wrapped around hers and she shifted with the gentle pull of her hands, shoulder resting against the wall. With his other hand, Charles lifted her chin. She let him, wishing they had dropped the honorifics and proper roles long ago.

"Rose." Her name, spoken so clearly by his comforting tones made her cheeks warm. Not a whisper as though her name was beyond his reach. He waited until she met his unwavering gaze. "As long as I live and have breath to give, I promise to protect you. If that means caring for your country alongside mine until you recover, then I will."

Rosealyn searched his face, looking for the hint of a lie, for the hint of uncertainty. And saw none. She smiled softly. "You're still leaving something unsaid, Charles."

"I have to find some way to protect you, even if I can't be by your side, because I can't imagine a scenario where I survive and you don't." He didn't flinch from her studying of his gaze, and her breath caught as he shifted a stray strand of hair from her shoulder.

"Still not saying it," Rosealyn whispered, her smile widening. His grip on her hands tightened for a brief second before he released them. Shoulders falling, her brows furrowed. From inside his obnoxiously bright coat, he pulled a set of carefully folded papers.

"Father's letter," she gasped. "But—"

"Azeiah brought them to me before I left." Charles frowned when Rosealyn set the papers aside.

"Those are not why you sat down beside me." She reached for his hands again.

Charles reached for the letters instead. "Did you already—"

"Later." Rosealyn stopped him from picking up the papers by intertwining her hands with his and closing what little distance remained between them. "I don't want to fight what I feel. Most of it I can't. The Gift makes sure of that. And there's this uncertainty—"

"We're both leaving something unsaid," he whispered as he shifted a hand out of her grasp. His palm was warm against her cheek.

"Then don't say it," she whispered back. "Show me."

His breath mingled with hers, and she closed her eyes.

"There you are." Her shoulders fell at the sound of Celena's voice.

"I'm not positive I'll see you again," Rosealyn whispered to him before the elf came closer, tilting her head until their foreheads rested against one another. She inhaled the scent of him—the coolness of the mountain air that always reminded her of snow—and opened her eyes. "Keep that sword close; I'm positive you will need it."

"And I am positive that, somehow, I will see you again," Charles said, ignoring Celena towering above them.

"We must leave with haste to avoid the incoming storm, Princess," Celena announced, breaking the spell.

Rosealyn glanced up at the elf and almost laughed, wondering if she would have found the same look on either of her parents' faces in such a scenario.

"We've waited too long already." Celena tilted her head, white hair falling to the side as her red eyes seemed to glow with the flickering flames. "King Charles, you know your presence would be of assistance in Violet Grove."

Charles stood, straightening his orange and red jacket and clearing his throat. "Christopher's presence will be sufficient, I believe." He looked between them, stone-like stiffness softening when he looked down at Rosealyn. "Jearnia will offer whatever aid is asked of it. I must accompany Ashtar." He grimaced, but the twist of his features didn't linger. "The soldiers listen to him, and I need to make sure he listens to me. That, and we need to learn Nasir's fate."

Celena nodded and glared at the still-sitting Rosealyn. Exhaling, Rosealyn grabbed the sheathed sword and letters and accepted Charles's outstretched hand to help pull her to standing. As she buckled the sword around her waist, she shook her head, trying not to laugh again, especially when Charles frowned and raised an eyebrow in question.

"The black looks better on you," she said, unable to stop the girlish giggle as she smiled.

"And the beige better on you." One of those rare smirks lit up his face before he rounded his shoulders and the banter disappeared. "Be careful and remember—"

"To breathe and watch the shoulders and feet," she finished for him. "I will."

"Good." Then his arms wrapped around her, squeezing her into his chest. At first she tensed and almost pushed away, shocked by his display of affection. But she returned the embrace, laying her head against his chest to hear the racing of his heart while his chin rested atop her head. After a moment, and a loud huff of annoyance from the elf, he bent until he could whisper into her ear, just loud enough for her to hear, "Don't you dare die on me. If you do, I'll never get to show you what we've continuously left unsaid."

51

Wooden beams crisscrossing high ceilings with occasional windows occupied Christopher's vision. This addition to the castle consisted more of wood than it did of stone, a simple factor making his room more welcoming than the original architecture. Far away from his brother's rooms, ones vacant for a decade. He wondered what his brother was doing and if his "new king" had given more thought to the compromise he mentioned but did not fully explain. The small wooden ball he tossed toward the ceiling fell back down long before reaching the wooden beams and smacked into his open palm.

When the door opened, he simply shifted his head to glance over. His aunt wore a deep green dress laced with bold red ribbons outlined in gold along the edges. As all women's dresses did, it held snug to her waist and chest with a series of buttons that ran up the back. Thin fabric swayed smoothly with each step she took. He hadn't thought to notice anything about their dresses until meeting the Orda'anian princess in clothing so different.

He switched the wooden ball to his other hand to avoid hitting his aunt in the face as he tossed it up toward the rafters again.

"Shouldn't you be getting ready?" Marsha looked down at him with crossed arms.

The ball went up again, but he let it thud into the bed beside him rather than catch it. It rolled into his side, following him as he shifted on the mattress.

"I'd be no good on a battlefield, Aunt Marsha." He winced at the memory of bruises and broken bones received throughout years of training sessions gone poorly. "*They* were the warriors. *They* were the noble princes. *They* were the heirs to the crown."

Marsha clicked her tongue and sat down on the bed next to him, picking up the wooden ball. "And you outlived them all." She turned the ball about as if hunting for a hidden compartment. "Almost all of them."

He grunted in response, snatching the ball from her hand and tossing it up once more. "I also brought Charles home." His fingers curled around the ball as he spoke. "I thought—" The words twisted in his throat. While rolling the ball with both palms, he sat up and crisscrossed his legs. "I thought I would enjoy being out of my brothers' shadows."

When he moved to toss the ball up again, Marsha grasped it. "Meaning?"

He sighed and fell back onto the bed. The new angle allowed him to see the sword his mother had gifted resting against the chest of drawers. "He came so willingly." He closed his eyes to relive the scene. "Laid down his weapons and did not fight Nasir when that gnarled grumpy old man snapped chains around his wrists." Christopher flinched, recalling the chains he'd placed around Charles's ankles each night of the journey. Worry made him do it. Worry that Nasir was right and Charles would disappear while he slept. Which would have meant failure for him, and Christopher knew what awaited those who failed his father's commands.

The mattress dipped when Marsha shifted away from the edge and pinned him with a stare that made her honey brown eyes glimmer just like his father's would when expecting an answer. A glare which always forced words from him.

"I will never have the level of resolve or determination that leading requires." He peered at the sword and glanced up at the sheathed dagger resting atop the dresser.

Marsha sighed and pushed herself to stand beside the bed. "Lukas was right. You are inordinately melancholic." A few footsteps mingled with the slight swish of her dress. "What were Nerida's instructions for you?"

After pushing back to a seated position, Christopher turned away. She, like her brother, thought the stories of the dragons foolhardy tales they could use to scare their children into obeying. He swallowed, hoping his tone would sound convincing. "She wanted me away from Father's sudden whims and away from the army. Just in case."

"Logical," Marsha whispered. "That's what they were before Charles won the trial. Now?"

Christopher bit his tongue lightly, trying to rework the moisture into his now raspy throat. "Charles asked me to attend Rosealyn and Celena to a summit in Violet Grove as Jearnia's liaison."

"I'm appalled Claude ever let an elf into this castle." Marsha's slippered feet shuffled against the wooden floor. "And will you go with them?"

He hesitated a moment, searching inside for an answer that felt like his own desires rather than a responsibility. And found none. Hands smacking against his knees, he stood and exhaled carefully.

"What will you do while we're gone?" Christopher grabbed several random shirts, random pants, and the silver medallion. His dagger and sword he'd keep around his waist.

She rolled the wooden ball between two open hands, eyes narrowed into slits, and broke into a smile. "Keep your mother comfortable. What else?"

"How is Mother?" Clothes stuffed into his bag, medallion cold against his chest, he fitted the belt around his waist and secured the dagger.

"Recovering," Marsha murmured behind him. "You haven't visited?"

"She was asleep when I did." Christopher cinched the tanned leather pack. "I didn't want to wake her. Besides Celena, the elf, already asked for the horses to be prepared."

"Storms can move quickly in this valley."

He slung the bag over his shoulder and turned to face her with arms crossed against his chest. "If I ever want Charles's trust, I need to do as he requests."

He watched her shift the ball from hand to hand. The rolling stopped, and she flung the ball at him. He caught it, palm stinging from the force of her throw. On her way out the door, she looked over her shoulder and met his gaze. "Trust is not easily won."

Christopher glanced around his room and tossed the ball toward his bed, but it rolled off the edge, thudding to the floor and continuing until it came to rest by his new sword. He squinted at the ball and then at the sword he had almost forgotten. A tightening of his jaw, a shake of his head that let his shaggy curls invade his vision, and he grabbed the weapon and secured it to his belt opposite the dagger.

Christopher stood next to the chestnut stallion who had become his companion for several journeys, rubbing one hand along his mane while waiting on the others. His brother and the Orda'anian princess looked at each other as though they never wanted to part but also like they would never see one another again. After several minutes, and a comment from the elf Christopher was too far away to hear, Charles and Rosealyn embraced.

As they did, Christopher studied Charles's demeanor. He had meant what he said about the man's resolve, an ability Christopher was positive he would never have himself. Otherwise, he would have asked to stay. Inside the castle walls was a place of comfort, a place he knew and would always be familiar with, despite the many painful memories.

Charles followed Rosealyn and Celena to their mounts, holding the reins for the princess's horse as she mounted. The kindness in his brother's eyes, the lack of the hardness he saw tormenting his other siblings and himself, clawed at his insides.

After speaking with the princess, Charles approached, and Christopher assumed the absence of emotion he had practiced since his first brother's death.

"I'm not sure if I should thank you or be angry with you," Christopher grumbled once Charles stood beside him. His older brother, decked out in the king's attire, smiled. Not a malicious smile of one who had ulterior motives or was about to threaten him, but of understanding and sympathy.

"See it as an opportunity." Charles glanced back at the princess with a quick flash of flushed cheeks. "I am allowing you to be Jearnia's voice at this summit." Searching gaze, selective words. Commanding, really. "We are lending aid to Orda'an even if the other countries do not."

Rather than spit out a retort, Christopher leaned forward and crossed his arms over the pommel of the saddle. "Understood, my King." He knew his tone dripped with animosity. Some day, he supposed he might get along with his older brother, but not until he believed his brother's words about forming a compromise. As he sat up straight, Christopher noticed the simple golden circlet atop his brother's head, and his brows raised.

"That's not Father's crown." The crown their father wore had been the crown of Jearnia for several generations. Possibly since its founding. Charles never explained how the damage had occurred, though Christopher had his suspicions.

"No, it is not." Charles spoke in a calm tone as he stroked the stallion's mane. "Let Father's sins die with him."

Christopher shifted, rubbing a gloved palm against his pant leg as if to wipe away the growing sweat. "If it's even possible."

That elicited a soft chuckle from his older brother, and Charles patted the stallion's neck. "Keep her safe, stay with her, and once this is over, we will discuss a compromise." Their eyes met again, and Christopher noted how Charles struggled between calm and worry. "You should probably fear that dragon, wherever he is, much more than you should ever fear me."

Christopher pursed his lips, thinking for a moment, and in a voice almost too soft for him to hear said, "Thank you." A slight nod meant Charles heard his whisper, and he tilted his head toward Rosealyn and Celena, who were both several paces down the hill leading into the city.

A part of him wanted to say more, to learn what future awaited him upon his return, but he didn't know what else to say. So he followed. Once more, he was leaving home for another's benefit rather than his own. Gripping the reins tighter, he glanced back at his brother who looked every inch the king he claimed to be. The set determination, the poise, and the appearance of a heavy burden weighing on him; Charles would not be the ruler their father had been.

By the time he rode alongside Rosealyn and Celena, they were beyond the castle gates, riding through Volante. Rosealyn looked back wistfully and turned her attention to the road before them and the small buildings on either side.

"I suppose these homes are larger than they appeared from the mountain path," she said, and he gave her a sidelong glance.

"They are not homes," Christopher explained. "These buildings house sla—" The glare she pinned him with made him bite his tongue, halting before he finished the word.

"I knew Jearnia utilized these plantations, the fields a form of servitude, but I did not think you would consider those who worked them slaves."

Her voice no longer carried the air of uncertainty from their first meeting. Now her tone was reminiscent of the one his brother had used on him hours earlier.

Christopher cleared his throat, surveying the line of small homes. "To be honest, I have no idea how many live in these homes. If one failed in doing what Father asked, he either sliced their necks or sent them to work in these fields. My uncle controls the northern fields of Volante, my aunt the southern." He lifted a shoulder and swayed with the horse's movement for several paces. "Sometimes Father would call them back, ask them the same questions, and if their answers were not satisfactory—"

The princess's darker skin turned ashen. "I'm beginning to understand how Charles could kill his own father."

He considered adding a statement in response to the princess's realization, but it was hard to decide if he felt anger or relief at his father's demise. Drunken tirades, impossible comparisons. The man's belief that Charles had died during his royal mission made it so none of the rest of them would ever obtain their father's approval. He tried not to let his father's words affect him, but he wanted to prove his worth.

While studying the brewing storms approaching from the north, Christopher rubbed a gloved hand along his leg and realized he had shed no tears for his father's death. A hollow void consumed his emotions. As always, he preferred to feel nothing rather than everything.

Storm winds nipped their backs, hastening their approach to the Guadelaide Lake. Christopher longed to dip his feet in again. To feel the tickle of the fish against his skin. An entire world awaited. One that, someday, he would explore. A simple meal of dried meats, rest, and the elf woke them when night still blanketed the world. Thunder roared in the distance, growing closer with each crack. A quick glance to the north revealed they had been right to leave when they did, before the brewing storms stalled significant travel.

52

Days of searching. Days without answers. Days where Eilon's control solidified or dissipated. His entire body surged with power as he circled the city of Vandyl from above. Most of the citizens had fled, racing from his flames in hope of survival. Others roamed aimlessly, gathering the broken pieces of their pathetic lives, trying to fend for food his magic would never allow to grow. One city, one field at a time, Eilon took what he could. Not enough, though. What he possessed now was nothing compared to what he had once wielded.

Soon he would recreate what the cruel world was so quick to take. He beat his wings and craned his neck, heating the simmering well of flame held deep within. By the time he'd realized what Magna had done when they had fought in that cave, Xannan's bond with the blade was too strong. His last great surge of magic created myth from legend. Then Eilon tried to break that bond.

After a century of fighting to regain even a sliver, a mere fraction of what Magna had trapped, he was no further than when he began. Clever matriarch. Trapping him to protect her own. Force him to scrounge for scraps. Piece by piece. Moment by moment. The land could only provide for so long.

Rain dripped from leaf to leaf before landing on Rosealyn's shoulder, and she shivered. Wintry winds whipped through loose clothing, though her soaked strands of hair did not move. A reminder this rain easily could have been snow, though she swore many drops of rain were closer to ice than they were water.

Try as they might, they could not beat the storm. Even surrounded by tall trees, the rain found them. Her drenched shirt clung to her body, same as her pants. Water dripped in steady beats from high above. Not loud enough to disguise the ever-present hum. She gripped the reins tighter, realizing she'd been tapping that rhythm against the small strips of leather, and listened instead to their surroundings. Each pace forward the group achieved created a sucking sound Rosealyn would have preferred living her entire life without ever hearing.

She swatted at a bug buzzing near her ear, muttering a curse when a leaf full of water dumped its contents on her head. After wiping the rain from her face as best she could, Rosealyn realized Celena and Christopher had stopped, so she did likewise. They'd arrived. Even through the haze, Violet Grove had a familiar ambiance. Like Andalova, the elven village boasted quaint homes with a meeting house at its center. She and the other leaders would stay in that building, so Celena claimed. Rosealyn disliked the idea of sleeping under the same roof as the Hoclians. Or the Alkaanians whose loyalties remained uncertain. It had been tough enough to travel with a despondent and mostly silent Christopher for several days. Celena's proximity brought a modicum of comfort. Not knowing who led the Tenoan council now, she wondered if she would finally meet her mother's cousin Ramon. She frowned. A foul taste accompanied the thought.

Rosealyn surveyed the homes. Vines grew along their sides, and she imagined how colorful this village would be at the height of spring. Not an inch of any home would be left without beauty. When Celena dismounted and led her mare into the stables, Rosealyn and Christopher followed. Thunder grumbled above them, and a flash of lightning lit the path of rocks leading through the streets. Rosealyn peered up at the sky, squinting at the clouds with a silent wish the first snows would delay until she'd reclaimed her home.

Once inside the stables, Celena approached a tawny-haired elf wearing light brown robes that billowed around him with the storm winds surging through the stables' open doors and hugged him. Rosealyn's brows raised at the display, and she cleared her throat, lifting the mare's reins.

"Arjun will care for them." Celena nodded toward the elf she'd embraced, who sighed at her comment. "The horses like you better than me. They always have."

"Probably because you always smell too much like a dragon." He faced Rosealyn and bowed his head. "Welcome to Violet Grove, Princess Rosealyn." She started to thank him, but Arjun shifted toward Christopher with another dip of his head and a slight twinkle to his red eyes. "And to you, Prince Christopher, though we expected your brother."

In response, Christopher grunted but said nothing. Arjun approached and led both Rosealyn and Christopher's mounts into empty stalls, calling on a younger elf to care for them.

The horses provided for, he paused at the entrance and said, "The other leaders await your presence."

Celena mumbled something incoherent, Christopher said nothing, and Rosealyn froze. Her chest became like a block of ice and she tried to grasp her dress-skirts only to remember she wore the shirt and pants Celena had gifted her at Andalova.

Rosealyn cleared her throat. "Please tell me I have time to clean up before meeting with them. I'd rather not look like I was drug through the middle of the Orda'anian plains during a thunderstorm."

Celena laughed, a sound much rougher than Rosealyn expected given the woman's often honey-like tone. A quick wave of her hand, Celena said, "A change of clothes again, I presume?"

"And me," Christopher said. He tugged his shirt until he could wring the edges and release a torrent of water from the cloth. "So much for avoiding the storms."

This time both elves chuckled, and Arjun said, "We were once known for providing aid. I suppose that can include replacing sopping wet attire with dry. I'll show Christopher to his room and let the others know the meeting will resume after the evening meal."

"Resume?" Rosealyn blurted out. "But I thought—"

Arjun winced. "I stalled as long as I could. Since three of five country's leaders are present they decided they could begin discussions on how to handle the situation." He lifted the hood of his robes, situating the material so rain would stay off any part of his head, making Rosealyn envious. His red eyes met hers from beneath the hood's rim. "Perhaps you can persuade them better than I."

53

Carved leaves tumbled and twisted along the edges of the table resting in the center of the innermost room of the meeting house at Violet Grove. Sky blue walls made the dozens of paintings adorning them bolder. Each of those paintings reminded Rosealyn of home. Gardens, city streets, forests like the one she'd traversed the day before. Many of the paintings blended together, forming larger images. The Shendaran Forest, the Vadamon Sea, the imposing castle of Cantadad, and the simplistic castle of Vandyl mixed with the major landmarks of Tenoa, Hoclia, and Alkaan. Very few held portraits of people. Except one. It looked familiar, as though she had seen it before, but Celena was the first elf she had ever met. The woman in shimmering white depicted within that frame was not Celena, though the two were uncannily similar. Rosealyn's gaze drifted back to the landscape paintings which reminded her of a childhood long ago, when her father would encourage her to venture outside the castle walls.

Rosealyn surveyed those at the table, reminding herself of each name as she glanced their way. Celena to her right in her usual garb of dark shirt and pants. Then her mother's cousin Ramon, whose loose gray shirt provided a stark contrast to his dark skin. Between Ramon and Christopher was an empty seat, which gave her pause for a moment. Beside Christopher sat King Nathaniel, who appeared several years younger than Christopher, and his thin, shoulder-length blond hair blended in with a pristine golden coat. Next came the dark-haired and dark-eyed Hoclian leader with loops of beads resting against her chest. That was the hardest gaze to meet, both because she had killed one of their citizens and because of how many of her people they had killed. Directly to her left sat Arjun, almost as if the two elves thought to protect her from those surrounding her.

She counted her breaths to ease the bubbling nerves and smiled. The counting would always remind her of Charles. But thinking of him and what they had almost shared made her breaths quicken, turned her hands clammy, and made her heart lurch in her chest.

In for two, out for two, not the right time to think about that hallway. Rosealyn gripped her sword's hilt for a brief second and offered what she hoped was a kind smile. She glanced at Ramon, envious of his loose, flowing garb. Hair cut short as though he had none, his eyes appeared a darker shade of brown than his skin. While her mind wanted to trust Ramon, an unfamiliar emotion swirled inside.

"I'm glad to finally meet you, Cousin Ramon." Simple introductions had already been given, but niceties always helped. "Tenoa will stand by me, correct?"

"It is your mother's wish." Ramon inclined his head with an almost reassuring smile, fingertips resting against each other as he leaned back in his seat. "And the council's, which I speak for."

Rosealyn returned her cousin's words with a silent, tight-lipped smile. When she looked away from Ramon, the muscles between her shoulders loosened and the strange taste lessened. The welling dread further dissipated when she turned to the young man sitting opposite her at the table. Where Charles had kept his hair short, Christopher let his hang loose with long curls abundant. With one hand, he pulled the curls away from his face. No matter how much she spoke with him or questioned him, Rosealyn did not know how to feel about Charles's younger brother. *The Gift trusts him, but not Ramon?*

"Once a plan is made, we'll let my brother know when and where to meet." Christopher's voice sounded dry, though he smirked at her. "As we discussed during the journey."

Rosealyn nodded, teeth tugging at her bottom lip. "No update from Nasir? Or about Vandyl?"

"I have heard nothing more, Princess."

"Xannan holds Vandyl," Ramon and Arjun said in unison. An awkward glance passed between the two, and Rosealyn rubbed her temples, staring down at a map of Ebios either Celena or Arjun had placed before her. She looked at the small dot which represented her home. Synda had torn her from there with such ease, and it would take a miracle for her to return. She shivered without warning, rubbing her arms. *If I ever return.*

"Cousin Ramon, you said Mother is in Tenoa?" Rosealyn swallowed and turned toward him again. After Ramon's quick nod, she looked back down at the map. "How did she arrive?"

"Out of thin air in the council room." His chair creaked. No surprise laced his tone. "What started as an almost imperceptible black cloud turned into Roseanne."

Rosealyn folded her hands and rested them on the map of the continent, wondering how to shake the chilling sensation Ramon's words brought. His description fueled a possibility as she recalled how the black cloud which took her father from the courtyard had been much larger than him. "Is he weakening?" She shared a glance with Celena. "Used too much strength to kill Father? What else has Eilon done? Unless—"

Images Rosealyn consistently pushed away surfaced. Soldiers, cooks, stable hands, all with fear etched onto their faces. All the Gift confirmed was that Vandyl had been attacked. The level of destruction, who lived or died, she did not know. Rosealyn pressed her lips together and flattened her palms against the table.

"Pardon?" Ramon's chair creaked again, and Rosealyn's quick glance showed he leaned forward with forearms resting on the table as he squinted at her. "I'm not sure I understand."

"I need assistance to retake Vandyl and annihilate Xannan." Rosealyn smoothed the map, pausing when her hands rested at each edge. Two day's hard ride, and she would be home. She lifted the finger covering Pasea and winced. "The more Eilon weakens, the greater chance we have."

"Eilon?" Ramon asked, and Rosealyn's quick glance took in the raised eyebrow and distant look in the man's eyes before roaming around the table to find both the Honorable Jordan of Hoclia and King Nathaniel of Alkaan leaning forward as well. A creak sounded, shifting her attention as Christopher settled back in his seat, blowing a wisp of curly hair from his face and crossing his arms while Rosealyn fought not to roll her eyes at the young man's air of arrogance.

"A dragon." Rosealyn rounded her shoulders. "A black dragon. Magna's enemy, and an enemy to us all." Her voice softened. "Celena, how does one kill a dragon?"

"I—"

Arjun held out a hand across Rosealyn to touch Celena's, and the elf paused, allowing Arjun to speak instead. "The dragons have returned, yes. But first, Xannan. With him gone, we can gift Praeteritum to another. Preferably someone younger and less difficult to trust." He moved his arm back to his lap, creating clinking sounds when he smoothed his robes. "Together, Princess Rosealyn and the other recipient can learn to wield the power of Praesidio and eventually destroy Eilon. Nevertheless, Celena and I will come prepared."

"But he's weak now." Rosealyn swiveled her head from one elf to the other in an attempt to stare down both as she spoke. "Why not annihilate him before he regains his full strength?" Both elves shook their heads, and Rosealyn had to bite back a curse, asking instead, "How does one kill a dragon, aside from a dragon-wrought blade?"

"You trap them," came the reply. But it didn't come from either side. It came from across the table. From Christopher. Who sat with that annoying smug smile on his face. "Father hated the idea that dragons could be real, but Mother insisted on spinning those tales." He drummed his fingers along the table. "Once they're trapped, only a weapon made by one of their own kind can truly kill them. Otherwise they are simply trapped."

Christopher pulled on the string which held his family medallion around his neck, lifting it over his head to set it on the table. The medallion clicked open to reveal a clear crystal with a faint black cloud pulsing in its middle. The crystal jutted at several odd angles but was no thicker than the medallion which had contained it. "Mother gave me the Jearnian crystal."

Rosealyn stared, mouth agape, while Jordan, Nathaniel, Celena, and Arjun pulled forth medallions of their own. She shook her head, rubbing at her temples with the points of her elbows digging into the table on either side of the map. "Did Father know too?"

Celena nodded, and the others all sat back in their seats, though the strange dark-hued crystals resting atop the table seemed to suck in what little light the room had left.

"You were born here." Celena tapped a finger on Violet Grove's marker on the map. "Whatever Phillippe saw when he first held you in his arms made him leave his medallion with us, made him perpetuate the theory many already believed that all magical creatures were only myth. The others believed these medallions to be elven gifts. And in a way, they are."

"More secrets," Rosealyn muttered under her breath. She asked so all could hear, "Are there any other crystals?" She rounded on Celena. "Any other insane secrets Father knew but never shared?"

All Celena offered was an unconvincing shrug.

"Five is sufficient, even for Eilon." Arjun rested his hand on her forearm, an action which made her tense, though it also eased a smidgen of rising anger. "As for your second question, that depends on what you already know." He lifted his hand from her arm, and Rosealyn breathed deeply to stifle the simmering emotions trying to coalesce. "We can trap Eilon, if needed, but we are here to assist you in annihilating Xannan first. Though, I must add, I'm grateful no shouting has occurred. Yet."

Rosealyn curled her hands into fists and flattened her palms atop the map again as she followed the elf's poignant gaze to Jordan. The Hoclian leader didn't flinch at the stare or move.

"The few who survived the battle at Pasea told me of what one would call a dragon accomplished before Phillippe left." Jordan almost spat the name, voice more gruff and guttural than any other woman Rosealyn had met. "We want no quarrel with a dragon. Who is this Xannan?"

"The Lost Prince." Rosealyn's tongue turned leaden. The pieces she thought had been so perfectly matched were tumbling out of place again. "My father's murderer."

"Ah," Jordan said with feigned surprise. "And what army does he have?"

"Mercenaries," Arjun explained when Rosealyn stared mute at the dark table before her. *Steady breaths. Use what is available to you and make it work.*

The adolescent King Nathaniel harrumphed. "The missing people mentioned at the last summit with Phillippe became mercenaries for this Xannan?"

She ignored the youth's question, for she did not know the correct answer, and whispered, "Xannan is a threat to us all." She lifted her chin, meeting the gaze of each without flinching. "We can eliminate him. Let us not allow our pasts to interfere with a bright future." Her gaze found Christopher's, and he tensed. "A future where we can live in harmony despite our differences."

She nodded to each as she named them. "Honorable Jordan, King Nathaniel, Praetor Ramon, I require military aid to reclaim my home, Vandyl, the capital of Orda'an. What say you in response?"

Jordan tsked and shifted the furs resting on her shoulders to retrieve a rolled parchment. "We will not help without something in return."

Rosealyn winced, rubbing her temples with her fingers. "I am willing to negotiate an agreement between our countries, Honorable Jordan." While thinking back through her studies on mediation, Rosealyn reminded herself to choose her words wisely. "Our trade routes are—"

Boisterous laughter burst from Nathaniel, and Rosealyn bit her lower lip so hard she was surprised she hadn't drawn blood. The young king waved a dismissive hand while holding the other to his stomach as the laughter turned silent but shook his body.

"I can salvage our trade routes." Rosealyn interlaced her fingers. "And we could include you in those."

"Not good enough." Jordan's voice was throaty, deep, yet somehow soft. It unsettled Rosealyn, making it more difficult to determine if the Hoclian leader was a woman as she'd assumed. "We want resources of our own. Land." Jordan pushed the parchment toward her. "Land that can prosper."

Almost the entire western border of Orda'an was marked, all but the diminishing city of Cantadad where Rosealyn's aunt resided as duchess.

"Too much. The priests would never approve this large of a trade." Rosealyn grimaced, lips twisting as she considered how to counter the demand. "I could persuade as far south as the Pasean fields, but those fields were our greatest producers and—"

"Pasea and its surrounding fields should suffice," Jordan agreed with a curt nod. "But it only gains you one troop. If losses are too great, we will demand more."

Rosealyn tightened her lips into a thin line but nodded her agreement. One matter settled, she turned to the blond youth. "King Nathaniel, what is your response? Will you assist in my retaking of Vandyl?"

"I have no quarrel with your people, Princess Rosealyn." A hint of laughter dripped from his tone and Rosealyn inhaled sharply at the reminder she had not yet assumed the throne. *Should have challenged Mother on that issue much sooner.*

"So I can count on several of your troops aiding me?"

"A few of them, aye. I refuse to lose my entire army to this conquest of yours." The laughter dissipated from his tone, though it remained apparent on his face. "If helping means you will not attack us later, then help Alkaan will."

"Thank you, King Nathaniel." Rosealyn bowed her head, and he returned the gesture. After another deep breath, Rosealyn turned to Christopher.

"Charles said to offer aid even if no one else does." He chuckled, and his curls swayed with the shake of his head. "I imagine his battalion is at or near the border, or at the very least has made it to the Guadelaide Lake." Words verbatim to their conversation that morning.

Another deep breath, Rosealyn turned to Ramon, whose grin displayed straight white teeth in a way that gave her pause. "What little aid Tenoa can provide our northern protectors, we will."

The tightness in Rosealyn's chest loosened. Barely. "Meet at the Cliff of Lycene in a week's time. We will march to Vandyl from there." She glanced over at Celena. "Or will that be too long? Too much time for Eilon—"

"A week to dragons is like seconds to you, Princess."

"A week, the Cliff of Lycene." Rosealyn nodded and turned back to the leaders. "Thank you all again for lending your aid. Orda'an and its people thank you."

She remained seated as the others left. Jordan's leathery face hid any emotions while the diminutive King Nathaniel had laughter in his eyes. Ramon flashed her another toothy smile which churned her stomach while Christopher lingered a moment after, a question in his eyes, but he left without asking it. She sat with two elves, beings her father claimed had gone extinct. A weak laugh laced with tears created a strange sound in her throat, and she pressed her fingers against her eyes to prevent her tears from falling.

"There is one more thing, Princess." Arjun's voice was even softer than when he interrupted Celena. Her body trembled with the mixture of laughter and sobs, and the elf's words did little to help. "A letter from your mother."

"Why didn't Ramon give it to me?" She stared at the envelope Arjun set in front of her. "That's not from Mother. It's not her handwriting. And my name is not Jaida."

"Not to the people of Orda'an, true. But for her, Jaida is your name, the one she gave you," Arjun explained. Though she had only known the elf a day, she preferred his soft tone to Celena's abrasiveness. A familiarity about Arjun made her believe she would truthfully answer any question he asked. "The Tenoan council insisted on Phillippe's marriage to Roseanne since she was the eldest, despite what Phillippe and Catarina, your mother, shared. I promised to deliver this to you when you found us. She explains the situation better than I could."

Rosealyn rubbed her arms, trying to warm away the chills as more pieces of the puzzle that had become her life tumbled. *Whatever happened to telling the truth? Whose side am I supposed to believe?*

Arjun and Celena left, leaving Rosealyn to stare at the envelope resting atop a map of the continent. Rosealyn leaned on her elbows, wondering if she could summon the Gift's ability. In the weeks since her father's death, she had avoided thinking about it, much less trying to use it. But the letter and the addendum from Gailin's journal added a new piece of information: the dragon's magic enhanced the Gift. The ability itself was within her, pulled forth when Magna allowed the Twin Blades to be gifted to Xannan and Gailin nearly five generations past.

54

Everywhere Rosealyn looked, vines snaked along beams, along doorways, even decorated the bed she occupied. The mattress enveloped her, much more inviting than the cold, wet ground she'd slept on for several nights. She twisted the unopened letter, squinting as the flickering lamplight danced across a name she refused to believe could be hers. Blankets almost too thick despite the waning winter months rested beneath her, cushioning her while questions about her entire life bubbled to the surface. Thoughts and emotions cascaded like a waterfall, each stream tumbling into the next without pause.

All except Christopher had left Violet Grove the moment the meeting ended. Rosealyn worried about trusting any of them, but she had little choice. She could not destroy Eilon or Xannan on her own.

The flowing handwriting of the letter's front reappeared. *Jaida.* Another twist of the envelope to be greeted by a dot of black wax. *So different from my name. Why is mine so similar to …* Mother's? What makes one a mother?

She set the envelope on the bedside table and hovered a hand over her sword briefly. Cumbersome, awkward, but it had become an inexplicable part of her. Without it and its incessant hum, she would feel lost. Shuttering the light as Arjun had shown her, she coated the room in blissful darkness. No windows, nowhere for moonlight to sneak in, no way for strange shadows to dance around her.

Sleep eluded her. Thoughts too tumultuous, too troubled for dreams. Then again, it was okay not to dream because the LeNoir Gift existed in sleep as much as it did in wakefulness. Another aspect of life both Gailin and her father had never mentioned. Whenever she succumbed to exhaustion, she stood amid a bloodied field. Shouts. Swords. People. Soldiers dying. Soldiers fighting. Her among them. Muscles aching. Lungs burning. Screams. Thuds. Mud. All such a whirlwind. Blood. So much blood. Too much. She shifted the blankets until they no longer weighed her down, curling on to her side in hopes she could find a place comfortable enough to assist in drifting to sleep.

Her father's reluctant acceptance of the LeNoir Gift seemed perfectly logical. Images she could push away or summon. Emotions were worse. When she tried, it was like being caught in a torrential downpour with winds threatening to pull her from the ground. Concentrating with eyes squeezed closed, two images flickered as though they were trying to converge into one. The flash of a blade pummeling toward her, but it switched to Charles sitting on a set of stairs. Repeat. Dread flooded her with the approaching blade, then a cooling calm engulfed her until a blinding flash overwhelmed what little she could see. All filtered by a simple acknowledgment—she could not stop it.

Wood creaked near the door and Rosealyn slid her hand from under the covers to grasp the hilt of her sword. Footsteps scraped against wood, searching for a quieter approach. Closer and closer until she could feel the person's presence above her. Whoever it was, they were listening. Despite her erratic heartbeat, she maintained a steady, even rhythm to retain the facade of sleep. *In for two counts, out for two counts. Repeat.*

Cloth ruffled. One of the elves? She had not met all of them. But both Arjun and Celena promised the elves were loyal to her father and thus to her. Another creak of the wooden floor, followed by a barely audible inhale. Rosealyn rolled off the bed to the opposite side, sword in hand, as a dagger pierced the mattress.

Light flooded the room when she opened the lamp. Air lodged in her lungs, Rosealyn swallowed and pulled her sword free of its scabbard. Insides twisting, she understood the earlier unease every time she had looked his way. Tight-lipped, Ramon wrenched the dagger he meant to bury in her neck from the mattress.

Anger stoked the simmering pot inside her that continuously threatened to boil over. Surrounded by liars. Surrounded by traitors. Was this betrayal? Against her? Against her moth— the woman who had raised her? Jaw clenched, she bore her gaze into him, enunciating each word in a low, menacing tone. "What are you doing?"

"Taking what I need." He grimaced at the bed which inhibited his path. "You should be asleep."

"And you shouldn't have missed." Rosealyn tossed the sword's sheath aside as Ramon jumped onto the bed and drew a second dagger.

She wouldn't attack. A motto she would hold until her last breath: defend, protect, do not provoke. One step to the side avoided his jump off the bed. Clumsy strikes, easy to avoid. None necessitated lifting her sword.

Engraved wood dug into her back, and she cursed. Stupid, so ridiculous to let him corner her. Light glinted off his daggers. Too close.

"What in the Blazes—" Her sword met his dagger, creating a ringing sound as she tried to tear it from his grasp. "Does family mean nothing to you?"

This time, Ramon's strikes formed a pattern. She ducked, wincing at the thud of blade meeting wood above her head. As she stood, she rammed her shoulder into his abdomen, shoving him backward. Muscles tensing, she flexed her hand gripping the sword and whispered, "Please don't make me kill again."

Ramon's laugh was strange and malicious. His words slithered into her, worming their way into her thoughts. "The dead can't kill."

Another rush of movement. Similar pattern. With her back pressed against the wall, she had nowhere to go. One of his daggers aimed for her throat. It would be a quick slash. A fatal one. No time to see where the other would land. She knocked the first dagger from his hand with her sword, preventing him from slashing her throat.

Ramon's movement continued and Rosealyn lifted her leg to kick him away from her. Before she could extend her leg, his second dagger pierced her thigh. She bit back a scream, shoving the pain aside as she followed through with the kick. Before he could regain his balance, she thrust her sword forward into his abdomen. Ramon grunted, reaching for the weapon embedded in her thigh, and gasped as she twisted her sword.

Teeth gritted shut against another scream, she shifted to regain her balance. The small amount of weight her wounded leg supported was too much. Warm blood trickled from her thigh to her ankle. Between the wall and her uninjured leg, she could stay upright. Barely. With a throaty screech, she pushed her sword in further and winced. *End them, before they end you.*

Blood trickled over his lips and she fell as he did, her sword still inside him. Shaking, she pulled the sword free and gripped the hilt. Gasps wet and raspy, Ramon reached for her sword. Head falling back against the wall, Rosealyn tugged the sword away from her dying cousin. Rather pointless. Red liquid oozed from him, coating the planks of wood flooring.

The door burst open, and Rosealyn lifted her sword. No matter a dagger remained embedded in her thigh or that she likely didn't have the strength to stand. Both Celena and Arjun paused at the entrance, observing. Less than a moment later, Christopher's head peered over Celena's shoulder, and he pushed his way into the room.

She wouldn't look. At Ramon's too still body or the elves, and especially not at Christopher. So she stared at the ceiling. Killing another hurt. It didn't matter if it was some stranger riddled with scars or a cousin she'd heard stories of her entire life. She knew how it felt when someone she loved would never return. Her own life protected, but at what cost? Another face to add to her nightmares. How many more would she add before her own life was forfeit?

Rather than continue entertaining those thoughts, Rosealyn studied the truly fascinating woodwork, trying to ignore the throbbing pain in her thigh. Vines flowed like the Guadelaide River, weaving and curving. Her gaze followed it until searing pain radiated from her leg and she screamed; Christopher had removed the weapon.

She glared at him, speaking through gritted teeth. "That hurt."

Christopher set the dagger coated with her blood aside, and she struggled to recognize what emotions he displayed. Pity, curiosity, and intrigue warred with one another, and he tilted his head. "So you kill them the first chance you get, regardless of what past you shared?"

It was a question, and a statement, to which she had no answer. Celena kneeled beside her, pushing Christopher aside, cloth and water in hand to clean Rosealyn's wound. Where the elf had retrieved them, Rosealyn had no idea. Arjun stood at the door a moment longer, holding it with one hand and fishing in the folds of his robe with the other. When he approached, he had a small vial with a dropper. Celena moved aside. Cold drops blossomed inside the wound, and the pain lessened.

Once the bandage was taut around her leg, she held out her hand for the sword. Christopher ran an already bloodied rag over the blade once more and obliged her request. Grip tight on the weapon's hilt, she let Arjun and Christopher help her back to the bed. It was awkward, skirting around her dead cousin. She leaned back against the headboard and stared at the ceiling.

"Please tell me none of you want this sword, too." She glared at Christopher as she spoke, but he gave a small shake of his head, and his expression conveyed concern rather than animosity. The swirling emotions calmed at his response.

"If we wanted it, you would not be here." Arjun searched the pockets of his robes, glass bottles clinking together as he pulled out several. After selecting one, he pocketed the others. "This will help you sleep and heal the wound well enough. You should, at the very least, be able to attempt a cautious walk in a few hours time." He shared a glance with Celena and handed her the bottle. "Celena will stay while you rest. Drink."

She grasped the bottle and frowned at Ramon's corpse. "He tried to kill me." She glanced at her sword. "For the sword?" Her lips twisted into a frown, and she hissed as Celena tied an additional bandage around her leg. "Could he have been lying about Moth—"

Her words halted, wondering how to refer to the woman she now knew was not her mother. The letter addressed to Jaida, who Arjun claimed was the same as she, sat unopened beneath the diminishing flame of her lamp. It cast shadows over Arjun and Christopher as they prepared to move Ramon from her room.

"Drink." Celena pulled the stopper for her. "I won't leave you alone. We will speak more when I wake you."

Without another thought, Rosealyn tipped the bottle back and drank, soon slipping into a blissful and dreamless sleep.

55

A shake of Rosealyn's shoulder jolted her awake. She winced when reaching for her sword caused a spike of pain to lace through her thigh as a sharp reminder of the wound. Celena tsked as she removed the sodden bandages, dripping more of the pain-reducing liquid into the wound—which appeared to decrease in size before Rosealyn's eyes.

"I have something to show you." Celena tied the bandage, and Rosealyn ground her teeth and tested a modicum of weight on her leg. *Invisible wound gone only to be replaced by another real one.*

Celena allowed Rosealyn to relinquish some of her weight on the elf as they walked through the hallways of Violet Grove's meeting house. Her birthplace. Which meant both Celena and Arjun knew about her birth mother. Had spoken with the woman. And her father.

She had no desire to read Catarina's letter. All it offered was proof of more lies.

Celena stopped at the entrance to a vast round room with a large tree of pink blooms in its center. Sunlight filtered through the open ceiling, alighting the tree surrounded by stone columns. A thousand burning candles flickered at the room's edge. Row after row. Before she could stop it, her left hand drifted. This room reminded her of Vandyl's tombs. Despite never finding her father's body, she would always consider that stone etched with her father's name to be his final resting place. She tugged at her lower lip. Replace the tree with the Orda'anian Blaze and torches in place of the candles, and this room could become Vandyl's tombs. Were these candles reminiscent of those who had survived a loss like she'd endured?

The scent of the blossoms, the warmth of the sun, and the stone walls all offered comfort. Celena, who seemed to abhor the robes Arjun wore and remained in her pants and loose shirt, guided Rosealyn to the room's center. Thigh throbbing, but no longer bleeding, Rosealyn hobbled alongside the elf. A cursory glance showed nowhere for her to sit, though she contemplated lowering herself to the floor.

"What now?"

Wind rustled through the blossoms, bringing their scent to her. A familiar scent that reminded her of her father. True calm, the kind she had not felt since his last embrace, enveloped her as she wrapped her arms around herself. Not even two months, and if she was being honest with herself, she hadn't paused to absorb her father's loss.

"You do as you said you would do." Celena moved closer to the tree, resting a hand on its bark as she peered up at the sky. "As the conduit between the dragons and everyone else, I will return to Magna to request her assistance before meeting you at the Cliff along with the others."

Rosealyn shifted her weight, releasing the pressure of the cloth wrapped around her wound as her muscles relaxed. "My *Gift* is useless now."

"What the dragons give, regardless of intent, is never useless, Rosealyn, simply misunderstood." Celena turned and folded her arms. "I saw how you looked at your cousin yesterday. Your Gift warned you. Trust in what it provides."

The elf handed her the unopened letter and walked away, leaving Rosealyn alone with the tall tree of pink blooms. Her father had a similar one once, but it had withered and died when she was a young girl.

She sank to the stone floor, left leg sticking out while tucking the other in close to herself. Sniffling and dabbing at her eyes again, she ripped open the letter. She paused. A strange combination surfaced in the pit of her stomach, and she reached to grip her sword's hilt, only to discover she had not brought it with her. One breath, two breaths. She closed her eyes and spoke into the breeze. "All life has a purpose, right? Even those we dislike?" She stared at the flowing handwriting on the front of the envelope. "But how am I to understand this calm dread?"

Footsteps echoed off stone. "Celena, I don't—" She glanced over her shoulder. "Oh, Christopher, I-I'm—"

"A calm dread, you say? Describes my entire life." Christopher's curls swayed as he shook his head. "I'm surprised you do value life after last night." He nodded at her outstretched leg and squinted at the fresh bandage. "How's the leg?"

Rosealyn scowled at the young prince and turned back to the tree. "I have no need of your taunting."

"That's not a pleasant way to speak with a fellow royal." Christopher sat down next to her with legs crossed and hands resting on each knee like he might meditate. "You don't need their soldiers. Challenge this Xannan to a rightful duel where you regain what is yours should you kill him, and he keeps it if he kills you."

"There's more to it than that." The flash of a plummeting blade seared into her mind. She gasped, arms jolting to steady her balance before remembering she was already seated. "Eilon—" She paused, pressing her lips together as she debated how much to share.

Christopher chuckled. "You don't trust me."

Rosealyn held her breath for a few seconds and shook her head. "I want to. You're Charles's brother. But … well—" She paused, wishing she could speak with Charles instead. He understood her, listened to her, and knew what to say. Warmth flooded her cheeks at the thought, and she leaned back on her hands. Small rocks pebbled against her skin, and she used the mixture of smooth surfaces and jagged edges to ground her emotions. "Your mother shared the dragons' stories with you?"

His questioning blue eyes searched hers with a churning of judgment and curiosity. At his small nod, Rosealyn added, "How did your mother meet them?"

Christopher squinted at the sunlight peering down on them. "She would not share that with me."

"Secrets," Rosealyn muttered. She drummed her fingers along the rocks, matching the ever-present hum. "Do you have aspirations for the Jearnian throne? To challenge Charles as you suggest I do Xannan?"

The blossoms of the tree were apparently worth intense study. Several long moments passed before he whispered, "Undecided."

Rosealyn swallowed and chewed at her bottom lip. "You would kill your…?"

Christopher's gaze slid toward her, and his expression turned quizzical, as if waiting for her to finish the question. He picked up a small pebble, tossing it into the air and letting it smack into his palm. "You killed your cousin." His eyes darted about as they searched hers.

Rosealyn did her best not to flinch, but between the throbbing in her thigh and her racing thoughts, it was impossible to control her expression.

"You need to leave now."

The young man inclined his head, turning away from her as she whispered, "Why can't people just tell me the truth?"

A short bark of a laugh caused Rosealyn to glance back. Laughter. She missed her father's laugh and Charles's slight chuckle. Even Lori's. Or Moss's or Azeiah's. Genuine laughter, not the half-hearted version Christopher had just given.

"It's a foolish endeavor." His tone changed, almost sympathetic. "One that will probably get you killed."

Each fading footstep was like a clap of thunder, matching the racing of her heart. The letter from her birth mother crumpled in her hands; she'd read it after killing Eilon and Xannan.

56

Charles stood with arms crossed and squinted at the city of Lycene. Behind him was one battalion of the Jearnian army. His army. But the tendrils of smoke rising from the city kept his attention.

Ashtar approached at his side and cleared his throat. After Charles's simple nod, Ashtar said, "A message from Prince Christopher and the princess."

Charles waited, jaw clenching when the general did not add to his statement. "And?" He studied the lines of smoke increasing within the city. It was only midday, but the fires burned strong.

"They plan to gather at the Cliff by the week's end," Ashtar grumbled.

It was likely all his brother had sent. If Rose had sent anything, the general did not inform him. Charles lowered his arms and turned away when Ashtar added, "The scout found Nasir and his men."

At this, Charles looked at the general. Lines etching the aged man's mouth and forehead deepened, and his tone softened. Ashtar stared straight ahead, looking beyond the city. Decades of death could wear on even the most seasoned soldiers. "Nasir and at least forty of his company are dead. The others must have joined this Xannan."

Charles opened his mouth to say something which could honor the dead, but he had forgotten the words. Only the Orda'anian blessing came to mind. He snapped his jaw shut, hoping Ashtar would see his lack of voice as sympathy rather than forgetfulness of his own country's customs.

Voice void of emotion, Ashtar added, "Vandyl was burned."

His stomach made a strange movement. Burned? What was left? Who was left? If he had stayed… The muscles along his jawline spasmed from the tightness of his clenched teeth. For the moment, he would concentrate on what lay before him.

"See the smoke?" Charles pointed at the wafting plumes close to them.

Ashtar responded in his usual manner—a grunted assent. Even with both Marsha's and Lukas's proclamations acknowledging him as the rightful king, the soldiers followed Ashtar's lead. Proper attire and kind words meant nothing when Charles sounded like an outsider.

"Lycene has been abandoned for almost a year," Charles explained. "Those could be survivors from Vandyl. Perhaps even Jearnians." He watched a plume drift into the sky, frowning at the memory of his brief sword exchange with Xannan outside this same city. "Or Xannan's group of mercenaries." Charles raked a hand through his hair, halting when his fingertips met the golden circlet. One day, he hoped the men would follow his orders regardless of what regalia he wore. "We need to know either way."

"Now?" Ashtar asked. "Or in the morning?"

Charles studied the general for a moment. "Now. I offered to assist and provide aid. That is what we will do. We have no reason to quarrel with the Orda'anians."

"So you say."

"And I mean what I say." If he wasn't careful, his head would ache from how often he ground his teeth together while speaking with the general. "We don't need the entire troop marching down there and scaring them. Ten should suffice."

Another grunt and Ashtar walked away, leaving Charles to contemplate if he should strip the general of his station. He recalled the interactions he had witnessed between Phillippe and Azeiah, their calm camaraderie, the ease with which they spoke to and with one another. Despite not always using Phillippe's titles, Azeiah's respect for his monarch had always been obvious. Charles tightened his lips, looking to the southern horizon in the direction of Vandyl. It was not the scent of campfires which floated along the breeze from the castle. Even from this distance, the barely discernible scent of burned flesh and stone threatened to upend his stomach. *One less worry, yes, but I should have stayed. I could have helped.*

He shook the thought from his head. One hand rubbed his chin, while the other gripped his sword's hilt, and Rose's words replayed. "Keep the sword close; I'm positive you'll need it." Such emphasis could not be ignored, though he refused to let her other belief fester. He would see her again, and he would help her reclaim her home. Simple knowledge of Vandyl's destruction was enough to increase the bubbling sensations within. One question dominated his thoughts, a question he should have asked the elf, or his mother, but hadn't. *How does one kill a dragon?*

The steady plod of horses' hooves along the grass pulled him away from those thoughts, jaw tensing when Ashtar tossed the reins to him. Without a word, he mounted and nudged the mare toward Lycene, glancing back once to make sure they followed. Satisfied, Charles refocused on the city. Months of abandonment should have meant dilapidated buildings, but they showed no signs of decay or disuse. They passed several singed buildings at the town's edge, and then he saw the people. More than he had expected, even given the number of plumes rising from chimneys, roamed through the city streets.

Dirt, soot, and blood covered their faces. All of them. His presence, combined with the Jearnian soldiers, made several skittish, but each appeared to have a task to achieve.

Some who walked about did so with pain inscribed on their faces. Charles held his fist to his mouth and failed to prevent a gag. Burnt flesh and death coated his nostrils. As the group of Jearnian soldiers approached, Charles dismounted and tossed the reins back at the general. Some of those moving about skirted around the newcomers or rushed inside or cowered beside a building. Others gave him a wary glance, and a few stared at him with the wide eyes of recognition.

Breathing slowly, he surveyed the city. The people's movement had a pattern, a logical organization amidst the dismal sight. A young girl carrying a bucket of water with clothing scraps draped across an arm hurried into a building to his right, and he followed. She nudged the door open with her shoulder, weaving in before it swung back shut, but he held it open for her. She murmured an appreciative thank you and continued inside.

While she walked with brisk purpose, Charles stood stiffly with one hand holding the door open. Rows of makeshift cots lay side by side, covering the vast room he had entered. Fatal moans mingled with those of pain, and whisking between the wounded were Lori and Alvin. Even with the dismal scene, Charles smiled; it was good to see familiar faces.

Lori kneeled next to a cot, frowning, closed her eyes, and bowed her head. A moment later, she stood and looked up at the newcomers. The other soldiers had followed him inside, and a hush fell over the room. Lori, wringing her hands as she always did when nervous, squinted at him and approached. "Captain?"

He nodded once and spoke to his men. "Do as Lori and Doctor Alvin tell you." Lori's gaze softened into a small, kind smile, though her hands wrung together incessantly. After letting the door swing shut behind him, Charles asked, "How can we help?"

Lori pursed her lips, focus darting to the men behind him before studying his bright colored coat. Charles knew she recognized their armor. She'd lived long enough to know. "We need more buckets of clean water to help clean the wounds. Those who could travel we brought here. Some refused to leave their homes." Her shoulders fell. "For many, it was already too late."

Her voice trailed off, head turning toward the scene which lay beyond her. Charles's chest tightened. "It's a miracle this many survived, isn't it?"

Lori nodded, gesturing to empty buckets near the door. "Use those." Lori turned back and began her swift movement through the people who had once kept the castle from disarray.

Charles followed, amazed some had survived the journey given their wounds. For once, he was grateful to know the Orda'anian customs, whispering the words each would wish to hear. Some he squatted beside were coherent enough to speak with him, after reassurance he was there to help. After a time, his sense of smell became numb to the rotting flesh, and he moved through the cots just as Lori or Alvin did. While they offered aid, he provided words of encouragement and asked questions of those who could answer them. He learned of the mercenaries' attack, of Xannan's arrival, of the sudden overwhelming flame which left many dead, and learned how

Moss had risen to the challenge of leadership. Rather than wait for more death to ensnare them, Moss had gathered groups, telling them to come here. With each new story he learned, Charles searched for the young soldier.

He squatted next to another cot and flinched. Half of the man's face was burned and oozed, but he was in uniform. Charles recognized the cut of the man's jaw, and the light brown hair cropped short. "Moss?"

The fatigued soldier nodded and turned to him with gaunt eyes which grew wider, absorbing all of Charles's appearance. Random holes and splotches of blood riddled Moss's coat.

The Lieutenant-Captain laughed with an almost obnoxious guffaw. The guffaw turned to wheezing and gasping; Charles waited. Glancing down at his clothing, he understood the laughter. A form-fitting coat of red and golden orange, the unadorned ring of gold he had commissioned not long after the trial resting on his head, black pants almost too tight for riding. The not quite contagious laughter was Moss coping with the shock of Charles's appearance. The regalia of a king had seemed necessary when leading men who questioned his authority. Now it felt ridiculous. The pants dug in at odd places, and despite the proper fit of the coat, he tugged at the ends of the sleeves absentmindedly throughout the day.

"I always knew there had to be something more about you." Moss laughed again.

Charles kneeled beside his friend, and Moss's laughter dissipated. "Azeiah?" Charles asked.

"Xannan," Moss whispered, saying the name as though he didn't believe he had seen the man. "So many dead."

"Where is General Azeiah?" Charles's insides crumbled at Moss's small shake of the head.

"Gone, before the fires." Moss coughed and winced, then inhaled sharply. "And then—"

Charles gripped Moss's shoulder and whispered, "May the Blaze of your ancestors carry him home."

A moment of silence passed between them until Charles remembered a detail others had mentioned. "Queen Roseanne?"

Moss shrugged. "Some claimed she disappeared, others say he killed her, too. I-I ran. Helped others, but we ran. We abandoned Vandyl to him." Moss turned to speak to the ceiling. "Like cowards, we ran."

While Moss continued to stare blankly, Charles wondered what purpose this room once served, aside from the infirmary it had become. "Seeking survival is not cowardice." Charles remembered the first time Phillippe said the same to him, remembered the calm it had brought. A glance toward the doors, and Charles saw Ashtar standing there, studious, observant, disbelieving.

"You did what you could, Lieutenant—"

"What does rank matter now?" Moss interrupted. "In case you didn't notice, Orda'an has fallen."

Charles grimaced, dismayed by the young soldier's acceptance of the words he spoke. Not knowing what else to do or say, Charles said, "I'll return once Xannan and Eilon are defeated. Between you, Lori, and Alvin, the people of Vandyl are in excellent hands."

The guffaw returned, and Moss lifted himself to his elbows. "What can you do that all of us did not?"

"I met the elves." Charles decided it was the most logical place to begin. "They will assist Rose in defeating Eilon and Xannan."

Moss squinted when Charles mentioned the princess by name. The wheels of the young soldier's brain seemed to click, roving over Charles's attire a second time. "You—your—" Moss fell to his back and laid one arm over his eyes, wincing when the cloth rubbed against the raw skin on the left side of his face.

"So long as people are fighting for it, Orda'an has not fallen."

Moss nodded his understanding. "But, sir, um." Moss paused, shifting his arm to study Charles again. This time no laughter accompanied it. "My apologies, Your Majesty, but with General Azeiah—" He swallowed the last of the statement, as though refusing to voice it aloud could bring the kind-hearted general back to life. "You would be our commanding officer now."

"A mantle I can no longer hold." Charles looked around the room again. "They already accepted you as a leader." He met the young soldier's gaze. "I may not be your king or your military leader, but I am here to help." He surveyed the room again, and his shoulders fell. "I promised to help."

Moss propped himself onto his elbows, but Charles pushed him back to a prone position. Charles stood, noting how the bustle they had interrupted had returned. He stopped his hand before it reached the cuffs of his sleeves, resting it on the hilt of his sword instead, and took measured cautious steps toward Ashtar.

"What now, my King?" Ashtar asked.

Eyes narrowing, Charles rounded his shoulders and surveyed the room again, heart sinking further. Such destruction ignited his desire to destroy both Eilon and Xannan before they did any more damage.

"I will head to the Cliff to meet Rose and the other leaders." He wondered if it had been Rose's choice to meet there or if the elves had recommended it. Strange myths surrounded that cliff and its waterfall. "Go to Vandyl. Keep Xannan there as long as possible."

In his periphery, Charles saw the curt nod and the general's tight-lipped expression. "I've been a part of much death in war," Ashtar whispered when Charles turned to him. "And your father's whims, of course. But this…"

Charles's eyes widened, shocked to find compassion flickering across the man's face. "This is not what I expected either." His shoulders tensed. "Stay alert, General. A fire-breathing dragon lies ahead. For one of us, or both."

Ashtar nodded without the typical grunted reply. "You'll need men with you, my King," Ashtar said, the pause less noticeable than before. "At least a few. You'd be a fool to go alone."

"Delay them, but do not initiate an attack." Charles nodded, tugging at his sleeves as he scanned the room again. Lori kneeled by another, face downcast. Moss held one arm over his eyes, as though he could hide from what surrounded him. Alvin, with dark sunken eyes, shook his head and stood.

Charles pushed open the door, intending to inhale a deep breath of fresh air, but even the air outside the makeshift infirmary tasted foul. Charles clamped his lips tight against the smell, his stomach a beguiling mixture of nausea and anger. He mounted his horse and looked up. The sky was a bright blue, unobstructed by clouds. No dragon in sight.

But at his side, the blade warmed, and he hovered one hand above it. If he gripped it now, he didn't think it would burn his palm, but it reminded him of Celena's comments that the Twin Blades called to one another. A similar magic had created his, according to his mother. The emanating warmth must be a warning. He nudged the mare into a gallop, not waiting for the soldiers Ashtar claimed he would need.

57

Another attempt to control the Lost Prince. Weaker this time. Eilon needed more. Wanted more. But the connection between Xannan's blade and the other formed a new obstacle. One which necessitated a change of plans. A new goal percolated. One he should have chosen long ago. Consume enough power to break through Magna's magical line, the one designed to keep him out. Specifically him. He swallowed down the brewing heat in his neck, holding it for when the young dragon drew near again. Time would be of use, and time he would have. A tap into the future brought hope and despair. The heat intensified, crawling up his throat.

One image, one peek into the past, and Eilon's tenuous hold on Xannan would break. A risk. A flap of wings above him, he twisted and released the flame he'd held. The young dragon escaped his aim only because she was small enough to be quick. He followed her path, growling to recreate his flame. As he beat his wings and gained on the white dragon whose feathers did not burn, Eilon's control of Xannan faltered.

New futures be damned. He would do whatever it took to remake all he had lost.

Rosealyn tugged at the lightweight armor, curious how it could protect her from the giant arrows both the Hoclian and Alkaanian armies carried. Or a dragon's flame. Beneath the armor she wore a gray dress. Its skirts had slits alongside her legs, and the sleeves hugged tight to her shoulders. To one side of the tent, Celena perched in silence. An air of annoyance and duty resonated around her as she answered every question Rosealyn thought to ask, and even those she should have. No answer on how to combine the swords, though. *If it's even possible.*

She shifted the tent flap aside. Two other tents bordered hers atop the bluff at the Cliff of Lycene. Below the cliff were the armies. No sign of Tenoa, of course. Or Charles. And Blazes only knew where Christopher had run off to. The flap fell from her hand, and she paced again. Four steps, pivot, four steps, pause, repeat. Today, they marched to Vandyl.

"Will you help?" Rosealyn tugged at the strange armor again. Sword wrapped around her waist, Rosealyn wished she didn't feel like a failure.

Celena shook her head. "I will protect those Magna deems worthy of protection. You are one of those. As is King Charles." A brief flash of a frown. "Should he arrive."

Rosealyn tugged at her lower lip. *A king, a man who killed his father, a man who really needs to stop holding back.*

Standing, Celena shifted the tent flap aside again. When she turned back, the bright red irises of the elf-woman's eyes had turned dark. Rosealyn walked out into the morning sun. Through the light fog, the Jearnian Hills rolled away from the river, though Rosealyn found no solace in the rippling water's incessant noise. Roaming beyond those Hills had always felt forbidden. But they were beautiful when one wasn't about to march to battle.

"Change of plans." Celena jerked her chin toward the open plains. "Look."

At first, her breath quickened, and Rosealyn froze, staring at the rippling waters of the Guadelaide. It ran off the cliffside, forming a waterfall along one edge. Fists at her side, Rosealyn's chest clenched. They were supposed to approach him, not the other way around. Any moment, the mercenaries Rosealyn was positive her mother had paid for would appear behind Xannan.

The ever-present hum blared in her ears. Faster and faster it reverberated inside her skull. She dug her nails into her palms, watching Xannan's steady approach with growing apprehension. No one joined him.

With the other blade in sight, she understood the earlier tugs. That longing to return home had been more than her own desires. A second hum joined the one which had become a constant companion. The swords beckoned for each other, desperate to be reunited. And from what Rosealyn could see, the Lost Prince could no longer deny that pull. She gripped the hilt of her sword and used one of the many calming exercises she'd learned over the years. A question of why and how remained, but heat emanated from her sword's hilt, caressing her palm with each pulse. It flared and Rosealyn cursed, shaking her hand and staring at Celena with an arched brow. The elf's eyes flashed a brief glowing red, and she offered a small bottle of liquid. Grimacing, Rosealyn accepted it, rubbing a small amount on her tender palm.

"No Ei—"

Words fell short as the largest beast Rosealyn had ever seen dipped below the clouds. Wings wide, Eilon hovered over the field and annihilated a vast portion of the Hoclian and Alkaanian soldiers with a single swath of flame. She wasn't sure if a gasp or scream would be appropriate and didn't have the chance to decide. Celena's hand wrapped around hers and pulled. They made it to the top of the path at the edge of the cliff, opposite where the waterfall drummed down. It didn't stop the screams from reaching her ears.

"Before night falls, those blades will become one; it is ideal you retrieve the combined blade, not him, and use it to kill Eilon," Celena said.

Rosealyn's mouth hung open, too stunned to stop the forward movement. That wasn't part of the plan. Not even close. Neither was Xannan and Eilon arriving at the Cliff. She should have returned home. Taken care of Xannan and his stupid dragon without the aid of useless armies. All of those men had been nothing but fodder for Eilon.

"Kill Eilon?" Rosealyn ripped her arm free of Celena's grasp, and the elf paused. "Xannan first. I can kill him. I'm sure of it."

Celena did not respond, which only increased Rosealyn's rage. So many dead without lifting a sword. The flame—so bold, so white and yet dark.

Red irises turned darker as the elf pulled Rosealyn along the bluff. Stone-faced Jordan in heavy furs and red-faced Nathaniel in shiny gold armor exited their tents.

"He's here!" Rosealyn shouted over her shoulder at them when Celena did not slow. Small rocks and upended roots threatened to send her tumbling down the path along the cliff's side. The sounds of battle she'd heard once before did not arise. Screams. Burned flesh. Nothing more. No clash of weapons. No guttural shouts or battle cries. No twang or concussive thud of arrows. Shrieks of death. Of terror. Every soldier she'd requested was only a feast for the beast they were supposed to help kill.

Keeping her footing was a slight comfort. When the path's winding quieted the screams, Rosealyn stopped, shoving off Celena's hand. She closed her eyes, and whatever air she tried to inhale did nothing. More deaths. Blood on her hands. Life seeping from glistening eyes, a comforting embrace she would never feel again. Hands turning clammy, she fell to her knees. Chest turning to blocks of ice, she berated herself for allowing fear to take over. One deep inhale to fill her lungs, and she flexed her fingers against the dirt and gravel beneath her as she exhaled.

The hum of the sword invaded every fiber of her being. "What happens when the blades combine?"

Celena reached for her arm again, but Rosealyn shifted away. "Answer me, Celena." When she stood and rounded her shoulders, the elf's eyes churned a deep red. "What happens?"

"Combining the blades might sever the connection to the LeNoir line." Celena's gaze darted over Rosealyn's shoulder, peering down the path. He was there. Now this close, she could hear his sword's hum alongside her own.

"I can't survive without it! Magna showed me—" She gasped. "You said to retrieve the combined blade. Praesidio?" Calm dread welled within again. "No. It's too risky. I asked for help." She glanced over her shoulder and shoved Celena aside to climb the path they had just descended. Away from the blade's call, away from her still-living ancestor, away from everything. She paused. Jordan and Nathaniel marched toward her. The pale king's skin was as red as a morning sunrise.

"An entire troop is dead!" Nathaniel lunged at her.

Rosealyn stepped aside from his charge, glancing between the two leaders.

"Tenoa isn't coming," Rosealyn muttered, as though it would appease his anger. "And I haven't the faintest idea what agenda Christopher actually follows."

"That beast has massacred my troops." Jordan seethed.

Rosealyn winced, glancing back down the path at the silently waiting Celena. "Half-truths, lies by omission, and flat out lies," she whispered. "Why did you agree to help?"

Jordan and Nathaniel exchanged glances, and after a moment's pause, Nathaniel shrugged. "Since she's asking."

Jordan grunted in agreement.

"Orda'an is already lost to you." The young king drew a line through the air with a finger, as though an invisible map stood before him. "Jordan and I plan to split it down the middle."

He jolted when Rosealyn pulled her sword and pointed it at his sparkling golden armor. Calm dread dissolved into seething anger. "And what makes you think Xannan won't come after you, either of you, next?" The second hum echoed against the first, and Rosealyn grimaced. "Xannan already has Tenoa. Does he have you as well?"

Jordan laughed, low and guttural. "If he did, I imagine his dragon would spare our people."

"I think the beast cares little for people, Jordan," Nathaniel added in his consistent overbearing loudness. "Thus why we came to help distract the armies so the good princess could kill the dragon."

Rosealyn frowned and lowered her sword. "I've barely managed to kill two people in my lifetime." She shook her head. "But a dragon?"

More screams answered her question. The blade hummed its odd song; the beat becoming more persistent. A blinding flash overwhelmed the sudden appearance of an image in her mind's eye. She couldn't stop that flash, whatever it was.

"This wasn't supposed to happen." Rosealyn rounded her shoulders. "Take your people and go. I'll take care of the dragon."

Both Jordan and Nathaniel raced back up the path, likely toward another way down the palisade awaiting near the waterfall.

Celena's hand gripped Rosealyn's forearm, but she shoved it off and rounded on the elf. "Where are Synda and Magna?"

The elf's lips tightened into a thin line, red eyes glowing for a brief second. "Magna is near. She must wait for her proper time." Another brief glow as Celena squinted at the sky. "Synda watches over King Charles. He's on his way." She paused, and the corners of her lips tipped down. "Alone."

But how… No. She shook her head. He could take care of himself. As could she. The asynchronous hums intensified, and Rosealyn's muscles tensed. "Will he survive the merge?"

At the elf's somber expression, Rosealyn swallowed hard. She could see his bright green eyes, could make out the shoulder-length blond hair, and could see he did not hold the sword. Even had she not been able to see him, Rosealyn would have been able to point to his location. The closer he came, the faster the sword's beating hum. And the faster her heart hammered inside her chest.

Rosealyn tugged at her lower lip, meeting the deep simmer of Celena's red irises. "Make sure Charles stays safe. Please."

One curt nod was the elf-woman's only response. Rosealyn looked up. White flame upon white flame mingled beneath a bright blue sky. No different than clouds floating. But this white was no cloud. Eilon's flame. And Magna's. She'd arrived. Rosealyn's jaw dropped, unable to tear her attention away as Eilon and Magna weaved between the other streams of white flame spewing at intervals. Neither went unscathed. The flame disappeared and returned with a vengeance. Magna weaved a second too late as Eilon's flame intensified. The flame from Eilon's maw turned an inky black. It stained the sky worse than the scent of burning flesh he'd left on the plains below.

58

Less than two steps away. Xannan recognized the sword's hum, recognized the woman who wore the braids his betrothed never got the chance to wear. Dark elven armor, simple gray dress, sword drawn. Footsteps cautious and delicate, she approached. Whatever words she said meant nothing. Not when the call of the other blade was so strong. He pulled his sword free and attacked. Calculated, controlled. He slashed, but she twisted and turned, avoiding each blow.

When she lifted the sword, he paused. Silver. The blade was silver. White. It had been white at some point. Yet the call emanated from it, one he had not heard for many years.

Another flurry of swings. More ferocious this time. He clenched his jaw, bracing for the impact sure to come if the blades met. Unless he could kill her first. So he increased his furor, increased the speed with which his sword moved. Closer and closer, until their blades met with the same explosive concussion he'd experienced once before.

The force of their blades meeting caused Rosealyn to stumble backward and fall to her back. She leaned up on her elbows, shaking her head and staring at the sword she'd dropped. Her hand hovered above its hilt as he approached. She grasped it, grimacing as she sprang to her feet to block his next volley of strikes. He understood the hesitation. Holding the hilt of his sword was like holding his hand inside a flame. And based on her expression, hers felt the same.

He moved in for another slash, ready for the concussion but not the images. They hovered above the meeting of the blades and faded quickly. Xannan's breath caught, watching his brother fall to his side in a cave, grasping at his throat as though he could not breathe.

Their eyes met above the image. This time Rosealyn swung her blade at him, and he parried. The humming crescendoed, but no concussion knocked them backward. Faint whispers of fog in the shape of someone he didn't recognize floated away before he could see more; tears trickled down Rosealyn's face.

The silver coating of her weapon disintegrated, revealing a crystalline metal of opaque white.

Xannan's next slash was weaker and showed him the truth. The carriage with his mother and his betrothed, Anna, right before it had burst into flame. And Eilon disappearing into the sky above it.

His feet slid as the princess pushed against him, the Twin Blades grinding against one another. Their beats synchronized, growing closer together with every passing second. Xannan saw the princess shift her grip, holding on even tighter, as though her strength would allow her to keep hold of the weapons as whatever magic this was began to work.

Xannan released one of his hands, grabbing the base of the other sword, its heat searing his flesh. Whispers of scenes they had both experienced, that every man who wielded the white blade had lived, flashed around them, growing brighter and more solid the longer the two weapons remained touching. Battles waged, fights won, ending with the princess inside a cave.

Heat branded his palm, forcing him to release his hold. An invisible weight bore down on them as the hums beat as one and the light grew ever brighter until a final blast forced them both to the ground.

Gravel pebbled against his back and into his hair. He tried to sit up, to move, to will himself back to his weapon. But he was stuck. Frozen in place as though two hands held him down. In his periphery, he noticed the princess was still.

He watched the faint rise and fall of her chest. "Curious."

Another bold flash of white light. Then darkness.

~   ~   ~   ~

Ears perked, Synda glided over the remains of the armies that had collapsed to flame. She considered gliding toward the weapon she had blessed. But he was too far.

Eilon and Magna weaved in and around each other. While Magna appeared the strongest Synda had ever seen the matriarch, the ancient dragon's leathery wings and faltering fire were succumbing to Eilon's marbled flame. The two rotated in a slow descent. What few claws adorned Magna's wings had broken. Synda's ears flattened as the two massive dragons approached the bluff. When Magna attempted to crane her neck back to the sky, to lift her body above the clouds once more, Eilon clawed her wing. Her flame coated him, and they drifted closer to the bluff. White fire mingled with black.

The bluff. They would land there. And Synda was too close to them. Tail feathers on fire, she waved them about to no avail—she would have to land. *Away. Not merged. Yet.*

Synda folded her wings back into her sides to land. Tail with singed feathers wrapped tight against her body, Synda sat on her hind legs and looked up. Tucked close to the cliff's wall, she listened. And waited.

Magna's stern warning after rescuing Rosealyn replayed—the matriarch would face Eilon. Communicating with him would be useless. They had no way to dissuade him from his path. Both she and Magna had seen such.

Soon Synda feared she would be alone. Tail feathers would fail in flight now. She could vanish back to the cave, powerless, or prove herself. With the unspoken rules she had broken, none would appear to assist, and her strength was a whisper of Magna's, a faint breath of what Eilon could wield.

Eilon approached a light emanating from the cliff's path. Growling, Synda formed what she thought would be a breath of fire, but not even a wisp of smoke spewed from her open jaw. Too young compared to him, the youngest dragon, the proof of their endangerment. The two walked parallel, one above, the other below, watching the light diminish. Fear rumbling deep within kept Synda's eyes forward.

Even the ancients of her own species could not surpass such wonderment. One of his outspread spiked wings could smother her. An orange glow radiated from his chest. A tail as long as his neck whipped from side to side behind him. Eyes peered down at her from the top of his long snout, but her gaze strayed to the spiked crown-like protrusions atop his head.

Wings tucked closer to her body, Synda curled her damaged tail around her feet. Head tilted, she churned the barely there flame inside her chest as Magna and Eilon's flames met again. The blinding light along the path winked out. Charles, the Jearnian king she'd followed, approached with his sword drawn.

Synda grumbled deep and approached the path as well, following his movement to the two unconscious wielders of Praeteritum and Futurae. Xannan's and Rosealyn's individual swords melded together, fighting between a clear crystal and a cumbersome black. Once Charles stood over the wielder of Praeteritum, he lifted his sword.

Synda jumped in front of him, wings spread to protect both wielders. Steam hissed from her open mouth, and Charles froze. Uncontrolled flame formed within, but Synda produced little more than a fine film of smoke.

Charles raised his sword again. Whatever fear showed in his eyes was not for her. Synda's breath fell deeper within, flaring as though she had drunk bubbling water. Her neck convulsed. The heat grew, expanding until it reached every inch of her neck. Synda stared at the ground, coughing several times like a bone had lodged inside. The burning intensified, her desire to growl heightening until she flung her head to the sky and roared. What came forth was not a roar. Flame. A small stream of flame sprouted from her mouth, singeing her tongue, and the last vestiges of heat dissipated.

A blinding light from the bluff. The call of immense power. First she growled, then flames crashed into one another between the ancient dragons.

Synda kneaded the ground, stamping it with her tail. Neck pulsing and shaking, Synda held the breath until she had no other choice. She had to release it, or it would burn her from the inside out. Her wings dropped as she released a flame-filled roar. Synda was smug despite her fear. The flame had awakened.

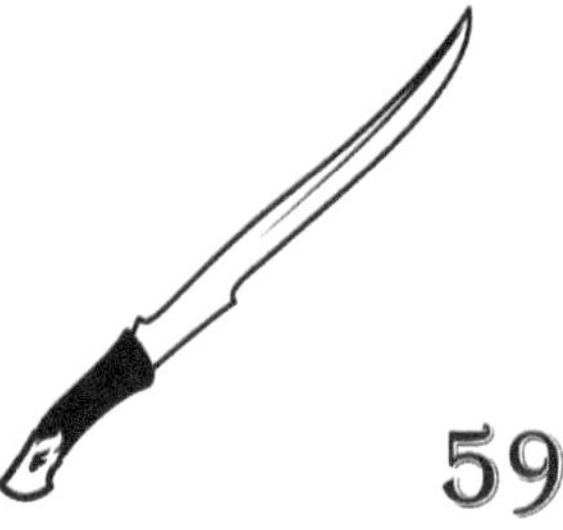# 59

Charles stood before a soft white dragon who would not let him approach Rose or Xannan. Two steps away, but every time Charles moved, the dragon growled. Based on her size and color, he recognized this one must be Synda. Above was Eilon. The third, who looked like she would soon fall to pieces if Eilon's flame hit her just right, had to be Magna.

A crystalline weapon lay between Rose and Xannan, pulsing in a rhythm matching the roars and fires of the two dragons above. He laid his sword down and tried to approach Rose, but Synda's wing shifted forward as though to swat him away. Seeing her white neck bright with its orange flame, he swallowed. His mother had told him about her encounters, but her descriptions had left much to be desired of the dragon's sheer size.

"He can't have it." Charles stepped forward, pressing his lips together when that orange glow in Synda's neck intensified. "She'll die if he takes it."

He fell to his knees, head pounding as an image of Xannan holding the blade lingered. "No." Charles reached for his own sword. Synda stamped her feet against the gravelly dirt path and growled, purple eyes an odd echo to her orange flame.

"I have to protect her." His words hung in the air, and the weapon continued its wavering between hues. From crystal to solid black to solid white, gleaming so bright Charles had to shield his eyes.

Synda covered the glowing weapon with one wing, long snout darting between Charles, Rose, and Xannan. Charles settled back on his heels, holding Rose's clammy hand in his own. Her breathing grew shallower as the blade grew brighter.

"Move, dragon," came a man's voice from the other side of Synda's outstretched wing. With an apologetic grimace, she lifted her wing to reveal Xannan holding the newly formed sword. Above, Eilon's flame orb disappeared, and he crashed to the grassy bluff. Magna followed, though her landing was even less graceful.

"Stay close to her," Xannan said, and Charles looked up in shock. No malice, no sordid overtone. Anger.

The words Charles tried to form fell flat and voiceless on his lips.

Xannan craned his neck, and the muscles of his bare arms tensed. "I have a dragon to kill." Without another word, Xannan marched up the path, glowing sword in his hand.

Worried his feet might go numb, Charles shifted. Synda stayed close. He could feel the warmth of her breath above him while his gaze darted between Rose and the dragons clawing at one another on the bluff. White flame gave way to black. Magna's wings shriveled into flakes as she collapsed to her side. When Eilon wrapped his jaw around Magna's neck, Charles looked away. The glowing sword caught his attention, and he followed it. Xannan prowled forward. No hesitation. One foot in front of the other, the Lost Prince approached Eilon.

"Magic?" Charles met Synda's purple eyes. Their color grew deeper, bolder, brighter, reflecting the increasing orange orb pulsing inside the dragon's neck. A growl which shook the ground beneath him came from the white dragon, and he crawled backward when Synda lowered her snout. But it was Rose the dragon touched. She gasped at Synda's touch but remained unconscious.

"She'll live?" Charles asked, hopeful. Synda gave no response, touching her snout to his sword resting on the ground and nudging it toward him. It was warm, but not the searing heat he'd once felt. And then the dragon disappeared.

The cave. She hadn't meant to go there, but the flame grew within her throat. Uncontrolled. She craned her neck to-and-fro, trying to find a position which allowed the heat to fester without distraction and found none. Her motivations, torn between protecting the princess and luring Eilon, fought against one another. Flame burst forth, uncontrolled, blackening the cave walls.

Synda coughed, wondering if it would always seem a bone stayed lodged deep within. And now the additional well. It wasn't inside her, precisely, but it was her. Magna was gone. Dead. Wings turned to ash, molten orb erased. All those years of giving, of protecting, of warning. And Synda had fled. *Coward.*

Synda paced the length of the cavern, spiked tail creating divots in the mud. An intense well rested inside, beckoning to be used. So she willed herself to return. It had just worked. No different than when she rescued the princess, no different than the times she had dared to spy on those Magna told her to avoid. But nothing happened.

Her kin wandered in the land beyond the mountains, unaware of the protection they had lost with Magna's death. Synda's own magic had grown tenfold at Magna's demise. But she felt a second well, larger than that which Magna shared, larger than Magna's last source of protection for her.

Too afraid to cough, lest she set more of the cave ablaze, Synda shifted her head to one side and pushed the flame deeper within. She had to exercise control, especially with the new well of power. To return and fight, she needed to be in control.

With Xannan awake, the merging of the swords complete, Eilon's access to his own well of power should be gone. No one could stop what Magna had set in motion decades past. Another swallow, another attempt to suppress the burn, another attempt to return, but fear held her there. A shift and a growth, Synda's flame burst forth again, uncontrolled. *Too much. It's too much.*

60

Head pounding, Rosealyn woke to fuzzy images that doubled. Tripled. She gripped her head with both hands and attempted to stare at a singular rock while focusing on not screaming. Her surroundings blurred, and every muscle ached. Both palms stung. Her head drummed abominably, and the rhythmic throbbing of the sword was several yards away from her. *Surely one would not feel such pain when dead.*

When Rosealyn finally dared to glance up, she found Charles. She tried to soak in his presence, to say something, but her visual of Charles blurred. When she tried to stand, he placed both hands on her shoulders to hold her in place.

"Stay here." That was a strange tone coming from him, much different from the man who'd handed her a dagger in the courtyard to protect herself or the one who'd gently caressed her cheek and almost kissed her. It was a command she didn't want to follow, so she tried to stand again. He pressed down, halting her movement. Intense throbbing radiated in every known muscle. And unknown, hidden ones.

His grip on her shoulders tightened and she winced as he spoke. "I can handle Xannan."

Rosealyn shoved his hands off her shoulders and pushed against the ground to stand. When she swayed, Charles gripped both of her arms, holding her steady. Breathless, Rosealyn whispered, "He wants to kill Eilon."

How she knew, why she knew, whatever the connection between the blades had done, the sudden thud against her back as Charles held her upright—nothing could have prepared her for what combining the blades had done between her and the Lost Prince.

She could barely focus on Charles as he said, "Then I'll help him kill the dragon and then kill him."

Rosealyn gripped his arm tighter when he tried to pull away, shaking her head once as she did.

"Kill Eilon? Please do." She was too afraid to speak any louder than a whisper for fear of increasing the thrashing inside her skull. "When the blades are connected, he and I are as well. It's like we're—" She grunted and grimaced. "Two pieces of one whole."

Charles shifted his head to one side, eyes flaring bright and flickering toward where the dragon and Xannan exchanged blows. She refused to let go of Charles's arm, not only for fear he would run after them and attempt to kill Xannan, but also out of fear she would collapse without something to stabilize her wobbling form. Every movement Xannan made, she felt. He weaved and slashed. No care where his sword landed or how. Nor any care if he himself became injured. An unabated fury gripped Xannan's approach.

Rosealyn fought his furor as her body became a training ground dummy. "Xannan is—" Words became difficult to form, teeth rattling together as the Lost Prince went flying across the bluff. "Eilon's power is … or was … inside Xannan's weapon." A hit to the shoulder. "But with the weapons combined, something's—" Vision blurred as though she'd been spun. "I think Eilon could kill Xannan now. And if he does, he'll get his magic back."

Her words a whisper, Rosealyn clenched her jaw shut as though grinding her teeth together would stop her from feeling the blows Eilon landed. So much burned, so much destroyed, so much simply erased from existence. Rosealyn shivered. She could hide the torment no longer. What started as a graceful lowering of her body turned into a fall when a very real wing slammed into Xannan.

"Rose?" Charles collapsed to his knees at her side. Gentle and caring, his hands roamed her abdomen. As his bold blue eyes softened and studied her, Rosealyn tugged at her lower lip, wincing and fighting the watering of her eyes. Pain. So much pain. Above, Xannan was blindsided by Eilon's wing—again—knocking him several yards and onto his back. She grunted, the wind knocked out of her as well.

"Connected." Charles halted his quest to find a wound that didn't exist and followed her gaze back to the bluff.

"I can't help fight—" A rush of heat as Xannan narrowly missed Eilon's blast of flame. "Every blow—" She pressed her lips together to prevent herself from screaming as Eilon clawed Xannan's arm. "I feel it instead of him."

Rosealyn inhaled sharply. "Is Christopher with you?"

"Christopher? He's not with you?" Charles asked in a near shout. Hands raised halfway to her ears, she winced and shook her head. Thankfully, his voice softened. "Why do you ask?"

"Only weapons forged by a dragon can kill a dragon." Rosealyn gritted her teeth. Eilon had knocked Xannan aside. Yet again. *Idiot of a fighter. Stab the damn dragon, please.*

"We have two, what's one more?"

"It could mean everything." Celena's white hair blended into pale skin when Rosealyn looked up at her. She assumed the other arrival was Arjun, but everything blurred again. "Go, King Charles, find your brother and return with him. Rosealyn will be safe with us."

"No." Her brows rose at the level of frustration Charles expressed. "Eilon is here now. Xannan is fighting him now. Rose looks like she may faint at any second. I'm not leaving her."

The elves' two heads doubled into four as Rosealyn attempted to focus on them, and Arjun said. "Fine. Follow me, King Charles."

Charles barked a single loud laugh that made Rosealyn wince. He reiterated in a tone of voice she had never heard cross the man's lips. "I said I'm not leaving her."

"Go." Rosealyn pulled her hand away from his approaching grasp. Any more contact would be too much. It was impossible to focus her vision. She could only recognize them by their voices. Everything was an insane, constant blur. Rosealyn shut her eyes as though it would stop the battering of Xannan's body, and hers, as he rolled along the ground. Such an attempt only made the bashing hurt more. "The quicker you kill Eilon, the better I will feel."

Arjun motioned for Charles to follow. After a forlorn glance, and an urging nod from her, Charles gave her shoulder a tight squeeze, and she tried not to wince. Once he turned away, Rosealyn buried her head between her knees, fighting the need to scream and yell as the invisible battering continued. Tears of pain flowed, uninhibited. Arms shaking, she reached for the unstoppered vial Celena offered. She tensed to pause the shaking, downing the liquid more quickly than she believed possible.

Nothing changed. Agony. Misery. Torture.

Hands held tight to her temples, Rosealyn resisted the urge to pound on her own head in hopes it might, ironically, alleviate the pain she felt. Every inch pulsed and throbbed. *Blaze take me if this gets worse. Death would certainly hurt less.*

61

Nothing hurt. Not a single blow from the beast's wings caused any amount of pain. No injuries, no wounds, no ailments, no weakening of Xannan's muscles or joints, no slow seep of exhaustion clawing at him. Even flying through the air after Eilon's wings rammed into him, the trees were still trees rather than a green blur.

Another blow landed him at the feet of an elf and the soldier he'd fought before the blade's strange reaction, though in much different clothing. Xannan grinned; the elves and dragons were old friends. And old enemies.

"Crystals?" Xannan jerked his chin at the aging bag looped around the elf's shoulder. He stood, brushing off his pants with a brief frown at the grass stains. A whistle warned him, as did the other two ducking, but the wing caught him and he slashed wildly at the leathery skin as it tossed him through the air. It lifted him up rather than backward and tore the blade free from his grasp.

After a brief roll along the bluff, he stood and searched for the sword. It was easy to find, considering its perpetual humming inside his brain, and its blinding, pulsing light. Sword back in hand, he raced toward Eilon, weapon poised to strike.

"Wait!"

Xannan ignored the voice, weaving beneath the beast's wing to land his first strike.

Eilon's roar rattled the ground. But not his bones. Xannan's grin widened. "Magic."

He pulled the blade from the wound he had bestowed. When Eilon's wings spread wide, he followed its outline to see the elf with the bag bending down to place an object on the ground. The decked out soldier strode forward, pulling his lackluster blade from its sheath. Xannan's weapon, his dragonsword, quickened its pulsing as the soldier came closer. Xannan frowned when the burst of light shimmered along the gold atop the man's head. *Not a soldier then?*

First the whistle, then the rush of wind. Xannan let the wing lift him into the air as he sliced Eilon's leathery skin. He tumbled to the ground and heat surrounded him, engulfing all of his frame. And still nothing. No searing wounds, no bubbling flesh, not even his clothes singed as the flame dissipated into a low, incessant growl. Head tilted, Xannan had the strangest feeling that it hadn't been the first time the dragon's marbled flame had surrounded him.

Not wanting to let the thought coalesce, Xannan raced back beneath the beast's wings, sword lifted high to sink it into Eilon's chest when he heard another shout to wait. He didn't. The blade sank until no glow remained visible. Weapon pulled free, he raised his arms wide to each side, refusing to flinch when Eilon's black-eyed gaze attempted to penetrate his mind.

Laughter filled his ears. His own laughter. Eilon had no control anymore.

"Whose death did you show me, Eilon?" Xannan shouted up at the great dragon, focus flickering for a second over to the elf. He had made almost a complete circle around Eilon.

Above him, Eilon's neck slithered. His flame turned from its wide swaths to small bursts, and then it was only smoke. In his wild thrashing, Eilon's bleeding wing had knocked the soldier turned royal to the ground.

"Charles, now!" came the elf's shout from behind Xannan. He looked to the royal, this Charles, as the man regained his footing, limping extensively as he approached.

Xannan snarled; he would kill the dragon. The orange orb in the center of Eilon's neck became his target. Eilon did not move. He was trapped. Irrevocably stuck until the crystal circle was broken. Xannan shouted, sinking the glowing blade in the aggravating pulsating orange orb with each word. "Beautiful, glorious, worthless, manipulative, magic."

A second sword struck in time with Xannan's last word.

Weapon pulled free and dripping with Eilon's life force, Xannan rounded on Charles with blade lifted. Emotions he did not understand swirled, and the once-clear vision blurred at the edges. Both men stumbled as Eilon fell to his side. An exhalation made Xannan's muscles tense until the orange orb dissipated and sputtered to nothing. No more breath remained to give such fire life.

Charles readied his blade, though he supported almost all of his weight on his left leg. "Eilon is dead."

Xannan inhaled deeply, finding the understanding red irises of the elf. He squinted at the young elf, recognizing the pudgier nose, the thinner slits to the elf's eyes, the tawny shade of the elf's hair. *It can't be.*

His neck tingled. "You had no right." Xannan's gaze lingered on the familiar and too-young elf.

"Rose is in pain."

When Charles stepped forward, Xannan faced him and lifted a brow. The man kept his weight on one leg, the other sporting a gash along the thigh that dripped blood. Xannan cocked his head to one side, and realization blossomed. The sword pulled from her life force, rather than his, though the dragonsword's pulsing had slowed.

Xannan shrugged and cleaned the sword of the dragon's blood on the grass. "And?"

"Split the sword again so she can use her half to recover?" Charles asked with so much uncertainty coating his tone Xannan could not bite back the laugh.

For a brief moment, he surveyed Charles. The bright orange and red coat, the grass-stained black pants, the wounded leg. He smirked. "No."

Xannan turned on his heel and walked away. The surrounding greenery dulled, the sky darkened, and aches coiled through each muscle. He barely felt the hand pull him back, and the punch to his face only served to further disorient him. Nose wrinkling, he dabbed at the small stream of blood running from his nostrils. Xannan laughed. All those fights with swords and blades. A fight against Eilon, the king of the dragons, and a simple well-placed punch was the injury that drew blood.

Charles raised his fist again, and Xannan held up one finger, waving it from side to side as the smirk returned. "Connected," Xannan said. The returning laughter cut off when several more blows landed to his nose, cheek, and jaw.

"It's her you're hurting." Xannan's head snapped back from yet another blow. More laughter seemed the appropriate response as he turned away.

"Where will you go? What will you do?"

"Live." Xannan curled his fingers around the glowing blade's hilt. "Where none can control me or what is left of him."

No footsteps followed him, so he continued walking forward. The effort to place one foot before the next grew more difficult. The once-blinding light of the blade fading, Xannan sheathed the weapon. Blurred landscape became darkness, muscles trembling as he inched his way forward. He walked along the bluff. Tendrils of tension slithered through him as he collapsed to the ground and lost consciousness.

62

The library. Her library. Their library. One place Charles always knew he could find Rose. But she was not there. He did not know where she was. Xannan had walked away, and by the time Charles had returned to where he'd last seen Rose, she was gone. Four days of travel, and such decay surrounded him. Except for these walls. A reminder of what could have been. Not even this room of the castle stayed unscathed during the beast's attack. Few of them had.

He limped along the path toward the stairs, fingers tumbling against the rise and fall of the books' spines. The scent of burned paper had finally dissipated, though the smell of anything burning still turned his stomach against him. When he reached the top of the stairs, he paused. On a step halfway down, in the middle of his path, sat a tawny-haired robed man rifling through the pages of a book. Arjun.

His once-injured leg protested each step, but eventually Charles lowered himself to sit next to the elf. Arjun continued his perusal of the text, his finger drifting across the page in a determined quickness. Charles tried to read over the moving arm, but he didn't recognize the language. "What now?"

"Do not get comfortable, Your Majesty." Arjun tapped his finger against the page. Charles stiffened at the honorifics; it was still odd to be referred as such. "There remains a side of this story which has not been told. Tell me. Where is Prince Christopher?"

"He's—" Charles didn't know. "He was supposed to stay with Rose, but—" Charles rubbed his leg. "I haven't seen him since he left Volante."

"How much did he study the stories your mother told?" Arjun's finger stayed put at a single line.

Charles fought the urge to be obstinate. "You should ask Mae or Christopher. But I suspect Christopher knows more than he shared. We always do."

Arjun glanced up, bright red eyes squinting at Charles, and looked back down, finger drifting again. "And no sign of Princess Rosealyn or Xannan?"

Charles shook his head, muttering. "Two sides, but only one truth." He raked a hand through his hair. "What do you think has happened?"

"Praeteritum and Futurae, the two halves of Praesidio, tethered themselves to the magic of the LeNoir line." Arjun's eyes churned a deeper red. "The issue with Eilon was both a trick and a mistake."

"What does that have to do with Christopher?" Charles rested one hand atop his knee and the other atop his thigh, away from the tender, healing skin. A few drops of liquid had knit his skin back together atop the bluff, allowing him and the elves to return to Vandyl within a day of killing Eilon.

"You and he have the only other dragon-wrought weapons, aside from Praeteritum and Futurae." The simpleness of Arjun's tone grated on Charles's nerves. "We prefer to know where said weapons are given the power they contain."

"Two sides." The first drops of rain from gray clouds, and he closed his eyes. She was there, in his mind's eye. There where they had both dropped all pretenses and honorifics, where they had just been themselves. The whispered plea left his lips before he could stop it. "Don't you dare die on me."

"I have no plans to die, King Charles." Arjun's gaze twinkled with a hint of laughter. "Nor will those blades allow one wielder to kill the other now that they've connected. Wound, possibly, but not kill." He turned back to the open journal. "That is, if I am reading my father's notes correctly."

63

Darkness. Tiny rocks. Caked mud. And dampness. A cave, Rosealyn realized after opening her eyes. Everything ached beyond reason. And the humming. So close she swore she could touch it if she just reached out her hand. The movement made her muscles twinge. Rosealyn lifted first to her elbows, and then pushed herself to sitting, only to groan. Water dripped rhythmically around her, and her stomach churned.

A cave she could handle. The pain of invisible wounds was, ironically, comforting in its familiarity. Mud squelched between her fingers as exhausted muscles screamed in protest. Somewhere close was the combined blade, the weapon that had chosen *him* over *her*. She reached in the direction of the sword's humming with a frown as her desire to annihilate her father's murderer returned. The hilt was still warm. With the dragon dead, there was only one…

Large hands wrapped around hers before she could pull the blade from its sheath. Muscles trembled as she strained to stand, to lift the sword and plunge. It buzzed against her palms with an intensity which shook her bones and made her teeth rattle, and she could barely lift it.

"I die, you die."

She froze. The tone, the cadence, was different. A sigh came from directly in front of her. Xannan was so close she could feel the warmth of his exhalation on her bare arms.

"I have no way of knowing if that's true."

"I do."

"What—" Her head rattled at the outburst. In a sharp whisper, she asked, "What did you try to do to me?"

It was a dejected, almost apologetic tone which responded to her. "War is one thing. Murder is different." He paused. "And the weapon literally wouldn't let me."

"That's not a very good apology." Rosealyn's gaze flicked toward the loud hum of the weapon. If she had hers, she would have already gutted him. But the two swords were one and the same.

"Maybe now you're awake we can finally get out of this cave." He sat down close enough his body heat warmed her right side. She shifted away, wincing as she used muscles that barely cooperated. "Every time I tried to leave you and take the sword, I ran into…"

Rosealyn rubbed her legs, pushing herself to standing and blinking rapidly, hoping the blinks would allow a stream of light to appear and help her see. The outline of him against the darkness became visible enough she knew he was no longer holding the weapon. She took a slow, deep breath, willing the ache of overworked muscles away as best she could. "Ran into what?"

"Nothing."

Rosealyn crossed her arms, rolled her eyes, and pursed her lips.

"Literally nothing." His silhouette shifted with the sound of his footsteps. "After a few hundred steps, it was like I hit a wall that wasn't there."

She grimaced as the effort to remain standing grated on her. "Still connected then?"

In the silence which answered her, Rosealyn barely saw Xannan nodding his head. "And, if I can see your exasperated eye roll in the darkness," he mused, voice the sinister taint she'd first known. "I imagine you cannot see your own fingers if you held them in front of your face?"

She tried holding her open palm in front of her face and squinted. The surrounding darkness had faded for her, and she could see the outline of not only her hands but also of Xannan's movement. It was a faint outline of his frame, but she gave a frustrated sigh instead, not wanting him to know her sight was also acclimating.

From her right, he chuckled, standing and wrapping the sword belt around his waist. "I saw that."

One of his hands grasped her forearm. Rosealyn shoved it off and took one step, fist raised to punch him. She willed her arm forward, though it felt more like falling toward him than a movement of intention. What little control she had over her own movement only made the pain worse. He didn't move, despite watching her movement. As her fist landed on his cheek, she felt a moment of painlessness. But the punch also jostled her own jaw. And made her knuckles sting.

He laughed again, almost comforting in its musicality. "Who do you think brought us here?"

This time, he gripped her shoulder to guide her through the cave. Rosealyn worried her scowl would become permanent if they did not split the blades in two again. Besides her own anger, however, she felt something else. Someone else. Him. More than just pain ebbed to her from him. She was inexplicably connected to the not-so-Lost Prince. A whirlwind of cascading emotions accompanied his physical ailments. He was lost, emotionally.

"Blaze take me, I'm as clueless as you are." She nearly face-planted after tripping on a small dip in the cave floor beneath them, the muscles of her thighs groaning at her. His grip on her shoulder steadied her. And the longer his hand rested on her shoulder, the less her muscles trembled, which only deepened her scowl.

"My portion held Eilon's magic away from him." Xannan's grip tightened to shift her movement away from another threatening mound. "Your portion of the blade is—was like a key. Gailin and I probably could have used it but never got the chance." His tone bordered on melancholic. "It must be the magic embedded in the swords that connects us right now."

They walked in somber silence for a time, Xannan's firm grip on her shoulder while she pretended she could not see more than mere inches in front of her. Each step brought a smidgen more light around them; they were in Magna's cave.

"Whoever brought us here already had the chance to kill us," Rosealyn said, grateful Xannan was behind her and could not see her squinting to see better as they neared the cave's opening.

"True." His voice turned gruff with the acknowledgment. "Though sometimes one does not wish for easy prey."

"So whoever brought us here wanted us alive?" She purposefully tripped on a mound of dirt to make Xannan think she could not see, though the hints of golden sunlight were visible in the cave's distance.

"Or," Xannan added, seemingly somewhat thoughtful, but he mumbled under his breath. "All I wanted was to live. Free of Eilon's control. And now—"

"Eilon's control?" Rosealyn interrupted.

"You saw the images, same as I."

Rosealyn gave a vehement shake of her head. "I saw the death of each ancestor, the Passing of the Gift and the blade from one king to the next, until your *murder* of Father."

"I understand your malice, Rosealyn. And accept you may never trust nor forgive me." He paused as they approached the entrance of the cavern. "Most of my actions during your lifetime—well, Eilon played on my own desires."

Rosealyn pivoted with fist raised, hesitating at Xannan's sole raised finger. A knowing smirk appeared as he waggled his finger.

"Stupid magic." Rosealyn turned toward the widening of the cave. "This is where Magna was when I met her."

"The small white dragon watching over us?" Xannan asked, curiosity coating his tone.

Rosealyn tugged at her lower lip, gaze roaming the empty cavern until she honed in on the vast opening, giving way to a thriving land. "That would be Synda," Rosealyn answered, eyes hunting the sky for the young dragon. Or any dragon.

From behind, Xannan hissed as though something burned him. When she turned around, the singular weapon was no more. The Twin Blades rested, unsheathed, on the cave floor.

In answer to her questioning gaze, Xannan shrugged and lifted his vest to inspect where the blade's hilt had rested. "It just happened." He gestured at the white blade, her half of the weapon. "One moment combined, the next in two."

She bent down and gripped her half, hand curling around the hilt one finger at a time. And became almost whole. "Something is still missing." She studied the solid white blade. But her arms no longer shook. The aches and pains suffered from being the training ground dummy for Xannan's carelessness were gone.

The empty sheath for the weapon dangled at her side, and she pushed the sword in before looking up to meet Xannan's gaze. Rosealyn truly observed Xannan for the first time. Xannan the person, not Xannan the image or the myth of the Lost Prince. No flinch, no taunting, no malice. And his weapon was more gray than black. A tickle of uncertainty nudged at her mind as he sheathed his own portion of the Twin Blades.

"I need to return to Vandyl." She announced it as though it were some proclamation. But the way Xannan's youthful green eyes bore into hers made her insides crumble.

"A warning, princess," he said. "Your home did not go unscathed."

The sword was out of its sheath and resting against the open skin bared by the odd divot in his vest before she could think more.

"I know that." Pressure applied, Rosealyn wondered if she could do it when her life wasn't being threatened. One shove to avenge all those Xannan had murdered. But there was pressure on her chest as well.

64

Jaida,

Do not trust Ramon. He claims battles rage across the Orda'anian plains. From what I have learned since arriving in Delphi, he waits for all other leaders to die. Then he would take their place. If I had known what turmoil awaited, even in Tenoa, I would have come sooner. I learned of the deals he made, of the plans he crafted, the plans which led to the destruction of the council. He is not the cousin I once knew. The world changed him, corrupted him. There's no other explanation for his decision to imprison Roseanne.

He seeks to unite all of Ebios under one ruling monarchy: himself. Where his thirst for power came from, I may never know. Working with Xannan was only one small piece of the puzzle he is crafting. It's clear Xannan used Ramon to make Roseanne trust him. But Ramon used him as well. I believe there are additional pieces, but I have little time.

I've written letters to you since leaving Vandyl, letters I've never sent. I pray this message finds you soon. You need proper warning. The LeNoir Gift, the ability Phillippe once held, is not designed to work as two separate pieces, but as one. Yes, your father explained what few glimpses he saw.

Phillippe had a mediator's heart. Please, dear Jaida, use words before swords. I fear what will happen if you don't.

Once I find my sister, I will find my way to you. Please be careful.

With love,

Catarina

END OF BOOK ONE

Exclusive
Bonus Chapter

CHARLES AND THE ROYAL MISSION

Charles shivered, hidden behind a line of trees whose shadows danced with the fading sunlight. Their fresh scent mingled with that of the drying blood on the nearby field. Hilt of his new sword gripped tight, he frowned. He'd had it less than a week and wasn't adjusted to its weight. The movement of his lips made the wound on his chin ache and he resisted the urge to touch the throbbing gash his father's signet ring had left.

Rainwater from the afternoon storm dripped from the leaves and onto his soiled shirt. Next to him, Nasir's grizzled features displayed his typical frustration, complete with arms crossed and a deep frown. For hours they had observed from their hideout. The skirmish had been a distraction. A distraction large enough to force King Phillippe of Orda'an to come to this border himself.

Charles drummed his fingers against the hilt of the sword, stilling the rising nerves. 'Kill the Orda'anian King', his father had commanded. To fail in this mission meant his own death. Unless he could escape whatever soldiers his father sent to find him.

Charles swallowed and winced at how even that movement shot a spike of pain through the open gash on his chin. He'd thought battles would last longer, that it wouldn't churn his insides to watch men maim and annihilate one another.

Bodies of soldiers whose lives became forfeit because of Charles's decision lay strewn about the blood-soaked and muddy field. Limbs hacked, guts leaking from abdomens, and the shuddering moans of those who had yet to succumb to their deathly wounds made a chasm of sorrow open inside his stomach as he counted the dead on both sides. He shifted his weight from one foot to the other, mouth drier than all those times he'd taken the blame for his brothers. At least the king joined this battalion.

"The time is now," Nasir whispered in a gruff tone. "If you wait any longer, you will fail." The mentor tapped a finger against his own dagger with a pointed look.

"I'll have to take out all of them, won't I?" Charles asked, the risen Jearnian emblem on the hilt marking his cold palm. Even in plain travel clothes, the gifted sword could reveal his identity.

"Don't make me kill you, boy."

Charles clamped his mouth shut; he had no desire to die that day. Nor did he want to kill anyone but his father had given him little choice. Skin chapped from the brutal winds off the widespread Orda'anian plains, Charles exited the line of trees with a single step. Then another. At fifteen years old, it was his duty to fulfill this mission and take his rightful place as Jearnia's next crown heir.

One more step and a black clad Orda'anian soldier with a white collar still carrying a bloodied sword shouted something Charles didn't truly hear. When the soldier's hand wrapped around his arm firmly and tugged, Charles let him. He needed brought to the king, anyway.

During the quick walk through the sodden dirt, Charles studied the soldier holding his arm with a vice grip. The white collar meant he was a high-ranking officer, one of the Banner-Captain's based on Charles's study of Orda'anian's army ranks. They halted near a group of men all dressed in similar fashion to the Banner-Captain. The Orda'anian held out his bloodied sword toward a nearby soldier in solid black who took the weapon and dashed off.

"This boy tried to sneak off with a stolen weapon, Your Majesty," the Orda'anian officer informed one of the men. Though others had the white marking to indicate rank, the one who turned toward them wore no formal insignia or crown, but he acknowledged his men's consistent brief bows as they passed near him with subtle nods.

Even without the title, Charles would recognize the man whose attention focused on him. Cropped blond hair, bold green eyes, and a commanding air labeled this as the king Charles would kill before the sun's last rays left the horizon.

Charles shifted his free arm, gripping the small dagger resting opposite the sword. Either would suffice. The method wasn't important, only the result. Accomplish the mission, and then return home. Simple. And insane to attack someone who could see snippets of the future.

"And if it's actually his?" The king frowned and sat on a nearby tree stump. Tugging a cloth out of his pocket, Phillippe methodically and reverently cleaned his own blade. Legend claimed the weapon had remained in the LeNoir family since Orda'an's founding and that the ruling monarch never let it out of their sight. Phillippe gestured at Charles with a faint hint of a grin. "The weight is new to him, yes, but he's been gripping that hilt so tightly I bet its design is now embedded in his palm."

The king held Charles's gaze while swiping at the blood caked to his sword. Charles bristled but maintained the king's stare. It started no differently than those from his own father, but then the Orda'anian king's eyes glazed over and lines creased his forehead. His wounded chin throbbed and his lungs ached to take more rapid breaths.

"Sire?"

"Finish setting up camp, Adrian," the king said without breaking eye contact. "Then prepare the dead for proper burials." He tilted his head with a sad smile. "I must speak with this boy. And search the woods. This young man did not come alone."

"Yes, Sire." Adrian released his grip on Charles's arm, bowed, and walked away.

Charles focused on studying his surroundings rather than rub where he worried Adrian had left a bruise. Several soldiers had skewered rabbits to roast over fledgling campfires that circled a lone tent in the center of the camp. Surrounded by the too familiar tang of blood and fearful sweat, Charles wondered how best to get Phillippe alone.

Voices murmured behind Charles, followed by Adrian's voice calling out, "Your tent is ready, Sire."

"Good." Phillippe inspected his sword with one last sweep of the cloth and sheathed it in an enviably fluid movement.

As Phillippe strode toward his tent, Charles chewed on his tongue and watched the soldiers work. Hands flexed at his sides, he counted the Orda'anian soldiers. Six tents around the king, up to four per tent. After Charles killed the king, he would have at least twenty-four soldiers to either fight against or evade. His throat parched further, arms tensing, jaw throbbing. Not just fight. I'll have to kill them, too.

The king entered his tent without glancing backwards. Charles counted his breaths and prodded himself forward with each. One quick stab, with all his might, before he had a chance to think. Shoulders rounded, blade loose in its sheath, his gaze darted between the soldiers busy with their tasks.

None watched his movement. He swallowed and flexed his hands before gripping the hilt of his sword again. Since he'd not noticed the Orda'anian army's general anywhere, he assumed that Phillippe's closest companion would be in the tent with him. Which meant he'd be fighting two men soon. Grown men who'd fought in more battles than Charles could even fathom.

Chest tight and arms tense, Charles approached Phillippe's tent.

Charles knew the king never brought over two hundred soldiers to a border skirmish. He also knew that Phillippe alternated between bringing either Banner-Captain Preston or Banner-Captain Adrian to the battles with him. Reports had taught him much about the king's habits and about the family who remained at Vandyl. The flame-like emblem on his sword-hilt grounded him. Steps away from the king's tent, Charles's resolve to land a fatal blow solidified. He'd killed once before; he could do so again.

His insides recoiled at the thought. His father made killing look so easy, made life appear so fleeting. He remembered the first time he had watched a death occur without flinching or looking away and recalled both his father's approval and his mother's admonishment. Fortunately, his mother had not witnessed his first kill.

The flame-like emblem on his sword's hilt grated against the tender skin of his palm. This was his task. Charles willed his hands to stop shaking. No soldiers approached; none viewed him as a threat. He bared a portion of the curved blade, wishing he had brought gloves to protect his grip from such clammy palms.

Charles studied the tent's entrance. Light flickered within, waning as the wind shifting through the lit candles. One more step and he would be inside. One more step and he could make his father proud. Both flaps flipped with the breeze. He tilted his head and searched for the king's shadowed silhouette. As he calculated how to react to where he might find Phillippe, Charles pulled his sword free of its sheath in a slow motion. The steel whispered against the leather. Before the tip was free, he tiptoed inside. A breath later, the weight in his hand disappeared.

Charles lunged, reaching to reclaim his sword from the king's hold. But Phillippe moved aside, seizing the back of Charles's shirt collar and pushing him to his knees. Cold steel pressed against the exposed skin of Charles's neck. He tried not to swallow, afraid that any movement on his part would be his last.

"This isn't the blade that kills me." Phillippe's grip on Charles's shirt shifted, but the steel against his neck didn't budge. The king tsked, squatting down to speak in Charles's ear, "A prince of Jearnia at a border skirmish." He shifted the blade away from Charles's neck and said, "The eldest, if I'm not mistaken."

All the air Charles had held inside when the blade rested on his skin rushed out of him. When the king released his shirt, Charles fell forward onto his palms. The rough hewn rug beneath him sunk with the weight and Charles remained there for several breaths. His gaze shifted from his sword that Phillippe still held at a ready position to the king's posture.

If he moved quickly, the dagger would suffice. It would make his father proud to use the man's favorite weapon. Before Charles could enact his secondary plan, Phillippe rested the tip of Charles's sword on the soft, wet ground beneath them. His stiff knees soaked in the moisture from the dirt that had seeped through the thin carpet. One fluid motion and Charles was positive he could pierce the king's heart. He tensed, readying for the strike.

"My demise will come by sword, not dagger." Phillippe lifted Charles's blade. The king's simple tone made Charles pause and appraise the light-skinned blond-haired man with a raised brow. Phillippe's attention remained on Charles's sword. "This is a nice weapon. You should be more careful how you wield it."

Unsure what to do or say, Charles flicked his focus from his dagger to the king's expression. Phillippe smirked down at him, so Charles scowled back and lunged, pulling his dagger free as he did.

Dropping the sword, Phillippe grabbed Charles's wrist and held firm. With his other hand, Charles punched Phillippe's arm, trying to free himself from the tenacious grip. Phillippe intercepted the blow. Using the momentum of his arm bouncing off Phillippe's, Charles twisted and rammed his shoulder into Phillippe's chest. If he could knock Phillippe down, maybe he'd have a chance.

He didn't. The king wrapped his arm around Charles's arms and midriff, pressing his back against Phillippe's chest.

"Brute force doesn't work the best every time," Phillippe murmured. When Charles widened his stance, Phillippe's grip tightened. The earlier amusement in Phillippe's voice transitioned to a commanding one. "Let us speak, calmly. Without weapons or punching, if you please."

Charles wriggled within the king's grasp, hand flexing on his dagger's hilt as he tried to shift the weapon to plunge it behind him. He was too young, too weak compared to the grown man.

So he elbowed Phillippe in the abdomen. Despite the release of a soft grunt, the tight band of the king's arms remained.

"Or elbowing," Phillippe said through gritted teeth. "I grow weary of your father wanting to claim my lands for his own. So, I shall propose an agreement."

When Charles shifted to elbow Phillippe again, the king shoved him forward. Charles stumbled and turned, raising his dagger to strike. His own gifted sword knocked the smaller blade aside.

Weaponless, Charles stood before the king of Orda'an, breaths quickening at the rushing realization. He would fail. His father would kill him. Punishment this time would be more than a backhanded slap that sliced open his chin. Chest heaving, muscles pulsing with the blood coursing through his veins, he curled his hands into fists and prepared to charge forward. It was better to die in the middle of this mission than be hunted for the rest of his days.

Even with that resolve, Charles went stiffer than a stone wall when the tip of his own blade rested against his chest.

"This agreement shall protect your life, the lives of my people, and yours." Phillippe's calm voice held none of the tension Charles could see in the arms keeping the blade poised against his chest. The point felt different than he expected. Not quite sharp and not quite dull, just pressure.

He scoured his surroundings, trying to find something, anything, to aid him in his task. A folded desk laid in one corner near the tent's entrance, accompanied by a worn suit of armor. Several smaller candles on wooden plates rested in the corners to give the tent a faint glow. Maybe if he set the tent on fire, it would disorient Phillippe enough. Or perhaps he could withstand the pain of grasping the steel sword and shoving it aside. But he didn't have a weapon, and taking the king's blade would prove difficult.

Shoulders falling, Charles followed the groove down the middle of his curved blade until he met Phillippe's unwavering stare.

"Live in Orda'an with my protection, including keeping your true identity safe," Phillippe said with a simple thoughtfulness, the sword steady between them. "I will send a message back with your companion that should Claude send any more of his children to renew the feud between our nations, they shall also die at my hand."

Charles swallowed hard; he had to protect his brothers and mother.

"I don't want to kill you," Phillippe said, though the sword did not shift away from Charles's chest. "I will if forced. As you have nearly done this evening."

"I'd rather die than live here," Charles seethed, debating how quickly he could duck from the sword's movement and attack again. But the slight twinkle in the king's eyes stopped him.

"That's a lie." Phillippe gestured with the sword toward the lone cot set out behind Charles. "Sit."

Charles glared at him and didn't move. With a heavy sigh, Phillippe lowered himself to the lackluster bed, laid Charles's sword across his lap and inspected the hilt. "You won't be getting this back. It'll make it too obvious where you're from."

Charles's heart lurched. "That's mine."

The king's enraging twinkle reappeared. "I know." Phillippe patted the cot beside him and repeated his earlier command.

Charles crossed his arms to hide clenched fists and scanned the tent for his dagger. It had been his first proper weapon, given to him by his father when he was barely eight years old. And he'd lost both it and his sword.

"I understand the hesitation." Phillippe twisted the blade back and forth as though studying his reflection in the candlelight. "But if you truly wished to kill me, you'd continue attacking. So. Sit. And we'll discuss whether you'll ever hold this sword again."

For the first time, Charles glanced at the tent's flaps. He could run. Run and never return home. Not as a failure. But Nasir would find him. Jaw aching from grinding his teeth, open wound on his chin pulsing in time with his thudding heartbeat, Charles plopped onto the cot next to Phillippe, arms still crossed, and hands still clenched into fists.

"Smart decision," Phillippe said, though he moved Charles's sword to lie on the cot opposite from where Charles currently sat.

"Like I said, I'll keep you safe here," Phillippe reiterated. "In Orda'an. You'll join my army, do as I command. That will include returning to your home to reclaim your birthright when it's asked of you. By then, you'll be ready." The Orda'anian king rubbed his chin of stubbled hair, tapping a finger against his jawbone. "It shouldn't be too difficult to make Claude believe you died trying to kill me."

Before Charles could stop himself, he glanced sidelong at the king. "So, I'll be a prisoner and my parents will think I'm dead?" Charles shook his head, shaggy curls drifting into his vision as he did. "Father won't believe anything without proper proof."

The thoughtful rubbing paused and Phillippe looked at him with mischief dancing in the man's bright green eyes. Charles's dagger reappeared in Phillippe's hands. The king rotated it. "A well crafted message, this dagger, and your ripped and bloody clothing should suffice as proof. Who is the man that came with you?"

For several breaths, Charles watched Phillippe with his dagger. All of him ached. The muscle between his shoulder blades spasmed, his throat felt raw from gulping down the frigid rain-coated air, and his toes squelched inside his boots. Wary the king would plunge that dagger into his heart, Charles whispered, "My mentor. He waits for me at the tree line."

A soft chuckle came from his left. "No name for this mentor of yours?"

His jaw was going to ache for days on end if he clamped it together any harder.

"This is a learning opportunity, Charles," Phillippe said as the dagger disappeared once more. It was a shock that made his heart pause for a moment. The king knew his position and his name. "I know your father's disposition and trust me when I say that not all men are the same as he."

Three options, none of them great. Agree to the king's offer, become a wanted prince, or return home to have his neck sliced by his father's dagger. His swallow was full of thorns, his voice dry as he asked, "And my brothers? Who will watch out for them? And Mae… if she believes me dead, it'll break her heart."

"You can choose our own path, young prince," Phillippe said. "I have known about this event since my father's death. Such a strange gift, to catch glimpses of the future. It's how I recognized you."

Phillippe's thoughtful rubbing of his chin resumed and Charles's fists unclenched beneath his crossed arms. Palms clammy, his once wet shirt now stiff, Charles glanced at his weapons again. The king had taken them so quickly, so easily. He could stay and learn. It might take longer than his father desired, but it could lead to success. With a singular deep breath, Charles pulled off his soiled shirt and held it out to the king. "Return my sword and I will agree to your terms."

Resting an arm against his knees, the king said, "The sword remains in my possession until I decide you have earned it back. If you reclaim this blade, you will keep the emblem covered until it is time to honor your portion of this agreement." Phillippe retrieved the blade, holding it so the faint candlelight glinted against the raised silver emblem of a dragon's head spitting fire. "Are you still in agreement or would you rather I kill you?"

A gust of cold air whisked through the tent, nearly extinguishing several candles. Bare-chested, Charles wrapped his arms around himself and rubbed. "I'll earn my sword back in less than a year." Charles flashed a glare in the king's direction before focusing on the ground beneath his tired feet. "And I agree to your terms."

"Good." The king's outstretched hand invaded Charles's vision. "The scabbard."

Unbuckling the sheath from his waist felt monumental. In some ways the weight of his father's expectations left his shoulders, only to be replaced by a new one he didn't quite understand.

After sheathing the sword, Phillippe stood and retrieved a blanket to toss at Charles. He watched it land by his feet and lifted his focus back to Phillippe's. Holding Charles's sword, dagger, and soiled shirt, the king had the audacity to smirk. "Azeiah will enjoy training you," the king said with that same annoying twinkle lighting up his eyes. "And I'll definitely enjoy watching him do so. Though I imagine watching you train my daughter will be even more entertaining."

Charles's jaw dropped. Train his daughter after being trained by his general? Teeth grinding against each other, Charles tugged the blanket around his shoulders and, despite being in the king's tent, laid down on the singular cot. Brown cloth surrounded him, and he stared at where the poles met to keep the tent upright. He would learn and infiltrate. And then, when the time was right, he would do what his father asked. One year. He could wait that long.

Also by

Cristen Jennette

The LeNoir Legacy Trilogy

The LeNoir Legacy

Published March 11, 2022

A Fractured Legacy

Published September 9, 2022

The Remnants of a Legacy

Coming Summer 2023

LeNoir Legacy Stories

The Crown's Inheritance

Published September 2021

The Twin Blades

Published Spring 2023

ACKNOWLEDGMENTS

Publishing a novel has been, for years, no more than a thought. Now, thanks to many, it has become a reality. This book, this story, has been through countless revisions and changes over the past decade. So it makes my heart extremely happy to say it is, finally, a completed novel ready to be shared with the world.

I'll be honest that writing this page seems scarier than writing the rest of the book. There are so many involved in the creation of any book. First, I must thank my parents. They instilled a love of reading in me during my younger years and without that proclivity, I may never have hit this milestone of publishing my debut novel. Reading stories others created solidified my idea that one day I could do what they did and write my own story. It may have taken a decent amount of time, but we're finally here! Also, thanks to my siblings, who let me read to them or with them when we were younger and who both read this story. I love that we all continue to read and enjoy literature in a variety of ways and hope we never lose that atmosphere.

While my family helped me believe that publishing could be a reality, it is friends and beta readers who truly made it possible. Reaching out to strangers to read my book was definitely the hardest part of this entire process, but I'm glad I did. Thank you to my beta readers for your supportive comments, poignant questions, and for the time you gave to help me make this book the best it can be. Without your commentary, this book would still be hiding in the depths of my documents and the far recesses of my brain.

A special shout out to my cover design artist, Stefanie Saw, who took my simplest descriptions and impressed me with her designs.

Last, but certainly not least, thank you to my current and future readers. You are the glue which holds author's together, which gives them the motivation to continue writing. So keep reading to your heart's content, dear readers, for more stories await!If you enjoyed this book, please consider leaving a review! Thank you for partaking on this journey with me and I hope you continue on to the next story.